MIDNIGHT OPS

MARK A. HEWITT

Black Rose Writing | Texas

The author grants the final approval for this literary material.

First printing

This is a work of fiction. Names, characters, businesses, places, events, and incidents are either the products of the author's imagination or used in a fictitious manner. Any resemblance to actual persons, living or dead, or actual events is purely coincidental.

ISBN: 978-1-68513-382-5
LIBRARY OF CONGRESS CONTROL NUMBER: 2023948133
PUBLISHED BY BLACK ROSE WRITING
www.blackrosewriting.com

Printed in the United States of America
Suggested Retail Price (SRP) $28.95

Midnight Ops is printed in Book Antiqua

*As a planet-friendly publisher, Black Rose Writing does its best to eliminate unnecessary waste to reduce paper usage and energy costs, while never compromising the reading experience. As a result, the final word count vs. page count may not meet common expectations.

To my buddy Mike, an incredible patriot, a good pilot,
and the inspiration for Duncan Hunter

MIDNIGHT OPS

"Politics is combat by other means."

–Carl von Clausewitz

PROLOGUE

CHAPTER 1

August 4, 2002
Naval War College
Newport, Rhode Island

The cream-colored 1965 Mercedes 280SL was waved through the gate without the driver being asked for her credentials. When the blue convertible top was down, she received an appropriate salutation from the security guards; *Good evening, Dr. McIntosh.* The armed men in black uniforms knew the car much better than they knew the driver. *The resident spook, at least that was the rumor.*

Dr. Elizabeth McIntosh negotiated the chicane of black and yellow concrete Jersey barriers placed in the aftermath of September 11; obstacles designed to stop a speeding suicide car bomber were imposing. She continued straight ahead for 200 yards, then took the curve up a short hill and made right turns into an elevated parking area for about 100 vehicles. She passed a dirty, old, bright-yellow Corvette without a license plate chained atop a road-weary trailer which was attached to an even dirtier black Silverado with Texas tags.

She pulled the Mercedes into her assigned parking spot, perfectly centered between the lines, not too far from the pickup and its precious yellow peril on a trailer.

It was Sunday, and there were only a few cars in the lot. That would change quickly. *I beat the rush of new students checking in.* As was her habit since college, she scanned the parking area. The only threat was the unusual truck-trailer combination that had parked haphazardly across a half-dozen parking spaces. It didn't encroach on her spot, and it didn't look like it would impede the flow of traffic into the lot. *Never seen one of those! It really doesn't matter where the Texan parks, as long as he gets his man-toys out of the lot before classes start tomorrow.*

The bespectacled fireplug of a woman slid out of the worn smooth blue leather seat, clutching her purse with one hand and holding a thick dull pumpkin-colored file to her chest with the other. As she walked toward the main building, a man in a dark business suit popped out of the pickup and made a beeline toward her. *Don't overreact! Don't make eye contact!* she cautioned herself. Then Dr. McIntosh heard an unusual baritone drawl from the man.

"Excuse me, Ma'am. Could you direct me to where I need to go to check in?"

She paused and turned: her eyes flitted between the car on the trailer and the man. *Obvious racecar. Probably Lucchese boots, French cuffs, top-tier suit…. This isn't the Grand National Stock Show.* The gravelly voiced Texan looked like a character actor from a James Bond flick; the Corvette was a manly toy built for burning racing fuel that would drive the environmentalists in the state barking mad. *It's a war college and it's Sunday.* She raised her eyes to see a reasonable facsimile of Steve McQueen smiling at her, or at least what McQueen's stunt double should have looked like.

She didn't smile. She pointed to the large building in front of her. Dr. Elizabeth McIntosh said, "Hunter, two-o-four." Information passed, the threat neutralized, she started back toward the building.

The man was instantly taken aback. He took a few steps to intercept her, and again the raspy baritone called out, "Excuse me, Ma'am!"

Elizabeth paused for a moment. She sighed and turned to him. Up close, he was very good looking and knew how to fill out a suit. She tried not to show her irritation. Her plan to get to her office and read the file she was carrying was looking less likely, as this Hollywood Texan could only ask insipid questions. "Yes?"

"I'm sorry, but how do you know my name?"

Irritation was replaced by confusion. "What's your name?"

"Duncan Hunter."

Confusion was replaced with a smile. *God, he is good looking.* "*Duncan*, you need to go to *Hunter Hall*, room two-o-four. Someone will be there to take care of you."

He flushed with amusement and embarrassment. Between blinks, he noticed the file she clutched to her chest as a shield was as thick as the ceramic plates in body armor. He committed the label to memory: CONFIDENTIAL REPORT. Duncan Hunter said, "Thank you very much. It's a beautiful car."

Dr. McIntosh softened, and smiled, and pointed to the car on the trailer. "Yours or mine?" *Why did I say that? Was that flirting?*

His baritone came alive with a smile and more information. "65 280SL, I believe. A rarity and a beauty. I worked for a Marine pilot who was restoring one back in the late 70s. You only drive it on Sundays?" Hunter was immediately embarrassed. That didn't come out exactly as he had intended. Before she could answer, he said quickly, "Mine is a 67 Corvette. Trailer queen, big block, eight fuel injectors, headers, pure racecar. I hope to do a little racing at Lime Rock, Connecticut on Sundays when the track is open, if the school load is not too onerous."

That was more information than was necessary. McIntosh slowly smiled. *Nice save! I thought you were going to intimate little old ladies only drive their cars on Sunday for church, but that was a nice recovery, Hunter...204.* Suddenly, Elizabeth softened. "I really wanted a baby blue '57 300 SL, but I was just a poor college student." She lowered her eyes, smiled. The banter had run its course. It was time to go.

Duncan Hunter nodded, threw her a smile and an informal salute; he returned to his truck, and from behind the driver's seat he extracted a glossy black Zero Halliburton briefcase. From a hatbox on the passenger's seat, he withdrew a white Stetson *El Presidente* and positioned it on his head. When Hunter closed the door, he turned to find the woman had scurried down the stairs and headed for the multiple doors of the war college main building. "That lady might be big, but she's fast." For a second, he wondered who she was. *Staff? Professor? Car aficionado? That is a fairly rare Mercedes.*

Hunter followed the signs for incoming students and presented himself to a uniformed guard behind bulletproof glass who asked for his civil service ID card. There were no more thoughts of the woman who had helped him as his card was checked against a roster; some unseen administrator had put his name on the list of new students — he learned something new, he was in the senior class. He was cleared to enter with a buzzer that magically unlocked the heavy door. Immediately inside the lobby, mounted eye-level on a concrete support, Duncan saw a large brass plaque. HUNTER HALL. Another plaque read: *Admiral Henry Kent Hunter served on the USS Missouri in the Great White Fleet's circumnavigation of the globe from 1907-1909 and distinguished himself during World War Two.*

He made his way through Hunter Hall, which was a part of the building and not a passageway, and found that he wasn't the only person in room two zero four. Someone took his transfer orders; someone took his picture. An elderly man handed him an access badge and a NAVAL WAR COLLEGE lanyard. A woman about his age handed him an information packet and a map of the college, and provided a few admonishments on what to do and what places in downtown Newport were off limits. He was assigned a room and given directions to the Bachelor Officers Quarters (BOQ).

Hunter drove past the gymnasium to what would be his home for the next eleven months. The truck and trailer required an out-of-the-way parking spot that would avoid pissing off any roving Military Police.

Across the street from the Navy Preparatory School, the nondescript, three-story BOQ with a small Navy-blue sign with a gold number 7 didn't inspire confidence. Having stayed at several substandard BOQs during his active service days, the building presaged likely Spartan accommodations.

He loaded his arms with his belongings and walked up three flights; he found room 307 was the corner suite. He unlocked the door, stepped in, and was shocked by the spacious two-room suite's large picture window. *This has to be an admiral's room!* After dropping his things onto a sofa, he walked to the window and with arms akimbo, gazed upon the NWC complex and Narragansett Bay with the Claiborne Pell Bridge in the distance.

"Sure the hell beats getting shot at. Hunter, you are the luckiest man alive." *Thank you, Greg Lynche.*

CHAPTER 2

August 4, 2002
Naval War College
Newport, Rhode Island

Dr. Elizabeth McIntosh made a pot of coffee and puttered around her office to prepare for the 530-or so men and women who would attend the next Naval War College class.

The sting of being removed as the Director of the National Center for Medical Intelligence was losing its sharpness. It had been five months and it would take a little while longer to get over it. With school about to start, there was no time to dwell on that event.

Elizabeth was grateful to still be working. She had worked for the CIA Director in the past. He had taken a personal interest in the final days of her career that had suddenly flamed out. He had been a new intelligence officer in-processing when he had seen her grandfather on his way out the door to retirement. *One out, one in.* As Director, he had reassigned Elizabeth to the George H. W. Bush Chair of International Intelligence as a twilight tour. She'd be out of sight and able to retire with a full pension.

Her duties at the Naval War College would be limited to being the Central Intelligence Agency's liaison to the school. She taught a different elective on the CIA every trimester. Dr. McIntosh had been the Acting Ambassador during the Joint Military Operations (JMO) exercise, teaching students how to use Agency-processed intelligence on the battlefield and in the fleet at sea. She also taught CIA History and Organization, and one of the CIA's more interesting offices, the Science and Technology Directorate, or what the NWC students affectionately called *Spy Toys*. Most active-duty students who attended the electives never interfaced with the CIA and learned a newfound appreciation for the mission of the intelligence community (IC).

Military and civilian students who had little to no exposure to the Central Intelligence Agency were fascinated with the CIA. Usually, the signup sheets for an Agency elective were filled within minutes of the class being offered.

In class, Dr. McIntosh answered questions about where America's spies come from and what prerequisites are necessary to get assigned to the IC; all the services had an intelligence occupational field. She was a little surprised to see an Air Force civilian in her elective class: *Duncan Hunter*. Elizabeth thoughtfully added, *204*.

When the time came during the final trimester, she always screened the student body for the key position of acting Chief of Station, an embassy's head intelligence officer for the end of course JMO exercise. No foreign nationals would be part of the exercise; the college hosted 55 mostly naval officers from allies across the globe. She and a panel of former senior intelligence officers made the selection. Dr. McIntosh assumed the role of acting Ambassador at the exercise embassy, and the acting Chief of Station would generally be the top, most distinguished student.

Dr. McIntosh was alone on the top floor of the main building of the Naval War College, at least none of the other staff had lights on in their office spaces. To ensure she wouldn't be bothered with a new student begging for a seat in her elective class or another faculty member who just wanted to visit, Elizabeth placed a towel on the floor against the sweep of the door to prevent light from spilling out into the hall. The message was clear: the resident spook was not in. She was alone at her desk; alone with her grandfather's confidential file, which now occupied the center of her desk and was illuminated by the desk lamp.

It had been a painful day. Turning over her grandfather's home to the Historical Society had required two final acts; removing everything from grandfather's office safe and relinquishing the keys to the house. Dr. McIntosh paused before opening the file. The Historical Society had demanded that if the colorful and spectacular floor safe was to remain in the house, it would have to be open for all to see. All contents would have to be removed and a locksmith would have to ensure it could never be locked again. The turnover had been a trying ordeal and would have been impossible during the school term.

She could still see that safe. Some things were indelible. Arcing across the top of the large two-ton floor safe, lettering announced the name of her grandfather's law firm in dull yellow-shaded block lettering: Donovan, Leisure, Newton & Irvine. The doors of the five-foot tall safe were exquisitely decorated with a painted scene of a covered bridge. The inner doors were embellished with faded yellow roses and daffodils. Intricate scrollwork dominated the corners of the doors. Proudly painted across the bottom of the outer doors was the manufacturer's advertisement of his work: Hall's Safe and Lock Co.

Elizabeth hadn't been there when the safe was moved into the house. But it had obviously been moved from the Donovan Building in downtown Manhattan to William Donovan's private office in his home, the oldest house in the borough in the Washington Heights neighborhood of Manhattan. As a child, Elizabeth had understood her distinguished-looking grandfather was a superb lawyer, a failed politician, and a decorated Army general.

As she grew up, her *Grandpa General* had ensured she received the finest education, a PhD in microbiology. *Grandpa General* said biology would not pay the bills and steered her to another graduate degree in international affairs. She graduated from the Walsh School of Foreign Service and became a Foreign Service Officer at the United States Department of State. A year later, she was offered a position as a medical intelligence analyst at the CIA. The granddaughter of William Donovan was shocked to discover her *Grandpa General* was more than a significant historical figure in the intelligence community. She had never been told *Grandpa General* had been the Director of the Office of Strategic Services (OSS) and a Medal of Honor winner.

It had taken a locksmith three days to open the safe without damaging it, and two minutes to open the safe-within-the-safe. The massive safe hadn't been opened since the General passed away in 1959. After the locksmith had opened the safe-within-a-safe, a thick, dusty, dark orange folder was found. *Maybe it was from an old trial.*

Safely in her office she could satisfy her curiosity about what secrets had been left locked up for six decades. CONFIDENTIAL REPORT was typed on a white label with a blue border, and binding the file was an odd tubular, fabric-covered elastic band which secured opposite corners. Remarkably, the band had some life left in it, and she opened the file. On top, there were dozens of loose-leaf official stationery with *Grandpa General's* law firm name emblazoned across the top. There were several photographs of what appeared to be from a bound notebook, and dozens of pages of handwritten notes which looked as if they had been cut out of a large journal. *This could be interesting.* She read the top line.

Journal entry: September 16, 1935 8:00 p.m.

Whose journal was this? she wondered. After scanning through pages of handwritten entries, Elizabeth came to a clue: *I was still recognized as "that American aviator," the Lone Eagle, and with that fleeting bit of fame I graciously turned offers of enhanced accommodations into private berths.*

She turned on her desk computer. After refilling her coffee cup, the computer was ready for her query: "Who was the Lone Eagle?" Elizabeth was dumbfounded by the answer. *Is that really possible?*

Dr. Elizabeth McIntosh scanned another dozen pages to confirm the author's identity. The dates of the journal entries were well before when *Grandpa General* was the head of the OSS. Elizabeth realized her grandfather may have kept the squash-colored file separate for other reasons.

Elizabeth slowly flipped through 80-year-old pages with the ancient cursive from The Lone Eagle's journal. Every page contained information that was more incredible than the previous page. She asked herself, *What am I looking at?*

CHAPTER 3

August 4, 2002
Naval War College
Newport, Rhode Island

Aware that adrenaline had hit her as she anticipated what lay ahead, Elizabeth went to her door and locked it. She topped off her coffee and returned to the yellowed journal entry of September 16, 1935. She repositioned the desk lamp for better illumination.

I write this from the sitting room of the Graf Zeppelin. I have neither compass or charts, but we set sail east, which means we are somewhere over the Atlantic.

I have been invited to Germany to attend the Nazi's next major rally. I had no time to dither. I raced from New York City, down the coast via railway, to catch this remarkable airship for a direct flight to Germany. Commercial transoceanic air service. I am still disbelieving I arrived in Miami in time, otherwise, I would have had to send my regrets.

The exhaust from the airship's engines is unlike the Ryan's; so much like a soft murmuring. It is more than merely muffled; there must be spark arresters on the exhaust. Everywhere I turn, I am amazed at the state of technology.

This airship is an engineering marvel, and from what I can see, as a commercial conveyance, is truly the world's most successful intercontinental airline. The crossing so far is remarkably peaceful and serene; much easier than the last time I flew to Europe. I must admit, I have seen enough ocean from the air to last several lifetimes. If we are going to travel to Europe again quickly, I wholeheartedly recommend the Graf Zeppelin. It is perfection: traveling comfortably, relaxing within the large gondola during the day, and at night in my own stateroom. Only a person of some means could do this.

I feel safe and secure; I have been very impressed with every aspect of this voyage. Passenger cabins are set by day with a sofa, which at night are converted into beds. The cabin is often cold, and some passengers wear furs and huddle under blankets. As I write this, I am reminded that we were instructed to remove any metal from our person that could cause a spark. We were given felt boots to keep our feet warm and to prevent sparks. The crew wear special flying uniforms of heavy dark leather with lambswool linings. I have a blanket over my legs. With that and my flying coat, I am sufficiently warm. And now that we have been underway for some time, there is no longer the smell from the Blau gas that was most noticeable when we boarded and when the airship was stationary. The galley staff is adequate and serves three hot meals a day in the main dining and sitting room.

The Graf Zeppelin is the consummate sum of German genius; the dream of Leonardo da Vinci. It is as breathtaking as it is incredible.

Via the wireless service aboard, my efforts to secure a hotel room in Nuremberg two days ago were for naught. I do not know how he knew I was aboard this majestic airship, but shortly after sending my telegrams of inquiry, I received a private telegram from Reichsminister Joseph Goebbels. As there is a Nazi rally scheduled and all hotels are filled, the Reichsminister intervened on my behalf and ensured I will have a hotel room upon my arrival. I am in his debt. He had not invited me to the rally, but the Generalfeldmarschall of the Luftwaffe, Hermann Göring. I was unsure how and why the Reichsminister took command of my needs. Herr Goebbels' cable was very explicit that after we dock in Nuremberg a staff car will pick me up, so I will not be burdened trying to find my way around Nuremberg, or to my hotel, or to return to the Zeppelinfield arena for the rally. After coming out of seclusion, I am surprised that my fame is still considered noteworthy in Europe.

Elizabeth caught her breath. *Are these….*

I am amazed at the efficiency of the Germans in finding me, or at least of Western Union. Although I am traveling on a diplomatic passport under an alias, I am still recognized. Fame has its limitations. Few people knew I had returned stateside. But when they found out where I lodged, even under an assumed name, the number of telegrams I received became obscene. It was time to leave. I miss flying, and only recently have I recovered sufficiently to focus on the maddening crush of airplane designers and builders who believe I can help them in some way.

I am so grateful for the German embassy's invitation. Another flying adventure. This airship is spectacular.

It is a blessing to have a wireless service aboard. The crew views me as an anonymous traveler. It is obvious the captain recognizes me, but he has not gone overboard in his praise.

But of course, as a world-famous aviator, I was invited to the bridge. I was somewhat displeased not to find the former company chairman, Dr. Hugo Eckener, commanding the flight. I had heard so many interesting and pleasant things about him. The crew still talk about Dr. Eckener with reverence, for it was he who conceived of the airship and the airline. The pilot, Captain Johann Ledford, explained that the radio direction finder of the Graf Zeppelin was probably on an order of magnitude more sophisticated than the rudimentary navigation equipment I used when I crossed the Atlantic. His remarks were given with the utmost courtesy.

Communication and navigation improvements are continually finding their place in aircraft. I was limited by a magnetic compass strapped to my thigh; now a loop antenna is used to determine the airship's bearing from the signals of any two land radio stations or ships with known positions. Behind the flight deck is the map room, with two large hatches to allow the crew to communicate with the navigators, who take readings with a sextant through the windows. Celestial navigation has been the standard for years when loop antennae are ineffective, as long as the navigator can see the stars.

While standing in the bridge, Captain Ledford refrained from speaking about himself but extolled the virtues of Dr. Eckener. Captain Ledford said he knew Dr. Eckener very well; that the doctor had earned a doctorate in psychology at Leipzig University and "used his knowledge of mass psychology to the benefit of the Graf Zeppelin" and the airline. I must admit I was taken aback by his boast, but Captain Ledford said Dr. Eckener identified safety as the most important factor in the ship's public acceptance of the first airline, and he worked to continue Dr. Eckener's policies. Hydrogen, the lighter-than-air gas that they use, is extremely flammable, so safety is paramount. In the gondola, we are isolated from the hydrogen.

Dr. McIntosh uttered softly, "So much detail...."

Captain Ledford reminded me that unlike seagoing ships, German airships are referred to as male. And while on the zeppelin, the crew uses metric measures of metres, kilograms, and knots per hour. He explained the Graf Zeppelin had originally intended to use helium, but most of the world's supply was controlled by the United States. Dr. Eckener complained bitterly that its export to Germany had been tightly restricted by the Helium Act of 1925. I was unaware of the U.S. law, but the Germans were very knowledgeable, as they viewed the restrictions as unnecessary and an impediment to air commerce.

Without the availability of helium, Dr. Eckener sought to prove hydrogen could be safely used in massive quantities, and took complete responsibility for the airship, from technical matters, to finance, to the itinerary of its years-long public relations campaign by which he promoted "zeppelin fever." I could sense people were being trained to accept that hydrogen was an adequate and safe replacement for helium.

CHAPTER 4

August 4, 2002
Naval War College
Newport, Rhode Island

She wanted to shout, but Dr. McIntosh caught herself and whispered. "He's collecting intel!"

Listening to Captain Ledford, I have come to accept that when Dr. Eckener ran the company, he was a master propagandist. His situational awareness was nonpareil, even when it was difficult to maneuver the airship because of the winds at NAS Opa Locka. Captain Ledford abided by Dr. Eckener's protocol to circle the landing area clockwise so that the swastikas on the airship's rudders would not be seen by the spectators on the ground. I assumed the ship turned anti-clockwise when in Europe. I should say Captain Ledford turned "him" anti-clockwise when in Europe.

This was something that I had never considered. Was it a tacit strategy that orbiting the naval air station in one direction announced the Graf Zeppelin was implicitly a commercial airship? What was the purpose of the swastikas? The Graf Zeppelin surely would have been viewed differently if spectators could see the swastikas on the obverse. Would it suggest that the airship could be a combatant? Whatever the rationale, Dr. Eckener's policies ensured that the swastikas on the airship's rudders would not be easily seen.

I vaguely remember reading the local English newspaper from Paris that President Roosevelt supported Dr. Eckener's request for purchasing inflammable helium for airships for commercial transatlantic passenger service, but that there was fierce opposition from the Secretary of the Interior, Harold Ickes. Ickes was concerned Germany would use helium-filled airships in war, and there was no compelling reason to change the policy or amend the law. I sense Dr. Eckener never forgave Roosevelt for not countermanding

Ickes' position, which forced him to use the more volatile hydrogen and Blau gas.

Dr. McIntosh turned to her computer and queried, "Blau gas." *That is so interesting…. More strategic intel….* She returned to the journal.

I hadn't thought of it before, but seeing the huge swastika when you were not expecting it could have definitely conveyed a threat, like a warlike Joan of Arc in chainmail, brandishing a cross which asserted her position and intentions. A Joan of Arc in a frock without any accoutrements would not convey any threat. I can see Dr. Eckener's command of psychology at work.

Admittedly, the airship captures the public imagination wherever it goes, and from the propaganda materials in the lounge, it was used extensively in advertising. I did not expect Captain Ledford to mention privately that Dr. Eckener had been an outspoken critic of the Nazi Party and had been warned about it by Rudolf Diels, at that time, the head of the Gestapo. When the Nazis gained power in 1933, the Reichsminister of Propaganda, Joseph Goebbels, and the Commander-in-chief of the Luftwaffe, Hermann Göring, sidelined Dr. Eckener and put Dr. Eckener's former first officer (who was more sympathetic to the Nazis) Ernst Lehmann in charge of the new airline, Deutsche Zeppelin Reederei (DZR), which has always operated German airships.

I knew the Treaty of Versailles had placed limits on German aviation. In 1925, when the Allies relaxed the restrictions, Captain Ledford said Dr. Eckener saw the chance to start an intercontinental air passenger service. I would have liked to meet that fellow pioneer.

Captain Ledford rattled off the airship's operating parameters like the professional captain that he is. The Graf Zeppelin's top airspeed was about 80 mph, as I surmised. The Spirit of St. Louis, which so capably carried me cross a hostile North Atlantic….

The Spirit of St. Louis? Dr. McIntosh wanted to shout, *Yes! Charles Lindbergh!* but caught herself. Softly, reassuring herself, "This really is Charles Lindbergh's journal! What was my grandfather doing with pages from Charles Lindbergh's journal? Strategic intel. Years before there was war!" *Years before there was an OSS.*

…had a cruising speed of about 100 mph when I began my journey and 110 mph as the fuel load decreased and I took advantage of the west-to-east

tailwinds. The Graf Zeppelin had a usable payload of about 33,000 lb. Captain Ledford remarked that "he" was slightly unstable in yaw, and to make "him" easier to fly, an automatic pilot was used to stabilize "him" in yaw. Captain Ledford said the pitch axis was controlled manually by an elevatorman who, as quoted, "…tried to limit the angle to 5° up or down, so as not to upset the bottles of wine which accompanied the elaborate food served on board." Since I never discerned any porpoising during the crossing, I must acknowledge the elevatorman was very proficient in his job, keeping "him" trimmed at all times.

The captain said he must go; it was time to prepare for docking. I am already packed. I have been invited to the bridge for the final phase of our flight, and I do not want to miss Captain Ledford at work bringing this massive beast to port.

Dr. McIntosh stopped when the journal entry ended. She was breathing harder than normal; she wanted to read it all, but she was exhausted. *This has been an incredible day. There are more pages. Many more. They are so interesting! And Grandpa General's notes. Why would my grandfather have pages from Charles Lindbergh's journal? I have to get out of here. Get some food. Get some sleep. I will visit The Lone Eagle again tomorrow.*

Elizabeth closed the file, returned the elastic band to the corners, and placed the file in the top drawer of a four-drawer safe in the office.

Outside, she inhaled the sea breeze. Her car was still in the parking lot, but now it was in the company of dozens of vehicles. The stairs leading to the parking lot held lines of new students checking in. *Off to Hunter Hall, two-o-four.*

The truck and Corvette and the Texan with the nice boots and deep voice, were gone. And for the first time in a long time, Elizabeth sighed.

CHAPTER 5

August 8, 2002
Naval War College
Newport, Rhode Island

Dr. McIntosh was standing on the dais on the right side of the 1,100-seat auditorium when she saw the Texan enter. *Now I know two students. Black business suit, bright red tie. No hat. No subtlety in that one. Yellow Corvette. He likes bright things.*

Duncan Hunter entered through a bank of doors from Spruance Hall at the top of the auditorium and walked down the port aisle. He sat four rows from the front, center on the podium. He didn't look around to see if anyone from his seminar class would be brave enough to join him. An adjunct college professor, he didn't have childish views about sitting at the front of the class; he would not retreat to the rear of the auditorium where the rest of the student body twittered in their seats.

What a great place to be! At a war college when there is an actual war going on!

He glanced at his two-tone Rolex, wondering when the presentation would begin. Then the class president, U.S. Navy Captain William McGee, walked in wearing the Navy's short-sleeve, white uniform and straining every stitch of those sleeves. The black man in the white uniform was awe-inspiring. McGee was big and muscular in the way muscle-builders are ripped and toned, packed with mass and definition. The man sported a gray flattop, wore small, round glasses, and his chest was covered in ribbons below the gold Trident badge of a SEAL. He strode to where Hunter sat and asked in a deep growling Barry White bass, "Would you join me up front?"

"Yes, sir; my pleasure," Hunter said, surprised at the request. Once Hunter had come around, he offered his hand. The former Marine Corps officer showed the utmost respect for the man with five Navy Crosses and shook the rock-hard hand.

"Bill McGee. As class president, I have to sit up front, and everyone's afraid to sit with me."

"Duncan Hunter. Retired Marine Captain. Glad to meet you, sir. I'll keep you company." They sat in the middle of the front row and chatted as old friends.

"Call me *Bullfrog*."

Hunter wanted to pronounce *Bullfrog* like John Fogarty of Creedence Clearwater Revival pronounced *bullfrog* during Green River. *I can hear the bullfrog calling me, aw….* Heavy bayou, Cajun accent. The big SEAL could have snapped him like a twig. But he avoided being a smartass and said, "*WILCO*. I'm *Maverick*."

Offstage, Dr. McIntosh intently watched at the interaction between the two men. They were complementary opposites. Hunter was a white man in a black suit, and McGee was a black man in a white uniform. *As opposites they seem to be getting along famously. Do they know each other?*

Hunter leaned over and said, "I haven't known many SEALs, but I went to flight school with one in '83. He was a SEAL during his enlisted days. He got a commission, and I think went off to fly A-6s. Like you, he embarrassed the rest of us pogues when he was in uniform with a boatload of ribbons and a SEAL badge. All the rest of the student pilots only had firewatch ribbons."

Scotty Beam. McGee broke into a wide smile, but before he could say anything, the assembly was called to attention. The NWC faculty and staff entered the auditorium led by the President of the Naval War College, a two-star Rear Admiral. A Marine Corps lieutenant colonel in a Class "C" uniform approached the lectern and asked the assembly to take their seats. Hunter smiled as he recognized the little lady who had given him directions to Hunter Hall. She remained on the platform. *Staff or faculty. Both?*

The colonel made a few comments that ensured no foreign students were present, then said, "This lecture is classified SECRET— NOFORN. I'd like to introduce Dr. Elizabeth McIntosh. Dr. McIntosh has been with the Central Intelligence Agency since 1975, serving in positions from field agent to chief of station to the personal aide of the Director. She currently holds the George H. W. Bush Chair of International Intelligence at the Naval War College and has held that position since August 2001. She is a graduate of the Walsh School of Foreign Service at Georgetown University. She was a Foreign Service Officer for the Department of State. She received a master's in international affairs from Boston College and a master's in National Security and Strategic Policy from the Naval War College. Dr. McIntosh received her PhD in Russian studies from Harvard in 1984. Ladies and Gentlemen, Dr. McIntosh."

Duncan smiled, shook his head unconsciously, and clapped for his second favorite spook.

Dr. McIntosh nodded to the class president, "Captain McGee, Mr. Hunter, and the class of 2003, on behalf of the CIA and the Naval War College, I welcome you to Newport and hope you have a great year."

Bill McGee gave Duncan an elbow.

Duncan was shocked to have been called out, outed by a spook, and tried to nudge back but the SEAL was as hard as a rock. *Whiskey Tango Foxtrot, over?*

Dr. McIntosh continued, "In the weeks after 9/11, the American public knew nothing of a top-secret interagency response. The first clue was a news report out of Afghanistan that a CIA paramilitary officer had been killed, and an American supporting the Taliban had been captured."

Dr. McIntosh explained the CIA paramilitary officer who died had been a Marine Corps officer before coming to the Central Intelligence Agency's Special Activities Division (SAD). In 2001, he was the first American killed in combat during the U.S. invasion of Afghanistan. Then, Dr. McIntosh introduced the other CIA paramilitary officer, another former Marine officer whose first name may have or may not have been his real name. He had survived the assault on the ground. She said, "His partner is here today to give you an eyewitness account of what happened at the Qala-i-Jangi compound near Mazari Sharif in northern Afghanistan. I think he even has some pictures."

For over an hour, the CIA intel officer talked while photographs projected on a screen behind him. When he concluded his presentation, the Naval War College clapped for two minutes, and then the lights came on.

McGee took the conclusion of the presentation to turn to Duncan and ask, "How does the head spook know you? You CIA?"

Hunter deflected. He had a cover to maintain and even though the CIA lady had blown it he didn't want to lie. "You wouldn't believe me. It's absolutely stupid."

"Try me."

Hunter berated himself; Greg Lynche told him not to get too cozy with any of the students. *They haven't been vetted. You must be very careful about who you talk to or meet. Keep a low profile. I don't want to lie, not to a war hero. But he is a SEAL. I'll wager he has been vetted. Crap, he can beat the crap out of me and kill me before I can blink!* Duncan smiled and told the story of how he met McIntosh in the parking lot.

Captain McGee didn't smile back. "That's pretty good. Now who are you really?"

"I was *Maverick* before there was Top Gun and Tom Cruise?"

The big man narrowed his eyes. "That I will believe. But I cannot fathom how you got here. You're an Air Force civilian. This is a school for naval types. You shouldn't be here unless there is a damn good reason."

Hunter smiled. *Busted, but I'm not going to give it up! That didn't take long!* Hunter frowned, nodded, and said, "This is not the place. It's a wild story, for another day, good sir?" They shook hands and agreed to meet in the classified library.

As Hunter departed the main building of the war college, McGee reversed direction and went straight to the Security Office. The pretty petty officer behind the desk asked, "Can I help you, sir?" When the security officer saw the class president enter his spaces, a completely unexpected event, he stepped from his office, but before he could render the appropriate greeting to a senior officer, McGee blew past him and said, "Close the door." Once the security officer's door was closed, pleasantries were not exchanged. McGee knew how to throw his weight around and asked for a full security brief on Duncan Hunter.

Later, at the base gym, Duncan Hunter met new people who played racquetball. Bill McGee took a moment to wander from the weight room over to the racquetball courts to watch Hunter smash a little blue ball. The two men exchanged waves. Hunter was a very good racquetball player.

McGee wondered who the man really was. *TS/SCI, accesses to include a Yankee White, and a polygraph? What stinkin' Air Force civilian has an Agency clearance with access to the President? Ok, asshole. We will find out who you really are and why you are really here.*

Chapter 6

August 8, 2002
Naval War College
Newport, Rhode Island

After depositing the Agency's paramilitary officer at the Providence Airport for the return flight to Washington, D.C., Dr. McIntosh zoomed back to Newport for another installment of her grandfather's papers and Lindbergh's journal.

Quietly ensconced in her office, Dr. McIntosh retrieved the file from the safe, sat down, and read:

Journal entry: September 24, 1935 Midnight.

I have gotten control of my nerves. I have left Germany.

Elizabeth McIntosh asked aloud, "What happened? Did I miss something?" She reviewed the pages she had already read and scanned the pages ahead; she convinced herself she hadn't overlooked something. The page before her was the next installment. She found sheets of stationery from her grandfather's law firm interleaved between Lindbergh's journal entries. *In Grandpa General's handwriting. A story within a story? Lindbergh's actions with Grandpa General's contemporaneous comments?* Elizabeth asked, "What has happened, Mr. Lindbergh?"

I boarded the North German Lloyd in Liverpool for New York. The trains in Germany gratefully ran on time, and I made all of my connections. I have not experienced an anxiety attack before, and I am troubled to admit it. Now that I have calmed myself, now that I am away from Germany, I can resume my observations.

Germany is recovering economically, as I rode on mostly new railcars that were most elegant and clean. I understand Herr Hitler's train is an immaculate example of German craftsmanship. Here and there I was surprised, even under an alias, I was recognized as "that American aviator," the Lone Eagle, and with that fleeting bit of fame I graciously turned offers of enhanced accommodations into private berths.

I am feeling much better now. I was so distressed, I became ill. I woke up in the middle of the night feeling as if some external force was suffocating me, like some demonic attack, but maybe that is too improbable to believe. The pounding in my head has subsided. Is it because I am away from Germany, Goebbels, or Hitler? I do not know emphatically, yet somehow, I suspect so. I believe they have harnessed the power of Satan. If war comes, I am concerned; would it become a spiritual battle?

I am well enough to account for most of my observations of the Nazi Rally. At least I have thought about them critically during my travels during the day. At night, in my sleep, my mind continued to solve the underlying questions, so that I now may be able to offer an explanation.

The ship's library does not have what I am looking for; I seek verification and validation of these thoughts. I can offer no proof, just my observations. I may be the most unqualified observer ever to partake of such a mission.

The mission. I will return to that in due course.

But first, I am well enough to continue my return journey. I am aboard the quickest available travel to the United States. My mission in Europe is complete to the best of my ability. I have accomplished what my president asked of me. However, I sense now my travel could have been for something more, for I did not see any Nazi aircraft as promised by Generalfeldmarschall Göring. There will be another time, he promised. When I have the time.

The challenge is to adequately describe what I witnessed. I am still exhausted, unsettled, and unsure of what happened on the seventeenth at the Zeppelinfield arena. "Spectacle" is insufficient to describe the VII Nazi Party Rally. It was a strange foreign feeling, and at the time I turned to the man with the foot deformity for answers, the Reichsminister, Joseph Goebbels, who rarely left my side. I had expected to be escorted and accompanied by the Generalfeldmarschall of the Luftwaffe, instead I was mesmerized by my surroundings and the man with a limp.

The structure we were on was modeled after the polished marble temples of ancient Greece where they worshiped Zeus. Some would think the structure *on which we were standing might be in some way stealing the historical legacy of the temples of the Greek gods, but they view Chanchellor Hitler as a god; they idolize Herr Hitler with something close to religious fervor.*

It is difficult not to see Nazism, with this Greek-like temple background, as an extension of an ancient religion. But there was something more. At the most extreme corners of the building were two raging fires emanating from a pair of concave fire pits. The architect, I was told, was Albert Speer.

Upon meeting Herr Goebbels, I found him to be incredibly intelligent and articulate. What one would expect of someone with a PhD in literature. I thanked him profusely for his assistance in my stay. I had recognized his face immediately from photographs. He is shorter than I imagined. By nearly a foot. I knew of him; in fact, I read about him extensively. Aboard the Graf Zeppelin, there were pamphlets about Nazi leaders, and I read them all. When I was introduced, he presented himself as an effeminate little man in a double-breasted suit, with a banal appearance, someone who would be expected to be stuffed away in the back office of a bank doing tallies, not to be seen by the public. In the United States, I don't believe he would ever have been considered for such a prestigious position as Reichsminister or its equivalent, whatever his professional qualifications.

He reminded me of a vile little proscribed book with a plain cover to hide the disgusting things printed inside. Still, I engaged him, for I had little option if I wanted answers to my many questions. I asked, "Dr. Goebbels, I am without words. What exactly am I seeing?"

The mouse of a man with rheumy eyes smiled thinly and took an inordinate amount of time replying to my interrogative. I do not know why, but I was suddenly struck with the notion that "the rally, the spectacle" before us might have been his idea, his creation. But instead of taking a bow for organization and presentation, he had deferred its importance, its genius, and subsequent ceremony to Chanchellor Adolf Hitler.

I learned from Herr Goebbels directly that his genius was the creation of an inexpensive radio, affordable to every German home, so listeners could hear the voice of their much-revered Fuhrer. Goebbels was proud of his radio, the volksempfänger, which he said massively boosted home radio ownership. Not having seen one, but knowing with whom I was dealing, I could tell the people's radio was designed to be a conduit for Nazi doctrine to reach German households. Clearly, the Ministry of Propaganda at work.

Yes, over 200,000 uniformed soldiers marched into the Zeppelinfield arena with the precision of German engineering, and the echoes of boot leather slapping cobblestones in synchronicity, was at once frightening and intimidating. It was a purposeful sound, one that I will never forget, like the roar of a nine-cylinder Wright Whirlwind radial at takeoff power. Once experienced, it becomes embedded in your mind. It was a truly fascinating spectacle — for that rally can only be described as a spectacle. It was loud and hurt my ears, which are not delicate; I've been around many aircraft engines. As far as I could see, every person and crimson flag and spotlight were placed with precision, just so, for a reason: to ensure the focus was placed on Chanchellor Hitler.

On the arena grounds, one in twenty soldiers bore a Nazi banner of scarlet emboldened with a white circle and black swastika. The swastika saturated my senses with every blink of my eyes. I tried to look away but found there were times I could not. In fact, I could look at the swastika, close my eyes, and the shadowy image of a white circle and black swastika was still visible against the eigengrau of my eyes. I do not know if this was a trick of the senses, but I found it unsettling. I tried not to look directly at any swastikas, but they were everywhere. I closed my eyes, and there were swastikas. It was at this point when my head began to hurt, as if my brain wanted out of the cranium, that it needed to escape. I believe the Nazi's use of the swastika created something akin to magical powers, turning the assembly into barking mad, mind-numb zombies.

I noticed the people in the reviewing stands with me turned away from what was happening with the troops on the ground. It was as if they knew they were supposed to enjoy the parade, but I sensed nervous laughter, as if they shouldn't be watching the magic on the field. When the Reichsminister said, "You need to turn away, we want you to come back, we do not wish to scare you in what could be a misunderstanding." Of course, I complied. Those who had turned away carried on conversations with one another. I admit I tried to peek, but I was unnaturally terrified to do so. I distinctly remember thinking, "Was that psychology or just a friendly warning?" just as Herr

Goebbels, without warning or segue, casually asked, "Herr Lindbergh, are you aware that Sunni Islam's four orthodox schools of jurisprudence implicitly permit necrophilia? I can show you our inventory. Ah! 10,000 fully vaccinated men, filing onto the parade ground." He had turned around to view the parade ground.

Inventory? Necrophilia? They were such odd statements that I thought I may have imagined them. When he spoke of necrophilia, I wondered if his use of inventory implied corpses, but for what purpose would anyone need corpses?

I am not wise in the ways of Mohammedanism or what necrophilia has to do with vaccinations unless there is a medicinal purpose. These topics dominated my thoughts for many minutes. Why did he mention inventory, and sex with the dead, and some troops being vaccinated? What were the troops being vaccinated from? Corpses? Corpses that carried diseases, like the plague? Was Germany creating a program to protect troops from biological weapons in the same way the armies of the Great War tried to protect troops from chemical weapons?

I was so confused. I could not conceive of a reason why vaccination was even part of the discussion.

Vaccinations are protection from some unseen disease.

Arms-length from all talk of inoculations, when Herr Goebbels returned to look onto the field, I returned to my observations on the field.

Surrounding the top of the arena were dozens of men operating movie-making equipment and being shepherded by a woman identified as Leni Riefenstahl. The night event was illuminated with at least 150 huge spotlights and a thousand torches placed at ground level, equidistant around the amphitheater's perimeter like the points on a compass. And hundreds of swastikas. It came to me that the Nazis may be using the swastika as a silent, unspoken weapon of propaganda. How odd, but very effective.

As if on command, 200,000 hands and arms pierced the air as 200,000 voices screamed, "Heil! Heil! Heil!" Riefenstahl's microphones likely picked up every word on the field and on Herr Hitler's platform. The men on the field moved with the precision of a machine.

Chancellor Hitler pranced from side to side on his platform, his chin raised and arm outstretched thirty degrees above plane. He appeared strangely satiated yet insouciant, and with my proximity to him, I could tell he was in total command. I do not know why I found this so odd. Rallies in the United States are celebrations, like the ticker tape parade when I returned from France and at the end of the great war. I did not know what I saw that day, but have had some time for reflection. People were delirious and overjoyed at the success of a person they did not know. At American celebrations, at least in New York City, there were people and American flags as far as the eye could see. The Nazi rally was something more intimate, like a group of men sharing the secrets that were contained within the pages of the Apocrypha. I learned it was a celebration of sorts, but celebrated differently and for a different reason.

Elizabeth sat up straight. *A celebration?* She lifted her arms up, in supplication, as if she were asking for divine guidance. She ripped off some post-it note papers from her desk and wrote, *Why mention inventories and necrophilia? I think inventory implies the living and not the dead. Sex traffickers use that term today. Why mention vaccinations? What were they celebrating? Acceptance into a cult? What was going on?*

CHAPTER 7

August 8, 2002
Naval War College
Newport, Rhode Island

Dr. McIntosh had a staff meeting and wondered if she had the time. She flipped through pages and determined she could read the rest of Lindbergh's journal before she had to dash out of her office.

We were standing five rows behind and above the Der Führer's platform. His arms behind his back gave him the appearance of a gray pigeon. The Reichsminister of Propaganda leaned into my ear and replied, "Herr Lindbergh, tonight the Nuremberg Laws will be presented to the public. It was a promise made by Der Führer, and he will keep his promise. But I believe your question can be answered this way; you are witnessing the power of enlightenment and propaganda. We understand the nature and necessity of human experimentation and propaganda; Americans and the British do not. At least I am certain your countrymen do not have this level of understanding of the mind or the necessary level of commitment to wage battle. American and British soldiers are drawn from the poorest of the population. Conscripts are rarely effective soldiers. They can be neutralized by the simplest of compounds. On the battlefield in the last war, troops, yours and ours, died by the thousands. These German soldiers have been protected and conditioned; they are extremely motivated and cannot wait to serve the Fatherland."

McIntosh wondered; *Did Goebbels imply they not only had a biological weapons program, but they had also developed vaccines to protect troops in the field from biological weapons? Why were they extremely motivated? Was there some sort of initiation rite? What could that be?* She sat straight up as if she had stuck her finger into a light socket. *Now, I think I know.* Dr. Elizabeth McIntosh audibly exhaled. She jotted a few words on another Post-It note and affixed it to the journal entry. *Did the Nazis* create the fear of biological weapons while protecting the troops with inoculations? For protection, did they demand fealty by forcing recruits in the ancient rite of sex with the dead?

I will research that. Goebbels knew young troops were impressionable and could easily be blackmailed. Of course, they would do anything for Hitler. I think that is how they got those troops to commit unspeakable acts with children and the dead.

She continued reading, "In this Germany, at this time, every person in this arena is turned and tuned to Der Führer; they are completely receptive; they believe everything he says without questioning a syllable; they will follow him to the four corners of the earth, if that is what he desires. They only breathe when he breathes. They understand through their power, he is powerful. These Germans view Der Führer as their savior – he has promised to deliver them from the poor decisions of his predecessors and the evilness of their enemies, and now their every waking moment is preoccupied with serving him. Yes, preoccupied! They receive enhancements to serve Chancellor Hitler unquestionably; they will die for him. See how he controls them with simple gestures. He can control them and speak to them with his thoughts. Your military and political leaders do not have this level of mental intimacy with the masses. It is through their anger as a group formation that Der Führer can focus his energies to lead them. For without him the Nazi Party would be nothing. What you are seeing is unique in military discipline."

I was astonished and wished Herr Goebbels would have explained why the troops, if I were to understand correctly, were inoculated to enhance their desires to serve Chancellor Hitler. I had never heard such words uttered before. It was a world alien to me. Vaccines were necessary to prevent illness; now they could enhance their desires to serve Chancellor Hitler? How is that possible?

It was more than foreign. I thought I knew what propaganda was, but Goebbels seems to have refined it or enhanced its effect with drugs; maybe even perfected it... as if a German soldier had been immunized and became a.... The word coming into my head is zombie, but even that is not adequate. Preoccupied, possibly, but that is Herr Goebbels' term. It is different, in a *different context than what we understand in America. He used the term "group formation." Of course, it is a formation, but Goebbels' definition is not my definition. There is a psychological component that I do not readily understand. I do not know what their definition really means, but whatever it is, the 200,000-strong crowd on the field obviously fed their energy back to Herr Hitler. Possibly they have become obsessed with seeking protection from the Jews. Maybe they were manipulated to become obsessed with seeking protection from the Jews. Through propaganda?*

This is a most unusual dictatorship. At this time, I still cannot adequately describe my understanding of the process that can take a peaceful farm boy and turn him into a mad dog obsessed with seeking protection from peaceful Jews. How can that happen? Through vaccination? Can a vaccine trigger an obsessive fear of Jews? By intravenous drugs? Can different drugs affect men to either be a patriot or preoccupied, fearful or obsessed? Is human experimentation with drugs a darker form of medicine or a branch of psychology? I wonder, if Germans refuse to be vaccinated, does the state have the power to take them to a doctor's office and plunge a needle into their arms? Is this what I witnessed? The more I think about this, I am convinced the Nazis believe they can do this. They just have to have a reason, which can be anything. And that could lead to involuntary human experimentation.

But I sense there is more, and I don't know if Herr Goebbels was trying to manipulate my mind with taboo talk of sex with the dead or observations that they were conducting experiments to make a better soldier.

I had heard that term earlier that evening. Chancellor Hitler negated a set of guidelines that governed the conduct of human experimentation.

I must say there was a striking similarity between the Nazi soldiers I saw that evening and the fictional zombie from the moving picture, "White Zombie." A man turns to a witch doctor to lure the woman he loves away from her fiancé, but instead he turns her into a zombie slave. Yes, maybe what I witnessed that evening wasn't a single zombie, but zombie slaves. Zealots turned on with a mental switch. There is something left unspoken in this context. Polite people do not discuss these things; they do not even think these things! But I sense…. the suggestion of necrophilia runs through all of it.

I must be going mad. Once that image has been implanted….

It appears as if the zombies on the field have abandoned their individuality and critical thinking artificially, using their minds, not to question the totalitarian controls that removed their basic freedoms, but to rationalize and evangelize them. They have become obsessively preoccupied with serving their master. If the biologics are not causal.... What if the Nazis are using the bodies of dead women?

I cannot write it.

An initiation rite to join a group, a clan? Is this how the Nazi leadership compels farm boys to swear their allegiance to Hitler? Goebbels' mind tricks are playing with mine!

I'm digressing. I retract my words on the matter.

My sense is that the Reichsminister Goebbels is something of a witch doctor. Voodoo without dolls to manipulate or stick pins into. Something has been implanted into their heads, and it is more than an idea. Which is of course, absurd and makes my head throb again, as if I were flying too high without supplemental oxygen.

Herr Goebbels claimed the soldiers would go home after the rally and work for the betterment of Germany. Instead of living their life of repetition and doldrums, they would be preoccupied – that was his word and he repeated it often – preoccupied with serving Der Führer. And if that meant they had to police their neighbors to work for a better Germany and not just selfishly for themselves, they would report them. I felt an overwhelming urge to vomit. I excused myself and bid my leave, and returned to my hotel. Thankfully, Goebbels expected my leaving early and his staff car returned me to my hotel.

The Naval intelligence officer I had traveled with to NAS Opa Locka had warned me that my hotel room would be searched while I was away. If so, I could not tell. But I dared not record my thoughts in my journal until I was safely away from Germany. It has not been out of my sight and has remained on my person since setting sail.

Elizabeth was captivated by the handwritten words. They made her tense and uneasy; she had experienced the feelings before when she had been caught peering at the pages of a banned book.

I have had some time to reflect on what I saw and experienced. For a moment in time, I believed the 200,000-strong masses were in some way hypnotized. Not the act of being hypnotized, but activating those who were already hypnotized, like turning on a radio to allow the tubes to warm up, a radio tuned to a certain frequency. I had heard of mass psychology for the first time when the captain of the Graf Zeppelin described Dr. Eckener's doctorate and work on the Graf Zeppelin. I could not then, and cannot now, comprehend hypnotizing the masses. Were they being inoculated to compound the effect? I do not know what to say; I had never considered it. I had never considered it possible; but now I'm convinced all of it is in action in Germany. A formation of the hypnotized masses.

It may be lingering effects from the rally, but that experience made me physically ill to the point I could not function. My head throbbed like some unseen hand was applying incredible pressure. I thought my temples would burst! My arm throbbed as if I had been inoculated with a thick needle. I was never so pleased that the aspirin in my kit finally obtunded the pain in my head from that sclerotic event.

I must rely on my eyes as I would my instruments when flying. As I have time to digest this bitter pill, I can state with conviction that with or without inoculations, I witnessed a quarter million people completely and totally hypnotized and transmitting to Chancellor Hitler that they are his to lead to a greater glory. For the greater good of Germany. This concept is foreign to me. I've seen hypnosis demonstrations. I know what I saw; it is a dichotomy, and it does not make sense to me. Even now as I write this, I am repulsed by the words, fearful that the men who dispatched me on the quest for information for my country will think of me as not up to the task, that I did not provide what they seek, that I am still quite mad from the kidnapping and the trial.

It may be helpful to continue my observations, some of which have been dimmed with the passage of time or the horribility of the ordeal, while others still strike me as if I were viewing them for the first time and are somehow, important. Am I missing something?

I remember distinctly the drab dress of the woman who adjusted recording equipment next to a spotlight which focused on Hitler. I asked Goebbels, "Is that Leni Riefenstahl?" and he acknowledged that it was. It was as if she dressed to be inconspicuous.

I noticed that Goebbels knew she was in the arena, but he never looked directly at her. He would rarely make eye contact with anyone. He shocked me when he smugly stated he had artfully manipulated her by using Adolf Hitler. His smile had no direction as he said, "I suggested Der Führer should personally approach Riefenstahl to film a strong Germany overflowing with Wagnerian motifs of power and beauty." Goebbels was quick to remark that he was certain she would do anything for Adolf Hitler, but not for him. It was as if it was something that was necessary to solve a puzzle or an equation. Goebbels was very proud of himself, getting others to do things they would not normally consider for money or prestige. I realized I had met a master manipulator, like the late Dr. Eckener. Herr Goebbels is so immersed in the psychology and propaganda that he is an expert, a maestro. I admit, I initially viewed him as a carnie, a trickster from a carnival. But no longer. I believe he possesses information on how to manipulate the mind that we may not have. If so, it is a talent which could be used for evil.

While Goebbels' assessment of the encounter may be entirely accurate, for you can never tell who is telling the truth in these events, I explained it to myself that, as the Reichsminister of Propaganda, he was keenly aware he had created a persona and reputation that could be offputting to others, like me.

Herr Goebbels was surprisingly open. He explained it was in the year of 1933 that Der Führer asked Leni Riefenstahl to direct a short film, "Der Sieg des Glaubens" (The Victory of Faith), to be shot at that year's Nuremberg Nazi Party Rally. That film was a success and was a template for her more famous work, "Triumph des Willens" (Triumph of the Will), shot at the Nuremberg Rally the following year.

He was very forthcoming on the details of the encounter. Herr Hitler asked Leni Riefenstahl what she needed; she was soon overwhelmed with unlimited resources and full artistic license for the picture. At that moment, I realized trust was a very powerful tool of propaganda, when in the right hands. Political power is a special tool, another silent weapon of propaganda.

I recall "Triumph of the Will" was widely regarded as one of the most masterful propaganda films ever produced. With its evocative images and innovative film techniques, it was an epic work of documentary filmmaking, and I believe it won several awards. I never considered why until this moment, *because it forever linked Leni Riefenstahl with the film's subject, National Socialism. And to Adolf Hitler.*

As one of the few civilians invited into the viewing stands, I wonder how anyone will ever believe this? Although the event was filmed, what I experienced was something you cannot effectively film.

We are sailing to America, and I will be grateful to see The Statue of Liberty and New York City again. I look forward to delivering my report. I feel safe now; no need to worry about my journal being purloined by a Nazi agent from the Gestapo. I must send a letter to the President, thanking him for allowing me to serve my country. After I disembark and meet my contact, apparently a lawyer and close friend of the President, I look forward to returning home. I sent a private telegram to him announcing my arrival in New York City. And I dispatched a private telegram to Anne in Paris. I miss her and the children so.

I know now that I was the correct choice to go to Germany, observe, and report those observations. Spywork can be so tedious. I am baffled by how I was selected for such a duty. Who recognized me for such a mission?

My successful solo crossing of the Atlantic put me in an enviable category of being the American who accomplished what others could not. And possibly the President knew I was sufficiently intrigued with the rise of National Socialism and Hitler's anti-Semitism, that I might receive special dispensation others might not be afforded. I can see that I would be more likely to get an invitation from Generalfeldmarschall Göring than nearly anyone else. I still had to be available.

Yes, I was surprised by the URGENT request from the White House. Apparently, some unidentified member of U.S. Army Intelligence in Europe had singled me out and requested I should visit Germany as a tourist. But if the occasion presented itself, I should inspect, if possible, the country's aircraft and air force, the famed Luftwaffe, and the construction of the other Zeppelins Germany has been constructing and operating. I sense I will need another trip or two to fulfill the President's request.

Since I did not announce my intentions, I wonder if I will ever receive the rest of the story. I will forever wonder if it was Army Intelligence who informed Herr Goebbels that I was on their Zeppelin to visit their country.

Or did the Nazis have spies in America? Did they know, in spite of my alias? Did they know I traveled by train with a Navy intelligence officer out of uniform to Miami (actually, to the Naval Air Station Opa Locka) in order to make the scheduled Atlantic crossing in the Graf Zeppelin in time to attend the Nazi Party Rally?

Am I still a hero to the Nazis? I am certain I left on good terms and was invited back by no less than the Generalfeldmarschall of the Luftwaffe, Hermann Göring. As a token of his sincerity, he promised to take me hunting and presented me with a Minerva chronograph, a 50mm mono-pusher wristwatch. These watches are worn by their military pilots.

I was not surprised Herr Göring had not done all his homework. It wasn't publicized and he was likely unaware I had written to the Longines watch company and described a watch that would make navigation easier for pilots. Longines has been producing aviator watches with tourbillon movements since 1931. The quality of the Longines timepiece is many times greater than the Minerva.

An offer of hunting? Stag, hare, fox?

I expect this report will be presented to the heads of U.S. Naval Intelligence and Army Intelligence. I wonder if they will be interested in what I perceived to be the mass hypnosis of a quarter million Nazis? Their unknown vaccination protocols. I cannot perceive what intelligence value there is to mentioning necrophilia.

Today, while eating German sweet breads and sipping tea on the foredeck, I read The New York Times article about the Nuremberg Laws as articulated by Adolf Hitler. They not only rescinded the old Wehrmacht's Guidelines for New Therapy and Human Experimentation, but they also imposed limitations on the rights of German Jews, stripping them of their citizenship and turning them into enemies of the Fatherland. The author accuses the Nazis of now being able to conduct human experiments without a person's consent, without limits. Nazis would celebrate such an event; I doubt the rest of the world would do so. Maybe it is because of my own views on anti-Semitism that I was unable to detect the newspaper's anti-Semitism. There was a quote attributed to Herr Goebbels: propaganda works best when those who are being manipulated are confident they are acting on their own free will.

I don't want to forget the episode when I waited for the great Nazi airship to make its approach at NAS Opa Locka. I had seen airships before in the skies over France, but no Zeppelins.

Finally, I still shudder at the thought that propaganda as I was led to believe, could be so inadequately described or understood in America. The German form of propaganda was finely tuned, as articulated by Herr Goebbels, it could turn an innocent young man into an unstoppable war machine. I have given this great thought; it is possible some forms of propaganda could be a more effective weapon in fighting wars than aircraft or tanks or battleships. What sliver I saw of group hypnosis possibly enhanced by inoculations suggested that a larger fighting force, like the whole German army, could be hypnotized to obey the word of one man, and then there would be no stopping men like Goebbels and Hitler from ruling the world.

In the U.S., military officers swear an oath of allegiance to the Constitution, not a single man.

Elizabeth nodded and returned the page to the file and closed it. She lifted her head and focused on a spot on the door. She realized the trajectory of the journal entries was basic spycraft. It came to her slowly. *Grandpa General was running Charles Lindbergh before there was an OSS.*

She said aloud to convince herself, "There were various departments with the executive which conducted American intelligence activities on an *ad hoc* basis, with no overall direction, coordination, or control. I know the Army and Navy had separate code-breaking departments... as did the State Department. What was his name? Oh yes, Henry Stimson deemed code-breaking an inappropriate function for the diplomatic arm. That's right, because 'gentlemen don't read each other's mail.' The FBI was not engaged; they handed domestic security and anti-espionage operations. So, it is possible *Grandpa General....*"

Elizabeth reopened the file and scanned the pages again, looking at who had been subject to the basic tradecraft. *Really just Lindbergh, although Grandpa General looks to have had contact with Jung or just maybe his research. Looks like Jung had discovered some interesting things on group psychologies, and Lindbergh confirmed them in Germany. That looks to be Lindbergh's mission. Validate and verify.* She came to an unexpected conclusion: *this is intelligence gathering in its rawest form. But it is more than that....* She said, "This file is probably the first successful intelligence gathering operations of Nazi Germany before there was an official Office of Strategic Services."

CHAPTER 8

October 10, 2002
Naval War College
Newport, Rhode Island

Bill McGee met with the other SEALs assigned to the war college for a running debrief. He had asked them to maintain soft surveillance on Duncan Hunter. The month-long informal surveillance on the civilian had turned up nothing unusual. McGee said, "I still want to know what he's doing here."

One SEAL asked, "But isn't he one of ours?"

McGee said, "If you mean Agency, then yes, but I want to know *why* he is here. The Agency doesn't send their intel officers here. If he keeps acting like a student, we'll terminate the coverage. Fair enough?"

McGee lamented that by all measures, Hunter was not only a good student, he just might be the distinguished graduate, much to the chagrin of the active-duty Air Force officers jockeying for the top grad and "must promote" performance records. Hunter didn't seem to try very hard as a student but still aced exams and read all the materials. McGee acknowledged Hunter being allowed to conduct classified research for Dr. McIntosh was unique. Even staff members were unaware of any student being allowed to do it, regardless of their security clearances.

The light surveillance on Hunter revealed he might have been a ladies' man, but he didn't exhibit any abnormal sexual tendencies. He had a couple of group dinners, only with the women in his seminar group, and only at the *Red Parrot*. He did not drink and always picked up the tab. Afterwards, he entered building 7 alone; his corner room was on the third floor. After class, he went to the gym every day, sometimes three times. He ran out to the mothballed aircraft carriers and back. Played intramural sports. Played racquetball in town. Every day he hit the classified library downstairs of the regular library for a few hours.

Sometimes he invited classmates for an adventure. The geographical bachelors in his seminar bonded as a group and played golf; sometimes they went to Boston for a ballgame and bought scalper's tickets. He and a classmate drove up to New Hampshire to check out old BMWs. Sometimes the group left the base and went to a racetrack in Lime Rock, Connecticut. Those times, Hunter retrieved his car on a trailer from a storage unit and raced it; they acted as his pit crew and then celebrated at the *Red Parrot* in Newport.

Except for the racecar, Hunter appeared to be a typical student doing typical male things with other typical male students, and doing typical male things with other typical female students.

McGee thought, *And he has a Blackberry. No one else in school has one. Only the senior officers at the Pentagon had access to that technology. And those leaders at the CIA.*

Then one of McGee's SEALs, Commander Jenks Arnold, said, "I think Hunter's under surveillance by someone other than us." McGee's interest was piqued, and he asked for details. "Well, this last time while I was staked out near the storage area where he keeps his car, I noticed a couple of Middle Eastern men intently watching Hunter. Hunter and a couple of his classmates were working on his racecar where he garaged it, eating pizzas, drinking beers and sodas."

"*Bullfrog*, it was hard not to stare," the SEAL commander said. "That's an incredible car. Loud! I was in the tree line above the lot and saw these dudes sneaking around corners. Their actions suggested they were scoping out the place. I thought they were casing the storage units, then I thought they were interested in the Vette. But the longer I watched, I wondered if they weren't watching Hunter, like I was."

"When Hunter and his friends were done, they rolled the car inside, put a car cover over it, locked the shed with a big padlock, and left. The dudes followed him out of the storage lot. Nothing else."

Lieutenant Commander Irving said, "That's where I picked him up. His classmates returned to base, Hunter went through the drive through at Taco Bell, and then he drove to the Newport Athletic Club where he plays racquetball with a bunch of old dudes. Five days a week. No deviations, so I went home. I didn't see anyone tailing him."

Commander Arnold said, "I left after ten minutes. I'm pretty sure they were watching him. They didn't see me."

McGee nodded. *Still a mystery....*

Then Arnold said, "But you know what else? Those dudes might be students here."

McGee spun his massive head around. He was instantly more interested. He made a motion with his fingers urging "more."

Arnold offered, "We just spent a year looking at Muslim men in Afghanistan, and there aren't many Muslims in Newport. There aren't many at school—I think the admiral said there were 30 or so from allied nations. Those foreign officers all have thick dark hair, so did the dudes in the lot. They weren't Hispanic like me."

McGee asked, "What makes you think you think they may be students?"

"A couple of days ago, Irv and I went to a Red Socks game in Boston; took the train. I swear I saw that dude leave a mosque near the ballpark and head for the train station. He was in another car and got off when we got off in Newport. I think I've seen him in the hall or auditorium—I never really got a good look at him in school. He's not distinctive and I cannot swear he's a student; the point is I didn't follow him. They all look alike to me."

Arnold asked, "What's it mean, *Bullfrog*?"

"Duncan Hunter has more people interested in him than us, and that is crazy. The man has the best tickets on the planet—I mean, *Yankee White*; access to the White House. Give me a friggin' break. A career spook, *35-year SIS*, vouched for him. Retired DO. My wife even worked for him."

Jenks said, "Maybe he's just a student."

McGee said, "Regular students don't know former CIA executives."

Arnold said, "*Bullfrog*, you want to continue this?"

McGee sighed and said, "No; I think the boy can take care of himself. But I would like to know who else has eyes on him, and if there is a foreign student surveilling a spook at school, I will flush that turd."

.   .   .

Zaid Jebriel, Lieutenant Commander in the Royal Saudi Navy, Saudi Intelligence Services, left the Boston mosque and headed for the train station for the return trip to Newport. The imam told the al-Qaeda undercover intelligence lieutenant that he had served the cause well. "Return and continue to observe the SEALs that murdered our brothers in Afghanistan. We are confident the infidel Hunter is *Cee-ah-a*."

Jebriel had explained, "The infidel surrounds himself with men and women."

The imam said, "Infidels are such swine. We have a secret weapon. You said he likes women. A woman will discover his true mission."

CHAPTER 9

February 14, 2013
Cologne, Germany

When the world's leading infectious disease and bioweapons expert, Dr. Salvatore D'Angelo, the Director of the Centers for Disease Control and Prevention (CDC), visited Germany, he stayed at the Althoff Grandhotel Schloss in Cologne. He was welcomed by Rho Schwartz Scorpii, not as a supplicant to the Supreme Lord Chancellor of the European Federation, not as a sycophant to the world's richest man, but as a titular business partner with the chairman of the *Ostgut Foundation.*

Dr. D'Angelo knew Scorpii had a public persona of flamboyance and glittering excesses. Most billionaire homosexual men in Germany did. The public story was that he had invested heavily in petroleum and biotechnologies, which became the source of much of his wealth. Scorpii supported progressive and liberal political causes overtly, dispensing billions in donations through his *Ostgut Foundation.* In liberal circles, everyone knew the history of the multibillionaire and that *Ostgut* was the name of the former railway depot from which the five-year-old Scorpii and his family had boarded a train for the Nazi concentration camps. Scorpii's *Ostgut Foundation* had donated over $10 billion to various philanthropic causes through third-party non-governmental organizations (NGOs), officially to reduce poverty, improve health, increase transparency, and award scholarships and fund nascent universities which would teach Marxism and Communism across the globe.

Rho Schwartz Scorpii had other interests in supporting socialist and communist nations that were committed to the destruction of capitalist nations everywhere. Most noteworthy were the accomplishments his European companies had made in state-of-the-art biological research and development. Scorpii provided additional funding to government leaders and researchers in biotechnology and bioweapons laboratories in Russia, China, and Iran to explore the universe of infectious diseases and viruses, and their potential for engineering as bioweapons. Through other NGOs, the *Ostgut Foundation* owned the controlling interests of virtually all of Europe's abortion clinics, as the human abattoirs had infinitely great and direct access to fetal remains for European biotech labs. American biotechnology firms were prohibited from using fetal remains for research and could not compete.

The quarterly meeting with Dr. D'Angelo was for business and pleasure. Young blood was the secret to eternal youth, and no one would believe the dapper D'Angelo was anywhere close to his biological age. All thanks to Lord Scorpii who traded a *soupçon* of luxury at his hotels for Dr. D'Angelo's gifts of lucrative U.S. government contracts and grants.

D'Angelo and Scorpii shared political and world views, and got along famously. They agreed the Nuremberg Code's *right to informed consent was a dangerous idea that must be dispatched like toxic waste.* One man plotted and the other exploited human desires for financial gain. Culturally, they agreed on much, such as it is better to abort an unwanted child than condemn it to a life such as Scorpii's had been: in the concentration camps, in the orphanages, abused by men for a lifetime of misery.

Scorpii's petroleum holdings generated billions annually; the wealth enabled his other business enterprises to grow. When over 100,000 children went missing in Europe each year, Scorpii perfected the business of finding the missing children and leveraging child sex trafficking among the rich and powerful for profit.

Many of the missing children were given safe harbor in child brothels as an adjunct of gay men's clubs. They were given nice clothes, food, and baths. Young boys would dress as girls to serve a discrete clientele who would be blackmailed for information and to incite military and industrial espionage. Scorpii's genius was creating a European network of blackmailed children to blackmail pedophiles.

Abortion clinics harvested body parts for the biotechnology firms during the day and for the pedophiles at night. They also harvested baby blood after some of the disposable children were tortured or frightened to death behind closed doors. This adrenalized blood was sold as *Ambrosia* to the lucky few who could afford it. It was marketed as a pathway to reduce aging, to give the most euphoric high of any natural drug known to man. But *Ambrosia* was also very addictive, requiring a fresh supply of adrenalized blood from murdered infants regularly. In the pedophile's language, elites D'Angelo and Scorpii viewed the unwanted or missing children and their organs as *inventory*.

Most recently, there had been four former senior Intelligence Officers assigned to the North Atlantic Treaty Organization (NATO) who had succumbed to the siren song of illegal child sex or sex with the dead. They were filmed in the act. They detailed their crimes in suicide notes, for they would not be blackmailed. They would not conduct espionage for any front company or NGOs clandestinely funded by the *Ostgut Foundation*. Two men took their lives while confirming the existence of the pedophile networks within the small discrete NGO, of child torture, child murder, and child organ harvesting as an accepted practice in Europe. Two others were found killed, disemboweled and castrated. These atrocities at the highest levels of government, in the multinational corporate sector, as well as throughout academic institutions and civil society were conducted in virtually every major city, mostly on weekends. One suicide letter concluded, "Satanic Occult practices are very real. And, I am so ashamed."

When Dr. Salvatore D'Angelo was a guest of the Althoff Grandhotel Schloss Bensberg, he met his benefactor in clothes he would not wear in America: a Versace suit, Hermés tie, and handmade shoes from Portugal. In the private office of the Supreme Lord Chancellor, Scorpii greeted the American with an ingratiating, "You are looking incredible, Salvatore! The *Ambrosia* is magic, no?" Pedophilic artwork dominated the walls of the old man's office.

D'Angelo bowed in deference to the man's age and position. "I feel better than I did when I was thirty. You are a magician, Lord Scorpii." They discussed the weather, the magnificent hotel, and Scorpii's stable of rare Mercedes 540K Special Roadsters used to transport special guests to the hotel from the airport. The special cars put Scorpii's special guests in a euphoric mood.

When the appurtenances of unproductive conversation had run its course, D'Angelo said, "Lord Scorpii, my government has ceased funding what I call 'gain of function' research. This is important work; politicians are not the best people to determine what critical needs the world's evolutionary biologists should be researching. If some of your people could submit, um, proposals for *gain of function* research without calling it *gain of function* research, I will be able to continue my research. This is important research. And of course, I will provide all the funding."

"Of course. Consider it done! Is there anything more I can do for you, *Salvatore*?"

D'Angelo said, "Not at this time. But I may need your help in a future endeavor."

Scorpii smiled and nodded. "When you are ready, Salvatore. When you are ready."

The men shook hands as Scorpii asked, "So, are you ready for the spa, *Salvatore*?"

D'Angelo raised his eyes to the art on the walls and nodded gleefully.

CHAPTER 10

May 23, 2014
2200 hours local

With a light touch on the screen of the handheld, night vision goggle-capable tablet (NVG), Lockheed Martin (LM) site lead Ralph Gilbert looked through the NVGs strapped on his head and selected the START icon. He looked up from the tablet, and the cockpit of the single-seat helicopter in which he sat instantly came alive in various shades of green. NVG-compatible instrument panel lighting signified that the AVIONICS MASTER switch had been flipped remotely, and the start sequence for the *K-MAX* helicopter had been received.

In seconds, the engine starter was activated by the aircraft's mission computer, and the intermeshing rotors turned as the powerful Lycoming turboshaft engine spooled up the massive gearbox. Gilbert momentarily pulled the NVGs away from his face to ensure there were no external lights visible on the *K-MAX*. When the aircraft achieved flight idle, he checked the tablet instrumentation to make sure that the engine throttle had been programmed to 100% rotor speed, N_R. Then Gilbert crawled out from the optionally manned, primarily autonomous aircraft. He closed and locked the canopy hatch.

A twelve-foot-high concrete segmented T-wall surrounded the maintenance shelter and protected the aircraft and support crew from al-Qaeda snipers overlooking the Kabul International Airport. Only those with night vision devices could observe the unmanned *K-MAX* pre-takeoff activities. The helicopter was virtually silent and the paint did not reflect light. That made launching the helo a little eerie. Machines are supposed to make noise, especially helicopters with turbines.

The aircraft's support crew was contracted to Lockheed Martin as part of a broader services contract. They were all wearing NVGs and body armor as they prepared the aircraft for autonomous external cargo load operations for its final flight in Afghanistan. A one hundred fifty-foot multi-layered nylon "long wire" pendant was connected to the aircraft's cargo hook centered on the *K-MAX's* belly. At the end of the long wire was the specially built circular carousel assembly, a metal wagon wheel device had four separate 25-foot short wires that were equidistant from each other. Each was connected to one of four piles of materials in cargo nets.

The contents of each cargo net would be delivered to one of four discrete and widely dispersed combat outposts between 12,000 and 15,000 feet of altitude of the Tora Bora, Afghanistan's mountain range of the Himalayas. Each load contained essential materials for the men in the field—colloquially described as the *Three Bs*: *beans, bullets, and band-aids*—food, ammunition, and essential supplies. Three loads for the troops; one classified load for an advancing SOCOM outpost.

Once Gilbert assumed his position away from the black rotorcraft, he touched an icon on the tablet to activate the autonomous program. As it had done almost every night for nearly three years, the servomotors worked the flight controls, and the collective pitch lever moved up incrementally, as if an unseen hand was pulling the collective stick. The unmanned *K-MAX* seemed to take an interminable amount of time to respond, but when it did, the helicopter slowly lifted off the ground with precision. In seconds, it had stabilized and hovered perfectly in ground effect. In near total silence.

Additional computer inputs to the collective resulted in the aircraft slowly gaining altitude. The aircraft climbed straight up. The flight computer and sensors aboard the helicopter allowed the *K-MAX* to take up the tension on the long wire, gently tugging the cargo load underneath, then maneuvered to hover out of ground effect directly over the four full cargo nets. Once the payload of over 5,000 pounds had been lifted off the ground, the aircraft deliberately transitioned from hover to forward flight and methodically departed for the mountains of the Tora Bora.

Gilbert and the LM men with NVGs watched the unnaturally quiet and unnaturally black-coated aircraft as it disappeared on its way to Americans in full battle gear. The troops at Combat Outpost Payne and other places waited wearing NVGs in total darkness on mountaintops for their stuff. Since the unmanned *K-MAX* avoided detection by flying at night at high altitudes, the enemy was unable to detect or direct effective hostile fires at the unseen and virtually silent aircraft. The aircraft may have been shot at, but the maintenance crews never found a single bullet hole in the metal airframe or the wooden rotor blades.

Gilbert had been there from the beginning and had been through it all. He wondered, *Would tonight be the one time the al-Qaeda got lucky and downed the aircraft?* He removed his night vision goggles and stared into the night. He sighed and reflected on the program that he and his men would soon no longer be a part of, all because of *politics*....

Kaman had been developing a version of the unmanned *K-MAX* since 1998. Their strange bug-like but incredibly stable and virtually vibration-free intermesher rotorcraft was originally designed for hauling logs out of remote forests. But it wasn't until Lockheed Martin provided the manpower and engineering expertise of its Electronics Division that the concept became a state-of-the-art autonomous combat resupply machine. Two helicopters were equipped with Autonomous Aerial Cargo/Utility System (AACUS) technology, which combined advanced algorithms with LIDAR (light detection and ranging) and electro-optical/infrared (EO/IR) sensors to enable a user or programmer to deposit a load of cargo on a tiny mountainous landing site no larger than the bed of a pickup truck. Virtually every night, every week, regardless of the weather. Three loads for the troops; one classified load for SOCOM. In virtual silence.

It wasn't lost on Gilbert and crew that every replenishment flight of an unmanned *K-MAX* removed at least a hundred ground troops who would have been assigned to a convoy that would have been exposed to al-Qaeda snipers and the Taliban's improvised explosive devices (IED) hidden in or beside the roads leading into the Tora Bora. Gilbert and his support crew proved the unmanned cargo delivery concept was more than viable. It had become essential; the standard in casualty-free, safe cargo delivery. Nearly every day, with the precision of a Swiss watch, the cargo was delivered at a prescribed time at a designated target. The expected arrival time of the first classified load destined for SOCOM was scheduled for midnight. Spec Ops warriors who fought in some of the nastiest conditions imaginable, above 14,000 feet where the snow never melts, would say, *The Midnight Rider is bringing Christmas, it's always on time, and we never hear it coming!*

The unmanned *K-MAX* had flown over 1,000 accident-free missions and had hauled over three million pounds of supplies, from Caterpillar generators and fuel bladders to MREs (Meals-Ready-to-Eat), flashlight batteries and toilet paper. As a group, the men of Quiet Aero Systems (QAS), contracted to LM, were proud of their contributions. Countless lives had been saved, as a function of casualties avoided since resupply troops in trucks had effectively been removed from IED-laden roads and sniper's crosshairs. The enemy couldn't kill what wasn't on the roads, and the troops in the hills were continually supplied with the materials they needed to press the al-Qaeda to the wall.

Back in Maryland, the Lockheed Martin Corporation bathed in accolades as the unmanned autonomous concept won aviation awards from *Popular Science* and *Aviation Week & Space Technology*. The Autonomous Unmanned Cargo Delivery aircraft was nominated for the 2012 Collier Trophy, but lost out to NASA/JPL Mars Science Laboratory/Curiosity project team for their successful Mars rover mission. (National Aeronautics and Space Administration/Jet Propulsion Laboratory).

As he walked back to the expeditionary maintenance hangar, Gilbert lamented that after tonight's mission, the aircraft would be sent home, presumably to Lockheed's Owego facility in New York where the program had begun or maybe dispersed to museums. The

QAS contingent would return to Elmira. Maybe when he got back home, he would be able to see his girlfriend again. *If she's even my girlfriend still….*

No reason had been given for removing the greatest counter-IED program on record. The Marine Corps had been so impressed with the six-month demonstration program that it had extended the use of the unmanned *K-MAX* helicopters indefinitely, keeping the two aircraft in use "until otherwise directed." Then, abruptly, the contract was canceled. The Marines in the mountains were pissed that their reliable resupply capability was being taken from them.

Al-Qaeda and the Taliban would immediately be back in business disrupting resupply missions and doing their part to send Americans back to the United States in body bags.

Ralph Gilbert wondered, *Who in their right mind would remove the unmanned K-MAX from combat? Well, I know who; will I ever learn why?*

•   •   •

The U.S. Air Force C-17 *Globemaster III* landed at the Elmira Corning Regional Airport during the hours when the airport was closed. It taxied to the eastern corner of the old Schweizer aircraft manufacturing business. Schweizer had initially been bought out by Lockheed Martin over two decades ago. Now belonging to Quiet Aero Systems, mechanics and avionics technicians poured from the hangars and helped the Air Force airmen push two white-plastic cocooned *K-MAX* aircraft from the cargo bay.

It was a slow and deliberate process; one they had done three years earlier in reverse, loading the aircraft for the war in Afghanistan. Removing the old war birds didn't require the same gentle, precise handling it had taken to load them when the pair of *K-MAX* helicopters left the QAS plant. This time, removal was accomplished in an hour, at which point the C-17 crew closed up their jet, bid their adieus, and departed the airport.

Gilbert and the unmanned *K-MAX* maintenance team had one final act to accomplish. Before they returned to their jobs at QAS, the unmanned *K-MAX* aircraft were moved into the far hangar for demilitarization and disposal at a later date. Gilbert and his men learned the unmanned *K-MAX* s were to be destroyed; a subcontractor would disassemble them and remove them from the QAS facility. Maintenance actions that would have preserved the aircraft for future use or for museum displays were not to be done.

Back in his distinctive red QAS shirt, Gilbert supervised the movement and placement of the aircraft to the far hangar.

Once the helicopters were in place, the ground crew uncoupled the towbars from the nose wheels and drove the tugs back to the refurbishment facility. Gilbert' job was not to question why; his job was to finish what he had started. He collected freshly signed non-disclosure agreements (NDA) that he would put on the CEO's desk before he closed and locked the hangar doors. He set the hangar's security system for the final time, closing that chapter of the greatest combat-proven aviation robot ever manufactured. Gilbert walked back to the corporate office, knowing his filthy car in the lot would not start.

But first he had to call a woman and let her know he was back in the U.S.A. This time, for good.

CHAPTER 11

June 1, 2015

"Thank you for tuning into this episode of *Unfiltered News* and welcome to the only true American on-line news network. From the formerly elegant city of Washington, D.C., where there is no difference between the communist message and the Democrat Party's message, we can report accurately the Democrat's propaganda arm is at it again. We have the video!"

"We thank our growing list of sponsors and the border blaster radio station, across the Rio Grande from Del Rio, Texas, generating an unbelievable 500,000 watts of power. Our radio transmitter is on Mexican soil, beyond the reach of liberal Democrat regulators and the censors of Free Speech, the American media. What they don't want you to know, they simply will not report it. Freedom is what makes this radio program and on-line telecast possible from coast to coast. I've got much to discuss. This is Demetrius Eastwood. Let's get your *Unfiltered News* rolling!"

"In the latest national polling, the Democrat Party hit a new alarming low, and the trend line is heading further south. We can only wonder if the Democratic Party will ever recover from the collapse. Massive blunders over the past 30 years have led to this turning point in Democrats' fortunes. The Democrat Party has been a stain on the nation since its founding in 1828 by a virulently racist president, Andrew Jackson. It has gone from dominating national politics to powerlessly criticizing Republicans."

"For the first time in the nation's history, the total number of registered Republican voters exceeds the number of registered Democrats. Chalk it up to Admiral McGee's leadership and his *Not Going to be Afraid Any More* initiative. Black women, single women, elderly women are the most common victims of violent crime. There are now over a million women who have the training to handle a weapon so they can protect themselves and their families with military surplus weapons. In those areas of the country where *Not Going to be Afraid Any More* has been implemented, violent crime against women is down almost 90 percent. No one has gotten hurt but criminals."

"The latest example that occurred just yesterday, a pregnant woman bravely defended her family from a would-be carjacker. A family from Missouri had been celebrating their daughter's eighth birthday. They marked the special day by visiting the zoo and waterpark. However, the celebration took a violent turn. With their three children in the backseat, the father was loading their vehicle in a parking garage, when a man assaulted the father with a tire iron. The criminal ran to the front of the car and threw open the driver's door, screaming, 'Get out of the car!' He began punching the mother, trying to get her out of the driver's seat. But she pulled a gun out from her purse and shot the would-be carjacker. The father suffered a broken collarbone and fractured ribs. The mother shot the thug in the head and the neck. He ran from the scene, collapsed, and died a few blocks away."

"The liberal media, led by the *Washington Post* and *The New York Times*, persist in demanding I delete the historically accurate account of the consequences of an unarmed society. Apparently, in all the media no one knows how to use the internet. The media never bring up the fact that Democrats and the Nazis and all totalitarian regimes were obsessed with gun confiscation. They used the most persuasive forms of propaganda to pry legal firearms from law-abiding citizens. If you have been paying attention for the past dozen years you know that saying the Democrats are obsessed with gun confiscation is a gross understatement. Every day they come out with a new scheme at the national, state, and local level to deprive Americans of their Constitutional rights. Their aim is to terrorize you, to change your mind. They want you to believe that the government will protect you."

"Admiral McGee reminds the media that perhaps the reason so many people are feigning outrage and offense to his *Not Going to be Afraid Any More* initiative, particularly in Democrat-run states, is that under Democrat-led policies, America has become soft on the issue of the Second Amendment. This suggests Americans have become weak, that the left's propaganda is working, that they are essentially offended by everything up to and including a snowflake in July. Let me say, 'An armed society is a polite society.' Thomas Jefferson wrote, 'No free man shall ever be debarred the use of arms.' He wrote this into the 1776 draft of the Virginia Constitution. Instead of playing defense, we need to ask the left, the Democratic Party, 'Why do you spend so much time trying to disarm Americans? What is your real goal?' There is a reason, and that reason is that the left embraces criminals, not the victims. These people, the Democrats, are not on the side of America."

"So, further in the good news category and related to Admiral McGee's *Not Going to be Afraid Any More* program, two illegal aliens, whose corpses will remain nameless, believed they could easily overpower the home-alone 12-year-old Molly Colmes when her father left to run to the store. It seems these crooks had not learned two things about the residents of the house they had cased: they were in South Dakota, and Molly had been a clay bird shooting champion since she was nine. Molly was upstairs in her room when the two men broke through the front door of the Colmes' residence. She ran to her father's room, grabbed his 12-gauge 870 Remington Wingmaster shotgun, and took up a defensive position at the top of the stairs."

"Molly showed remarkable courage defending herself and her house when the first criminal ran up the stairs to the second floor. He caught a near-point blank blast of skeet shot from the 12-year-old's knee-crouch aim. He suffered fatal wounds to his abdomen and genitals and collapsed at the foot of the stairs. Criminal number two, apparently right behind the idiotic number one criminal, took a blast to the chest, tumbled down the stairs, struggled out the door, and staggered out onto the porch where he bled to death before medical help could arrive."

"The police report said that one of the illegal aliens had been armed with a stolen 45-caliber handgun he took during another home invasion. That victim was not so lucky; he died from stab wounds to the chest."

"Ever wonder why stuff like Molly Colmes' encounter with criminals never makes NBC, CBS, PBS, MSNBC, CNN, or ABC news? We cover the news they will not carry. A 12-year-old girl, properly trained, defended her home and herself against two murderous, illegal immigrants, and she wins. She is still alive. Molly Colmes was well trained by her NRA Instructor father, and she knows what gun control is all about!" Eastwood clapped in the studio, applauding the actions of the brave young lady.

"Two things just in, two more churches were destroyed by fire over the weekend and the FBI has removed the last terrorist from their Most Wanted Terrorist List. Church fires are becoming a trend. And no more terrorists on the FBI's Most Wanted Terrorist List should be a cause for rejoicing, but that news appears to have been met with indifference in the corrupt news media. Maybe there will be a film at eleven."

"And before we go to break, have you heard of the Democrat Party's latest effort to censor Americans and talk radio, like me? New cars will not be equipped with AM radios anymore, with Ford leading the way, proving the left's lunacy once again. Apparently, they never heard of the National Emergency Broadcast System. AM radio baby. Rush Limbaugh turned AM radio into a powerhouse, and liberals just can't have that!"

After a break and commercials, Eastwood continued. "Another good news story of a person with *huevos:* reports that the giant Sequoias, the largest trees in the world, were in danger of being totally consumed by fire were met with indifference in the capital building in Sacramento. It was California's largest fire in decades. We were a little surprised to learn that for two years the Governor has refused to allocate any funding for aerial firefighting. Instead, he proudly said that they are testing new modeling that predicts where active blazes would spread and deployed an ignition detection system that relied on aerial sensors. Sounds like another faculty lounge idiot saying they don't need firefighting assets when there are forest fires. Instead, they will test a detection system. What are they looking for? Flames?"

"It sounds a bit like rearranging the chairs on the deck of the *Titanic*. The California Department of Forestry and Fire Protection, or Cal Fire, issued a solicitation for innovative ideas, laying out narrow parameters rather than the traditional funding request for firefighting efforts. Again note, no firefighting assets when multiple fires were threatening the park."

"So, as Sequoia National Park was threatened with several encroaching forest fires with a dangerous rate of spreading, two QAS FireFighter Martin *Mars* aircraft, built in the 1940s, the *Hawaii Mars* and the *Philippines Mars*, the largest operational flying boats and converted water bombers in existence, flew from their home base in Canada to Mono Lake in the Sierras. After four passes to take on water, they completely doused the Manzanar Fire that threatened the Sequoias."

"The CEO of QAS *FireFighters* took a hard line. 'The citizens of California are not being well served by their governor. Instead of taking decisive action, he postured like a strutting chicken saying his way of firefighting is the wave of the future. Use technology to predict where the fires will be. If that doesn't work, if the Sequoias were destroyed, it would not be his fault or the fault of California. It would be nature's way of things. All things green. As the California governor was screaming at me, telling me we could not intervene on the out-of-control fires around the Sequoia National Park, I said, 'Sue me.' Our firefighters on the ground are also using drones to drop 'dragon eggs,' self-igniting plastic balls filled with potassium permanganate. Dropping dragon eggs as a proven method of targeted fire-starting is essential with wildfire prevention. Not computer models or sensors. It may sound counterintuitive, but it is an established firefighting tactic to burn through undergrowth to prevent buildup of potential fuel for an unregulated blaze. Just before the dragon eggs are dropped from a drone, the ping-pong sized balls are injected with glycol which starts a reaction causing combustion within 30 seconds."

"The governor doesn't think California needs to spend money on protecting their national parks, so Canadian QAS *FireFighters* took action. And they provided proven preventative measures in fire-prone areas. Ya'll in California, take up a collection and recall that guy. Your fire is out, and your governor is an idiot. America's Sequoia National Park is safe. Consider it a gift from Canada to the people of California."

Eastwood added, "That is incredible. That is a real American patriot — for a Canadian! And the QAS *FireFighters* are reportedly at Amistad Lake, outside of Del Rio, Texas where our transmitter is located, preparing to tackle another fire deep inside Mexico. We have photos of the two bright red flying boats landing at the lake and two of their red helicopters. I have to tell you; these are truly remarkable aircraft."

Eastwood decided against another QAS *FireFighter* story in his stack of stories. A QAS firefighter helicopter had gone missing while flying to a Canadian airport. Instead, he mentioned in another comment the CEO of QAS *FireFighters* offered. "One final comment from the firefighters in Canada. The CEO of QAS *FireFighters* mentioned the Canadian government has also sided with the California governor in the stupidity department. They do not think there is a need for firefighting assets either. All that's required is the same failed modeling that predicts where active blazes will spread and deploying an ignition detection system that relies on aerial sensors. With a single bad policy, Canadian forests are now threatened by liberals. They don't need firefighting equipment like the *Mars* flying boats when there are forest fires. No, what is important to the Canadian Prime Minister is a detection system. QAS *FireFighters* is looking to get out of Canada and redeploy its operation to the U.S. Maybe Del Rio would be a nice new home."

Eastwood sighed into the microphone. "Also, thought for the day: calling an illegal alien an undocumented immigrant is like calling a drug dealer an unlicensed pharmacist. Just thinking."

"Next subject. Although it is early, Democrats have lost virtually all advantages, as we are seeing Republican's cruising to victory under the leadership of Admiral McGee. Stories of women protecting themselves, like young Molly Colmes, are popping up all over the country in rural areas, but increasingly also in the cities. Liberal media are not covering these stories but conservative media is. Democrats have not appealed well to rural or minority groups, and their oversensitivity has led to nonsensical words such as 'Latinx,' alienating a key constituency of blue states. No longer are pollsters suggesting it will be a red state wave, but a red state tsunami. Will it really be that easy? Also, send videos of electric vehicles on fire—we'll post them on our page. So far, we have three hundred. That's it for today! Eastwood out!"

CHAPTER 12

June 30, 2015

Anyone who knew anything about the late-60s early-70s, five-passenger Learjets would know huge engine nacelles were indicia that major modifications had been made to the fuselage to accept a pair of larger, state-of-the-art turbofan engines.

The Lear on the ramp may have had new engines installed at one time, but now the aircraft that had once been the joyride of the rich and famous and had graced executive terminals worldwide, appeared to be a spent shell of its former glory. With one look at this Learjet, the casual observer was likely to notice its paint, which was dull, coarse and scratched like the opaque headlight covers of salvage yard cars. The paint had faded to the color of old eggshells and was no longer smooth, but textured like a hen's egg. The Lear's paint told a sad tale of years of neglect. Maybe after the expensive engine modifications the money ran out and there were no funds to strip and re-paint Bill Lear's flying masterpiece.

Contributing to the image that the aircraft was a derelict were windscreens covered by a faded denim apron that was tied to remain in place, even in high winds, to protect the cockpit from the sun. There were none of the required serial numbers on the tail or engine cowlings—a sure sign that the jet had been taken out of service long ago. With crappy paint, no serial numbers, and the cockpit hidden behind a scrap of cloth, the Lear was obviously on the fast track to be broken up and sold for scrap, a heartbeat away from being disassembled and crushed.

But if one were to open the aircraft door and step inside the Lear, an incongruity would be seen. The cabin had that new car smell. The windshield transparency was crystal clear. The Lear's cockpit had been updated with advanced, fully digital electronic displays, the same multi-function panel displays (MFD) and best-available technology that were found in the newest corporate jets rolling off assembly lines in North America. The Lear's interior was also as fresh and modern as the oversized turbofan engines outside.

If one had been versed in the nuances of restored jets, one would have noticed other subtle changes on the outside. A new cambered wing had been installed. Subtle aerodynamic improvements had been made to reduce stall and approach speeds and improve maximum speeds. There was a new fuselage fuel tank for longer range as well.

Maybe the Lear would reside in the private hangar of a rich aviation aficionado or a movie star who had money to throw away on aviation toys. Some suggested it was a restoration challenge, a science project of a Commemorative Air Force (CAF) colonel who might also have a warbird or two in a very large and pristine climate-controlled hangar. Despite it being on one of the busiest airports in America, no one had any time to reflect on it; it was to be ignored.

For the people who lived and breathed aviation, the people who worked on the flight line, the Lear was unique, a flyer with new tires but without numbers. It was one of a handful of aircraft allowed to fly incognito, keeping the Lear's flight information private. With no serial number emblazoned in big black numbers on the tail or engine nacelles, no one could track the jet to destinations in the U.S. or abroad. The owner and aircraft operator had been granted an exception to policy to delete those things for security concerns.

The goal of the owner of the Lear was to not only create a hot little rocket ship, but to create an illusion.

CHAPTER 13

July 15, 2015

After the usual annual kabuki dance in a closet with an Agency polygrapher, Duncan Hunter was surprisingly enjoying his anonymity as the Agency's only airborne assassin of terrorists. If CIA Director, Greg Lynche, got out of the Congressional hearing on time, they would have their meeting, and *Maverick* would debrief the boss on his successes in Colombia, the Middle East, and Africa.

Hunter walked through the double doors of the main entrance of the Original Headquarters Building, across the large granite CIA seal inlaid in the floor of the main lobby, past the OSS Memorial and the statue of Major General William Donovan, and through the access control point.

In the quiet solitude in a corner of the CIA cafeteria, Hunter reflected on how far he and Lynche had come, and the obstacles Lynche had overcome to put their special access program (SAP) on the fast track to success.

Hunter acknowledged that Greg Lynche had a connate sense of when America's national security priorities were about to change. So he had put into place special assets necessary to conduct manned aircraft surveillance operations in the Middle East. And Colombia. And Africa.

The main problem appeared to be related to an old in-house Agency moratorium. When Francis Gary Powers was shot down over the Soviet Union in 1960, embarrassing the country and the CIA, Director Allen Dulles declared there would be no more manned flights over hostile, dangerous, or denied territories. The strategy of having local Colombian pilots perform aerial eradication work using armored crop dusters with bulletproof glass canopies was not the best solution.

The CIA leadership thought that the aerial eradication program would be an unqualified success; but because the countries on the program suddenly prohibited the use of herbicides, saying they created birth defects, it had actually been an abject failure. Even in armored crop dusters, before the prohibition, local pilots were not motivated to bomb mountainsides of coca with herbicides when the cartels shot at them with automatic weapons. When they were not being shot at, too many pilots crashed into the mountains where updrafts and downdrafts often proved fatal. It had been Greg's desire to have Agency pilots perform some of the out-of-country counternarcotics (CN) work, like aerial surveillance of drug labs in Colombia. Despite the billions spent on aerial eradication efforts in nine countries, drugs increasingly flowed into the U.S. Democratic-run states legalized marijuana and lessened the penalties for harder drugs. The left was winning the war on drugs.

In 1967, newly assigned Chief Air Branch Greg Lynche was tasked to improve the substandard aerial counterdrug and counterterrorism activities in Colombia. Quarterly program effectiveness reviews showed the aerial eradication and surveillance programs were not meeting expectations in South America. Narco-submarines were now crossing the Pacific and the Atlantic and making deliveries to the U.S. and Europe.

By chance, Lynche became aware of a U.S. Navy aeronautical engineer who had designed a low-noise-profile prototype aircraft that would have direct application for the military's low-altitude nighttime reconnaissance missions in Southwest Asia. The engineer had tried to find a government sponsor to put the concept in production with little luck. Lynche could see that such an aircraft could change the face of the war on drugs, and proposed the CIA Director fund the fragile U.S. Army project with the approval of a staffer known as the top counternarcotics specialist in Congress. The CIA Director approved Lynche's proposal, and he monitored the "Quiet Thruster" (QT) program at a distance.

What he found was stunning. Lynche slapped a top-secret, national security interest designation on the Naval officer's design and the Army's nascent program. This instantly complicated program progress and increased the cost of research and development (R&D). Lynche was present in the CEO's office when the proof-of-concept took to the sky. It was a heavily converted Schweizer glider with a muffled engine occupying the glider's rear seat. An engine-reduction gearbox was bolted between the engine and pilot, and a torque tube ran over the top of the canopy to drive an oversized and slowly turning propeller which kept supersonic waves from forming. And it had multiple mufflers to keep the exhaust quiet.

The first QT was anything but cute. It was the strangest Rube Goldberg contraption ever devised for low-level quiet flight, a wholly new category of spy aircraft. When all the concepts to quiet the aircraft were incorporated into it, test flights determined the altitude at which a blindfolded crowd could discern the wingbeats of an owl or when a QT flew overhead. With every new development to optimize quiet flight, the Chief Air Branch was forced to slap more top-secret classifications on the means and method: multiple mufflers, state-of-the-art propeller design, a trade-secret prop speed, and a proven operational altitude where an enemy could not detect they were under surveillance.

The initial propeller for the QT was handcrafted out of seasoned birch stock by a noted propeller designer and builder. Two QT-2s built at the Lockheed facility at the San Jose, California airport under the highest security measures proved their effectiveness with a demonstration program in Vietnam. Lockheed engineers turned their attention to the challenge of designing a quieter platform for production. For the production YO-3As, depending on mission, there would be three highly specialized propellers developed by MIT's acoustics laboratories; each prop was specifically tuned for a discrete altitude, airspeed, and propeller speed. The day the Army showed the effectiveness of each quiet propeller, Lynche slapped them with a top-secret classification.

That was also the day when the Navy, Air Force, and Marine aviation acquisitions managers opted out of the classified quiet aircraft program. The U.S. Army program manager, a colonel, was told by a Congressional staffer that there was no support from the services and there would be no funding for quiet aircraft production. The program was to be canceled. When Lynche heard the news, he called the New York congressman directly and offered Agency money to fund a short production run of aircraft. The U.S. Army program manager agreed to use a six-bladed prop that was noisier than the quieter more expensive propellers. To compensate for the compromise, operational aircraft would have to fly at a little higher altitude.

In the span of a few hours, the quiet aircraft program went from aviation novelty to program cancelation to limited production. To avoid interfering with the Army's Table of Allowance, which listed the number and type of aircraft the Army was authorized to have, the quiet aircraft were designated "prototype demonstrators" to determine their effectiveness in a combat setting. They had six months to prove themselves. In 1969, the Lockheed Aircraft Corporation built and delivered eleven prototypes to the U.S. Army. The Air Force packed the aircraft into two cargo jets and delivered all eleven to Vietnam as quickly as they rolled off the factory floor in Pasadena, California. Greg Lynche was ecstatic. He had his quiet aircraft, even if the Army possessed them. Now all he had to do was get the CIA Director's moratorium overturned or amended and hope the U.S. Army wouldn't crash any of the aircraft.

The new aircraft were pressed into combat as soon as they arrived in country. Every night at midnight the YO-3As went out. Every night, they detected advancing North Vietnamese soldiers between layers of jungle canopies using first-generation night observation device systems (NODS). The night vision sensor operator became a forward air controller who guided naval gunfire or artillery to destroy the Viet Cong. Passenger and cargo planes leaving Air Force bases in Vietnam were being lost to Viet Cong sniper fire until the YO-3A began flying, detecting the snipers who had cleverly concealed their firing positions close to the air base in holes, caves, and other "hides." Identifying the precise locations of snipers from the air allowed troops with flamethrowers to extirpate the guerilla snipers from their hides and immolate them.

The enemy who had been making headway, was suddenly demoralized. They retreated. The tide of war had turned with the introduction of the YO-3As until word of its successes reached the Oval Office. A Presidential decree stated its mission was complete and demanded the Army's quiet aircraft be returned to America at once for disposal.

The Army's experiment with quiet airplanes, with hundreds of missions flown by YO-3As had been a resounding success. The aircraft were never detected at night, and not a single aircraft sustained any damage from the enemy. The U.S. Army's general staff were livid that their game-changing nighttime surveillance aircraft were being pulled from the battlefield. The YO-3A proved its mettle in combat every time it took to the skies. Yet it was being removed from Vietnam for no apparent reason.

Of the eleven YO-3As manufactured for the Army, one had been lost in a landing mishap, but ten survived. Once they were returned Stateside, they were sent to Davis Monthan Air Force Base in Tucson to be dismantled and scrapped. The Chief Air Branch, who had quietly funded the aircraft, tracked their movement out of Vietnam and scheduled disposal. He requested the Army transfer the excess war birds for counterdrug missions, but the Army refused.

For national security purposes, the counterterrorism expert and Congressional staffer suggested the Army issue an official press report that all the YO-3As prototypes had either been destroyed in Vietnam or were destined for Army aviation museums around the country. Salvaged aircraft would be put up for auction.

At that point, Greg Lynche leveraged an established CIA shell company with one of the highest procurement priorities to purchase the salvaged aircraft for experimental flights. NASA was also interested in a single YO-3A with a previously secret wooden propeller to explore "quiet flight" performance envelopes. The intervention was timely. None of the YO-3As were destroyed. Four YO-3As went to Army museums. Five of the disassembled YO-3As were purchased by private entities and stored in shipping crates in a warehouse in Fredericksburg, Texas.

In 1995, on the eve of Greg Lynche's retirement as the Agency Director of Operations (DO), the number three person at the CIA, the Chief Air Branch declared the YO-3A aircraft that had been stored in Texas for 23 years as excess and sold them to Lynche for one dollar each, U.S. currency. Lynche finally had his airplanes, and he had used his position as the DO to remove the Dulles moratorium on manned aircraft over restricted areas. The CIA could now be in the aerial counternarcotics business against the drug cartels. They could also use them in the aerial counterterrorism business against the Muslim Brotherhood in the Middle East where there were no anti-aircraft systems, and manned aircraft could be used with impunity.

Most of the Muslim nations, close allies of the United States, were also at war with elements of the Islamic Underground, specifically their assassinations and sabotage arm, the Muslim Brotherhood. Any American help with targeting a burgeoning terrorist problem was welcome.

All Lynche needed was a pilot, and not any pilot would do. He had been tracking a very special person since the 1970s when his name first appeared on a list from a secret CIA screening program that nearly every child, government worker, and contracted executive in America had taken: Lynche's "17 Nails" special access program challenge. A newly minted Marine Corps Sergeant, Duncan Hunter, stood out from the rest of the country in high-level aptitude and problem solving, and complex pattern recognition. Lynche never tried to recruit the Marine who seemed to be on a fast track to a commission and flight school, but he monitored Hunter's progress and held his file in abeyance.

The "17 Nails" SAP was shut down by the CIA Director when an unintended consequence to the nationwide testing was detected. Researchers determined there was a political correlation between those who did well on the test and those who didn't. The test results showed that those who leaned left politically had a great deal of trouble solving or were unable to solve the 17 Nails puzzle and had little ability to recognize patterns. Those who leaned right politically solved the 17 Nails puzzle easily and were able to recognize complex patterns quickly. Thirty years of testing consistently concluded that complex, high-level, problem solving and pattern recognition were more prevalent in those on the right of the political spectrum. At age 21, Duncan Hunter set the record for how fast the puzzle could be solved. It was not a surprise to Lynche that Hunter registered as a Republican.

Eventually Lynche got his man, just as he had gotten his YO-3As. Under the initial special access program *Wraith*, the YO-3A's old night vision periscope system had been replaced with a fuselage-mounted, extendible Forward Looking Infrared (FLIR), with FLIR repeater scopes in each cockpit. The configuration proved to be very effective in its first mission, Hunter as the pilot and Lynche as the sensor operator located hostages and sex slaves held captive by the FARC (*Fuerzas Armadas Revolucionarias de Colombia*; the Revolutionary Armed Forces of Columbia) high in the Colombian mountains. Lynche had recorded the night's first mission on a VHS tape and gave Hunter a copy for a job well done.

But as more capabilities, like the drug crop eradication system, *Weedbusters*, were added to the basic aircraft, the YO-3A proved to be a spectacularly effective drug war fighting capability. The once industrial-looking prototype YO-3A had been continuously upgraded and was now a sleek, modern, and powerful warbird that didn't allow for any frippery. It located drug labs, FARC camps, and drug submarines in Colombia and fields of opium poppies in Afghanistan. The FLIR operator could see the high-resolution thermal images of those people protecting the vast opium poppy fields while *Weedbusters* lasers used ultraviolet (UV) radiation to kill or damage the emerging baby opium poppy plants.

The drug cartels expected noisy crop dusters spraying herbicides to fly over their poppy fields as they had in the past. As a countermeasure, the Islamic drug cartels always put children in the poppy fields at night, for the mighty Americans were considered weaklings when it came to children. The crop dusters would not spray herbicides on the poppy when children were present. When the children who slept in the poppy fields were not covered in the powdery herbicides yet large sections of the poppy fields continued to be devastated, the men of the cartels became enraged. The crop dusters no longer came to Afghanistan, but their protected fields were still being decimated by an unseen agent. The al-Qaeda retaliated and killed those who were not responsible, the innocent farmers and abused and sold the farmers' children.

After fifteen years of improvement, the UV light aerial eradication process eventually achieved probabilities of kill that approached 100%. No children were ever harmed by the laser. With the new technology, Hunter transitioned from irradiating thousands of mature plants over several nights to irradiating millions of nascent budding poppy plants in a single night, turning the YO-3A into the greatest counternarcotics success in the Agency. It was a different kind of spyplane, and the pilot who flew it was a different kind of pilot. Since everyone had believed the official press reports that all the YO-3As had either been destroyed in Vietnam or were hanging in museums, no one suspected the YO-3As—affectionately called *Yo-Yos* in Vietnam—was again active, this time in low-level counterdrug and counterterrorism roles.

To keep it a secret national asset, the special-purpose quiet aircraft always received special handling and the highest movement priorities for counternarcotics and counterterrorism missions. After almost twenty years of moving the YO-3A and her crew into and out of high-risk locations under Duncan Hunter's leadership, the program execution had been refined to an art. There had never been a mission abort in the program's history. No aircraft were ever detected, no aircraft ever returned from a mission with bullet holes.

.   .   .

After Duncan had waited a few hours, the Director's secretary found Hunter in the cafeteria and informed him the Director would not be able to see him and rescheduled him in two weeks. Not surprised, Hunter thanked the woman and left the building.

He passed the A-12 OXCART on display outside in the back lot of the CIA's New Office Building on his way to a hotel room at the JW Marriott where he would meet up with his wife.

CHAPTER 14

July 30, 2015

After another successful intelligence collection mission, *Maverick* touched an icon on the center multifunction display to activate the autonomous flight software. This energized the automatic takeoff and landing system (ATLS), turning the YO-3A into a robot. He programmed the Global Positioning System-fed (GPS) autopilot to return to his initial take off point. As always during the programmed hands-off landing profile, he was a little nervous letting the computer do all the work. With his hands and feet off the flight controls and throttle, *Maverick* first feigned terror at touchdown and then smiled during the hands-free landing. There wasn't anything like the YO-3A.

The ATLS program had again worked as designed, and after rolling out on the concrete runway, astride the centerline and spinning the *Yo-Yo* 180° at the tail end of the LM-100J, *Maverick* shut down the engine, turned the AVIONICS MASTER off, and gingerly climbed out of the cockpit. Flying low level at night was stressful and exhausting, but not as intense as flying the Phantom which could leave thirty-something-year-old pilots looking like they were a hundred. *Maverick* had a bad back after an ejection from an F-4 and often after *Noble Savage* missions his mechanics would apply lidocaine patches to his lower back.

The night's work had *Maverick* finding well-hidden drug labs, FARC campsites run by sex slaves or hostages, and locations where low-profile vessels and 70-to-100-foot long, narco-submarines were being built to smuggle tons of cocaine to America and Europe. The most common route for drug smuggling was to the United States, the world's largest consumer of Colombian cocaine.

All the clandestine imagery was recorded without alerting the cartels. Before boarding the civilian *Hercules*, *Maverick's* final act was to provide the Embassy's Chief of Station with a video recording and GPS coordinates of the FARC camps and the illegal activities, which would be disseminated to the Colombian military, intelligence, and law enforcement communities.

About every six months, the FARC would be destroyed, hostages and sex slaves would be rescued, and submarine manufacturing would be decimated by the Colombian army. *Maverick* flew low over the Colombian riverine network to locate the thermal signatures of new drug labs hidden under thick jungle canopies. New members of the drug cartels were busy upstream of Colombian rivers building a new fleet of ocean-going submarines. Detection occurred when sudden flashes of thermal energy in the FLIR between layers of jungle canopy gave away their positions and activities. Over the years, the FARC enterprises became noticeably smaller largely because *Maverick* knew when and where the cartels' new bases of operations were likely to be. The cartels and narcoterrorists followed a pattern.

•   •   •

In less than four minutes, the YO-3A crew of Bob Smith and Bob Jones had disassembled the aircraft, ripped off the speed tape, disconnected the flight control cables, twisted the quick-disconnect (QDs) fuel lines and electrical connections until they were separated, pulled the different-sized clevis pins from the fuselage lug fittings that joined the wings in place, and removed the very high aspect ratio glider-like wings. Smith and Jones positioned the wings into wing cradles on a wall on the inside of the YO-3A's container, a modified shipping container. A *Hercules* crew member attached a high-speed winch to the tailwheel; a mechanic controlled the speed of the fuselage moving up the cargo ramp and stopped its movement when the YO-3A's main landing gear tires hit their stops inside the container. That was the moment the pilot of the idling QAS LM-100J programmed the throttles for takeoff. Once the four-engine cargo aircraft was airborne, with the susurrus of the airstream moving across the airframe, *Maverick*, Jones and Smith crawled into sleeping bags for the ride home to the Baltimore-Washington International Airport (BWI). The airplane's container would be staged on-site at BWI's cargo facility within a small QAS warehouse. Then Duncan and his crew would take one of Hunter's business aircraft to Elmira, New York, home to the QAS aircraft refurbishment hangars. Except for some unexpected maintenance issues, the YO-3As never left their containers stateside. The movement of the *Yo-Yos* into and out of BWI had become routine.

Once stateside, Hunter confirmed his appointment and visited CIA Headquarters, but the CIA Director, his former business partner and mentor, was usually overloaded with meetings, conferences, and the occasional Congressional hearing. Greg Lynche would make an appointment to see Hunter, but the vicissitudes of the office meant he rarely kept the appointment.

Even with a blue badge that allowed him to be in the New Office Building, Duncan Hunter was an infrequent visitor and walked about in total anonymity. A check of his Rolex told him he was running early. Never one to pass up the chance for a hot meal, Hunter found himself sideling through the serving line at the Agency's cafeteria and finding one of his favorites on the special board: beef and noodles. Being early was going to pay unexpected dividends. The contracted polygraphed cafeteria worker loaded his plate. He found a seat next to the line of ponytail palms which framed the glass walls of the eatery. While Director Lynche received an anal probe from Democrats on the Hill, Hunter enjoyed his meal.

As Hunter dined, he wondered, *How many times would Director Lynche get asked by some brain-dead liberal lawmaker, "What happened to President Mazibuike?"* The fleeting wry grin on Hunter's face was replaced by a shake of his head. *You know he's dead, and you know where he was killed, Congressman. He died in Dubai.* Hunter loaded another fork full of beef and noodles. *But they will never acknowledge he was a traitor. They would go ballistic if they ever learned I killed him before he could kill me. He was the protected one. We all thought, why him? We must have been locked in a paradigm, unable to see what was in front of us. But then we figured it out. He really was the chosen one. The Democratic President of the United States was the titular head of the Muslim Brotherhood in North America.*

Greg would not allow his socially liberal, fiscally conservative emotions to get the better of him today. He just has to get away from the Communist psychos in the Senate without his blood soiling his suit.

Because they had no one else to blame, the Democrats in Congress attacked Lynche for losing their leader. They always blamed the CIA. Lynche would tell them, once again, that "…the CIA doesn't engage in assassination. The CIA does not know the whereabouts of former President Mazibuike. The CIA has not retaliated against him. The CIA has not assassinated him. President Mazibuike resigned from the presidency. It is the responsibility of the Secret Service to protect President Mazibuike. The CIA has no interest in him or his whereabouts; now or ever."

Hunter sighed; *I wish Lynche didn't have to endure their BS. I can tell it's wearing him down. The left worked so hard to get Mazibuike into office, and it was a massive shock to their system when he quit. Every month at Capitol Hill was the same. As the head of the CIA, Democrats blamed Greg. But Greg is protecting me; still protecting me. When will he finally say enough? That was the left's way. Aggressive activism from mental disorders. When will he push away from the pier at the Annapolis Yacht Club for the last time and never look back?*

Mazibuike was an Islamic president who co-opted and debased America's electoral process. Mazibuike was exactly what the Islamic Underground and the Muslim Brotherhood required in their quest to destroy America so Islam could dominate the world. Yes, I diverged into uncharted territory, but I swore an oath to defend the Constitution of the United States against all enemies, foreign and domestic. I didn't promise any usurper of the Constitution would go unpunished.

My darling bride considers me one of the men who unhesitatingly fights evil with every breath they possess. A husband is indeed fortunate when his wife holds him in the highest regard, and I am so blessed. Nazy told Greg that everything I had done for our Nation confronted the domestic enemies within and eliminated the terrorists who have been working to defeat America. Greg agreed and said I was worth whatever bullshit propaganda the Democrats in Congress threw at him.

Once again, the Director's secretary sent his regrets, "Maybe next month." Greg never showed for their meeting.

Hunter didn't have time to wander through the Agency's museum and rendezvous with Nazy too.

CHAPTER 15

August 17, 2015

Hunter breathed freely, grateful that Lynche was talking to him again. *Maybe Nazy was finally able to peel him off the ceiling.* He swung his eyes left and right, and then upward to marvel at what CIA aviation had been able to accomplish in such a short period of its history. The disparate black shapes suspended from the ceiling of CIA Headquarters looked futuristic or alien, props from a science fiction movie. They were not subtle.

They were partial-scale silhouette models of the U-2 and the A-12—the *Blackbirds*—and the supersonic picture-taking drone, the D-21. Gifts from Lockheed. An actual single-seat A-12 was mounted on display outside CIA Headquarters. Hunter thought the aircraft should have been spent its final days inside a museum. *I know, I know, I know; that requires a lot of space…. Aviation intelligence artifacts require a lot of space. Non-aviation types making crappy decisions about airplanes.*

There had been talk of suspending one of his YO-3As with the Agencies *Blackbirds* once the program ran its course, once there were no men on the FBI's Most Wanted Terrorist List or the *Disposition Matrix*. But it was just talk. As long as the secret *Yo-Yo* remained on an active special access program, no one needed to know what the last couple of directors had used to find and eliminate over a hundred of the world's worst terrorists.

Hunter exhaled audibly. He had come a very long way from the days of Allen Dulles, one of the first Directors of the CIA. Hunter smiled at the thought of Director Dulles rolling over in his grave if he knew what the CIA had him doing in Africa, the Middle East, and South America in a manned aircraft.

He had time and wandered over to the CIA's bookstore and museum. Once inside, Hunter spied something new: a ceramic-coated CIA sign in majuscule to advertise the address of the original CIA Headquarters. A placard announced the newly formed agency had taken over the 2430 E St. NW site from its wartime predecessor, the Office of Strategic Services. President Eisenhower had called CIA Director Allen Dulles and ordered a sign be placed at the entrance. The President believed that the E Street address was well known as CIA Headquarters and that the absence of a sign fooled no one.

Hunter moved from display to display; he was especially interested in the secret Soviet files that told the story of how Soviet spies in American aircraft manufacturing plants stole plans for America's first generation unmanned or remote-controlled airplanes. Nazy Cunningham, Duncan's wife and the current Director of the National Counter Terrorism Center (NCTC), had analyzed the journal of a Soviet intelligence officer, who casually mentioned Stalin had awarded medals to several Communist infiltrators in America. It was all done in an effort to start a war between Germany and the United States by sabotaging the Nazi's 800-foot zeppelin *Hindenburg* when it visited the American East Coast.

Hunter looked about but could not find any reference how Joseph Stalin directed a Soviet Navy submarine to pull Amelia Earhart off course in her around the world attempt. He frowned; there were no displays or placards of Soviet subversion, nothing about Communist loyalists in the United States who were stopped from stealing schematics and plans of America's naval vessels, frontline fighters and bombers, the *Concorde*, and even the Space Shuttle. Instead, there were personal histories of the men and women of the Office of Strategic Services, the fabled OSS. *Like Pete Ortiz. Big Bird's dad; my RIO's dad was a war hero! Two Navy Crosses while assigned to the OSS.* The stories of Communist infiltration of American institutions were probably the histories that would never be declassified or featured in the museum. Like the planning model for the raid on Osama bin Laden's compound in Abbottabad, Pakistan or the Kennedy assassination, some documents would never be declassified.

He would tell the Director the museum curator needed to update the displays. They were old and tired. *Even the International Spy Museum had built a new building with new displays.*

Hunter stopped and read one display in the Historical Collections: bat bombs. *OSS Director William Donovan appointed Dr. Stanley Lovell as the director of research and development at the agency. Dr. Lovell was a renowned industrial chemist, and a blue-sky thinker long before the phrase even existed. He envisioned catching bats for the "bat bomb" – tiny incendiary devices which would be attached to bats, which were then released into enemy territory.*

Hunter thought, *That was probably the best they could do at the time. Trying anything to gain an advantage over the Nazis. Now we have drones to do that. Now I have Firestarters, no thanks to S&T.* He grinned and sidled to another display that caught his eye: *The Cuban Missile Crisis.* The six-foot tall glass case featured an actual U-2 pressure suit and a model of the 1962 U-2. A lot of history there that will never be released to the public.

Hunter paused at the display for a moment of reflection. *And I won Francis Gary Powers' Rolex Datejust at auction. His son, Gary Powers Jr., said that a few months after his father returned to the U.S. after the famous prisoner swap in 1962, he used the money the CIA paid him to buy himself a Rolex. He said his father had found a new appreciation for life and freedom. He owned other watches, but the Rolex Datejust was the one he wore daily.*

The next display featured a long-barreled pistol in profile. The placard read: *the Hi-Standard .22-caliber pistol was "ideal for use in close spaces or for eliminating sentries." Developed by Stanley P. Lovell for the Office of Strategic Services, the pistol weapon was flashless, silencer-equipped, and designed to kill without making a sound.*

The next paragraph made Hunter smile. *How quiet was it? Maj. Gen. William J. "Wild Bill" Donovan, the Director of the OSS, was so eager to show off his agency's latest lethal gadget that he took a Hi-Standard and a sandbag to the Oval Office. While President Franklin D. Roosevelt was busy dictating to his secretary, Donovan fired ten rounds into the sandbag. FDR gave no notice and never stopped talking, so Donovan wrapped his handkerchief around the still-hot barrel and presented the weapon to the president, telling him what he had just done.*

President Roosevelt remarked, "Bill, you're the only wild-eyed Republican I'd ever let in here with a weapon!"

Now that puts the special in special trust and confidence. Hunter turned and found something new.

The 1968 Project *Aquiline* was envisioned to be a small drone, to be kept as close to bird size as possible with the current state of technology — as if there was a bird that was five feet long, 7.5 feet wide, with a takeoff weight of 83 pounds. The largest known flying animals, like the reptilian *Quetzalcoatlus* with a wingspan of over thirty feet, about the span of a Piper Super Cub, wouldn't have made a very good platform to conduct unmanned surveillance either.

83 pounds? Seriously? Looks like Da Vinci's ornithopter. No wonder it never got off the ground. Maybe that sounded like a good idea at the time but small and silent is still the ticket in this business. Like our old Blackguards. Maybe it's time for another model entirely. Hmmm....

He crossed his arms and read how planners wanted to use a nuclear powerplant powered by a single pellet of uranium so the bird would be able to stay aloft, flapping its wings for months. Hunter shook his head and marveled at the concept. He read that the drone, which was supposed to act as a robotic spyplane and courier for secret payloads, was never completed. *Aquiline* never became operational but the concept proved invaluable in the decades-long development of unmanned aerial vehicles (UAVs). In the early 1960s, Agency personnel figured out how to use physics to quiet an engine and its propeller.

Like the YO-3A. Hunter read the brief sheet for Project *Aquiline*:

February 15, 1968
Col White Program Manager

Development of a miniature surreptitious aircraft vehicle system which with its growth capabilities would penetrate with relative impunity, thousands of miles into denied territory such as the Soviet Union, Red China, and Cuba to collect critical technical intelligence, support in-place agents, or perform other Agency missions. It is small, flies low and slow, having small visual, acoustic, and radar observables that can outfox defenses rather than overpower them. Inexpensive and unmanned, low-risk and minimal investment. Inoffensive and unassuming characteristics compared to overflight aircraft and large drones, make it more politically palatable. Lightweight propulsion systems and long-range navigation systems will give this an operational range of a thousand miles.

Hunter thought, *Which is what I do now. Collect intel, support in-place agents, and conduct other Agency mission as required.... Sounds like a Yo-Yo. But.... Hmmm.... That gives me some ideas.... The state of technology today is light years ahead of what was available back then, and I suppose the displays are a complex concinnity of intelligence artifacts. There is still nothing like this place on earth.*

A snap check of his Rolex prodded him to leave the history of the Agency behind him for the temporary companionship of the Director. His mind raced. *Could the boys in Fredericksburg come up with a corvine version of Aquiline? Maybe the color and size of a raven? The RC crowd makes tiny jet motors for remote-controlled aircraft. We need a capability that would allow a bird to penetrate our airport laser protection systems being rolled out at airports but would keep a drone out. Don't want to zap harmless birds like one of those rotating Ginsu knives they call wind turbines.*

I'm certain the boys in Texas can tweak the system to distinguish between our slow-moving feathered friends and the speeds of drones. Fixed and rotary wing. I'll see what Bong can make out of this idea. I remember in my high school biology class we dissected cats; the school got dead cats from a company that euthanized pound cats and dogs for biology classes. Could you get dead ravens?

The Director of the Central Intelligence Agency, Greg Lynche, found Hunter in the museum. Hunter warmly greeted his old friend. Lynche began, "The Colombians are eternally grateful. Their military raided those locations and freed over fifty sex slaves." *Several kids, too....* "I understand they seized four 37-foot, blue-water, narco-subs like what they found in Spain."

Hunter nodded an acknowledgement. The details were more than he expected. Most of the time, Greg just moved to the next mission. There was always work to be done.

Lynche dropped his head a bit. "We have known each other a long time, *Mav*. I wanted to suspend *Noble Savage*, but Nazy was adamant *I* needed more time. I blamed you for taking advantage of the situation. I shouldn't have. Nazy is quite a woman. She helped me see you were more than entitled to respond the way you did. He abused his position and tried to kill you and hundreds more. I knew it was true. I didn't want to see it." *Must have been my liberal upbringing.* "I think I never really believed Mazibuike could have been so bad. It took me a while to see that you were right about him all along. Why I wanted to give him the benefit of doubt, I don't know."

Hunter smiled and thought, *He can't say decapitated and defenestrated.... And yes, it is sometimes a challenge dealing with a left-leaning best friend, but you came around to my way of thinking. I didn't rub your nose in it. That took a lot of courage Greg. And, I forgive you.* Hunter offered his hand and Lynche gladly gripped it then covered Duncan's hand with his free hand to solidify his commitment to Duncan. It was an unexpected gesture, like the one he had received from an old Air Force colonel, long ago.

Still holding Hunter's hand, Lynche continued, "Nazy was right, and I came to my senses. You did what had to be done. Now I need you for another one, if you are willing."

Hunter nodded, *For you, Greg, always.*

"Nazy will give you the particulars."

Hunter smiled and released the old spook's hand. They had been through so much, and the death of another terrorist who killed

Americans wasn't enough to break the bonds of friendship; even if that turd had been the former president.

A pat on the back and Lynche was gone; a man on a mission. Hunter was left with his thoughts. *Nazy was able to change Greg's mind. Poor Greg; he didn't have a chance. Every senior intelligence service officer in the intel community was bewitched by her. British accent, exotic looks. Every executive's eyes lingered on her face, her incredible cat-like eyes, amazing cheekbones, full lips, extraordinary laugh, the distraction of her unbelievable figure, and the best-looking legs in the country. Yes, she was a distraction to the surrounding people, men and women. Nazy was, by far, the most spectacular woman at the Agency. And, I am the luckiest man alive, because she is my bride.*

But Greg had come to know there was more to Nazy than her physical beauty; it was just the beginning of her gift. She was a real intelligence officer, always on point, yet unpredictable and surprising. The talents she brought to the CIA analysis division were unmeasured. Her perspicacity and ratiocination came from a deep place. She was a master manipulator in her own right, for the side of good. As a senior analyst, Nazy brought passion to every assignment. Her work, her leaps of logic were raw, unapologetic, and very brave. But always on target.

The daughter of a Jordanian Supreme Court Judge, Nazy had been educated at Oxford and Yale. She had been a Muslim apologist, a left-wing activist, and a battered wife. When she had tried to flee Jordan and return to the safety and freedom of the United States, she had been caught. After working for a few weeks at a fast-food restaurant at Boston Logan Airport, the Transportation Security Administration (TSA) arrested and jailed her when an informant claimed she was carrying a stolen passport. Two male Muslim TSA agents escorted her to a van and drove her to the Boston Islamic Center; the imam there gave her an ultimatum, either work for him or she would be deported back to Jordan and returned to her enraged husband, who would surely kill her. If she were allowed to live in Jordan, it would be a life of punishment and violence under a *burka*. Her mission was to spy on an American who was friends with America's most celebrated killer of Muslim men, *The Black Shadow*. She cringed every time the imam touched her sleeve, "*You should be honored to serve Allah!*"

The imam arranged an apartment and an immaculate red Mercedes 380 SL for her. That would surely impress the man from Texas and help establish her bona fides. Marwa Kamal was to contact the man at the Newport Athletic Club. She tried to spy on Duncan Hunter, but he saw through her. She was a terrible spy. Hunter asked if he could help her escape the clutches of the Muslim Brotherhood. The CIA gave her a chance to be an American patriot; they changed her name and her life. When she became Hunter's wife, they worked together to stop the Islamic invaders and America's domestic terrorists from defeating the United States.

•   •   •

Hunter left Headquarters, and for the first time since becoming a contract pilot for the CIA, he didn't go by the A-12 mounted outside on his way out of the compound. Lynche had given him an apology, a thank you, and a new mission. For the fine points, he would be briefed by Nazy. She had been on Capitol Hill with Greg and she had returned to her office at Liberty Crossing. Nazy's debrief would be after hours, in the privacy of a cleared hotel room. With a *Growler*.

But Hunter had another project banging around in his cranium. He couldn't get the idea of a new and improved version of *Aquiline* out of his head. When that happened, Hunter knew to listen to his conscience; there was magic being made across synapses and neurons. Once away from Headquarters, Hunter scribbled some notes on a 3x5 card he always carried.

Hunter went to pick up his business partner, Arsenio Bong, at the well-known-to-those-who-were-well-known diner across the street from the entrance of CIA Headquarters. As he entered the packed restaurant, he avoided knocking over the former Speaker of the House, a Republican, who was balancing a coffee and a partially eaten cinnamon roll in his hands. With apologies offered and accepted, Hunter found Bong behind a newspaper. Bong could see Hunter had "that look," so the men expedited their departure.

Watching Hunter and Bong leave, the former Speaker of the House said to the former Democrat Senate Minority Leader, "You can't swing a dead cat in this place without hitting a spook."

The former Minority Leader said, "Please Newt, this place is so jammed, you couldn't even Swing Time."

CHAPTER 16

August 17, 2015

Duncan drove Nazy's up-armored H2. Every few months he would get it out of a storage locker near McLean to keep the batteries charged. The vehicle hadn't gotten a lot of use since the last time the Muslim Brotherhood had attempted to assassinate her on her way to work. President Hernandez said she could no longer drive, and the CIA Director assigned her a security detail. Duncan donated six black Escalades from his armored car business; three for Nazy and three for the Director.

Hunter's destination was Ft. Meade, in Maryland. He was going to the library inside the National Security Agency Museum. As he drove on I-295, he debriefed Bong on *Aquiline* and what he wanted from the scientists at the QAS Science and Technology laboratory in Fredericksburg, Texas. "And, I'll need an *AeroDog*."

Bong asked for clarification, "*AeroDog*? Do we have such a beast? Did we build something for you? I'm not familiar."

"Not yet. I'm thinking of a four-wheel design where the wheels morphs or pivots onto their sides and work as propellers, turning the *Aerodog* into a quadrotor drone. Using AI, it will make those determinations autonomously."

Bong looked confused.

"Wheels that are also rotors or incorporate propellers. A shrouded propeller can be a wheel turning on an axle. It just needs a folding mechanism. It doesn't have to be large. If the AI determines it needs to roll or fly behind me, it does it without my input — unless I tell it to. Its real purpose is to get people to look at it — with a spinning red laser — and not at me and then hammer them with UV LEDs. But the best part, it should be disposable. I don't want to pick it up. That's it, make it disposable; lithium batteries to immolate it if I have to leave it."

Bong said, "You are an evil genius, sire."

Hunter laughed and explained, "Let me tell you a little story. It was the day after April Fool's Day, 1994. I had just been fired from my job at the Cleveland Hopkins International Airport because I wouldn't hire a couple of dozen Muslims who couldn't pass the piss test or the FAA background check. Too much *shisha*, apparently. I went to my racquet club one last time. My buddy, Bobby Sanders, five-time National Racquetball Champion, told me, 'Don't worry, you were in the wrong job.' He said, 'Duncan, you're educated, a really smart guy. I'm a bus driver. Maybe you can't fly any more, but you can teach. You should be a teacher, a professor, an inventor. People need what is in your head. There is a special place for you. Cleveland is just not it. Keep at it. Someone will eventually figure out you're a superstar. I fit in here, in this world, but you don't. I will miss you, my friend. Go home to Texas, and I'll look for you at the National Singles. You can buy me lunch at Whataburger and dinner at the Spaghetti Warehouse in Houston.' The man was a genius, on and off the court. He could see what others could not. Well, I drove out of Cleveland and headed for Texas. On my way, I took a month-long break."

"You took a break?"

Hunter laughed and said, "Hard to believe, huh? Well, I did. I towed my '67 Corvette Sting Ray racecar and did what you and I do when we want to clear our heads. Solo road trip. No work, no racquetball, no girlfriend, no radio; nothing but me and my thoughts. I drove to places I had never seen. I saw America. Stopped in places like Sport Wade's in the tiny town of Weldon, Iowa where Monica made a great lasagna. I looked up a name from my past and met this old Navy *Corsair* pilot. I saw farmers, working men, great cooks; real Americans. It took over a month for me to get to Texas."

"I didn't know you had a racecar."

"Still have it. It's in a hangar in Jackson, Wyoming along with a few dozen collector cars. I've been pretty proud of that car. I was all of

38, 39. Retired from the Marine Corps. I had flown the jet from my childhood dreams, and I had the Corvette, also from my childhood dreams. That Vette does things that I can't even believe. Every time I take anyone for a ride, we just start laughing hysterically because we're scared shitless. It's so agile and so powerful, and that V8 with straight headers make the most wonderful sound on the planet. It's a great car, a pure racecar, for me to play with. Like your Porsche."

"79 930 Whale Tail, turbo!"

Hunter grinned. "A very nice Whale Tail."

The normally Saturnine Bong grinned and nodded for a long time.

Hunter continued, "I had taken the company that fired me to court. Wrongful dismissal. Won my case. Bought gold coins with the settlement because gold was dirt cheap. Anyway, I had been on the road for a couple of weeks, and I was getting a little lonely. I'd cruise around, find a hotel, and park. I would sit in my room and write my thoughts in my journal. I'd walk around town, go to dinner, sit at my own table, re-taste anonymity, and think unencumbered thoughts like, why would Muslims want to take security jobs at an airport where TWA had a direct flight to Tel Aviv? Was the goal to plant a bomb on that jet? Was the goal to kill hundreds of innocent people or was it my imagination? Two years later a TWA jet was blasted from the sky and I knew exactly how they did it. The FBI ignored me but Greg Lynche confirmed it through his contacts. Stuff to consider for a journal, not to be shared with just anyone."

"Write it down or you will forget it. Like *Aerodog*."

"Exactly. While I was laid up back in '88 recovering from a bad ejection, I completed my PhD and filled journals with my thoughts. Counterterrorism thoughts. Designs. Still in a hospital bed, I realized I could recognize patterns where they were not readily apparent. I also realized I had some patentable ideas. The last three years I was on active duty, I made some money off the royalties of a couple of inventions designed to thwart or defeat terrorists trying to harm the U.S. In the beginning, it was airport security stuff mostly."

Bong said, "And how to make mechanical things quiet?"

"That came later—but you get the idea. Anyway, I had been offered the job in Cleveland and was ready to put down roots...."

"But you had a problem. You can't stop thinking."

"I did, and when I realized the problem with the Muslims who demanded jobs at an airport was bigger than me, I talked to my boss who freaked out and said, I had to go."

"He used to be a colonel in the Marine Corps, and then he was a vice president. He didn't want to lose that position; he thought that if he acknowledged what was on my mind, what needed to be done, like call the FBI, report the strangeness of it all, he'd be let go too. I didn't really realize there was so much fear in America. Remember, this was after the first World Trade Center bombing, the *Bojinka Plot*, and Oak-City. Flight 800, two years later. So, a seed had been planted by my buddy Bobby Sanders. On the road, the seed germinated. Lots of seeds germinated."

"Like *Aquiline* today."

Hunter smiled and nodded. *Exactly!* "In my little mind, law enforcement was behind the power curve. Some things you can predict. Terrorists are so clumsy, they will tell you what they are going to do, if we only listen. If you can see they have a pattern in the way they do business." *Like radical Muslims banging on the door of an airport. Where there was a TWA 747. Full of Israelis heading for Tel Aviv.* "Some things require action; some things are just necessary." *Like keeping radical Muslims from accessing the airport security of Israeli-bound jumbo jets.* "Also, like *Aquiline* today, I realized I had a knack for seeing troubles before they developed. And I saw how to stop those troubles before they could kill people. Innocent people."

"Like the Muslims at the airport wanting to work airport security."

"Exactly."

"You were Nostradamus."

"It's a gift and a curse." The men laughed.

Bong smiled, "And that's why we take road trips. To let the mind wander and explore."

Hunter grinned and said, "A couple of years ago, I asked the Agency's S&T for a remote-control machine gun and, of course, they said, 'You're a stinkin' contractor, we can't let you have that.' So, I know our lab guys in Texas could come up with the next best thing in robotic weapons; something that could fire tear gas, stun grenades, maybe sponge-tipped bullets. But most of all, I felt if I ever needed to be on the ground, because I could see I needed that capability, I'd need crowd-disabling weapons; non-lethal disorienting weapons. I needed a remote -controlled vehicle with a spinning red laser pointer that would catch the eye of any onlooker, then use UV LEDs to blind anyone who was dumb enough to look at it. A miniaturized version of *Weedbusters* for ground ops, if and when I was ever dumb enough to operate on the ground. And I think there is a market for micro-batteries and bug-sized robots, and maybe *Aquiline*. If the IC isn't developing them, they will want them, I'm sure. And if the IC doesn't want them, as long as I am in this business, I may need them."

"Bug-sized robots and silent and stealthy *AeroDogs*, and black birds that can do surveillance and more." *Like deliver a Firestarter.*

Bong said, "I know the boys and girls in Fredericksburg can make something lightweight, and a laser and UV LEDs to blind enemy crowds will be better than any gun. A wounded soldier could still get a weapon on you, but no one could target you on the ground after encountering *AeroDogs* with UV LEDs. Would the blindness be mostly temporary?"

Hunter continued, "From the *Yo-Yo*, the level of damage depends on power and the altitude. If I had a need for *AeroDogs*, I'm not worrying about hurting someone's eyes. If I'm on the ground for some ridiculous reason, I need to be able to stop them before they can stop me. It needs to be instantly disabling, incapacitating, and they can't be able to think of anything else but their own survival."

"Like a .45 to the knee." Bong continued, "I love that idea. I'll see what they can muster up. I think we just upgraded the lab with the latest rapid prototyping machines, 3D printers. They should be able to knock something out in a hurry. And if it is small, that's better yet."

"Great. It will never be Geneva Convention friendly. I don't give a crap. When you have to tango with terrorists, you want to go home after the dance. If I have to litter the dance floor by blinding my adversaries, so be it."

"*Screw 'em!*"

"Exactly." Hunter thought, *When using a powerful UV laser, blindness and the severity of eye damage is predicated on altitude or slant-range, and wavelength. The wavelength of our earlier Weedbusters version was more of a cutting tool at minimum altitude; it had the same wavelength industry uses to etch hard metal parts, like turbine blades and compressor hubs. Greg almost had to fly in the weeds to get close enough to shred a sniper's eyes to prevent him from killing me. Someone is always saving me.... Now we have a kindler gentler wavelength in Weedbusters.... At design altitude, blindness is temporary. Fifty feet lower and the damage is permanent. Electric burns...gas bubbles form in their eyes....*

"Duncan, I'm sure you're envisioning an RC truck chassis to be able to negotiate stairs, but would you want it to be able to race across a lake? I've seen videos of RC vehicles being able to do that."

Hunter appreciated the info and considered the idea, "Probably not the first generation. But an *Aerodog* needs to be able to fly up to or fall off of a one-story roof and still be functional. If I'm climbing out of a *Yo-Yo*, it has to be rugged and smart enough for me to be able to toss it into the air and work. Hardened. We'll need two of them. A primary and a spare."

"*Aquiline* 2.0 and all of those options—less a gun of course—are doable. We'll need some time to integrate everything and harden it."

Bong added, "When we have them for you to val-ver (validate-verify) *AeroDogs*, I'll need you to download a controlling app to your Blackberry. It will follow you like a puppy. You won't have time to drive it like an RC car or manually fly it unless you want to."

"*Programmable.* That's what I'm thinking. Perfect."

"You're a wretched evil person, Duncan Hunter. I would hate to be on the other side of an *AeroDog*. I'm glad to be on the right side."

Where does he come up with those names and why does he want that capability is anyone's guess, but he is the boss.

"I know. I don't know when I'll be able to use it, but trying to develop it when I actually need it is not the right time. I want to build a toolbox of capabilities. Silent weapons. Where we put the extra effort into making it quiet. Especially *Aquiline* 2.0. I see a need; maybe not now, but definitely in the future if we are still hunting rabbits." *We'll have to call it something….*

The tall retired colonel from the National Reconnaissance Office (NRO) smiled at the Bugs Bunny reference. *Terrorists multiplied like rabbits.* He said, "We have time; thankfully these are things in our wheelhouse to develop. Also, there is an upgrade to the *Yo-Yo* app to account for the capabilities of the new helmet. I can download it for you."

Hunter didn't hesitate; he offered Bong his Blackberry to download the YO-3A's controlling app. He'd check it out the next time he had the *Wraith* strapped to his back.

•   •   •

They walked around the NSA museum and took in the Cray computer displays and of the various three and four-rotor Enigma machines the Nazis had developed and used to ensure secure communications with aviation and submarine forces. They also studied the Venona transcript display which proved Alger Hiss, an assistant to the Assistant Secretary of State, had been the Soviet Union's greatest spy to infiltrate the U.S. Government. They spent time in the library going over old NSA research.

An hour later, Duncan returned Bong to the BWI executive terminal on the other side of the airport where the QAS Lear was parked. Then, whenever she got away from HQ, he was off for a night with Nazy.

CHAPTER 17

April 13, 2018

Carlos Yazzie wanted to argue with the delivery man. He had expected a yellow Corvette delivery, however, the man had three 1957 300 SLs and paperwork. Two black, one blue; a Gullwing and two roadsters. Carlos knew there had been a delay in the restoration of the three Mercedes. Having them delivered early was a complete surprise. He looked them over. *A blue convertible? That's unusual. The Captain doesn't have a single blue car in his collection. Oh, well…. Now he does.* Knowing each of the Mercedes' were worth over a million dollars each, his job was to store them and maintain them, not to drool over them. *They are engineering perfection and were as sensational today as they were the day they rolled out of the factory.*

Yazzie shook his head. *Whatever the color, if these cars don't do it for you, you probably should just collect stamps.* Carlos beseeched the gods above and asked the sky, "Where am I going to put these?"

The delivery man moved million-dollar cars daily and said, "Not my problem. I just deliver them. And I'm early, so I get a bonus per my contract. Please sign for them and note that they arrived before the 'must deliver date' and without damage."

Yazzie looked at the man and thought, *I'm going to need some help.* Technically, Carlos had room in the hangar, he just didn't have room for three more two-seaters *and a jet* when the *Captain* returns. *The Captain will be abroad for a few more days, and he'll just want me to take care of them. So, I will.*

Three sparkling rare Mercedes on a delivery truck, in the springtime sun of Jackson, Wyoming brought onlookers. He convinced the delivery man to help him drive the two black Mercedes into the aircraft hangar on the other side of the airfield. Yazzie drove the robin-blue car safely inside the hangar then disconnected the cars' batteries and covered each of them with their own custom-fit car cover.

After closing the door and locking up the hangar, Yazzie marched to the other end of the airport to leave when his cellphone went off. He didn't recognize the number but took the call anyway. After several minutes of back-and-forth discussions, Carlos leaned against the doorframe outside the airport manager's office. He was at a complete loss. *Where am I going to put another car?! I need another aircraft hangar!*

The *Grand Sport* had arrived.

CHAPTER 18

November 4, 2019

A couple of hours had passed since the severe weather system had moved over Prince Ali Base in southern Iraq. The wind had been so strong that the control tower was seen to librate against the sky. Puddles filled depressions in the taxiway and runway.

The Air Force Special Operations weatherman had a head of steam as she made her way from the weather shop at Base Operations through the line of security people on the flight line, to the man in the strange black flight suit. As she approached, *Maverick* stuffed a hand in his flight jacket pocket and activated his *Growler*.

Without salutations, she stopped and said, "We've had frontal passage and target weather is now favorable." *Maverick* nodded and thanked the petite blonde in the green camouflage battle dress uniform. He deactivated his *Growler*. He walked to his sheet-covered airplane which was hidden under a fifteen-foot-thick concrete bunker. It was one of a handful of bunkers that hadn't been bombed before the invasion of Iraq. American JDAMs, Joint Direct Attack Munitions, proved fifteen feet of concrete wasn't enough to stop them from destroying what was parked inside.

Maverick took off on an easterly heading, and the GPS symbology on his visor signaled the instant he crossed the Iraqi-Iranian border. Using the enhanced night vision systems in his helmet, he located the only real threat of the mission. A few miles from the border he saw the infrared image of a Russian-made S-400 *Triumf* anti-aircraft battery. Radar-guided surface-to-air missiles (SAM) that could kill him and his aircraft before he could blink an eye.

The YO-3A had radar homing and warning (RHAW) equipment to detect SAM launches, and provisions to carry multiple countermeasures—flares, chaff, TROJANs—but *Maverick* rarely used them or the decoys. The black nanotechnology coating provided a passive radar absorption capability. The *Wraith* hadn't been picked up by the fixed-based radar system in Iran during several previous incursions. But each time *Maverick* encountered an anti-aircraft battery he was reminded that he had been targeted once, not by radar antenna, but by the thermal imaging system of a *Stinger*, probably a purloined Man-Portable Air Defense System (MANPADS) from the inventory of Gaddafi's Libyan army. That night, *Maverick* and his YO-3A, had been shot down by an infrared-seeking surface-to-air-missile. That *Yo-Yo* had not yet received the latest nanotechnology in radar absorption paint. He didn't want to give any enemy the opportunity to shoot him down again.

Fixed defensive radar systems were now easy to penetrate because the *Yo-Yo's* new nanotechnology coating not only absorbed radar waves but also absorbed 99.96% of the visible light spectrum. As a result, the YO-3As hadn't been detected by any of the Russian's best radar systems. The threat of detection would be from the thermal sights of a portable anti-aircraft missile system. The YO-3A was quiet and could not be detected in the visible light spectrum at night, but it still had a thermal signature.

•   •   •

The S-400 was in the same position as during a previous excursion into Iran. This time, the missile battery was unexpectedly illuminated like an Atlantic City casino. People were walking about, suggesting the site was out of action even though the S-400's antenna was pointed toward Iraq. *Maverick* lowered the FLIR into the airstream when he entered the "cone of silence." He focused on the high-resolution thermal image of a technician smoking a cigarette outside the command-and-control van of the S-400. *Maverick* could make out a jagged scar across the man's cheek. At less than 200 feet above ground level (AGL), *Maverick* monitored the actions of the man to see if the radar site had detected the silent aircraft that had just overflown him. There was no reaction. *Yep, like I wasn't even there….*

Maverick wasn't unreasonably rejecting all modern equipment in favor of an archaic aircraft, but he and Greg Lynche had found the highly specialized airframe and propeller combination was the only true solution in conducting special aviation activities, like extractions and insertions. With all its cockpit upgrades, coating, weapon and sensor technologies, there simply wasn't anything better than the YO-3A to get into and out of a hostile country undetected. The enemy searched the skies for high-flying jets, not for slow, low-level propeller-driven airplanes that could slip under their radar coverage.

The weather system and rain had moved out of the area, but it remained nubilous. No moonlight illuminated the land, which was an advantage for an incursion into Iran. The administrative phase of the flight gave him some time to listen to a medley of some of his favorite songs. He selected Murray Head's *One Night in Bangkok* and programmed the recorded music on the thumb drive to play until it was time to set up for the extraction.

> *Can't be too careful with your company,*
> *I can feel the Devil walking next to me….*

The new helmet and night vision systems upgraded to white phosphor integrated in his visor would soon display the complete battlefield in shades of white-blue. Now the NODS just displayed white-blue desert and rolling hills. The thermal imager, the FLIR, didn't pick up a single heat source. No reds, no yellows. No animals. Just shades of white-blues. Perfect. *No need to get excited yet.*

At twenty miles out, the GPS confirmed he was on course. At a couple of hundred feet above the ground, he was still not audible to humans. As *Maverick* approached the pick-up point, he programmed the control stick aft and gained some additional altitude to see if there were any thermal images of people or vehicles on the road or in the area. There was nothing in view at that altitude, so *Maverick* deployed the aircraft's laser designators, reduced the throttle, and slowed the aircraft. At the target speed, he engaged the reduction gearbox. Its twelve drive belts slowed the prop and made the YO-3A silent for an even lower altitude. The three-bladed wooden propeller provided just enough thrust for the glider-like aircraft to maintain altitude.

At four miles to target, *Maverick* allowed a passing thought, if all continued to go well, the thermal image of the person to be extracted would be the only thermal signature projected onto his visor. The color thermal imagery in his helmet displayed no hotspots anywhere. Two miles to go.

In his periphery, the 8-day clock on the instrument panel showed midnight. On-target pickup time. When he crested the final hill, the FLIR image in his cockpit scope and helmet came alive with color. There were probably a hundred yellow-orange-red thermal images of helmeted soldiers carrying AK-47-style weapons moving in the NVG-white-blue background of hills and trees.

Ambush. Crap!

He scanned the thermal image in the middle of the valley. The defector was in the prone position as briefed, his arms spread out as directed by his Agency contact. He appeared to be alive.

Maverick shut off the song blasting in his helmet. He took stock of the situation. *But I haven't been detected….* From his vantage point, with the FLIR deployed, *Maverick* could observe the actions of the ambush troops. Their thermal images suggested that their focus was on the defector in the middle of the field. As he made a standard rate turn, the men on the hill were displayed as continually moving, red-hot thermal ants in the tree line.

Now what to do? This op has been compromised. I could turn around and leave; no one would ever know I was here. I could just shoot the defector, get the hell out of Dodge. But killing him assumes he was complicit. We don't know if he is the one who informed the authorities that the Agency was coming to get him.

In case the ambush troops were equipped with night vision or thermal devices, *Maverick* flattened the aircraft's turn to starboard to keep the thermal energy of the aircraft's muffler system from being detected by IR devices. He monitored the situation on the ground and engaged the ALTITUDE-HOLD feature of the autopilot. He took inventory of what the men in the hills were carrying and what they were doing. *Maverick* still could not discern if anyone on the hill was carrying NVGs or hand-held FLIRs. He zoomed in on the image for better details. The collective actions of the men on the ground suggested he had not been seen or heard. If he had been detected, there would be gestures pointing skyward. But there were little more than yawns.

Maverick mulled over what to do. *No one would blame me for abandoning the lift when there were a hundred troops in the hills with AKs, rocket-propelled grenades, RPGs, anti-tank weapons, and machine guns. But, so far, no NVGs; no FLIRs. Surprisingly, no MANPADS!*

I don't want to go home empty-handed…. There is a way. Means taking a chance. A couple of chances…. Luck needs to be on my side.

He scanned the valley and the hills again; he enlarged the imagery for greater resolution. Larger versions of the men in the field filled his visor and the FLIR screen. He found what he was looking for. A few of the officers had night vision goggles but were not using them. He lowered the Terminator Sniper System (TS2) into the airstream and powered it up.

Those are straight NVGs. They still cannot see me, because they're not looking directly overhead for me. They are looking down on the target and checking the avenues of approach for a rescue helicopter. They're expecting a helo. If they were to look up, they would see me. But they are not looking up.

In over twenty years of hunting terrorists at night, only one person had ever looked up into the night sky, as if he had been forewarned. Briefed. It was natural to look ahead, to the side, or behind, or from an elevated position to look down, for that was where an expected threat would come from. People do not naturally look up when they are focused on an event on the ground.

Maverick silently climbed to get a better view of the entrance road to the shallow valley.

Dozens of vehicles on the other side of the hill displayed on his visor in shades of white-blue, but there were no high-resolution thermal images of anyone in or near the vehicles.

I have the advantage; now, do I have the balls? He answered his own question by lowering the *Weedbusters* drug crop eradication laser system into the airstream. The additional drag required more power; he bumped the throttle slightly to add RPMs and maintain altitude. *Maverick* placed the infrared laser designator on the back of the outstretched defector and programed the *Weedbusters* fire control system to make a hundred-foot eye-safe circle around the man. The fire control computer would blank the designated area and not allow the laser beams to enter the eye safe area.

Now or never, big boy! With the aircraft configured for offensive maneuvers, *Maverick* rammed the throttle to the firewall for two seconds. Takeoff power RPMs propagated into the valley. The additional RPMs rumbled through mufflers designed to kill exhaust noise at low RPMs, not take-off power. Supersonic shock waves cracked off the tips of the propeller. He countered the increase in propeller torque with rudder inputs.

The FLIR's thermal imagery registered the instant a sudden noise surprised the men in the hills. It appeared to be coming from the center of the valley, but higher up, in the air. As if the men's movements had been rehearsed and choreographed, they all looked up at the same time to locate the origin of the noise.

Maverick mashed the trigger on his control stick and engaged *Weedbusters*; ultra-violet radiation swept the valley and irradiated the eyes of the soldiers. The effect on their optic nerves was instantaneous; all the soldiers recoiled as they were blinded by the white-hot energy of the invisible laser, leaving their eyes opaque. *Maverick* wasn't convinced everyone in the hills was incapacitated. He squeezed the *Weedbusters* trigger again and again.

Men screamed and wailed; all they could see and feel was an angry white-hot torch had been applied directly to their eyes. It was like having fully dilated eyes and then being exposed to the arc of a welder's cutting torch at point-blank range. Men uncontrollably blinked, trying to rid the white infiltrator. In seconds, they panicked, for they were certain their eyes had been burned out of their heads. *Maverick* targeted the men with NVGs. In sixty seconds, three bodies lay on the ground, terminated by laser-guided Terminator Sniper System rounds.

The TS2 featured an electronic-targeting constantly computing impact point system and boasted a probability of kill of 98% at three miles. The gun on the YO-3A was so accurate that the bullet with the tiny seeker head and wings would hit within an inch of a laser-designated fixed target at ten miles.

When *Maverick* was sure none of the soldiers would be a threat to him, he retracted the FLIR, the TS2 gun, the laser designators, and *Weedbusters* into the airframe to prepare for landing.

•   •   •

Maverick and his passenger landed at Imam Ali Base an hour before sunrise. The Chief of Station at the Baghdad Embassy watched as the *Noble Savage* men helped the blindfolded and handcuffed defector from the back seat of the black spyplane, onto the wing, and onto the ground. Bob Jones removed the man's handcuffs but not his blindfold. They ushered the blindfolded man into an awaiting Cessna Caravan.

Maverick, sans helmet and skullcap but using a *Growler*, provided the Agency man a quick debrief.

"They were expecting someone. I'm sure they thought it was going to be a helicopter. There were about a hundred soldiers, all armed. I could have returned to base or killed him, but I got him out. The problem is I left a calling card. Three tangoes down and a hundred blinded. They know we were there. They do not know how, but they know their bait guy is gone and their assault force was neutralized by an unknown weapon. That information will get out. I don't know if the problem is on their end or yours. Either way, you have an issue."

Maverick lamented to himself, *And if I'm going to keep doing these, I will have to change the way I do business.*

The Chief of Station hung his head to consider *Maverick's* insight. It was an extraction, but it may have unintentionally ruined any further extractions and infiltrations.

Once the YO-3A was disassembled and inside the *Globemaster III*, the mechanics secured the sheet-covered aircraft into its container for the return trip to the U.S. By the time the Cessna with the extracted passenger was airborne, the C-17 had started engine number one and was working on a clearance to depart.

Inside and buckled in, *Maverick* thought, *To get him out of there, I ruined the eyesight of a hundred Iranian soldiers, maybe forever. That's an inconsequential price to pay for all the Iranian bombs that have killed U.S. troops in Iraq and Afghanistan. My actions will leave a mark. I should have carried chaff and flares. I should have used flares to get them to look up, but I still got them to look up. Like the old days. Maybe I got away with one. Time will tell.*

CHAPTER 19

December 16, 2019

Marine Security Guards stood at attention and opened the West Wing doors at the precise moment the President of the United States entered the grounds of the White House. President Javier Hernandez walked across the patio and took the lectern as the assembly of some 200 politicians, military officers, Supreme Court Justices, and family members applauded.

President Hernandez said, "Thank you very much. Thank you. Members of Congress, members of the Cabinet, honored guests, and fellow Americans. It is my privilege to address you tonight from the Rose Garden of the White House. We are gathered together this evening for a truly momentous occasion. Joining us this evening are former Directors of the Central Intelligence Agency, Greg Lynche and William McGee. Director Lynche, Director McGee, America owes you a profound debt of gratitude for a lifetime of noble service to our nation. Thank you for coming for this passing of the torch."

Polite applause rippled across the gathering.

"One of the most important appointments a president can make is the appointment of the Director of the Central Intelligence Agency. Leading the nation's intelligence agencies is a unique and critical responsibility, requiring special trust and confidence to protect the United States of America. This nation has been blessed with the superior leadership of CIA Directors Greg Lynche and Bill McGee, and the Acting Director, Nazy Cunningham. America's new CIA Director will be every bit a champion for freedom as the head of the intelligence community. Ladies and gentlemen, I'm pleased to nominate another exceptional American, the former Supreme Allied Commander

European Forces, General Walter Todd III as the Director of the Central Intelligence Agency."

The assembly stood, applauded, and cheered. After applauding the man to his right, President Hernandez recited the general's curriculum vitae, General Todd III took the lectern and gave President Hernandez thanks for his trust and confidence.

CHAPTER 20

December 16, 2019

After the President's announcement nominating the new CIA Director, Demetrius Eastwood, war correspondent extraordinaire, left the White House grounds and took a taxi to Washington's Union Station. He secured a first-class ticket on the Acela, AMTRAK's express train. On the way to New York City, he wrote articles for the *Washington Times* and the *New York Post* about the President's unusual nomination for CIA Director.

It wasn't an issue that another military man would occupy the top spot in the intelligence community (IC) again, but that President Hernandez's choice for CIA Director hadn't come from the intelligence community. Virtually all the other military officers to hold the top position at the CIA had made their reputation in the IC. Todd was unique; he came from the Air Force's fighter community.

Eastwood thought, *General Todd III flew F-22 RAPTORs. Big deal. He'll have plenty to learn. Today's jets are electronic wonders and the pilots are computer operators. Why was this guy even considered? Presidential decisions — you just can't figure them out sometimes.*

While on the Acela, Eastwood also prepared the script for the weekly radio broadcast that he would give before he and former CIA Director Bill McGee returned to the campaign trail.

Upon arrival at New York's Grand Central Station, Eastwood found the pococurante, no-questions-asked, mob cash-cab to take him to the Main Post Office; from there he would walk across the street to the new 7 World Trade Center and disappear into the elevator stack in the lobby. The owner of the business space had allowed Eastwood to turn the office into a suite, an apartment, and a recording studio.

Dory Eastwood entered the unmarked door at 2613 and silenced the CIA-level security system before it could emit a triple-decibel piercing tone designed to make an intruder's ears bleed. As was often the case when an itinerant correspondent comes home for a pit stop after a month on the road with a presidential candidate, he was exhausted. For security purposes, he knew his movements should not be as predictable as a liberal being given a thimble-full of power at nine a.m. and abusing it by noon, but a worn-out man could always find an excuse to deviate from an efficient, economical, and safe itinerary. Besides, it had been a few years since anyone had tried to kill him in the building's garage. Eastwood had a good memory; he still remembered every detail of the Muslim Brotherhood's failed attack. That day he had been lucky. And, thankfully, they hadn't been back.

Work had precedence over food or a shower or sleep, so Eastwood hurried through the apartment's eclectic furnishings to his office desk. He emailed his articles to the two most conservative newspapers in America. After a brief bathroom stop, he got to work behind the microphone with his script before him.

"Thank you for tuning into this episode of *Unfiltered News* and welcome to the only true American on-line news network. In the city that never sweeps, the stench of dope and garbage is everywhere. New York City, the Democrat Party's failed social experiment, is here for all to see."

He repeated his opening schtick, thanking sponsors and blasting Democrats and the media. "This is Demetrius Eastwood. Let's get this show rolling!"

"Last evening, in the Rose Garden of the White House, President Hernandez nominated a new CIA Director. Choosing a general officer instead of a career intelligence officer, he nominated Air Force General Walter Todd the Third. General Todd was the Supreme Allied Commander Europe (SACEUR) of all commands of the North Atlantic Treaty Organization for three years. That's NATO for liberals following along. Many consider the nomination somewhat puzzling, since General Todd isn't from the intelligence community but from the fighter aircraft community. President Hernandez's previous selections for CIA Director, CIA careerist Greg Lynche and Admiral Bill McGee of SEAL Team Six fame, all had intelligence community backgrounds and helped dismantle the socialist and totalitarian policies of the former president. There is nothing to suggest Director Todd will be any different from the CIA Directors President Hernandez has nominated before him. And for that, we are eternally grateful."

"We sadly report another three churches were destroyed by fire in Bakersfield, Chicago, and Detroit. Authorities are investigating but since we started tracking them, we are finding more of them. Are there any fires of mosques? Curious minds want to know."

"New for today, we have reports of archaeologists in China unearthing a secret underground bunker complex with interconnected rooms and tunnels that was used by Japanese scientists to conduct experiments on humans during World War II. Because of the atrocities conducted there, researchers are calling it 'The Forgotten Asian Auschwitz,' and the 'horror bunker.' It was discovered near the city of Anda in northeast China. Records uncovered reveal the bunker was used by the Japanese army's infamous Unit 731 when Japan occupied China from 1931 to 1945. Built by the Japanese in 1941, the bunker was running nonstop until Japan's surrender at the end of World War II. Records show the lab was Unit 731's largest research site. Its exact location had been lost for 75 years, until now."

"Apparently, Unit 731 began as a Japanese-run public health unit, but it quickly expanded its research to include grotesque biological and chemical warfare experiments using Chinese, Korean, Russian, and American captives as test subjects. Researchers at the Provincial Institute of Cultural Relics and Archaeology who unearthed the bunker, said that its discovery 'highlights the ongoing legacy of Unit 731's atrocities and their impact on global efforts to engage in biological warfare.'"

Eastwood paused and said, "Isn't it interesting? The Nazis, and now the Japanese, were conducting the most horrific experiments on men, women and children. In China, Japanese researchers exposed individuals to dehydration until they died. They killed men inside spinning centrifuges. They injected women and children with diseased animal blood; some were exposed to high levels of X-rays. Some were operated on without anesthesia, and some were kept inside low-pressure chambers until their eyeballs burst. Unspeakable crimes."

"Unearthed records detailed how plague-infected fleas were bred in Unit 731's labs and dropped by low-flying planes over Chinese cities, causing disease outbreaks that killed hundreds of thousands of people."

Eastwood paused for effect and said, "But, this got my attention. Following Japan's surrender in September 1945, the U.S. Army covered up evidence of the gruesome experiments and secretly granted many of Unit 731's leaders' immunity from prosecution for war crimes in exchange for their research. These men were later taken to Fort Detrick in Maryland — which was the center of the U.S. Cold War biological weapons program between 1943 and 1969."

"I will not ask or accuse indiscriminately, but rather state the obvious. It is well known from his bio that Dr. Salvatore D'Angelo began working on biological weapons programs at Fort Detrick in the 1960s, before moving on to the Centers for Disease Control (CDC). I wonder if, in addition to the Japanese version of Mengele and his band of mutilating men, did they — the CDC — have Nazis working there as well? Dr. D would know. All of a sudden, some of the things that have come out of his mouth recently, where he was caught channeling old Goebbels, make sense."

"I think it is time to take another look at what the maybe no-so-good doctor has said about human experimentation. We'll discuss those on a future show."

"Which reminds me, there are 10,000 stains on our collective history; why are they mostly Democrats?"

For the next hour, Eastwood talked about current events and Bill McGee's campaign. He closed the last hour of his show with, "As you know, my thoughtful and informed audience, the left is horrified by the prospect of another Republican President. Evil is marshaling its forces against America. The Democrats plan to run Senator Neil Burgess, an African-American astronaut, a Navy man, and a radical to face Admiral McGee in the general election. More than ever, we need a sound and rational voice to counter the bullshit from the Democrats and their corrupt media."

"And, just when life appears to be headed back to normal, our friends at the CDC are warning Americans a deathly new pathogen has arrived on our shores, and you better line up for a vaccine. Have you heard of this? You haven't? I hadn't either. But if you were to check the alphabet networks, you'd find out what the former Director of the CDC, Dr. Salvatore D'Angelo, is claiming. Apparently, there is an outbreak of *Monkeypox* — yes, *Monkeypox* — has been reported by the London-based newspaper, *The Times*. *Monkeypox* is in a growing number of countries — and of course that includes the U.S."

"Just today, the CDC issued a warning to *some people* about the potential new viral threat." Eastwood paused for effect. "*Some people? Can I say, some people?* Yes, *some people* that the cowardly CDC will not identify. You wouldn't know who these *some people* were until you read way down into the article of the London newspaper."

"We've always wondered why President Hernandez shitcanned Dr. D'Angelo, and now we are getting some answers as we review the latest gallinaceous and bovine narrative from the CDC. Specifically, although the *risk to the public is low*, get vaccinated. *Against Monkeypox?* The CDC is reportedly deploying crack teams of health officials to set up vaccination centers all across New York City. The former CDC Director has been urging people to avoid close contact with sick people with skin or genital lesions. *Genital lesions?* How is someone supposed to know to avoid sick people with *genital* lesions…unless…. CDC, is there something you are afraid to say? Spit it out!"

Eastwood grinned. He was having some fun with the serious topic. "The former CDC Director, Dr. Salvatore D'Angelo, who is treated like the president with taxpayer funded security, is warning Americans they must get vaccinated against *Monkeypox*, that is *must*, as in Do Not

Pass Go, Do Not Collect $200 kind of must. The current acting CDC Director is being interviewed on liberal networks and reporting that *Monkeypox* infections have been reported in 16 countries. They are advising afflicted people to tell their doctors if they've been in contact with someone infected with *Monkeypox,* or if they've been to an area where the infection has been reported in the past month."

"So, let me get this straight, the former CDC Director is screaming we have to get vaccinated to stop the *Monkeypox* pandemic, while the current acting CDC Director suggests if anyone has been in contact with someone with *Monkeypox* or has been to an area where the infection has been reported to tell their doctor? Why is anyone listening to the former CDC Director? Oh, that's right, he's a staple of the mainstream media, a camera whore, and the liberal networks have him on contract. Who is right, and what are you trying to say, CDC? What is going on? Inquiring minds want to know."

Eastwood looked up into the camera and asked, "What does the World Health Organization have to say on this *unprecedented outbreak* of the rare disease *Monkeypox*? Well, you have to read 20 paragraphs down into *The Times* article, because the American media will not report on this, to find their take, the CDC's ever diminishing credibility's take. The CDC says that this was a *random event*, but *The Times* says there was some risky sexual behavior going on at two recent mass events in Europe. Oh, now we understand."

"Doesn't this sound like the AIDS epidemic all over again? It has the same cast of characters at the heart of the issue. Gay men. If I remember right, just months before AIDS broke out in New York City, the CDC was testing a new hepatitis B vaccine targeted specifically toward gay men in Manhattan. Dr. D'Angelo was everywhere. On the Communist News Network and editorials in *The New York Times* and *The Washington Post.* Within months, purple lesions began appearing on the skin of the vaccinated gay men. Yet the hepatitis vaccine experiments continued with gay men in New York City, Washington D.C., San Francisco, Los Angeles, and on children in South Africa and Nigeria. Every future hot spot for the AIDS epidemic. Now it is

Monkeypox; the CDC wants everyone to take a vaccine when gay men are the receivers and transmitters."

"The American media and CDC will not give us the truth about who has been infected with *Monkeypox*, but overseas official media who are not censoring or propagandizing the issue, will articulate it for their readers. America, we have a problem with our media. It may be time for torches and pitchforks to exorcise those demons from their gargoyle perches."

A look of abject disgust washed over Eastwood face. He shook his head. "If you were to read 24 *paragraphs* down in *The Times'* article, I'm certain you would be *astonished* to find that there were two other events that the WHO, not the CDC, was investigating. A recent Gay Pride event in the Canary Islands which drew some 90,000 people, and thousands of cases that were reported after men visited a Las Palmas sauna. This is exactly the reason I have never stepped foot in a public sauna and never will."

Dory continued, "The former director of the CDC, I'm fairly certain that's the Center for Democrat Control, that bomb-throwing attention whore, Dr. Salvatore D'Angelo said, 'It's unusual that we are seeing cases happening in several countries at the same time. We've never seen that.'"

"I'm certain he hasn't. What a fake. Why does the media keep returning to this charlatan for comments? The President fired Dr. D'Angelo, but the mass media assures you he is as pure as the driven snow and is on top of this one — no *double entendre* intended."

"At a Congressional hearing, he dismissed concerns that U.S.-funded Chinese scientists had lied about performing risky gain-of-function (GOF) research. Then he praised the microbiologists and research scientists in China as competent and trustworthy while the CDC Inspector General (IG) said a publicly disclosed grant was simultaneously funding ethics training for Chinese. So let me get this straight. The Chinese needed ethics training over research misconduct and publication fraud? It seems Dr. D'Angelo still runs the CDC with an iron fist; there isn't anyone at the CDC who will speak on the record."

"Not even the CDC's most highly remunerated staff member, the CDC's Monkeypox Coordinator, Yiannis Makropoulos, who *The New York Times* has recently reported is a Satan-and-occult-obsessed gay man who recently donned bondage gear for a speech at a biomedical conference. Apparently, bondage chic is the new business attire for government employees. It makes you wonder what the hell is going on at the CDC."

"I think *The New York Times* needs to be relegated to the tabloid rack, or better yet, as Leon Trotsky would say, 'Go where you belong from now on—into the dustbin of history!"

"The CDC's own IG said it's no secret that China's been hugely obstructive. I think we have beat that story to death. More to follow, when I know more."

"I have much more to say on this topic. Look for my article on the *Monkeypox* scam in *The New York Post.* There *is* a disease destroying America and that is *Donkeypox.* Call your Congressman. There needs to be an investigation into this man and the CDC. And just to let you know the Hernandez Administration is monitoring the situation, the White House assures us that if and when the time is right, they will create a *Pandemic Response Office.* The PRO. And until then, we'll move on from amateur hour at the CDC and FDA to another topic."

The topic had once energized him, amused him, but now the fatigue that had chased him back to New York City for his radio show was scratching at him like rats fleeing a sinking ship. *Wrap it up!* He sighed, "That's enough for this week. Thank you for dropping in. Please pause to remember and offer prayer for our service members who are *the tip of the spear* defending you and me and all of America against all enemies, both foreign and Democrats. Also, we received about fifty new videos of electric vehicles and windmills or solar farms on fire—please send yours and we'll post them on our page. And, do not miss the next episode of *Unfiltered and Unspun!* Eastwood, out."

PRESENT

CHAPTER 21

July 1, 2020
Salve Regina University
Newport, Rhode Island

It had been a quiet day for the Provost at Salve Regina University. Summer school was over and there were no students or faculty to foul up her reverie the one day she was off. She was used to the bustle of academia, but now she didn't want to be disturbed. In Elizabeth's experience, unnecessary calls at home were usually bad news or someone selling something she didn't want. Poll takers were the worst. Dr. Elizabeth McIntosh didn't take calls after dinner.

Her cell rang. She exhaled in mild exasperation. She leaned over to see who it was; it could be important; it could be trash. A half-frown telegraphed she didn't immediately recognize the name or number of the caller. At the third ring, the number and the name suddenly seemed to be familiar enough to warrant a chance. *I can always hang up; I will block it if it is a pollster!*

She answered before the next electronic entreaty. To Elizabeth's surprise it was Dr. Ronald Stephens, Dean of the Walsh School of Foreign Service at Georgetown University and the OSS Society Chairman.

"Elizabeth, Ron Stephens!"

"Dr. Stephens, what a surprise. I haven't heard from you in years. What can I do for you?"

"Well, Elizabeth, we would love for you to present the *OSS Society William J. Donovan Award* this month. You are at the top of our list every year to recognize a member of the intelligence community with the award named after your grandfather."

Hmmm, again…. She asked, "Who did you select this year?"

Dr. Stephens was ecstatic she hadn't cut him off like she had in previous years. He had tried several times to get Bill Donovan's granddaughter to become more active in the OSS Society, but for whatever reason she rebuffed all of his earlier invitations. This time he had sweetened the pot. He had done his homework. He said, "The person to receive the *OSS Society William J. Donovan Award* would be one of your former students from the Naval War College."

Glad I answered it! "I'd be delighted!" she gushed. *The Naval War College. What an incredible assignment that was!* While the man droned, Elizabeth thought the award should go to the student she couldn't forget, Duncan Hunter. But she had read about him being killed and being interred at Arlington National Cemetery.

He was a native Texan with a huge heart and a knack for details. He was equal parts affable and academic, surprisingly quick to crack a joke or rattle off trivia from memory. He definitely knew how to make the girls' heads turn.

That was something. My heart was just crushed. Tried to put all of that business out of my mind. The media showed the President and the former CIA Director following the caisson, walking in the pouring rain. That man, Hunter 204, had to be something…. Greg Lynche called…I thought he was being hyperbolic. We had no way of knowing. He was something…special.

The OSS Society Chairman finally revealed who the recipient would be. "Our awardee will be Rear Admiral William McGee, the former CIA Director."

After disqualifying my favorite, I'm not surprised it will be awarded to the nation's most decorated man in uniform. He worked at the CIA and was a Navy SEAL. And let's not forget, he was the CIA Director. Of course. Duncan Hunter and Bill McGee were inseparable at the war college. How interesting and dynamic those relationships were…at that time.

"Yes, Captain, Admiral McGee was one of my former students at the war college. It will be nice to see him again, and he is running for President! He has come a long way from leading the first Navy SEAL Team into Afghanistan to find Osama bin Laden. Those were incredible expectations for any person. At the war college, the rumor was that he was washed up. He didn't find the master terrorist; he wouldn't make admiral. For failing an impossible mission, the Navy kicked him to the curb. But the President promoted him to the CIA Director, and now he's an admiral and a Presidential candidate. He certainly landed on his feet."

Elizabeth thanked the OSS Society Chairman, for his time and consideration, and said she would see him soon.

She moved to her window, struck a pose of reflection, and remembered. *It's been about twenty years.... We invaded Iraq in 2003. I guess that's 17 years. Don't do math in public, Elizabeth! I remember the massive Navy Captain, but mostly I remember his sidekick. I could tell that man was a dynamo.*

Dr. McIntosh would never admit it to a living soul, but from the moment she met him, she had a thing for him. Faculty-student romances were taboo. *He wasn't just another good-looking student who was passing through. There never could have been anything between us. He thrilled me, but I was an overweight excuse for a spook, fired from a job I loved, and was too much of a coward to fight that weasel D'Angelo.*

Greg Lynche.... I had long forgotten about him. He and I were both skinny aides to the Director. He was knock-kneed and I had fallen arches. He went off to become the Chief Air Branch and Director of Operations, and I went off to get another PhD. He was appointed Director by President Hernandez. Greg had goals, but I remember he wasn't a ticket puncher. The day he called and said that Duncan Hunter was not just any student, but family who required shelter. He asked if I would look out for him. Family, as in the CIA family. One of the code words for undercover, covert action. I did, but Duncan was an Air Force civilian, if I remember, contracted to the Company? I thought it was impossible until I remembered Duncan was on a SAP. The standard rules don't apply when someone is on a special access program.

Elizabeth smiled at the old memories. They were great, spectacular memories. *I took Duncan in and gave him permission to conduct some classified research. No one ever volunteered for the extra work required of true classified research. Field trip to Navy Intel in Washington, D.C. With Lynche's call, the faculty's assessment of him, and my observation, I assigned him to be the Chief of Station (COS) for the JMO (Joint Military Operations) exercise. He completely blew us away. Every JMO position, every person in the senior class had a script, except the COS. With no script for the COS position, we thought he was just ad libbing.*

I'll never forget what he said. 'Madam Ambassador, I know where the terrorists are located and where they are going. They are on a path to attack the oil storage tanks on the coast near the shipyard. I also know where the hostages are located, and I have video.' What a jaw dropping assertion for a simple exercise. Where he came up with that FLIR tape…. It was as if he made that tape out of thin air. I don't think I ever asked where he got it. But that tape changed the trajectory of the whole joint exercise. McGee was the acting Secretary of Defense.

Isn't that strange? Always McGee and Hunter. They were such an odd couple, but not really. They were men of action. McGee chased bin Laden to the gates of Hell. Duncan was the class honor man. Who knew what that man did? I knew exactly what Duncan did in 2003 but couldn't tell you who was Chief of Station during any subsequent JMO exercises or any other class honor man for the whole time I was at the college. Those two, they left their mark on that school. I have known a lot of impressive people, but Duncan and McGee are one and two in my book. It is too bad he's gone. The country sure could use more people like him.

She returned to her chair and desk, and contemplated what it had been like since she retired from the Agency and took a position at Salve Regina University in Newport.

The university kept her occupied, so there was little time for her to return to the file in her bottom drawer, the file from *Grandpa General's* safe. She loved to read the old intelligence collected from the famous figures her grandfather was interested in, and her grandfather's accountings, as well as his analysis. She knew that the file, looking through 1940 glasses, would probably make for a good book.

Without a thought, Elizabeth reached into her lower desk drawer and pulled out the eighty-year-old file. *Grandpa General* had used the law firms' stationery to record his meeting with Charles Lindbergh. *I still remember: The Lone Eagle.*

Law Offices
Donovan, Leisure, Newton & Irvine

I found the six-foot-three famously familiar boyish face in the crowd on deck, looking about for a face he did not know, waiting to disembark. Once a gangplank had been installed and passengers shuffled down the incline, I made haste to meet the Lone Eagle. At the end of the gangway, I stepped in front of Lindbergh and offered my hand and the challenge: Our business is like men to fight.

Charles Lindbergh was seriously taken aback by my abruptness. The U.S. Naval Intelligence Officer assigned to travel with him to NAS Opa Locka at the beginning of this mission had forced Lindy to memorize the challenge and response. Lindbergh recovered, smiled, shook my hand and completed the ending to The Cavalier's Song Poem by William Motherwell: And hero-like to die!

I introduced myself and said, "Welcome home, Colonel Lindbergh." Before we departed the pier, Lindbergh's eyes fell to the blue bowknot rosette with thirteen white stars on my left lapel. I knew that Lindy also had one, that we were survivors, not mere mortals.

He acknowledged the rosette immediately with a smile and said he had received an identical rosette years ago. He looked as if he shamefully regretted not being able to wear his. Sometimes it was the tiniest and simplest of things that distinguished great men. Although I could tell Lindbergh did not consider himself to be a great man, Congress and the Nation begged to differ. They had authorized him to wear the special rosette in lieu of the Medal of Honor for completing the first nonstop flight from New York City to Paris.

He tried to explain why he was out-of-uniform. President Roosevelt's letter had been explicit that he was not to travel with the rosette. Lindbergh had complied with the unusual directive, but made mention that he had resented it. It was at that moment Lindy realized who I was. I smiled at his discovery. Yes, I was that Bill Donovan, a fellow Medal of Honor winner.

It wasn't the time or place to compare medals. I was still embarrassed to be the only person in America to have received all four of the United States' highest awards. Prior to discovering the rosette on my lapel, Lindbergh had known little about me, other than we might both have known a line from The Cavalier's Song Poem perfectly.

I believe Lindbergh was as impressed meeting me as I was meeting him. Charles was more impressive in the flesh than newspaper or magazine photographs had led me to believe. I could tell he was a serious man.

We rode to Delmonico's in the Duesenberg with the top down. It was freezing, but there is nothing like feeling the wind on your face in a motorcar. Lindbergh noticed my wristwatch and was fascinated with my automobile. I could tell he appreciated quality and superior craftsmanship. He asked politely about the watch and the car.

I said, "This is a Duesenberg Model JN convertible. Clark Gable has one exactly like this one, but his is buttercream. And this is a Swiss Rolex Oyster square button chronograph; antimagnetic; it's called a 'La Moneta,' with register, tachometer, and telemeter; reference 3233. That's how they detail Swiss watches; they have reference numbers."

He said the car and the watch were magnificent, and they were. I said, "There are many parallels between fine automobiles and fine watches, and the relationship between Rolex and the fledging auto racing industry is amazing."

We had some minutes before arriving at Delmonico's. I said, "My analysis is that the previous war was a mindless exercise of political power. When the United States entered the war, Germany knew it had lost, because there are few things that can negate the strength of a free superpower awakening from its slumber. The next war will be a test of psychologies, of which we know very little. Germany has a head start, and the United States is woefully unprepared to face a newly militarized and arrogant Germany. The British and the Americans do not know Stalin is secretly rearming Nazis within the Soviet Union, and providing them with training on new aircraft and tanks. Germany will soon show the world what they have been up to, but for now they are not an official belligerent. I asked the President if he would engage you to do some reconnoitering for us. I am grateful, and I know your travels have been fruitful."

I would not apologize for manipulating the President to conduct some needed intelligence work. I said, "The Nazis are rearming Germany with *crazed fanatics, and the U.S. has to catch up with military intelligence if we are going face a militarized Germany again."*

At this point, Lindbergh offered me his journal.

I said, "Colonel Lindbergh, I only require the pages recounting your journey from the time you left Miami, to your observations when you arrived at the Nuremberg rally, until your return. And anything noteworthy when you left Germany. I am not interested in your private thoughts before this mission. Your diary was to bait the Nazis and it proved your bona fides to them."

Lindbergh was taken aback.

I said, "We needed you immediately; we had a very special mission and it required precise timing. I convinced the President we needed to borrow you. There wasn't anyone else who could do what we wanted. America borrowed you from your family at one of the most difficult times in your life, for a very short period. My analysis of the situation was that we needed your celebrity to break the ice in a Germany secretly preparing for war. We needed an accomplished aviator to get inside, to see how they have sped up their aircraft program, but possibly more importantly, to experience their rally. Over all other famous pilots, I suspect the Nazis have had you in their gunsights for some time. They know your politics and are very interested in you. If they had access to you, they hoped to turn you, to overcome your allegiance to America, and to legitimize their agenda. I would be shocked if they haven't invited you back to Germany."

"Repeatedly." Lindbergh confirmed.

I said, "You passed their first test. They will want to have another go at you soon; you can count on Göring wanting to fete you. Pilot to pilot. You'll be at home in Europe, access to you will be direct. Herr Goebbels' brainchild is propaganda and mind control. Göring is an old fighter pilot, and his brainchild is the new Luftwaffe they are creating in Russia with the help of Uncle Joe. They will want to show off their air force for you. I'm counting on their arrogance and motivation to impress you. They want to establish their credentials on the world stage, and they will entice you with their greatest awards. The French awarded you their Legion of Honor; you should expect something more impressive from Germany. Something more impressive than a watch. You know medals always impress Nazis."

Lindbergh said, "I understand," but I know he did not fully.

I said, "Their awards are propaganda tools; psychological tools designed to manipulate your mind. To turn you to their side. You will see."

I believe Lindy was embarrassed that someone he had just met could read him so well.

I continued, "I know you did not want to leave France or your family — we did find you on sabbatical in France, didn't we? Good. We had you living in England."

He said, "Normally, I am."

I said, "We brought you to the U.S. on business so we could send you back on the zeppelin. We needed an aviator's assessment of the Graf Zeppelin's technology. I appreciate what you have done, as does the President. America needed you to get what we could not get. We are not organized to conduct spying. We have no method of recruiting spies or operating spy schools. One of these days we will be able to conduct special operations. Soon we hope to be greater than the British Special Operations Executive. Until the President can establish an 'intelligence office or agency' dedicated to collecting and analyzing intelligence, we have to rely on very patriotic civilians with very special or unique qualifications."

"It was a Herculean effort to get you to Nuremberg on their airship, although the Nazis think they were the ones that lured you out of your personal exile. They sense you may be angry with America, that you're anti-Semitic, and they will go overboard the next time."

Lindbergh agreed my analysis was correct.

"They know and we know your position of non-interventionism, even if some of your statements about Jews and race have led some in America to suspect you are a Nazi sympathizer. President Roosevelt and I know you have never publicly or specifically stated support for Nazi Germany. It is those perceptions that made you an ideal candidate for our needs. We know when you had the opportunity you condemned the Nazis in your public speeches and we believe you do so in your personal diary. That is why the President asked you to take your journal with you, but not to mention your mission in

any way. We fully expected Goebbels would secure a hotel for you, if only for their Gestapo to enter your room, and find your diary of your private thoughts about your travel to Germany. They certainly photographed its pages. We can play the intelligence game too, although we are not officially organized to do so."

Lindbergh was silent.

I said, "At present, we have Naval and Army intelligence-gathering structures, but we are a very long way from having a national dedicated spying apparatus. If you are willing, you will become our chief German asset. You will not be used too much. We have to maintain the appearance that you're a private citizen in self-exile. I will be in the background; I will not be your handler. That job may be handled by the military attaché at the Berlin Embassy. I expect we will use you one or two more times, but no more. We're going to Delmonico's for the best steak you have ever had, before you head back to Europe. If you do not want to participate any further, there is no need to go to Delmonico's, and I can put you on the next available scow heading to Europe. You can go home to France or England like nothing ever happened. Pretend that you had some personal business to attend to in Germany and the U.S., and once that was completed, you went home. You will be compensated for your time."

Lindbergh was incredulous and asked, "You want me to spy for America?"

I assured him, "Colonel Lindbergh, you've just been spying for America. This is the nature of the work. My question is, do you want to continue? If your allegiance is to another country or ideology, like racial or political homogeneity, then our conversation is through. In everyone's eyes, mine, the President's, you're an American hero. We know you've been through the worst pain and suffering a person can endure. Rational men are saddened by your loss, as am I. Patriotic people look up to you with awe. You have been in the Army Air Service; you are an Army colonel in the Reserve. You were awarded the Medal of Honor, and I have always believed your service and sole allegiance is to America. But I also know that you, The Lone Eagle, could be of critical utility in our nascent intelligence establishment. Joseph Stalin has quietly rearmed Adolf Hitler. Nazi Germany is very interested in you. They *are collecting people who can help their cause while other men of intellect are leaving. Doctors, scientists, physicists, aviators. They have a nose for war. Goebbels and Göring and Hitler would love to bring you over to their side. It would be of immense propaganda value for them. What we are asking could very well become a burden to you and your family. The Boche are preparing for another war, and we are unprepared. Your propaganda value to Nazi Germany cannot be measured, which is why you came to my attention."*

Lindbergh sighed and said, "Bill, I would love to have dinner with you at Delmonico's."

I held out my hand and Lindbergh shook it. I said, "Welcome aboard, Charles."

Dr. Elizabeth McIntosh closed the file. She had read *Grandpa General's* complete file, from start to finish at least a dozen times over the last seventeen years. Every time she learned something new. Every time she finished and closed the file. But this time she was left with a question: *shouldn't this be in the hands of the CIA's museum? The future OSS Director conducting intel before there was an OSS? And who knew Lindbergh was spying for America? This doesn't belong in my bottom drawer simply for my own pleasure.*

Then it came to her. She knew to whom she would gift *Grandpa General's* CONFIDENTIAL REPORT.

CHAPTER 22

July 1, 2020

About every six months for the past ten years, American and Nigerian intelligence officials of the Boko Haram Task Force huddled at the U.S. Embassy in the capitol city of Abuja for another round of interdiction missions. The goal was to stop the al-Qaeda affiliate, Boko Haram, from operating in the upper third of the country and neighboring Chad. Nigerian forces provided the intel, the U.S. provided the means.

Bizarre was the only accurate description of the relationship between the Boko Haram and the Nigerian government. First, a Boko Haram raiding party from Chad would be eradicated in Nigeria before they could decimate a village. Then, five months later, another raiding party would surprise the authorities with an incursion that hadn't been detected through a nascent intelligence network of dedicated Christian villages. The Islamic raiders would strip the life of the village, sending the women and children to the sex trade, killing the husbands, terrorizing some for the blood sacrifice, and forcing other sons and brothers into serving Islam.

Compounding the difficulties of detecting the whereabouts of the Boko Haram network in Chad was the simple fact that the leadership of the Nigerian military could not keep a secret. The rank-and-file Nigerian soldiers were terrified of the al-Qaeda and Boko Haram. Previous military encounters had resulted in Nigerian soldiers being captured, tortured, publicly beheaded or eviscerated.

Complicating the challenges of the Nigerian intelligence officers who had been trained in America, was the political atmosphere. Christian presidents increased the numbers of military and border control officers in the north, sufficiently deterring the Boko Haram from raiding Christian villages. Muslim presidents wouldn't fund military efforts in the north, essentially firing a starter's pistol for the Boko Haram's next incursion into unprotected villages and its riches of Christian children and women.

It had become a vicious cycle. The bloody conflicts had transitioned from single-shot rifles in the 1960s to fully automatic AK-47s in the 80s and 90s. Weapons were brought into the country by the tens of thousands by the international arms dealer, Viktor Bout. He totally weaponized civil war in Sub-Saharan Africa. Bout armed criminals and mental disorders, and transformed poor destitute African children into adolescent warriors, and then into insidious mindless maniacally driven killing machines, operating with assembly line efficiency. The Russian Bout was a shadow facilitator, arming not only designated and up-start terrorist groups and insurgents but also the powerful and rich drug cartels around the globe.

If it wasn't Bout providing arms, then it was the former American President Mazibuike who, before he resigned and disappeared, authorized nearly $1 billion in arms sales to the Muslim Brotherhood president of Nigeria. American foreign aid was not used to fight Boko Haram or other al-Qaeda affiliates, but to fund the terrorist groups clandestinely. When the Muslim Brotherhood attained the presidencies in Nigeria and Egypt and Algeria, Islamist parliamentarians in those nations immediately kowtowed to American foreign aid requirements of legalizing abortions and dismissing laws against homosexuality. Cultural time bombs designed to destroy Christianity in the country.

Armed with Bout's weapons, paid for by American taxpayers, Boko Haram raided large Nigerian villages in the north, killing the men, stealing female children, and raping the women. The male children were captured and given an ultimatum: join the Boko Haram and swear allegiance to its leader or suffer the consequences. A machete would amputate a foot to punish the unwilling. Sometimes the bloody stump would be thrust into hot pitch to cauterize the wound. Sometimes the child was left to bleed out. The butchering of

Christian children was part of the plan. It usually took only one writhing screaming amputee to telegraph the message that the alternative to the pain and suffering was dedicating their life to the Boko Haram and Allah. The goal was to stay alive.

But there were other reasons for the Boko Haram to kidnap children. They publicly tortured their young victims, waiting until the maximum amount of adrenaline had been pumped into the victim's body, then the torturers tapped the child's carotid artery. Some in the Boko Haram elite believed that consuming the fresh adrenaline-saturated blood of a terrified child created a high with dramatically increased senses, hallucinations, and feelings of euphoria. The al-Qaeda affiliate preferred the blood of children, believing the younger the child, their blood was more potent and possessed rejuvenating effects. The techniques of harvesting this blood had been passed down through secret societies and cults for centuries. Raping the conquered dead and human blood sacrifice had long been part of the rituals of many cultures in Africa.

The Boko Haram Task Force at the U.S. Embassy was briefed on at least 20 people who were reportedly killed in a Christian village in Plateau State. The Task Force initially believed the attack was the work of Boko Haram. However, as more military reports came in, the Americans cautioned the Nigerian intelligence service that the attack was probably not the work of Boko Haram, for the raiders were not wearing uniforms and were uncharacteristically destructive. The Boko Haram favored a more hit-and-run style of attack. The Americans had their own intel sources who said Christian victims and survivors claimed the attackers were Fulani terrorists. Women and girls were not kidnapped; white men were not killed.

The Chief of Station explained, "Fulani herdsmen have terrorized Christian communities in Nigeria's Middle Belt for years; it's a clear intent to target Christians. Their attacks on Christians are inspired by the Fulani's desire to take over Christian's lands by force and impose Islam, because desertification has made it difficult for them to sustain their herds." He added, "Residents of the community vociferously criticized the government, since it took two days for police to arrive in the villages." The Nigerian intelligence officers were forced to admit their intel was incomplete.

The Chief of Station would not communicate the other aspect of Islamic conquest, that Islam implicitly permitted or condoned sex with children. He didn't want to further inflame the passions of the Nigerian Christian intelligence officers. The Chief of Staff concluded, "We know Christian ministers in northern Nigeria are continually at war with the Boko Haram cult. The Boko Haram has made it a point to terrorize communities near Chad and Cameroon. Wherever they found the white men of God, they killed the white men of God who preached blood sacrifice was evil." The Chief of Station noted, *Every day, north Nigerian Christians see persecution beyond anything experienced or imagined in America.*

A handful of American and Nigerian intelligence officers constantly juggled the political and religious permutations of whoever was sitting in the presidential palace. With a Christian president, the quality of the intel trended positive. The Americans sometimes relied on a resource that they had used several times. No one knew who it was, but the deep resonating baritone was again on the radio. "Visitors from the north are inbound." He was referred to as "the Texan" because of his accent.

The only hint that the Texan was in the area was the single radio transmission confirming a raiding party had crossed into Nigeria from neighboring Chad and was making its way toward one of several potential communities.

The Nigerian intelligence officers had been deeply suspicious of the radio transmissions, but over the years they had learned to trust the sonorous voice of the Texan. During the period between radio calls, the Chief of Station reassured the Nigerian intelligence officers that their "asset was in place and wouldn't let them down."

Minutes after the staticky rumbling voice came over the radio, the Boko Haram would be utterly destroyed. No one at the U.S. Embassy knew how, but the evidence of carnage told a consistent tale. When the *voice* radioed that the area had been cleared, the Nigerian military moved in to confirm the attack, count the bodies, and conduct clean-up operations of the dead. The exit wounds of the dead were uniformly the size of a number 1 soccer ball.

The Nigerian intel officers didn't know how the Americans did it, but they expressed their appreciation to the men whose unknown asset saved hundreds of Nigerian lives. The intel officers recognized that their government should be more consistent in funding and collecting intelligence all the time, not just when a Christian president was in office.

•   •   •

Twice a year *Maverick* visited the Boko Haram's hunting grounds as the hunter. Tonight, he had a plan and moved quickly to configure the YO-3A for attack. He threw the switches to lower the high-caliber single-shot gun and the laser designator (LD) from their stowed positions in the belly of the YO-3A. And he activated *Weedbusters*, the aerial eradication laser. It took a few seconds longer for *Weedbusters* to unfold from the aircraft's belly.

Maverick waited for the aircraft's special purpose systems to lock into place in the airstream; gun targeting information and symbology were superjacent onto the black and white FLIR image on the visor of his nearly half-million-dollar helmet. An NVG-capable light meant *Weedbusters* was down, locked in place, and ready for use.

Weedbusters was the ideal weapon to incapacitate masses of terroristic men on the ground. Operating at 265 nanometers and the proper altitude, the UV laser could instantaneously sear the optic nerve of the human eyeball, blinding anyone in the path of the scanning lasers.

He chose a member of the Boko Haram who would live for a few more hours. With the laser designator, he drew a circle around that man and programed the *Weedbusters* to blank the inside of the circle so that the UV-C laser would not enter the area where the man was standing. *Maverick* rammed the throttle to takeoff power for a couple of seconds, then returned it to the QUIET detent.

Every man of the Boko Haram looked skyward to the growl of an unexpected aircraft motor. *Maverick* activated the *Weedbusters* lasers. He saturated the killing field with UV-C except for the man within the no-laser circle. He electronically *acquired* the lone man with the Terminator Sniper System but did not allow the system to *track* him.

Maverick didn't shoot him; he was taking a chance. He hoped he could get the man to flee. In a few seconds, he would know whether the gambit would pay off.

All the other men instantly recoiled after being hit with the blinding UV-C. They dropped their weapons and dropped to their knees. Their hands went to their eyes but the damage was already done. The unaffected man was bewildered by his comrades' actions. He spun around as his comrades shrieked and fell.

Maverick looked for advantageous angles and placed a laser dot on the chest of some of the men who *doubled-up*. Laser-guided bullets from the airborne gun passed through the terrorists like a plasma cutter through hot steel. Every six seconds, *Maverick* targeted and killed another pair of terrorists. *Maverick* scanned the area looking for any Boko Haram escapees.

He had effectively disarmed the Boko Haram. None of the thousands of bullets from their AK-47s with huge banana clips were fired. None of the Christians of the village were injured.

The single unaffected Boko Haram man freaked and ran for a vehicle. *Maverick* smiled and let him run. He caught up to the speeding truck and made lazy Ss overhead to keep from overrunning him. After an hour of hard driving, the Boko Haram getaway vehicle entered a remote village in Chad and stopped. In the FLIR, *Maverick* saw dozens and dozens of men pouring from mud shacks with thatched roofs. The escapee gesticulated wildly to the group. Instead of targeting the man's sternum, *Maverick* shot him in the ass in profile; the bullet passed through cheek-cheek-crack-cheek-cheek. Being shot in the ass was still a mortal wound.

Maverick ran the YO-3A's throttle to the stop and back. Startled men looked up; *Maverick* activated *Weedbusters*, blinding everyone in the village. He targeted the remaining Boko Haram and decimated them with the laser-guided rounds from the TS2. Chest shots; no ass shots.

He grabbed ten *Firestarters* from his helmet bag, set the timers for thirty seconds, and tossed them out from an access door in the cockpit near his elbow. Grass-thatched roofs in the village caught fire immediately.

•　　•　　•

The clock on the aircraft's instrument panel read just after three a.m. when *Maverick* radioed, he had completed his mission over the northern savannah of Nigeria. It was time for the troops to move into position to clean up the bodies of the Boko Haram men he had shot. The Chief of Station was surprised *The Texan* was so late in reporting *Mission Complete.*

Maverick returned to the Abuja airport before daybreak. His ground crew removed the wings of the YO-3A and rolled the airframe and wings into its special container in the back of a white LM-100J, the civilian version of Lockheed Martin's C-130J cargo workhorse. When the *Yo-Yo* was safely aboard the *Hercules,* the aircrew closed the aircraft ramp and upper door and started its engines. From engine start to takeoff took ten minutes. The LM-100J departed Nigeria for Roberts Field at Monrovia, Liberia.

•　　•　　•

When Nigerian soldiers entered the Christian village at sunrise, many of the men and women of the village protested the lack of government protection from the murderous and evil Boko Haram terrorists. Instead of burning the dead terrorists or allowing the soldiers to cart off their bodies, the men and the boys of the village dug several deep pits and tossed the remains of the Boko Haram into them. One villager slaughtered a pig and cast the blood of the animal into the pits until blood covered the dead Muslim terrorists. Once the pig was drained of its blood, four Christian men threw the swine's carcass atop the Boko Haram. Soldiers filled in the pit so lions would not make a meal of the men or the pig.

Once the fires in the Chadian village that was further north had burned out, rapacious animals left their jungle sanctuary and fought over the multiple carcasses there.

CHAPTER 23

July 13, 2020

The CIA Director of Operations had given the President's Daily Brief (PDB) as the Director monitored the process. Director Todd had been in countless meetings over his forty-plus years in uniform, but he found the PDB unique. It included highly classified international intelligence analysis, information and status of covert operations abroad, and information from the most sensitive U.S. sources or those shared by allied intelligence agencies. The PDB fused domestic intelligence from the Defense Intelligence Agency (DIA), the National Security Agency (NSA), the Federal Bureau of Investigation (FBI), the Department of Defense (DOD), the Department of Homeland Security (DHS), and other members of the U.S. Intelligence Community.

After leaving the Oval Office, the Senior Intelligence Service executives shared the Director's limo back to the CIA compound. They convened on the seventh floor of the New Office Building. Todd went straight for the phone.

• • •

Duncan's Blackberry buzzed with the ringtone, *Secret Agent Man*. Once the connection was made, Director Walter Todd allowed the encryption to catch up; there was always a delay. When it had cycled, and he heard a barely audible *hiss* in the background, he said, "I need you." As soon as the three-word transmission was completed, he ended the conversation and looked at the DO.

Nazy Cunningham looked radiant in a white and black polka-dot silk dress which featured a high neckline, ruched waistline, and puffy cuffed sleeves. She sat in one of two chairs in the front of his sprawling wooden desk. Todd asked, "Like that?"

She said, "Just like that, and now I have to get to work."

•   •   •

Those three words might have meant nothing to an eavesdropper on a descrambling listening device, but to the receiver, the words meant work, a mission. Duncan Hunter closed the connection on his Blackberry. *Now, that there's an Air Force general in charge, I have to change that ringtone to Wild Blue Yonder, or something.* He exhaled; the next call on the hand-held device would be from his wife. *I'm waiting for the details, Baby….*

•   •   •

Nazy smiled, nodded. Todd had activated *Noble Savage* for a mission. The next step, she would provide the details just as soon as she could extricate herself from the boss' office.

There was still an uneasiness between the two intelligence executives. She didn't know Walter Todd. He hadn't come from the IC. Apparently, Todd and Duncan had substantial history, and if Duncan said Todd was a trustworthy patriot, then it was a fact not to be debated. But it would take time for the number one and the number three persons at the Agency to build a relationship.

Now that her husband had been officially notified of the lift request by the only person authorized to do so, she had to provide the lift details to Duncan. As Nazy stood to take her leave, Director Todd asked, "Nazy, now that we have *Noble Savage* activated, can you tell me what the Scorpii affair was all about?"

Nonplussed, Nazy returned to her seat, crossed her legs, and said, "Director Todd, it is a very complicated…."

"Nazy, I have time. Please."

I don't have time now! She didn't let her exasperation show. "Let me start with this: Christianity is a celebration of good and life, the rejection of evil. The left's worldview is a secular alternate religion; they celebrate death. Those on the left engage in the alternate religion and have done so, in America, since the civil war. In Europe, it's been going on for centuries. European secularism has largely driven Christianity underground. Your pilgrims broke from the Church of England, escaped the tyranny they experienced, and made plans to settle in the New World."

"Mohammadanism Muslims were the only group powerful enough during the Crusades to displace Christians; they celebrated their conquests and converted the grandest Christian churches into mosques. It's actually been a battle for millennia. The Crusaders stopped Islamic raiders and drove them back to the Middle East and in Europe, underground. They still exist and we call them the Islamic Underground."

"I apologize if this sounds like a lecture; it is not."

"No, no, please continue, Nazy."

"Good and peace and life are normal conditions of a Christian heterosexual man; evil and chaos and death reside in the secular where they have sex with anything and demanding it be called normal, as in normal for them."

"A psyop?"

"Yes. Indeed. Rulers of the left view themselves as megalomaniacal secular gods. Hitler, Stalin, Mao, the elite of the Democrat Party."

"How?"

"You can see some of it in the difference in foreign aid when Republicans are in power and when Democrats are in power. Democrats insert themselves into the internal domestic politics of foreign countries, demanding anti-discrimination laws be passed to protect homosexuals and the other sexual deviances contrary to the indigenous culture. These Christian countries reject the cultural interference, but if that is the only way they can get foreign aid...."

"So, they are poor and need the money...."

She nodded. "Or if they reject American funding, they take the Chinese's money in trade for natural resources. The Chinese are not interested in changing the culture. Their focus is on resources. This is how America loses the foreign aid battle with China. Republicans provide foreign aid based on need, to help their militaries, their medical communities, or their commercial infrastructure. The last time I was in Monrovia, Liberia, the airport equipment had 'Gifts from The People of The United States of America' stenciled on the side. Republican presidents enable those type of things to occur through the Econ offices in the embassies. Democrat presidents mandate Democratic Party agenda items, such as requiring a country to allow abortions, decriminalize homosexuality or similar actions which are counter to their culture."

"Now, Europe is secular, but after the war their anti-Christian sexual-deviant religion was disorganized. Rho Schwartz Scorpii changed all that. He built an empire upon anti-Christian gay clubs and hotels that served homosexual men, and he became the dominate factor in child sex trafficking throughout Europe."

"That was the reason for those assessments in the PDB."

"Yes, sir. Always. A country is and can be leveraged by the sexual activity of their elites. We polygraph our intelligence officers to determine their trustworthiness. If they lie about their sexual activities, they can be blackmailed, but more importantly, they prove that they cannot be trusted."

"Continue."

"There were some other activities Scorpii found to be lucrative."

"Like?"

The subject wasn't a pleasant one. Nazy chose her words carefully. "Director Todd, for forty years Rho Schwartz Scorpii maintained a steady supply of children for the sex trade, mostly those who had run away from home or had been abandoned, or were in orphanages. Some were stolen off the streets. In Europe, that amounted to well over a hundred thousand children each year. He developed an espionage monopoly through his network of child brothels and gay men's clubs. He recruited homosexuals and lesbians who had been purged from DOD and NATO's militaries, but he also focused on recruiting the poor performers at America's intelligence agencies, NATO, and the Federal Bureau of Investigation. He funded abortion clinics throughout Europe which trafficked fetal remains for the range of pedophilias: child sacrifice, cannibalism, satanic rituals. The secondary purpose of abortion in Europe is to feed the anti-Christian pedophilic left."

"Satanic rituals?" *Feed the pedophiles? Seriously?*

She nodded and continued, "In Europe alone, human trafficking is a $32 billion-a-year business according to our World Factbook. $150 billion worldwide. Child sex trafficking is the fastest growing criminal enterprise in the world, and it is all connected through social media. The missing children of Europe were his business' *inventory*, for gay men, for pedophiles. A direct quote from his journals. As are some of the code words used in the child sex trafficking business."

"Such as what?"

"The FBI has a listing that goes back to 2007 when American social media networks and President Mazibuike and *Mazibuikism* came onto the scene. It references Italian food; *pizza* is a girl; *cheese* is a little girl but *cheese pizza* is child pornography. Hot dogs are boys, pasta means little boy, and *map*, that is a minor attracted person; another term for pedophile. There are key words for buying, selling, trafficking children, or sexually explicit materials, or to arrange child sex activities."

"In Scorpii's hotels there were content menus which listed children harming themselves, children engaging in sex acts with animals; there were options to arrange for meet ups. Those sorts of things. Abortion clinics, morgues at medical schools in the U.S. and throughout Europe, also had content menus, selling body parts from donated cadavers and allowing buyers to come to the morgue to choose which parts they wanted. Abortion clinics specialized in fetuses and the harvesting of body parts. Biotechnology labs would have a list of desired body parts and visited during the day; pedophiles at night. All detailed in Scorpii's journals."

Not Navaho Code Talkers. And I don't want to know what they do to body parts. Todd shook his head. *Crazy.*

"The line of business that directly affected us was the network he built that used children to compromise NATO intelligence officers and other officials throughout the NATO countries. There has been an epidemic of NATO employees, primarily in Brussels, being charged with espionage, but there was virtually no mention of their involvement in child sex trafficking or child pornography. Extreme child abuse."

Human... inventory? Director Todd replied, "Yes, I lived through what I thought was a dark period at NATO when I was in Brussels. It always seemed like there was someone involved in espionage, but we were in Europe, surrounded by socialist, communist, and increasingly Islamist countries. What do you mean by child sacrifice, cannibalism, and satanic rituals? I really haven't heard of anyone actually doing those things until now."

Nazy quietly sighed. "Director Todd, just today eighteen people were arrested in New York City in connection with child sex trafficking. They had used the same child for seven years. Another case, in Europe; after paying his mother $1,000, a child trader was caught trying to take an 11-month-old baby out of Ukraine to traffickers where they could get 25 to 40 thousand dollars selling the child's organs. These things happen everywhere, all the time, but are rarely reported by the media. After Scorpii's death, all throughout Europe, law enforcement leaders were no longer being bought off by Scorpii. They are finding groups that were harvesting the blood, organs, and body parts of children for cash. Scorpii's abortion organizations commercialized these events. They murdered children of every age, placed organs into containers, and passed those containers on to biotechnology labs and pedophilic black markets. And sex with dead...*females...* is a huge problem among the elites and the Muslim men who invaded socialist countries. The problem is everywhere. The media will not cover it because Scorpii had not only paid the media to ignore the problem, but he paid law enforcement to look the other way. Now that Scorpii is dead and no longer paying for protection, we believe some of the Europeans will try to continue child sex trafficking as long as the media chooses not to get involved. The media were incentivized for too long to not report on it."

Todd realized Nazy was much more informed on world views than he was. She had been delivering the PDB for years. Todd asked, "Why?" and listened intently.

"One half of our Congress are Socialists, anarchists, and Islamists who are actively working together to overthrow the West. Not the military externally but the government internally. These groups also routinely visited Scorpii's hotels where they would sleep with children."

"Scorpii's foundation wasn't only an amalgam of Marxist secular thought, Scorpii leveraged those ideologies to commercialize child sex trafficking. The satanic global elite had a sponsor who could orchestrate everything from hunting children for sport to drinking the adrenalized blood of children to using pedophilia to blackmail pedophiles. Europe is dealing with President Hernandez's directive and the collapse of Scorpii's empire, and there are now reports from the BBC of international judges examining charges against Scorpii's foundation. A former Marine Corps military judge and Agency general counsel heads the international tribunal. The charges are for facilitating child rape, kidnapping, torture and murder to benefit the members of the global elite known as the Ninth Circle, a satanic child sacrifice network."

Todd looked as if someone had stolen his dog.

"Scorpii's minions orchestrated child sacrifices in the catacombs of Catholic cathedrals, on private estates, and on military bases in Belgium, Holland, Spain, Germany, Australia, Ireland, France, England, and the U.S. We analyzed the info for accuracy and applicability, and passed the information from Scorpii's journals to the international attorneys general. The first week they received our intel, that information allowed law enforcement to find over 35 mass grave sites of children in Ireland, Spain, Canada, and Germany. They were pits full of children, reportedly appearing to be between the ages of two and seven, who had been carved up and disposed of like so much waste. These nations' respective governments initially refused excavation, until we reminded them, we had Scorpii's tapes and we would be releasing them soon."

We have the tapes.... Director Todd asked, "Was the CIA named in any of these Ninth Circle activities?"

Nazy said, "Yes, Sir. Scorpii had identified the former Econ Chief in Berlin. He had arranged hunting parties for some businessmen and congressmen from the U.S. to hunt and kill children. Scorpii's groups organized virtually everything. He provided children for European royals, prominent government ministers, priests, bishops, clergy, judges, politicians, aristocrats, military men, and others."

Dumbfounded, he asked, "How?"

"Director Todd, we provided some of what was in Scorpii's journals to *Whistleblowers* and European law enforcement, through third party means, as proof of what he had orchestrated in Europe for the elites, and now there are an increasing number of reports coming out of Europe's international tribunals detailing how children were drugged, stripped naked, and raped. Some had their blood removed, or were hunted down in the woods and killed. That is according to this week's eyewitness testimony before the International Common Law Court of Justice in Brussels. For the record, we provided some very limited information from Scorpii's *pumpkin*."

Pumpkin? Pumpkin? Pumpkin? Oh yeah, from North by Northwest. Scorpii's treasure trove of evil. Todd shook his head in amazement.

"In one of Scorpii's journals, he became livid when a woman gave an accurate accounting of the human hunting parties of the global elite. A former member of the Netherlands criminal drug syndicate, known as Octopus...."

Todd said, "Never heard of them."

"… testified that victims for these human hunting parties were obtained from juvenile detention centers in Belgium and Holland. Some children apparently eluded the hunting activities and escaped; several of them have sued the men involved."

Incredible.

Nazy continued, "I received the transcripts of the trial from our Chief of Station Berlin. One woman was an accessory to torture, rape, and murder sessions of drugged children that were performed before a group of high-ranking Netherlands officials. She recalled being driven to hunting parties throughout Europe, most recently in Belgium, close to Brussels, where she had prepared two boys and a girl, ages 14 to 16, to be hunted and killed by, I'll just call them global elites. Several former child sex slaves said the human hunting party that they were involved in was heavily guarded by the Netherlands Royal Guard and that the King of Belgium was present. Other eyewitness testimony said children and youths were forced to attend the human hunting parties. Some of the hunters had sex with the corpses of the children they caught and killed. Some deceased boys' penises were cut off. Allegedly, there was a Dutch countryside palace where the penises were displayed like trophies on a wall. There were reports of satanic sex, where men engaged in ritualistic consumption of adrenalized blood, and reportedly, experienced a high from the adrenaline when they murdered a child."

"That is sick. I'm almost sixty and I have never heard of such a thing."

Nazy said, "You've heard of snuff films?"

Todd nodded.

Nazy said, "Scorpii created centers in virtually every country in Europe to conduct snuff operations for the Illuminati elite so professional harvesters could acquire adrenalized blood to sell; they traded in child pornography. A victim is tortured or told they will be sacrificed in the arena, which increases the amount of adrenaline that flows through their body. We have many of those tapes in a vault."

"Arenas?"

Nazy nodded. "In his clubs, sometimes in private auditoriums, but for the elites, on private estates or in private castles. But mostly, in his hotels where he could control the videotaping of the blackmailed."

Director Todd turned his head away for several seconds. *I'm familiar with deer mating season, the rut, when adrenaline and other hormones drive bucks into a frenzy to mate. Do people go crazy when they have adrenalized blood?*

Nazy continued, "Adrenalized blood, however, is not the end. Like addicts seeking a stronger hit, some prefer the purest, most potent form. Scorpii called it *Ambrosia*. His people collected it with a syringe from the base of the neck or spinal column; the smaller the child the better, according to Scorpii's own writings. Scorpii provided *Ambrosia* to Europe's elites. *Ambrosia* was even used by the Nazis' elites. After the war, it was sold on the black market in Europe, Africa, and the Middle East. Exorbitant prices. Scorpii processed the missing children of Europe and made millions. Maybe billions. We have not completed the analysis of his journals...."

"I had no idea."

Nazy offered a half-grin. "Welcome to the intelligence community, Director Todd. It only gets worse from here."

CHAPTER 24

July 13, 2020

Todd shook his head in wonder.

Nazy continued, "As Duncan has said, 'Not everything is as it seems; not everything is peaches and cream.' We deal with the worst of society. Information from Scorpii's journals tells us that most satanic sacrifices include some consumption of blood and sometimes even the consumption of body parts. These are provided by Europe's abortion clinics, which were controlled by Scorpii's NGOs. Scorpii's clinics were also involved in harvesting children's bone marrow."

"Why?"

"Reportedly, as an anti-aging solution."

Todd thought, *The Secretary General of NATO was a client. The houses of royalty….*

Nazy continued, "Before you on-boarded, I briefed the President that Europe was the model, NATO was the immediate target, and America is the next goal. Narco-terrorist groups like the FARC and Boko Haram trade sex slaves for cash. They can make more money from children than drugs."

"How?"

"They can only sell a bag of dope once but they can sell a child several times a day."

My God.

Nazy continued, "The old KGB, now the FSB, will do anything to get to NATO's classified information. In the early days, the KGB subsidized Scorpii's early male clubs. Scorpii knew social norms quickly degrade under liberal rule, and he wanted to export his model to the United States. Under President Mazibuike, when the social media companies took off, abortion clinics expanded their organ harvesting offerings to the biotechnology firms — many of which were a cover for child sex trafficking, child sacrifice, cannibalism, and satanic rituals involving murdering a live-birth child. All this to get men and women who were entrusted with secrets to pass intelligence to those not authorized to have it."

"I was never briefed on these things."

Nazy nodded sympathetically. "Scorpii's enterprises thrived in the socialist countries."

"What about here?"

"Director Todd, the world's largest child sex trafficking ring was busted in Europe, in Germany, and no one has been held to account for it. But these things happen here too, just in a different form. Democrat led states began letting their pedophiles out of prison and reducing the penalties for illegal contact with minors. Statutorily, we cannot do anything in the United States; this is the purview of the FBI. DOJ."

"Which you say isn't doing their job."

"Neither the FBI nor the media. The media is silent on the issue of child sex trafficking because of who the customers are. The FBI is fully aware of who the customers are, and yet they sit on their hands."

Director Todd shook his head.

Nazy nodded. "The FBI is fully compromised, rotten to the core, and has essentially become a clean-up company for the Democratic National Committee. The DNC. The DNC controls the media and social media. At our security briefs, our employees and contractors are told to avoid social media. We tell them the East German *Disintegration Directive* program was a pre-electronic form of social media. The government cannot restrict free speech, but social media can. Democrat leaders tell the social media companies who and what they want censored."

"Censored? Really?"

Nazy frowned and nodded. "It controls... to destroy — how do I want to say this? Social media is designed so the Democrat Party can fully *control* the electorate, the elections, and the narrative. Scorpii's social media companies and those in the U.S. connect and promote a vast network of accounts openly devoted to the commission and purchase of underage-sex content and activities. If necessary, social media can destroy the lives of people who get in their way. I can arrange a much more detailed brief on the subject." *I really need to go and activate Duncan.*

"Nazy, you are doing fine." Todd shook his head. "I knew something was going on, but as SACEUR, I never had time to indulge in the goings on of the Secretary General of NATO. He was a strange little man, incredibly well-connected, as were some of the diplomats and general officers from our allies." *And they weren't polygraphed and probably had sex with children and spilled their guts. I cannot even fathom killing a child. It is so difficult to believe.*

Nazy said, "Yes, sir. From Scorpii's journals, the Secretary General was a frequent visitor at Scorpii's hotels. You were not, but you were approached several times. It was the only time you were mentioned. Scorpii annotated you had been approached, but he lamented you had an unusually strong bond with your wife and children. As for the Secretary General, Scorpii provided him children. And *Ambrosia*. We have the documents…*and the tapes* of the Secretary General and thousands more officers and CEOs and Chairmen from industry across Europe. Royalty. A British prince and many Americans who were so preoccupied with having sex with a child they dismissed the notion a fellow pedophile would record them. It's the mentality of a mental disorder, like what the Secretary of State, Henry L. Stimson, often quoted that, 'Gentlemen do not read each other's mail.' The European elites were of the belief that fellow pedophiles don't record each other's activities."

"But Scorpii did."

Nazy nodded. "He did. We have ten thousand of his tapes. Video recordings."

Royalty too? On tape? Oh no…. Todd nodded. "That probably explains why NATO's Secretary General committed suicide when the President issued his ultimatum."

Nazy nodded and continued, "In many ways pedophilia and child cannibalism in Europe was the exclusive purview of the royal families and the wealthy, high-ranking military men. The elites. Ours, theirs."

"Ours?" inquired Todd.

"Sir, when I said CEOs and Chairmen from industry, I meant not only billionaires and leaders of companies but also America's elites and Democrat politicians, millionaires from industry. Hollywood elites. They constantly made the pilgrimage to Scorpii's hotels in Europe, under official travel, for sexual encounters with children. Men and women. They were all provided *Ambrosia* as a hotel service, or they could purchase *Ambrosia* for export. Scorpii said the blood was collected largely from Europe's abortion clinics and missing children, about 100,000 a year for twenty years." *For a higher high....*

That's a lot of blood.... "And we have the documents?" *And the tapes?*

"Yes sir, that night at the White House when you were announced as Director McGee's replacement, I confirmed to President Hernandez we had Scorpii's *pumpkin*. We had all of Scorpii's journals and diaries, and CDs from his clubs, many hotels, and castles that had been converted to specialty hotels throughout Europe. That's where he recorded the powerful having their way with the innocent."

Todd said, "So we have Scorpii's *pumpkin*, and that is why President Hernandez threatened Europe with sexual Armageddon...."

Nazy said, "Actually sir, just to be completely transparent, before the *pumpkin* was in our possession, the Attorney General told the European Ambassadors that America would leave Europe and let Russia have their way with them if they didn't shut down the child sex trafficking and ancillary related events throughout Europe. We maintain those other records at an off-site location called the *Library of Diaries*."

"There was chaos that day in Brussels, but I never had good info about what had actually happened. So, President Hernandez threatened them?"

Nazy nodded, "That one Presidential decision effectively shut down Scorpii's billion-dollar *Ostgut Foundation*. That was the source of all their funding. Scorpii used NGOs, front companies, shell companies to fund worldwide leftist causes from Germany. He was paying off local police forces when gays and children were involved and had streamlined the harvesting and distribution of *Ambrosia* worldwide."

"We suspected all of this was going on in Europe but we had no proof. Our goal was the *pumpkin*. Duncan brought Scorpii to the United States; essentially an impromptu rendition. He flew him to the Anderson Cancer Center in Houston. The doctor who saw him before he died said that he had raised Scorpii's arm and saw a tattoo: 15482. The medical team realized the man near death was a survivor of the Nazi concentration camps. He had to have been a child when he was tattooed. We know through other documents that Mengele had a particular interest in using children for experimentation. Mengele tattooed the children as do today's child traffickers." Nazy touched the back of her neck to illustrate where the child traffickers tattooed the children.

"The rest of his story in the 1940s was that the Jewish underground was secretly taking the orphaned children to Palestine, but Scorpii would not go; he told his story how he had found a cache of gold coins and watches after the Allies bombed a synagogue. The Nazis used that synagogue to melt the gold fillings and watches of the dead from the concentration camps. That cache of gold allowed Scorpii to start his businesses."

Todd frowned. He made a throat-cutting motion. He had had enough of Scorpii and NATO's Secretary General. He was disgusted with himself because he had known the Secretary General was dirty, but at the time he could not conceive just how dirty. He hadn't been able to ask for an investigation. He'd had his suspicions, but he could not ever imagine the strange, exotic and foreign activities of that man or the elites on the left.

"So, let me conclude with concentration camp survivor or not, Scorpii's journals confirmed oligarchs like him ruled the world, at least the European world, using a system of social media to facilitate their pedophilia. It is a greater problem than anyone can conceive." *The President wouldn't ignore their heinous crimes; he showed great courage and used the power of America to blow up Europe's deviant enterprise. And, Duncan was there to make it all happen.*

Nazy was grateful Todd had enough. She wanted to put the ugliness behind her too and get out of the office. Duncan was waiting. She waited to be dismissed.

For several seconds, it was quiet in the CIA Director's office as Todd pondered what the left in Europe had been able to get away with, and what the left in America was trying to make normal and acceptable. He hadn't ever been political. He had shied away from it. This was all new ground.

Nazy allowed some time for Todd to process and assimilate what he had heard. It didn't look like she would be able to leave. *There's still much to brief him....* She broke the silence with, "Sir, new subject. Part of the *Noble Savage* special access program is the *Disposition Matrix....*"

Todd narrowed his brows and thought, ... *Disposition Matrix?* He asked, "What's that?"

"Sir, when you energized Duncan for a recovery, that was one element of *Noble Savage*. Another element of *Noble Savage* is our office's responsibility to find and track the world's worst terrorists. These are men on a list of the CIA's and the FBI's top 100 terrorists in ranked order. Through contacts on the ground that we developed over the past twenty years, we determine and locate the heads of the disparate terrorist organizations, wherever the intel takes us. Those on the *Matrix* have been exclusively Muslim men, with a few exceptions of some drug cartel chiefs and the international arms trafficker, Viktor Bout, who was captured in Thailand. We, the National Counter Terrorism Center, determine who they are and where they are, and if we can, we monitor them for their habits. When the President gets a request and permission from the heads of the countries where these groups are operating, he notifies me during the PDB, and we prioritize them for elimination."

"Did he do that when we were in the Oval?"

"Not this time. If the President had a request from an ally, he would have handed you a folder. It would have contained the authorization to deploy *Noble Savage* assets."

"Ok."

"This one was internal. You activated Duncan for an internal recovery mission for the Agency by saying, 'I need you.' You would do the same thing for an insertion or a rendition. For specific foreign targets, where the leader of an ally needs help with eliminating their terrorism problem, we require Presidential authority. When Duncan started on the program there were hundreds of intelligence targets on the *Matrix*; now there are none."

"Who knows of this *Matrix*?"

"Since its inception, only four people know of the *Matrix*: the Director, the President, me, as I compile and update the list, and the program manager, Duncan. He has the only aircraft capable of performing the various missions."

"How does it happen?"

"Sir, the President gets a private request for the U.S. to help eliminate a nation's radicals or terrorist group. These are all mass murderers and these countries are not organized or equipped to deal with mass murderers. The presidents or prime ministers of these countries authorize the U.S. to find and eliminate their mass murderers for the good of their nation."

"Got it."

"What Duncan does is never recorded. You have a copy of the *Disposition Matrix* in your personal safe. I can brief you more thoroughly on it or give you a tour of the *Library of Diaries* when you wish."

The CIA Director's three telephones were lit up. He intercommed his secretary to push all of his calls to the Deputy, unless it was the President. "I'm in conference with the DO." He replaced the receiver and said, "Nazy, I had little clue. Director McGee said he would give me a more thorough debrief of my duties and responsibilities when his campaign came this way." Todd paused for several seconds to collect his thoughts. Then he used Hunter's call sign, amusing Nazy. "Is *Maverick* rewarded for his work?"

"If you mean, does he get paid, 'yes'. He is a contract employee. He's been an Agency contract employee for over twenty years."

"Has he received personal awards?"

"Duncan has received five Distinguished Intelligence Crosses. The most of anyone at the Agency."

Director Todd let that information set in. "For finding terrorists and eliminating them?"

"Yes and no, sir. There is more to the *Noble Savage* special access program. On two occasions, Duncan rescued the passengers and crews of 747s that had been hijacked. One was a British Airways jet. The Queen knighted him, Knight Commander of the British Empire. The other was a Qantas aircraft that had been electronically hijacked. He has also located or effectuated the rescue of several hundred hostages and sex slaves in Colombia, Somalia, and 300 girls from the U.A.E. Most recently there was an American gentleman in Mali and a SEAL Team that had been captured in Syria. Those men were about to be executed by ISIS, but Duncan stopped it."

300 girls from the U.A.E.? Todd was taken aback by the information. *My God Maverick, what did you have to do to stop a SEAL Team from being executed? Maybe I don't want to know. No, I want to know.*

CHAPTER 25

July 13, 2020

Director Todd was quiet for several seconds, assimilating the information. He asked, "ISIS?"

Nazy half-nodded. "Duncan found them in a remote part of Syria, near the ancient city of Palmyra. ISIS was using a tourist hotel as a base of operations and conducting executions under the awnings in the hotel parking spaces. He has been doing these for a long time and knows where and what to look for. He's something of a savant and has a gift of recognizing patterns. The awnings protected ISIS from surveillance satellites or unmanned aerial aircraft with sensors and cameras. Duncan flies so low he can look under parking lot sunshades. There were about 60 men and children that night; ISIS had prepared the children to execute the SEALs. Those children had been groomed to murder."

"But Duncan stopped them."

"Yes sir, Duncan stopped the execution of American soldiers. And the SEALs were rescued unharmed."

How? Todd looked at a very somber Nazy Cunningham who did not want to provide the details of that night. He realized that *Maverick* must have killed the children who were going to execute the SEALs. He thought, *This can be an ugly business.* "From an airplane?"

Nodding, Nazy continued, "Director McGee said, 'Duncan has a nose for finding those who do not want to be found.' He knows what to look for, and has been instructing his partner how to read or 'cut sign.' Illegal aliens and terrorists moving through dirt or sandy areas leave traces where they have been and indications where they are going. They leave clues what they are doing. They act or respond a certain way when they believe they are not being observed. Duncan amplified those skills from his time in the Border Patrol. There they tracked aliens who were in the country illegally."

Todd considered what she said and added, "I understood *Maverick* had busted up a drug cartel operating in Del Rio. That's how I came to meet him. The Border Patrol Chief there in Del Rio said he needed to get *Maverick* out of the Border Patrol and out of Texas; drug cartels were hunting for him and had attacked him at his home. I hired him, and I think it was the CIA who had the Air Force send him to the Naval War College until things blew over."

Nazy smiled. *And that is where I met him.* "For the longest period, Duncan was our only resource. Now he has help. There are two active YO-3As."

And no one on the FBI's Most Wanted Terrorist List.... Todd nodded, "I've seen one of them. *Maverick* showed me and told me a little about what his aircraft was capable of doing. That has to be an amazing aircraft." He explained, "Fighter pilots fly jets with offensive and defensive capabilities. Military observation aircraft have passive detection capabilities. *Maverick's* airplane is a low-level offensive aircraft tailor-made to surveil and engage an enemy at night. Remarkable." *Weird black coating, had a gun, as I remember Maverick telling me.* "Who is his partner?"

"A former squadron mate of his, Link Coffey." She said *mate* as if she was a barmaid in an English pub. "They were captains together. Flying F-4s. Coffey went to the FBI after the Marines and retired as an assistant director. When he was assigned in Europe, he assisted *Interpol* in dismantling networks involved in the child sex trade and the exploitation of children. Child pornography."

Todd sighed, considered the information, and then shifted gears, "What's the deal with the FBI?"

Nazy said, "Sir, if you mean what is the problem with the FBI, under the previous president it had become completely infiltrated with Islamists, and to a lesser degree, communists. The current FBI Director wouldn't support Director McGee's designation of the Muslim Brotherhood as a terrorist organization."

"Which it is, I think?"

"Yes, sir. Of course, it wasn't always like that."

"What happened?"

"After the first World Trade Center bombing in 1994, the FBI instituted a *Muslim Outreach* program. It was a presidential initiative and except for the DOD's *Don't Ask, Don't Tell* law, *Outreach* was probably the single greatest mistake or act of treason committed by a Democrat President. It reorganized the FBI leadership to be more sympathetic to Muslims. Muslims are peaceful, however, what *Outreach* really did was allow al-Qaeda sympathizers and the Muslim Brotherhood to infiltrate the FBI."

"When President Mazibuike was elected, his *Muslim Outreach* initiative exploded in scope and encompassed not only the FBI, but the entire Intelligence Community. The members of the Muslim Brotherhood who infiltrated the FBI orchestrated massive sting operations on Catholics and Jewish people across the country. It was stealth *jihad*. They infiltrated dozens of Catholic churches and synagogues hoping to find domestic terrorists among the traditionalist Jewish and Catholic congregations."

"How?"

Nazy said, "A radical Muslim is always at war with infidels. Every radical Muslim is an Islamist. The 'how' is that there probably isn't a single mosque in the United States, or in all of Europe, that isn't run by or under the control of Islamists. When you enter the house of the believers, you're met with radical Islamism. They go to mosque for that purpose, to receive the word on what and who to attack. They use peaceful Muslims as a cover for their activities. They are the soldiers in a holy war with the infidel. Imams preach 'the mosques are their barracks and the domes of the minarets are their helmets.' They are always at war with the infidel, in this case, the white man, and they believe they cannot be defeated."

"It's not yet insurrection, as in France, it is stealth *jihad* that is a red light for America which they run every day."

"As soon as Muslim men cross the imaginary line and become radicalized, they are pushed toward more hate and anger. They train to fight Christians. Kill Jews. The American population is, by and large, unarmed, and U.S. citizens, normally Christians, are routinely murdered."

"But the media...."

"The American media must be considered an extension of the Democrat Party. Reporters' affiliation is around 98% Democrat. Islamist attacks on Republicans and Christians harass and intimidate, sometimes with individual murders which are rarely reported. They avoid mass murder because those generate much scrutiny and response from law enforcement. When those are not reported...."

Director Todd said, "It's like they never happened." Todd had difficulty accepting the DO's analysis but he knew it was true.

Nazy could tell Todd wasn't convinced. She continued, "What you see from the media—reporting on some stories while ignoring others—is a very sophisticated form of propaganda. The media espouse the Democrat Party narrative. The reality is that virtually every Muslim country in the Middle East and Asia has a police force *and* a secret police force. The secret police force is specifically organized to investigate and stop radicals from committing mass murder in the name of Islam."

"So, you are saying the National Counter Terrorism Center...."

"Correct. It is task organized as a clearinghouse of law enforcement and IC to investigate and stop radicals and terrorists from committing mass murder in the name of Islam in America."

"And, you are the Director?"

"Yes, Director Todd. These Muslim men become fully proselytized, radicalized. They believe Islam is the one true religion. They are hardened mass murderers whose goal in life is to kill as many Americans as they can. Our Muslim allies have a similar problem with their mass murderers."

"I had no idea. That's incredible, Nazy."

"Yes, sir. So, with no contrary information, these Muslim men are taught to believe that their holy warrior training that takes place in an imam's office or in the basement of a mosque, also happens in American churches and synagogues. Of course, this isn't true. The mosques were once under surveillance by the FBI, but now they are under the protection of the Federal government."

"That's our FBI?"

"Yes, Sir. President Hernandez has tried to clean house at the FBI with an Executive Order (EO) that requires everyone at the FBI who comes into contact with classified information to be polygraphed. Most of the legacy *Muslim Outreach* people refused to be polygraphed and were let go. But the ones who remained at the FBI have tied up the EO in the courts under judges who were appointed by Democrat presidents."

"Muslim men in the FBI had their priorities: protect Muslims, hurt Christians, and kill Jewish people. But the Democrats in Washington made a pact with the FBI leadership, so they turned a blind eye to the evil things Democrats in Washington were involved in: child sex trafficking, child sacrifice, cannibalism involving children, satanic rituals involving children, adrenalized blood, child murder. The same thing Scorpii did in Europe."

"The Democrats still control the FBI. The answer to their recovery is not the creation of new rules, but a renewed fidelity to the old. Radical Muslim infiltrators were identified and expunged; justice needs to return. It will come down to the integrity of the people who take an oath to follow the guidelines. Additional rules and regulations or more training would likely prove to be fruitless if the FBI's guiding principles of 'Fidelity, Bravery and Integrity' are not engrained in the hearts and minds of those sworn to meet the FBI's mission of 'Protecting the American People and Upholding the Constitution of the United States.'"

The discussion of the FBI was a good diversion. He didn't want to hear of those rituals involving child murder any more. Todd was numb; he realized he had stopped listening and had starting focusing on Nazy's sing-song melodious British accent, her hair, her face, and her eyes. Pendulous breasts. *She has beautiful eyes; too bad no one looks at them.* He caught himself and asked, "Say again?"

Nazy summarized, "The FBI had turned overtly hostile, politically. They investigated Washington Republicans and dismissed Democrat Party malfeasance. What was happening in Scorpii's Europe was also happening in America, but the FBI wasn't interested. Democrat politicians, CEOs, millionaires and billionaires, and Hollywood were fully engaged in the domestic child sex trade. The FBI could not be bothered to investigate, and the media focused on trivialities or manufactured Republican crimes."

Todd was quiet for some time. He blurted out, "Five DICs?"

Nazy didn't like going over old ground but accommodated the new Director. She nodded, "Duncan had also saved the lives of the President and his family—on election night. A group of rogue intelligence officers from the National Clandestine Service tried to shoot down the President's helicopter. Duncan parachuted to the roof of the MGM Grand Hotel across the Potomac River to stop them."

Parachuted? From what? His airplane? Todd shook his head in disbelief.

"That information is only known to a handful of people. President Hernandez and Duncan have known each other since his days in the Border Patrol. President Hernandez was then Congressman Hernandez of Val Verde County."

"He is an amazing man. *Maverick* is an amazing man."

Nazy smiled. She liked hearing her husband was "an amazing man." She knew he was, but it was always good to have it validated. She said, "Director Todd, he's taken 200 elite terrorists off the battlefield. Once, the *Disposition Matrix* was full; now there are no names. There was also a time when he and Director McGee stopped the Iranians and the Chinese from developing...." Nazy caught herself, "...Duncan and Director McGee eliminated the Ayatollah Khomeini Institute of Virology in Iran. From the records we took from there, they had developed gene editing technologies and brain-controlled weapons to crush dissent, and they were manufacturing ethnic-specific bioweapons for use on Israel." Nazy imperceptibly shook her head. *And the CDC director bragged that if Bill McGee is elected President, then he will have to deal with an outbreak, a pandemic. I am so grateful President Hernandez fired him. But I fear D'Angelo will not go away.*

It looked like Todd was trying to retrieve long lost memories. Squinting, he said, "Was that about the same time when Iran had a problem with their nuclear power plant? Like, one of their reactors blew up?" *She has the most amazing green eyes…. Subtle smoky eyes….*

Nazy nodded. "That was a different mission, Director Todd. Duncan also irradiates the multi-billion-dollar opium poppy crop in Afghanistan every year. The al-Qaeda believe it is a fungus or something, and they keep trying to cultivate the fields like before. Opium is now cultivated elsewhere, mostly in Mexico."

Todd scrunched his face, "Damn, *Maverick*. What did he use?"

"One of Duncan's many patents is called *Weedbusters*. It's an ultraviolet laser, actually a multiple laser head on his airplane that is tuned to kill opium poppy, coca, and marijuana. Every year in early April, when the snows recede from the valleys of the Himalayas, he flies into Afghanistan. His *Weedbusters* laser system irradiates newly sprouted poppy plants to the point they are so damaged that they either die or are unable to put up a mature bulb which contains the alkaline sap used to make opium, heroin."

"Amazing! That's brilliant!" *It has a gun and a laser – what else?* "I said Duncan had busted up a drug cartel. My memory is getting better. I remember the Border Patrol Chief asked me to transfer *Maverick* to the Air Force and this retired CIA executive…"

"That would be Greg Lynche. The Director before Director McGee. And these drug cartels couldn't exist without China or Russia or the Islamic Underground."

Todd grinned. "That's right. Lynche and the Border Patrol Chief asked me to send *Maverick* to the Naval War College in Newport. I thought they had lost their minds—an Air Force colonel can't send anyone to the war colleges – I might have been able to stop someone from going – but I believe it was Lynche who had already facilitated the orders. Lynche had incredible pull. He must have been able to get the Director to act on his behalf. All I know is that *Maverick* left Del Rio for Newport to hide out until the crisis across the border blew over."

Nazy smiled and said, "I suppose I can tell you that's where I met Duncan."

Todd rocked back in his seat as if he had been gobsmacked. Astonished, he thought, *Seriously?* He motioned to the slightly embarrassed woman to tell him more.

Nazy said, "It is a very long story, Director Todd, and we have much to do – can I tell you later?"

"I'll hold you to it."

As Nazy sighed, she was teleported back to Newport. Where she had first seen him. On a racquetball court. *He asked me out. Duncan hired an ancient white Rolls Royce to take me to dinner, to the Red Parrot. I wore the most decadent dress I could find. Painted red enamel on my nails for the first time. He knew I was in trouble. I told him I was supposed to spy on him; I was a terrible spy…. He took me to his room at the Naval War College. He was so tender and thoughtful.* Nazy accidentally kicked one of her shoes across the Director's office. Now she was really embarrassed. She stood up, retrieved her shoe and said she had to get started activating the specifics for *Noble Savage. Duncan's been waiting!*

Todd sucked air as he watched her go. His eyes fell to her ankles and legs before rising to her departing ass. *She looks so much like a young Sophia Loren! Good Lord. How does anyone get anything done around here?*

CHAPTER 26

July 13, 2020

Nazy returned to her office in a huff. *I have work to do and he wanted to play twenty questions! I am really upset! Bloody hell. He still doesn't have an idea who he is in that job.* Once she rounded the door to her office, ignoring the secretary, Nazy began calming down. *Talk about throwing your toys out the pram!* She sat at her desk, one hand holding a land-line to her ear, and one hand fiddling with the James Avery cross suspended from her neck. Nazy began coordinating the rendition flight with the embassy in North Africa. She bounced a foot in a black Valentino pump as she waited for the encrypted line to connect.

Organizing special access program missions required great effort to ensure the people on the program would not be subject to retaliation. Moving a terrorist prisoner from Africa or the Middle East always infuriated the worldwide Islamic Underground.

Sending Duncan off for a few days meant Nazy probably wouldn't see him before the OSS Society Dinner. And she had bought a devastating gown just for the occasion. It seemed there was always something urgent that required his expertise, that had to be done as quickly as possible. With his special purpose aircraft, Duncan was the only option the CIA had for the very sensitive work. Renditions were a different matter requiring a different aircraft.

After she liaised with the Chief of Station at the U.S. Embassy in Algiers, Algeria she contacted her husband.

She got right to the point. "Do you think you'll be back for the Donovan Award? I wouldn't go, but it is Bill and I spent a fortune of your money on a new gown that is guaranteed to stop your heart. But, if you will not be there, I'll wear a suit."

Duncan howled at the imagery. "I know Bill's receiving it; now that we know, *we* have to go. There are just some things you just don't miss."

"His wife cannot come. She's taking care of her mother. The leaders of the IC will be there. Bill would understand, but I don't want to go unless you are there."

Duncan's smile could be heard over the line. "I know, Baby. Be there. I paid for all of us to attend just so you would get all dolled up. You *will* wear that new black turtleneck…?"

Nodding unconsciously, Nazy cooed in her husky, traditional English accent, "That's the plan. If you can make it. But I'm not going to dinner in a stunning frock unless you are there." She breathed deeply in anticipation of making herself ravishing for Duncan. Thoughts of him taking her after dinner made her fling the Valentino up against the modesty panel of her desk. She rolled her eyes and stopped bouncing her leg. Her free foot tried to locate the errant shoe. *Concentrate!* she admonished herself. Freed toes found her shoe, but it would not cooperate. She gave up and slipped the other one off. *Barefoot on the seventh floor – the old directors would have a fit knowing there was a female DO who was running around barefoot with bare legs in the Agency.* She giggled at herself.

Duncan listened to her giggle like a schoolgirl, then got back to business, and said, "Let's get this show on the road. If Kelly and I start soon, I'll have a good chance of making it. Depends on the winds; I have to get in and out of there while it's dark. Midnight ops. Always know, I can't wait to see you. Save me a seat. Oh, I'll need a *beacon*…."

"You will like what I got."

"Baby, I already love what you got."

She smiled. "You know what I mean. Anyway, we'll place a beacon on the roof of the limo. My detail will expect you." *That's another way of saying he plans to use the jetpack, and that thing scares me.*

The adventuresome Hunter grinned as Nazy provided the procedures and location for the rendition. In his rich authoritative baritone, "Thank you, baby. I'll be there. Love you." He raked a thumb across his brow knowing Nazy would have reciprocated with a tug of her earlobe.

Nazy sat back in her chair and remembered how exciting it had been, the first time, the second time. Her foot stopped bouncing. *Snow fell outside Duncan's room window, obscuring the Newport Bridge. He held my hand. My attraction to him was immediate and all-encompassing... He treated me like I was porcelain. It was magical. No one had ever treated me that way. I don't even remember why I told him, "I want to go ice skating, I may never get another chance."* She continued her daydream, *That was the night I became unleashed, unburdened from Islam and the Muslim Brotherhood. He took my hand as we stared out the picture window of his room. Over a foot of snow had covered the cars and trucks in the parking lot. I had nothing! Nothing to wear. But Duncan bundled me up in layers of his large, long sleeve T-shirts, sweatshirts, and sweat pants. I still have that yellow Corvette sweatshirt; I was so thankful it was big enough. That was the night Marwa Kamal looked like a resident of a homeless shelter. That girl is long gone.*

She fingered the gold cross on the chain like a talisman.

He worried about me, worried that I'd get too cold. I was so excited to be free; I just wanted to experience everything! I was so bundled up; I could barely move! I assured Duncan that I'd be warm enough, even in that subfreezing weather. He took me to a skating rink, because that's what I wanted to do. No other man would do silly things in ridiculously snowy weather just to please me.

He got down on his knees and laced up my skates, looking deeply into my eyes. His eyes never left mine. Duncan took me by the hand and carefully led me out onto the ice. There was no one else around. I had so much fun I nearly hyperventilated! Although I couldn't keep myself from falling, I never did. Duncan was always there to catch me. To save me. He bought hot chocolates from a machine, and we laughed at my near-spills. I remember telling him, "You're an amazing man, Duncan Hunter. I think you really would do anything for me." He said, "Of course, I would!" That was the moment I became his forever.

STOP! Get back to work!! Nazy grinned at herself for being solipsistic and dutifully complied. *We'll be together soon.*

•   •   •

Hunter called Wulfkuhle, his head mechanic who had been supporting him since the very beginning of his Border Patrol days. The loyal and responsible man, with all the clearances and polygraph, would drop what he was doing to make Duncan's rendition jet ready for flight. Next, he called Kelly, his daughter. He told her he needed her help with a continuous flight; they would be tag-teaming pilots like big rig team drivers making a bicoastal, over-the-road trip. Reflecting on the last few minutes, Hunter could see that the new CIA Director was learning the job, benefitting from having Nazy there to coach him in the finer points of turning him into an intelligence officer instead of a retired military pilot.

Hunter sighed. *Another rendition flight. Greg and I met in the cafeteria to discuss the work. Not quite ten…maybe twelve years ago, I guess. He told me they couldn't use their jets anymore because there were too many Tailwatchers who monitored and scrutinized every move of Agency aircraft. It pained him to add to my duties, but he knew I would do it right. It would take some time to get everything into position to do them properly. Regular contractors would cut too many corners to maximize profit, but I wouldn't do that to him or the Agency. I told him, "I'm on contract to do whatever you need me to do, and I'm willing — I just want to do it right so it does not impact the Agency in any way. I'll need a little time, but you can always have confidence that when you send me out, we will exceed your expectations. My way, Tailwatchers will never know you are back in the renditions business. We have a jet that's impossible to track. And it can be configured for the nasty work."*

And to think, this one makes thirty-one terrorist dirtballs taken off the battlefield and given a cell instead of a million-dollar Hellfire to the face.

CHAPTER 27

July 13, 2020

Hunter expected this rendition flight would be like all the previous ones. Some newcomer who had hit the FBI's Most Wanted Terrorist List had thoroughly screwed up. Would it be because their suicide vest hadn't detonated as designed by Iran's Islamic Revolution Guard Corps (IRGC)? Did the terrorist leader repeatedly mash the detonate button on his suicide vest to no avail? He wouldn't have known that the men from the National Clandestine Service Special Activities Division or DOD's Special Operations Command had used a powerful signals jammer, one powerful enough to sterilize a bull while disrupting any nearby electrical switch. That allowed their men in black battle dress with black keffiyehs and black weapons to close in and taser the terrorist, making him flip and jerk and squeal like a stuck pig, incapacitating him instantly.

The identities of the terrorists were immaterial to the rendition crew. Their names might hit the media in weeks or months, or never. *Not my concern. I just pick up and deliver. Make sure my shots are all up to date and we are all on the anti-malarials and anti-parasitics. But this one will be more challenging, simply because I need to attend the OSS Dinner with Nazy. She'll be at the Ritz-Carlton, and if I'm on time, I'll be blowing out of Manassas after going through decontamination. That means loading the jetpack, exposing myself to the elements, and the public. I'll be a stinkin' UFO. Oh, well, all in the name of love! Lucky, I'm in Elmira. I have a tux in the office somewhere…. I had the tailors adjust it to hide the Python. How they screamed, 'We can't do that to an Armani!' but they did it, anyway. And I'll need some oversized flying coveralls. I can't show up to the dance looking like I had been dragged across a stockyard.*

Whether by design or accident, whenever the CIA found themselves with a terrorist they would rather interrogate than vaporize with a million-dollar missile, they called Duncan Hunter. He had made himself and his company, Quiet Aero Systems, *indispensable*. A firm fixed price contract for aviation services, to be determined. While other private jet owners raced around trying to deliver the lowest cost, technically acceptable service to the Agency's classified request for proposal, Hunter invested heavily in the technologies to ensure his jets and business aircraft could not be detected or tracked by the Muslim Brotherhood or the media or the Russian's *Tailwatchers*. On each rendition flight, there was little if any profit.

He was able to keep his flight information private so that no one could track his jet to the Middle East or North Africa, the originating locations of all rendition flights. It required the Agency, specifically Director Lynche, to make a formal request for the Federal Aviation Administration (FAA) to develop a program to allow high-visibility people the ability to fly incognito. The CIA's Air Branch vehemently opposed the public sharing of certain Agency flights or having their senior executives tracked. A jumbo jet full of passengers was blown out of the sky because CIA executives aboard the jet had been tracked by the Islamic Underground. The FAA immediately allowed special handling of corporate and business aircraft, for a fee of course, which was gladly paid.

Other aircraft were still required to be part of the ADS-B, the Automatic Dependent Surveillance-Broadcast Exchange. This technology had allowed aviation to evolve from using ground-based radars to using satellites to report aircraft location. With the waivers, information used by air traffic controllers and other aircraft about the location of movie stars and CEOs in flight were no longer in the public domain. These aircraft could change their International Civil Aviation Organization (ICAO) identifier frequently while in flight.

The genesis of the program resulted from a communist front group that had forced the Agency to change their rendition procedures. A secret and, at the time, unknown resource was headquartered in

Moscow. *Overwatch,* as it was called by its designers, was a shady group *The New York Times* called *Tailwatchers* in the U.S. The CIA was forced to acknowledge that two rendition flights, each carrying a terror suspect, had refueled on Diego Garcia, a British island territory in the Indian Ocean. Earlier U.S. assurances declared none of the secret flights since the September 11th attacks had used British airspace or soil.

The public disclosure and Agency request forced the FAA to introduce a Privacy ICAO Aircraft address (PIA) program. This allowed certain aircraft owners to apply for temporary aircraft registration numbers which were not attached to any other plane, thus allowing people to fly anonymously and rendering their aircraft untraceable. The PIA program didn't involve a fee to get a temporary ICAO address, but it required a ton of paperwork. Aircraft serial numbers, N-numbers in the vernacular, were tiny, insignificant, and strategically placed on a painted aircraft fuselage where they could not be seen or photographed. Moscow-based *Tailwatchers* relied on telescopes and cameras from hotel rooms or apartments to see the big black N-numbers displayed on engine nacelles, the fuselage, or tail of regular aircraft. But on PIA aircraft, serial numbers could not be read, even from high-powered telescopes.

Duncan had things to do while he waited for his daughter to arrive in Elmira. He fully stocked the jet with consumables — food, water, snacks — and checked the contents of the jet's large customized Middle East first aid kit for fresh anti-malarials and anti-parasitics. Hunter activated the PIA program with a radio call.

His rendition jet was on the ramp in Elmira, not in Manassas where the rendition crew was located. Hunter had agreed to meet with the aircraft owner of a World War II Curtiss P-40 *Warhawk,* made famous as the aircraft of choice of *The Flying Tigers.* A shark-mouthed *Tomahawk* was being restored by Hunter's mechanics in Elmira. The owner wanted to talk price. Hunter made the man an offer and was about to return to Virginia in preparation of McGee's big night when Todd and Nazy called.

The cabin of the Gulfstream G-IVSP was specially configured with two seats for security guards and plenty of floorspace to lash down captured terrorists who would be shrink-wrapped and strapped to stretchers. At the rear of the cabin, an oversized waterproof bag containing the jetpack rested on the floor like a pile of luggage. A single seat belt secured it so it didn't roll around. A dark suit bag from Armani hung in the tiny coat closet.

How am I going to do this? James Bond always made it look easy. Hunter estimated how much time he would need for the PIA protocol. *Forty hours? Twenty hours of wearing a mask. Ugh! I'll at least have some help.*

An old unmarked Lear landed and disgorged Kelly Horne near the QAS Operations Office. She bounded out of one jet, ran up the stairs of the Gulfstream, and pulled the door closed. She kissed her dad on the cheek and crawled into the right seat of the cockpit.

Hunter had been flying the Gulfstream solo for much of the time he had had it and hadn't flown with his daughter for some time. The last time had been another rendition flight to Jordan. Kelly had sworn she wouldn't do another one. But when dad asked, the petite redhead surprised him again. Hunter thought, *Maybe she has a short memory….*

With over 200 terrorist interdiction missions, thirty-plus renditions, countless rescues from African pirates and the FARC, and annual trips to Afghanistan to eradicating a half-million hectares of opium poppies, Duncan Hunter knew his way around the Middle East, Africa, and South America as well as a blind man knows his own room. But most important of all, *Tailwatchers* had been rendered blind to his jet.

CHAPTER 28

July 13, 2020

Shortly after the QAS Gulfstream departed, the unmarked Lear 24 moved to the airport's taxiway. A blindingly bright landing light led the way as the jet taxied to the far end of the Quiet Aero Systems hangars, turned 90° to port and shutdown. Considered a poor man's jet by many, the Learjet was markedly quieter on the ground than the other jets of its era.

A single pilot lowered the cabin door from inside and stepped out. He walked across the tarmac to the north side of the hangar, accessed the security system, opened a set of double doors, and disappeared inside. He moved with confidence; he was totally familiar with the procedures of opening the hangar doors. Two cocooned and one mission-ready helicopter beckoned. Once the segmented hangar doors fully opened, the pilot walked to a tug with a towbar attached to the nosewheel of the strange, black, two-rotor helicopter. He pulled the helo out of the hangar, looking over his shoulders occasionally, and positioned the helicopter on the north-east side of the hangar. It was near a dozen Learjets waiting to be refurbished that were parked along the edge of Sing Sing Creek. Once the rotorcraft was in place, he checked its rotors would not interfere with any suspended wires or the adjacent building. Then he dismounted the tug, uncoupled the towbar from the nose wheel, and installed a grounding wire from the helicopter to a grounding lug in the concrete pad. He accessed the battery, hooked up the quick-disconnect, locked the battery access door, and returned the tug and towbar to the hangar.

An insignificant red light in the helicopter's cockpit flashed every ten seconds to confirm the aircraft had electrical power.

Five minutes later, the hangar doors rolled closed and the security system was reset. The pilot walked back to the Lear, fired it up, taxied to the runway, and departed to the south.

After depositing the boss' child in Elmira and moving the old helicopter out of its hangar, Arsenio Bong's next stop was a little airport in Washington, D.C. Washington National.

CHAPTER 29

July 14, 2020

Halfway across the Atlantic *Maverick* said, "We'll wear flight suits on the return trip."

Kelly turned and asked, "Flight suits?" *Why would we wear flight suits in a corporate jet? For a rendition?*

Maverick nodded. "These are special and cost about a hundred grand apiece."

The look on Kelly's face was abject incredulity. *$100,000? For a flight suit?* "What makes them so special?"

Maverick continued, "Well, they actually cost millions to develop. Lawrence Livermore National Laboratory scientists developed a breathable, protective smart fabric designed to respond to biological agents. Like the previous guys we have chauffeured to GITMO, our next boy is the epitome of a biological hazard and I'm not taking any chances with him. The flight suit's innovative material can autonomously react to microscopic dangers in a live biological environment."

She asked, "It's wearable for a long time? I thought you could only wear CBRN stuff for a few minutes." (Chemical, Biological, Radiological, Nuclear.)

Duncan nodded. "*This* fabric incorporates breathability and protection in the same garment for safe extended use. It's a technological marvel and wears like a regular flight suit. When you touch it, you'll know it's not Nomex®. Not rubber, like the old biohazard suits, but it is slick."

"They're not fire retardant?"

"No, but they are special. They confront biological threats like viruses and bacteria, and chemical agents, like sarin gas; the material provides a barrier and neutralizes all of them."

Kelly said, "Sounds like a technical marvel."

Maverick said, "After twenty years of R&D in chemical and biological warfare protection, they developed a multi-layered multi-functional material. The base layer comprises trillions of aligned carbon nanotube pores, graphitic cylinders with diameters 5,000 times thinner than a human hair. Very cool."

Kelly asked, "Nanotubes, like the paint on the *Yo-Yo?*"

Maverick nodded. "It's exactly like the coating on the YO-3A, only woven in a fabric!" *Maverick* continued what was essentially a capabilities brief. "The nanotubes transport water molecules through their interior. This ensures a level of fabric breathability, but the real magic is that the nanotubes trap and block biological and chemical threats down to the size of the smallest virus, largely the same way the paint traps radar signals on the *Yo-Yo*. Just the unseen threats our petri-dish terrorists carry. When we are done with the rendition, we just throw them into a dryer with UV lamps, and the UV kills any trapped pathogens stuck in the nanotubes."

"You're so smart."

"Not me—these were developed when Bill was a SEAL. For him and his guys. They operated in some crazy environments."

"But haven't you been working UV sterilization efforts? Irradiating poppies and killing coca with the UV laser, UV drones that kill bugs after renditions. Dad, I've seen your office; what do you have, twenty patents?"

"Thirty, if you count all the quiet technologies we developed. There's a reason I take my anti-malarials and anti-parasitics religiously and wear that flight suit when I'm over Africa and the Middle East. You never know what bug you will run into. I even carry potassium iodide tablets."

Kelly tried to form a question. "But…"

"But not this time. And, I know what you're thinking. Yes, when we return to Manassas, we still have the showers and UV disinfecting equipment. So, once we get off the jet and through decon, we can go home. We're on final into Algiers. You can go suit up in the cabin."

Kelly thanked her dad and left the cockpit. She was amazed that the black flight suit was everything her father said it would be. *It is slick! It feels a little strange to be standing in the middle of the jet in just my bra and panties and socks.*

When Kelly returned to the cockpit, *Maverick* moved to the cabin to suit up with the nanotechnology flight suit, matching gloves with leather touch points, steel-toed flight boots, and lightweight spider web body armor. He finished the ensemble with a Colt *Python* with a laser pointer in a plastic zip-lock bag slung under his arm, and a Kimber Model 1911 ACP with a silencer strapped to his ankle. He reentered the cockpit.

The approach into Algiers International Airport was uneventful. Kelly Horne, a former U.S. Air Force jet pilot, flew the instrument approach and landed the business jet expertly. It was just another routine North African evening as dust blew off the Sahara; the suspended dust and sand only impacted visual flight operations minimally. Kelly mentioned she was grateful the Algerian airport didn't require any of the runway lights-off, spiral approaches that were required to land in Afghanistan and Iraq. Apparently, there were no snipers taking shots at arriving aircraft here.

Duncan double clicked the interphone switch on the yoke and was on the radio to Approach Control and to Ground Control on a specific frequency manned by the Algerian Secret Police. The ATC controller told them, in technical English with an Arabic accent, where to turn off the taxiway and where to taxi the Gulfstream.

Kelly was directed to stop the jet and shut down in front of an open hangar. A refueling truck positioned itself parallel to the Gulfstream, ready to refuel the business jet. *Maverick* opened the aircraft's cabin door and lowered the airstairs. A twinge in his back reminded him to get Kelly to apply some patches. An ambulance and four black cars waited inside the structure that would easily hangar the large business jet. One man attached a tow bar to the Gulfstream's nose wheel. Once the jet was refueled, another man drove the tug slowly, straddling a painted line on the floor. Segmented hangar doors closed behind them by electric motor. When the doors were fully closed, the hangar lights came on.

Maverick knew from previous renditions that the prisoner was loaded inside a closed hangar to prevent potential *Tailwatchers* with telephoto lenses identifying and tracking a rendition aircraft. To prohibit *Tailwatchers* from identifying the Gulfstream, it did not display any serial number on the engine cowlings or tail. The G-IVSP was just a white jet with inch-high black numbers and letters on the bottom of the engine nacelles being towed into its hangar in Algiers.

Maverick met three CIA men on the spotlessly white painted floor. They shook hands. The Chief of Station said, "It's midnight, and you are early. We only have one tonight. There will be two officers to accompany you." One CIA man offered N100 particulate respirators. *Maverick* knew the medical-grade, maximum-filtration carbon filters trapped and blocked about 99.97 percent of bacteria and viruses. As he expected, he knew the detainee was likely infected with the terrorist's biological trifecta: tuberculosis, plague, and probably a weaponized virus straight from an Iranian or Chinese bioweapons lab, or even a post-Saddam Iraqi bioweapons lab that the press was loath to identify as Iraq's weapons of mass destruction programs.

The captive on the stretcher was wrapped from chin to toe in plastic film. The Agency had learned how to prevent an uncooperative detainee from shitting and pissing all over himself just to make it as uncomfortable as possible for the aircrew and intelligence officers transporting him. Terrorists were less likely to be a total biohazard if they were fully "prepared" for flight. This terrorist, like the others, had been stuffed with laxatives to empty his bowels hours before flight, and he had been sedated. Earplugs were stuffed in his ears, and he wore sound suppressors. A ball gag wouldn't allow him to speak or spit if he woke up.

To ensure intelligence officers were fully protected from infectious diseases carried in the man's lungs, a full-sized spit shield covered the terrorist's face to prevent him from shooting snot out of his nose. A black mask covered the man's eyes to prevent him from recognizing the intelligence officers or anyone connected to the rendition. The mask also protected his eyes and face from the UV lamps suspended over his head. Agency men wore respirators throughout the flight to further protect themselves from any of the highly contagious bacteria or viruses a detainee might carry. In theory, infectious viruses released with each exhalation of the detainee were promptly killed by the UV lamps.

While the detainee was being loaded aboard the jet, *Maverick* walked around the aircraft inspecting the jet's landing gear, flight controls, and engines for the turnaround flight.

With the diseased detainee aboard, Kelly wasn't sure if it was safe to break the form-fitted seal of the N100 in order to eat or drink anything. She had learned from her father in preparing for earlier rendition flights, to put everything in bags, and she was glad that she had. Even his Blackberry was in a zip-lock bag. Rendition flights were nasty work on so many levels. Personal safety was paramount.

Maverick watched four Embassy people manhandle the shrink-wrapped terrorist on a stretcher. When they finished, he silently shook hands with the men. The Chief of Station overseeing the operation slipped a challenge coin into *Maverick*'s hand. Global Response Team. *Those boys and their coins!* He thanked the intel officer, adjusted his mask for better comfort, and ran up the airstairs. Once back inside, *Maverick* pulled the aircraft door closed behind him. From an overhead cupboard, he brought out an aerosol spray to saturate the interior with a gaseous insecticide to kill any fleas, ticks or mosquitoes that may have hitched a ride on the detainee. It was the same aerosol flight attendants released in aircraft cabins to kill malaria-carrying mosquitoes which slip into commercial carriers transiting African countries.

He glanced at the stretcher and the two men in chairs with their N100s. He gave them a gloved "thumbs up" and a questioning look with raised eyebrows to ask if they were ready to go. Thumbs up were returned. *Maverick* entered the cockpit and closed the cockpit door. He gave Kelly the challenge coin and told her to wipe it down.

When Kelly had flown jet trainers in the Air Force, she had worn a positive pressure oxygen mask that provided life-sustaining aviation breathing oxygen (ABO) at 99 and 44/100 percent purity. Now she wore the N100 particulate respirator to prevent potential airborne diseases from entering her lungs. Once the aircraft engines were started, the pilots would go on the aircraft's closed ABO system.

The hangar was again darkened before the doors were opened. The crew who had pulled the Gulfstream into the hangar pushed the jet outside and turned it 90° until the nose wheels straddled the taxi line. Once the tow bar was uncoupled from the nose wheels, *Maverick* started the APU and the engines.

As Kelly tried to sleep, he flew the published departure toward the Atlantic, then turned north and set a course for the Ireland airport at Shannon for fuel and head calls.

They took turns sleeping and flying; flying was monitoring the autopilot. Refueling in Ireland was quick and uneventful. Everyone but the terrorist was allowed off the jet to take a bio-break and get a fast hot meal.

Based on the forecasted winds, they waited aboard the Gulfstream until *Maverick* was assured of an evening landing at Guantanamo Bay, Cuba.

Landing at Manassas with time to spare was the real goal. Getting the terrorist to his new home in the tropics was a secondary priority.

CHAPTER 30

July 15, 2020

Why Are Children Coming Down with Monkeypox? Part 1
The New York Post
By Demetrius Eastwood

Several months ago, the former Director of the Center for Disease Control, Dr. Salvatore D'Angelo, went on the record and said, "If Admiral McGee is the Republican nominee or wins the election, he can count on having to deal with a major pandemic. He will have to declare a national health emergency, for which the country is not prepared." With 6,000 or more cases to date, the CDC has declared there is a Monkeypox pandemic across the country. The CDC believes they have their election pandemic.

Regardless of the curious timing of this declared Monkeypox pandemic, is Monkeypox actually a pandemic, or is it something else designed to scare the American public?

The CDC of old, that is before the election of President Mazibuike, had researched Monkeypox for forty years and concluded it was a sexually transmitted disease. There is a vaccine for Monkeypox. You can find it in the Army Field Manual. It and the smallpox vaccine are effective treatments for Monkeypox.

But yesterday's CDC is not the same CDC of today. Today's CDC cannot say Monkeypox is an STD for fear of upsetting the gay community of the Democrat Party. Apparently, gay men have the power, and upsetting gay men is not allowed.

Until Dr. D'Angelo went on record to attack Rear Admiral McGee, we always thought the CDC was apolitical. They were doing the work necessary to keep Americans safe from a range of infectious diseases.

Now we know better. We are wary of anything Dr. D'Angelo has said or done. Anything he says needs to be scrutinized thoroughly before being accepted. What is happening at the CDC today is a case study of clandestine politics; a government agency doing their part, trying to influence an election.

The CDC insists that prior studies of Monkeypox outbreaks show that most cases of Monkeypox report close contact with an infectious person. They are reluctant to say what role direct physical contact has. In instances where people who have Monkeypox have traveled on airplanes, no known cases of transference of Monkeypox has ever occurred in people seated around them, even on long international flights. It is noteworthy that several outlets, like CNN and Scientific American, have confirmed Monkeypox is a sexually transmitted disease, an STD. It seems, however, Dr. Science and the CDC is trying to turn an outbreak of Monkeypox among gay men into a national pandemic.

Politics aside, who is getting Monkeypox? If Monkeypox is a sexually transmitted disease, then why are children coming down with Monkeypox? In America alone, we have confirmed there are currently nineteen cases of children and one case of a dog being treated for Monkeypox. How do children and dogs get Monkeypox when multiple news outlets, overseas newspapers, and hospitals say it is uniquely transmitted by sex between men?

If children are getting Monkeypox, and they are, where are the police reports? There are none, because it is gay men and pedophiles who are fueling the Monkeypox outbreak. That part of the story is to be censored. This is how you know your media are corrupt.

Children with Monkeypox sores should be compelling evidence for a law enforcement investigation, an indictment for criminal felony sexual assault on a minor, and an obvious conviction. But there are no reports of a sexual assault on these children because the media and the Democrat Party have censored these cases.

Monkeypox cases are, reportedly, continuing to increase worldwide, and the CDC and Dr. D'Angelo say it is a pandemic here.

But we are supposed to ignore the obvious criminal sexual assaults and evidence. If there are Monkeypox sores anywhere on a child, that is direct—not circumstantial evidence of *transference*—but direct evidence of a sexual assault, that illegal contact with a minor has occurred. We call them assaults because that is what they are despite what a corrupt media offers. This is aiding and abetting a criminal.

Mainstream media can and does ignore criminal sexual transgressions against children. Are they now scrubbing these sexual assaults to make the evidence of children with Monkeypox go away "like it never even happened?"

Are the media interfering with criminal investigations when pedophiles assault children? This seems to be the case. The alphabet media and local newspapers are ignoring how children get Monkeypox sores. Evidence of Monkeypox sores on a child is proof of statutory sexual assault on a minor. The unreadable obfuscating diarrhea spewing out of *The New York Times,* or anyone from the liberal corrupt newspapers, Democrat newspapers, or alphabet networks that cannot report how many people were shot over the weekend in Chicago, suddenly spew unmitigated dishonesties and say the link between the two hasn't been clearly established.

Liberal networks and newspaper companies who are more than a century old have lost their way and are now the propaganda arm of the Democrat Party. No longer are they the Fourth Estate. Now they are Fifth Columnists. Joseph Goebbels would have envied our media.

Children come down with Monkeypox for only one reason: Monkeypox spreads through sexual contact.

Where are the police reports?

CHAPTER 31

July 16, 2020

After his opening monologue, Demetrius Eastwood dove right in, "This is Demetrius Eastwood. Let's get this show rolling! *Ooorah!!*"

"Every once in a while, I find it necessary to update my reporting. So, this episode is dedicated to continuing the discussion we had on the CDC's bogus Monkeypox pandemic. They have ignored the crisis created by gay men; they have fostered the sexual assault of children by pedophiles who have infected children with Monkeypox. And, the White House promised that when the time was right, they would establish a *Pandemic Response Office*. And today they did. The *PRO*, led by the Vice President, will monitor potential pandemics, like the one foisted onto America, Monkeypox, and take action."

Dory Eastwood took a short break for his sponsors to make some money. After six minutes, he returned with a new subject.

"Big-box legacy newspapers have rarely been considered *good* — their century-long reputation for covering up Democrat criminal activities and tragedies cannot be disputed. One decent article out of a hundred crappy ones does not make a great newspaper. For example, Walter Duranty of *The New York Times* received a Pulitzer Prize for a series of glowing reports about the Soviet Union while denying the widespread famine, particularly the Holodomor. Yet another Pulitzer Prize–winning American journalist and war correspondent, who is best known for his stories about ordinary American soldiers during World War II, Ernie Pyle, is rarely cited. He was killed in action. He was from a small newspaper. So, when there are reports from hard working journalists in minor newspapers overseas, of children with Monkeypox, one can be certain the big-box legacy media were also aware of those stories but *chose* not to investigate these sexual assaults on children."

"The former CNN reporter, the great Chris Plante is fond of saying, 'The most insidious power the media have is the power to ignore.' And sometimes the media screws up and tells the truth. *The New Yorker* knows the truth. Now that there is a Monkeypox epidemic among gay men in the active reportable universe, *The New Yorker*, a Democrat magazine of some repute, is embarrassed about a report and the timing of one of their articles. Specifically, last year in their exposé, *The German Experiment That Placed Foster Children with Pedophiles*, *The New Yorker* profiled 'a government experiment' that placed neglected children in foster homes run by pedophiles. These children, according to the article, *appeared* to be in a 'homosexual relationship' with their foster fathers."

"Only a blind man wouldn't see this coming. This is the epitome of willful ignorance and journalistic malpractice. And government tyranny."

"Now, how could something like that happen? Is there an established link between homosexual men and pedophiles? When do gay men cross the line and become child sex predators? Is the original diagnosis by the American Psychiatric Association (APA) correct? It defined homosexuality, the sexual disorder that had been classified as a mental disorder for forty years, as those who have an unnatural preoccupation of having sex with other males. The implication has always been unstated but now *The New Yorker* knows and reported: regardless of age."

"It's funny how pedophilia, a sexual disorder still profiled in the *Diagnostic and Statistical Manual of Mental Disorders (DSM)*, hasn't received the same level of violent activism that demanded homosexuality be removed from the pages of the DSM. For decades, members of the APA were systematically terrorized by homosexual activists who claimed they were being unfairly stigmatized for simply being in the pages of the DSM. How many of them were caught *in flagrante dilecto* and certified by the courts as convicted *pedophiles*? The voting body of the APA eventually capitulated to the domestic terrorism, first softening, then changing the diagnostic language in the DSM that the sexual activists considered offensive. Ultimately, the APA voted to remove homosexuality, transvestitism and transgenderism from the DSM, although the sexual disorder *pedophilia* remains."

"This demonstrates that violence against a civilian target pays off in the long run."

"As you know, pedophilia is a different type of sexual disorder. The pedophile's preoccupation is children: an abnormal interest in children, such as being involved with child pornography or the desire to have sex with children of either sex—apologies to the trannies out there, there are only two sexes. Pedophiles are predators, and when they act out against children, they commit criminal child abuse. Sexual activists, particularly in blue states, are aggressively trying to legalize and normalize pedophilia. Recently, there have been reports of convicted pedophiles being interviewed on camera discussing their exploits with children when they were troops in Vietnam. These are criminals."

"You cannot justify sexual assault on a child in any shape or form. We can only hope the Republicans in Congress can fix this mess; Congressional Democrats pushing for the legalization of pedophilia are acting like domestic terrorists."

"While our Federal Bureau of Investigation has also been acting like domestic terrorists, we find there is a law enforcement branch in the country that hasn't been infiltrated. I'm talking about the U.S. Marshals Service who announced this week that 1,300 missing or endangered children were recovered as part of a six-week, multi-state initial effort dubbed *Operation We Will Find You.* "

"Rear Admiral Bill McGee spoke to President Hernandez on the creation of these initiatives that Washington Democrats refused to consider, such as *Not Going to be Afraid Any More* and now *Operation We Will Find You*. The U.S. Marshals Service said the children they recovered included runaways as well as abductees by non-custodial individuals. With technical support from the National Center for Missing and Exploited Children, *Operation We Will Find You* resulted in the recovery of over 1,200 additional children. The U.S. Marshals Service referred 28 cases to law enforcement agencies for further investigation of crimes such as drugs and weapons, sex trafficking, and sex offender violations. *Operation We Will Find You* is a great example of how the U.S. Marshals Service continues to prioritize child protection while the FBI looks the other way."

Eastwood took a moment to applaud the Marshal Service. He continued, "The article goes on to say that these missing children were considered some of the most challenging recovery cases; 1,300 one week, 1,200 the following week based on indications of high-risk factors such as victimization by child sex trafficking, child exploitation, sexual abuse, physical abuse, and medical or mental health conditions. Also, the U.S. Marshal Service established a Sex Offender Investigations Branch, a Behavioral Analysis Unit, and a Missing Child Unit. It's about time the country is taking child sex trafficking, missing children, and child abuse seriously."

Eastwood spoke for another two hours before closing with, "Tonight is going to be a special night. Many of you know I'm covering the presidential campaign of Rear Admiral Bill McGee, the former CIA Director. Tonight, he will receive the *OSS Society William J. Donovan Award* in Washington, D.C. Catch my next show, and I'll tell you all about it."

"That's all I have for you this evening. Thank you for tuning in. We'll be back in a few days for another episode of *Unfiltered News*. Be careful out there—the Democrats are a violent party threatening to burn down everything. That Party is a lunatic asylum and an open-air dumpster fire. 'Semper Fi' to all of my Marine Corps brothers and sisters. And as always, I would like to close this broadcast by saluting the men and women of the military, first responders, law enforcement, the farmers and the factory workers, and all the law-abiding citizens across the fruited plain who make this country work. God Bless America. Good night. Eastwood, out."

CHAPTER 32

July 16, 2020

It took longer to refuel at GITMO than it did to offload the Agency's human cargo. *Maverick* and Kelly blew out of Guantanamo Bay Naval Base and made a steady port turn to avoid overflying Cuba.

Hunter broke several Gulfstream speed records on their return to the United States and brought the aircraft to a stop in front of an unmarked hangar at the Manassas Regional Airport an hour and ten minutes after taking off from GITMO. *Maverick* felt stiff as he disembarked the jet after the almost a 40-hour mission. His athletic, redhead, and freckled daughter said she was exhausted and would probably sleep for two days. *Maverick* acknowledged and said into the mask, "There's still work to do, and I don't have time to dilly-dally." Kelly smiled at her father.

They entered separate locker rooms with industrial showers designed for personal decontamination. *Maverick* fired up his Blackberry, still in its zip-lock bag. He found the app he was looking for and energized it with a touch of his index finger. Then he put it down to finish the decon procedure.

A few hundred miles away, a helicopter came to life.

On separate sides of the decon facility and still wearing the N100s, *Maverick* and Kelly stripped off their clothes and showered with soaps designed to kill any of the superbugs, such as tuberculous and methicillin-resistant staphylococcus. Underwear and the particulate respirators went into medical waste hazardous materials bags to be burned. Duncan knocked off his two-day vibrissae with a razor. Once finished, they donned sleep masks, and felt their way through Hunter's newest invention, a sterilization chamber that resembled an upright tanning bed with six-foot vertical fluorescent UV bulbs operating at 265 nanometers. A single pass through the opposing banks of ultraviolet lamps killed any residual viruses and bacteria hiding on their bodies. In the sterile area, they removed their sleep masks and donned fresh clothes.

Outside, the trained aircraft decontamination crew had been busy. They wore Tyvek® HAZMAT suits as they sterilized the interior of the rendition aircraft. A single four-rotor drone the size of an electric griddle, with dozens of C-band UV LEDs mounted above, below, and along its four corners was guided through the aircraft door by remote control. Once the decon tech closed the aircraft door, the autonomous program kicked in and the drone flew to every corner of the jet. It flew near the floor, near the ceiling, in-between seats, and through the cockpit. Pulsed xenon ultraviolet light LEDs flooded the cockpit and cabin with enough C-band UV to kill any bacteria and viruses that may have become attached or lodged in hidden nooks or crannies of the interior.

When electrical power was connected to the aircraft, the cabin interior lights illuminated and specifically designed UV-C lamps mounted in the Gulfstream's HVAC ducting were activated to irradiate viruses and pathogens that may have entered the aircraft air conditioning system. Once the flying machine returned to its starting position at the aircraft's door, a decon tech opened the cockpit door and removed the robot.

Maverick bounded out of the decon chamber in gym shorts and unlaced running shoes. He entered the sterilized aircraft and removed his suit bag. He handed his jetpack to the decon crew and gingerly took the airstairs one at a time. He looked back at the Gulfstream and patted the fuselage.

Kelly helped her father get dressed in his shoulder holster, boots, and tuxedo. She applied three lidocaine patches across his lower back and tied his tie. Duncan stepped into flying coveralls and donned his YO-3A helmet. She helped him strap on the jetpack, even though Duncan really didn't need the help. To Kelly's utter amazement, it took mere seconds for Duncan to activate the jetpack. He lifted a few inches off the ground and slowly turned 360°, once clockwise and once counterclockwise. Then with a shot of blue exhaust, he headed toward Washington, D.C.

Kelly drove north toward Maryland, fighting the I-95 traffic in the Jaguar her father had given her. She was a bit envious of her father. He had much more faith in the jetpack and its propulsion system than she ever would. She would have loved flying it, but her dad said it was very temperamental and difficult to maneuver.

With the boss and the female pilot departing the remote hangar area, several other men set to work on the outside of the Gulfstream. It was refueled, both engines received an engine oil check via a military-grade, spectrometric oil analysis. The tire pressures were checked and topped off with nitrogen. Before being towed to a stand-alone corporate jet hangar, the aircraft's exterior was washed, the interior's carpets were shampooed, and the leather seats were treated and wiped down.

If it was needed for another rendition, the G-IVSP would be ready.

CHAPTER 33

July 16, 2020

The tinted windows of the black government armored Escalade obnubilated any view of who was inside. When the Cadillac stopped under the awning, the Ritz-Carlton doorman was supposed to step toward the vehicle and open the door. Instead, he was politely shunted to the side as a member of the security team disembarked from the passenger door and opened the rear door for her boss, the CIA Director of Operations, Nazy Cunningham. The DO slipped out of the leather seat, turned 180° and placed an infrared (IR) beacon on the roof of the vehicle. Held fast by a magnetic mount, the device was the size and shape of a Hostess Snowball, and flashed a tiny red light every few seconds to show it was working. With the beacon in place, Nazy scanned the sky for something that was not there yet. But it would be soon; she was certain. He hadn't called, but he had promised.

The security team and the doorman offered to escort her to the front door, but Nazy said it was unnecessary. She wrapped her shoulders with a silver fox stole and headed for the door.

Like lions when a gazelle wanders onto the savannah, every head in the Ritz-Carlton lobby turned when Nazy Cunningham entered.

The reception area for the *OSS Society William J. Donovan Award Dinner* was packed with the members of the IC; mess dress uniforms or tuxedos and formal evening gowns were required. Diamond necklaces and earrings adorned the women; gold Rolex *Daytonas* or *Presidents* were hidden under French cuffs closed by a mélange of intricate or diamond-studded cufflinks.

One wall of the reception area was dedicated to a long portable bar with a dozen white-shirted, black-jacketed, bow-tied attendants. Ritz-Carlton's finest mixologists could concoct any drink imaginable;

patrons swizzled their beverages themselves. Champagne was served nonstop, while the doyens and deans of the IC filled a tip jar with dead Presidents, mostly crisp Grants and Franklins peeled off thick moneyclips.

Along the opposite wall under a colorful banner of his book covers, an author of espionage thrillers was autographing copies of his books for an excited crowd. Some took pictures with the old fighter pilot, a former contractor to the Agency who once held a TS/SCI clearance. He famously wore Ian Fleming's stainless-steel Rolex *Explorer*.

The man of the hour, former CIA Director Rear Admiral William "Bill" McGee, saw Nazy approaching. He spread his arms wide and announced, "Nazy, it may not be politically correct, but you are absolutely breathtaking. You sure clean up well!" Nazy walked into the arms of her former boss and gave him the classical Middle Eastern three cheek kiss reserved for family members. The massive African American and the tall, lithe former Muslima made an incongruous sight.

When Bill McGee released her, Nazy looked into his eyes for confirmation and asked, "Do you think Duncan will like it?" She spread her arms wide.

He reached for one of her hands and held her at arm's length. He inspected her like he had inspected sailors as a commander of U.S. Navy SEALs. Over the left breast of her gown, Nazy wore a single red-white-dark blue-light-blue bowknot rosette of the Distinguished Intelligence Cross. McGee wore the light blue with white stars Congressional Medal of Honor rosette on the lapel of his tuxedo.

Tonight, Nazy wore her hair up. Normally when she moved, her silky hair covered her shoulders and resembled flowing ink. Tonight, a doublet of diamond teardrops adorned her ears. A diamond wrap-around bracelet and a woman's platinum Rolex *President* decorated her delicate wrists. Her gown was form-fitted and highlighted her supermodel curves. The men and the women in the room found it difficult to look away; she was the cynosure of the evening. She was elegant and regal, with the mien of a queen.

Nazy watched as McGee kept his eyes above her chin. He finally nodded. She passed inspection. Looking into her platinum green eyes he said, "We're going to have to have paddles — someone will have to be standing by with paddles. I'm afraid you're going to stop his heart!" McGee grinned and squeezed her hand. *He better get here soon! She's going to give me a heart attack too!*

Nazy laughed at the compliment but smiled heartily. *What are they doing with the temperature in here? It's freezing!* She repositioned the fox stole to keep her girls warm.

In her periphery Nazy saw her boss. She released her grip on McGee to ensure Director Todd was properly introduced. The Director of the CIA was speechless. He had seen her at work in Brooks Brothers, Burberry, and Ralph Lauren work suits, but never in a gown. He concurred with McGee's assessment of Nazy's striking beauty with a simple nod. He thought: *there is something going on with those two, and it's not because she cleans up good!* Although he was new to the CIA, he was an expert on military awards and knew what McGee's award was, but wasn't informed enough to know what personal Agency award Nazy wore. Todd displayed his personal awards as a rack of miniature medals on his tux.

As the former Supreme Allied Commander Europe and an Air Force General, he was comfortable with the upper echelon of society, but the *hoi polloi* of the intelligence community was about to give him a nosebleed.

McGee introduced Eastwood as his press agent and presidential candidate historian to Director Todd. The ramrod straight, former military men shook hands vigorously; Todd covered Eastwood's hand with his left as a sign of respect.

Now that Rear Admiral McGee was running for President, all publicity was on his terms. He had spent a lifetime avoiding the media, but he knew Demetrius Eastwood was a unique asset, a one percent conservative reporter in a field totally dominated by liberals. He was a Republican, a patriot, a close friend and on the right side of history.

Nazy waited her turn, then also hugged and kissed Eastwood in the classical eastern three cheek kiss. Not everyone got to hug Nazy, but Eastwood and McGee had saved her life years before. She was tonight as she had been when they first met her, a long-haired bombshell and first-string demigoddess. She had a beauty that took a moment to take in.

Eastwood thought, *No one can be friends with a woman who he finds attractive. He always wants her. But the rules are different with a woman you rescued from criminals that had to be killed in order to free her. Then a savior; now a protector.* Since then, McGee and Eastwood had become part of Duncan and Nazy's family.

Retired Lieutenant Colonel Demetrius Eastwood was the only reporter allowed into the evening's festivities. Not only was he McGee's press agent and campaign historian, he represented himself as the host of the *Unfiltered and Unspun* radio show on the internet. His single line of miniature medals awarded during multiple combat tours in Vietnam paled by comparison to Todd's. Yet the white-haired, crewcut septuagenarian had earned—and lost—his clearance and access during the Reagan Administration when he was a member of the National Security Council. Eastwood was all smiles as he stood with the heavyweights of the Agency. He had yet to interview CIA Director Todd, but hoped he would leave the event with a future appointment.

The other man who joined the group wasn't new to McGee and Nazy, but he was to Todd and Eastwood. Arsenio Bong was a tall Asian-American Retired U.S. Air Force Colonel whose 30-year career had been mostly with the NRO. Nazy had always thought Bong was a bit difficult to assess. She couldn't get a good read on him, but he was always polite, and Duncan trusted him implicitly. Bong repeatedly shuttled her to Manassas when she returned to the U.S. from vacations with Duncan or from their home in Jackson Hole, Wyoming. He flew a completely refurbished and innocuous Lear 24 on the FAA's PIA program. He had also flown her and her security detail from Texas and Wyoming to Virginia several times when Duncan had been away on a mission. He hardly said anything to her; he treated her like the senior intelligence service executive that she was. Nazy was vaguely curious about Bong, but his name rarely came up in conversation with Duncan.

Admiral McGee introduced Director Todd and Eastwood to Bong. Bong wore a dozen miniature personal medals.

Director Todd asked, "Bong? Are...."

McGee answered, "Yes, like Colonel Bong — the World War Two fighter ace and Medal of Honor winner. And 'no,' no relation. Bong was NRO and has been one of our senior business partners for years. Bong took over as the CEO of the training center and the QAS businesses when I came to D.C."

Bong was succinct, "That's correct."

Eastwood was intrigued and lifted his glass to Bong.

Arsenio Bong explained, "Several years ago, Duncan asked me to establish a geopolitical intelligence and consulting firm; we help clients identify threats and opportunities. When Bill became the CIA Director, the training center, QAS corporate, the lab and Quiet Recoveries International (QRI) were all dumped onto my plate, so to speak. And about five years ago we gained a firefighting company in Canada. With that acquisition, Duncan rescued the last of the giant flying boats used to fight forest fires. And you may not know, but last year Duncan and QRI discovered over one hundred rare and iconic cars that had been stolen in Europe and America. They were in several hangars at multiple airports scattered across Europe. We reunited them with their owners."

Eastwood asked, "Like what?"

Bong said, "Well, we recovered the iconic 1963 Aston Martin DB5 car used in the early James Bond films, *Thunderball* and *Goldfinger*."

The group of men were impressed. Nazy was indifferent. Todd asked, "How?"

Bong said, "Much of our success in that was from our commercial intel work."

Eastwood offered to fetch fresh drinks for the spooks but no one was ready for a refill.

Bong took a moment to acknowledge the author at the table and said, "I swear I have seen that guy before; does anyone know him?"

Nazy smiled and said, "Duncan knows him well. He helped bust a local espionage ring. When he was signing books at the International Spy Museum downtown, he noticed some Arab women who always wore *Shalimar*, always in traditional dress and headscarf, and they always ignored him totally. Sometimes there would be men in thobes in the bookstore, too. He knew they were up to something. They didn't buy his novels but every time they came into the bookstore, they always loaded up with books on the Mossad and anything associated with Navy SEALs. Every time. When they paid in cash, the sales manager alerted the author who dropped a text message to Duncan...."

Repositioning her stole, Nazy continued, "...who told me. I informed the FBI who couldn't be bothered. They were running a training school out of a local mosque in Virginia, but the FBI refused to surveil them, so we contracted Colonel Bong. He observed them and concluded that they were developing training manuals from the books they purchased from the Spy Museum. They were using the Muslim Brotherhood's special operations units in the Middle East, the SEALs, and the Israelis special operators as their models."

Bong nodded. Todd and Eastwood were surprised at the revelation; McGee was not.

Nazy continued, "The school was in a mosque in Fairfax, and Colonel Bong found out they sent trained men all over the Middle East and Africa to hone their skills. I heard sometime later that the Islamic Cultural Center there had caught fire, and their budding terrorist school was put out of business." Suddenly, there was nothing left to say.

Eastwood thought, *An Islamic terrorism school in Virginia was put out of action?* The rest of Nazy's story was simply incredible and he wished he could have reported on it. *I would love to look into that....*

Fire has a way of cleansing evil.... McGee nodded, smiled at Bong, who smiled back and then both men searched the room for threats.

Todd searched the room for anyone else he knew.

Bong lowered his head and did not look at anyone for several minutes. *There is a reason that woman could get free drinks at any bar....*

Nazy sighed and searched the room for her husband. *He isn't exactly late but he still isn't here. He promised....*

Nazy, McGee, Eastwood, Bong and Todd couldn't think of anything else to say, so they scanned the ballroom looking for the fashionably late Hunter. McGee figured Hunter wouldn't wear a disguise for this august group of the OSS Society and the IC.

McGee broke the momentary quietude and commented, "While we are waiting.... Last Halloween when we attended the *Pumpkin Papers Irregulars Dinner*, I told Duncan that his disguise made him look like leech bait. I don't think he needs to worry about being recognized with this crowd. These old dogs are definitely not his crowd." He smiled at Nazy. "He'll be here."

The men laughed; Nazy nodded and smiled. After a few seconds, she sighed. *Come on Baby!* She kept her eyes on the entrance to the ballroom as she waited for Duncan.

McGee, Todd, Bong, and Eastwood subconsciously surrounded Nazy when they weren't conversing with the leadership of the IC. She was unusually tall for a Middle Eastern-born woman; she was taller than her mother by a foot and inches taller than her father. She was nearly as tall as Todd, Bong, and Eastwood. She was extremely hard to miss. The black, long-sleeved, floor-length, turtleneck sequined gown looked as if it was from a designer shop in Beverly Hills.

Todd thought, *I hadn't really thought about it before, but Nazy is a very striking woman in the classical sense. Almost as if she was royalty. Was she born to the purple? If not, she would give the doyennes of Europe an excellent run for their money.* Another quick surreptitious scan of her body left him wondering, *Why does she always cover up her arms and chest?*

McGee and Eastwood knew it was more than modesty. Nazy used length and sleeves to hide her scars, but Eastwood was convinced she also went for the dramatic just to make Duncan's knees buckle.

Eastwood spun around; his eyes scanned the ballroom entrance — still no Duncan. He needed another drink.

CHAPTER 34

July 16, 2020

Flight data symbology filled his helmet as Hunter made his approach directly to the Ritz-Carlton Hotel. He continually consulted the GPS navigation information projected onto his visor as he found and closed on the illuminated building. At the same time, he found the IR beacon that flashed every few seconds on Nazy's Escalade. He guided on the Caddy and expertly adjusted the throttles to set down in front of it, momentarily astonishing her security detail inside. Security agents standing guard near other vehicles converged on the man dropping from the sky.

Maverick shut down the earsplitting jetpack. Two members of Nazy's personal security detail waited until it had been silenced before disembarking from the limo. Still wearing his helmet, he flipped up the visor and asked, "Miss Cunningham's superstars, I presume?" The women nodded. Pointing to the rushing armed guards he asked, "Could you call off the dogs and give me a hand?" One woman waved away the approaching slack jawed and curious security teams, declaring "He's a friendly."

He removed his helmet as if it was a baseball cap. The helmet and all the metallic parts of the jetpack had been treated with an experimental nanotechnology coating that absorbed over 99.95% of any light that hit it. The nanotechnology erased any three-dimensional features; the helmet was just black like the outside of bowling ball — but without depth perception. *Maverick* flipped over the strange black void and shoved his skullcap into it. The helmet also had earcups, padding, and a boom microphone. He handed it to the other woman on Nazy's security team. It was only then that she could determine that the weird bowling ball-shaped void was actually a pilot's helmet.

Maverick asked that the IR beacon on Nazy's Escalade be taken down and turned off. When that was done, she opened the rear doors of the Escalade for him so he could secure the cooling jetpack and helmet inside. In a moment reminiscent of an old James Bond movie, *Maverick* unzipped the flying coveralls from chin to crotch revealing his tuxedo underneath. He shrugged off the sleeves and stepped out of the overalls. He roughly wadded up the flight suit and tossed it in the back of the Caddy. He repositioned the helmet on top.

And then he was gone, jogging toward the entrance of the Ritz-Carlton in black crocodile boots and an Armani tuxedo. Nazy's security team lead said, "You see the strangest things in Federal service. Jetpacks. Coveralls and a helmet that sucks light. Jetpack pilot in a tux. Cowboy boots—*Yee haw*! Miss Cunningham sure has interesting friends."

"You know, that might be her husband."

"I heard she was gay."

"A lesbian would not wear that gown or that jewelry. No, she has a man, and wears a wedding band. I think we just met him."

"You might be right."

•   •   •

Just as the concierge stepped into the reception area and began malleting the Deagan Dinner Chime to signal the crowd to take their seats in the dining area, Duncan Hunter splashed his way into the room. He signaled his presence, waved, and hurried to the best landmark in the room—the mastodon-sized Bill McGee. Where McGee was, Nazy would be close by.

When she saw him, Nazy's smile lit the room. McGee thought he had heard the unmistakable shriek of the jetpack outside of the ballroom; he grinned and said, "That lad knows how to make an entrance."

Todd, Bong, and Eastwood smiled and concurred. *The boss is in the house! There's got to be a story about why he was late!*

As the concierge herded the Donovan Award patrons into the dining room, Hunter caught up with Nazy. He gave her a passionate hug, an eyelock, and a long kiss—electricity sizzled between them. Duncan stepped back for a moment and admired the view. He told Nazy, "My word, you're the most beautiful woman in the world! Is there an *arrière-pensée* behind this amazing gift?"

Nazy's smile should have melted the buttons on the Armani. The ultimate gift; Nazy had her man. After flying halfway around the planet to pick up a scumball for the Agency, the effulgence of the Ritz-Carlton's bright lights, Nazy's beauty, and medal-bedecked friends was a welcome sight and worth the effort to arrive almost on time. Duncan's tux sported no medals or rosettes, but it hid a six-inch Colt *Python* admirably.

As the crowd in the ballroom took their seats, they watched the raffiné woman with her entourage of former and current CIA Directors, show unexpected attention and *amore* to a man that they did not know. *Could the Director of Operations really have a man? She wears a wedding band, but her sexuality has always been in question. Then this man shows up, no awards—maybe he's a civilian. And it looks like he obviously thrills her. The book on her has changed. If is she married and this is her husband, who is he?* None of the most senior men and women from the IC and law enforcement recognized him, but they couldn't take their eyes away from her or the dynamic, intimate group who would obviously occupy the head table.

Knowing where Duncan had been, Todd wondered how Hunter had made it to the award ceremony. *To Africa and back? It's not possible! Laws of physics and all that!*

McGee and Todd got a fast hearty handshake, Bong and Eastwood got smiles and fist bumps.

McGee leaned into Hunter and asked with a touch of concern, "How are you doing? You look like shit."

Hunter groaned in McGee's ear, "A lack of sleep will do that to you. Feels like my ass has been pressure washed, and parts of me might be frostbit. Other than that—*peachy*." With one arm around

Nazy's waist and another stolen look into her green eyes, he said, "I'm doing fantastic. Things couldn't be better."

McGee chuckled and slapped Hunter on the back. He knew it to be true. Hyperbole wasn't Hunter's forte; going above and beyond was his way of life. He remembered what some of the women at the Naval War College said about Duncan, *I swear he's the most interesting man alive and we know nothing about him.*

Hunter had been exposed to the elements for a longer time than was reasonable. His arm was around Nazy, but now she was providing a little support to him. Hunter had mentioned that the jetpack was physically and mentally demanding to fly for even short periods. Nazy run her hand to the small of his back to confirm he had patches. *Thank you, Kelly.*

McGee shook his head perceptively. *It's a wonder he's still functioning after coming all the way from the decon site.* McGee looked askance. *I have new appreciation for what it took for him to fly to the top of the Burj Khalifa. God, that was a night.*

McGee gestured at Hunter's partially disheveled condition. The helmet had given *Maverick's* hair a case of the unrulies that a comb could not tame; his cheeks were as roseate as he was tired. He understood why his friend was not only exhausted but bedraggled. McGee recognized all the signs of over and above professional pride. He had been there, done that and had the t-shirts and the medals to prove it.

Maverick fully inflated his lungs, smiled broadly, and said, "Admiral McGee, sir. There are some things you just don't miss."

McGee expressed the obvious. "True. Director Todd, can a guy who looks like he had been in the trunk of an abandoned car at an airport parking lot... for a month... really be working for you? He could give the place a bad name."

Everyone within earshot smiled or laughed.

Totally beat and limp, Duncan nodded and smiled at the crack. *Maverick* said, "You can bet after my little stunt I'll be reported as a UFO.... I don't think I caused any accidents this time."

Todd and Eastwood looked at each other with confusion. *UFO? This time? What was the other time?*

Bong was amused.

McGee explained, "One winter night Duncan made an approach to the Dallas Convention Center helicopter pad atop their parking garage. Drivers on the freeway were more interested in a man flying a jetpack than the road, which created a massive pile-up."

Hunter shook his head and nonchalantly said, "I flew over 95 and crossed 66 and 123. Just tried the direct route to remain above the powerlines." He smiled at Nazy. "And, as promised, I hurried."

While Bong had seemed pretty sincere when the group first met him, he became quite waggish once he got comfortable with them. "Sounds like quite a harrowing flight."

Todd and Eastwood looked at each other with concern. Bong knew Duncan had taken the jetpack; he lowered his head for a moment of thanks for *Maverick's* safe flight before returning to the present.

Nazy understood immediately; Duncan had obviously taken the jetpack from Manassas to get to the Ritz-Carlton in Tyson's Corner. She looked at him, smiled wide, and thought, *Of course, he is exhausted, and he did all of that to be with me.*

Duncan found the strength to stand without her support, offered her his arm, and escorted her to the head table. He pulled a neon green *Growler* from his tux pocket.

McGee and Nazy thought the use of a *Growler* was unnecessary for the night's festivities, and their eyes told him so. But maybe Duncan had something to share that he didn't want the eavesdroppers to know, like flying the jetpack in front of God and country. Bong glanced at the device for a second and then looked away. He knew what it was and had seen Hunter use it before.

Duncan smiled, coughed, and nodded. He palmed the *Growler*, switched it on, placed it in the middle of the table, and covered it with a program. A green light flashed every few seconds.

Nazy, McGee, Hunter, and Eastwood knew that when activated, the *Growler* generated a bubble of electronic noise and prevented anyone and anything from electronically eavesdropping on their conversation. Nazy hadn't briefed Todd on the capability, but apparently McGee had done so during his out-brief because Director Todd muttered, "*Growler*" like a tour guide would announce a Wal-Mart store in Beverly Hills.

Hunter adjusted the device so it would not interfere with the emcee's microphone.

Bong remained amused. *Glad to be here, a pleasure to serve.*

It didn't matter that the room was full of men and women with the highest security clearances in the land. There was no conversation he and *Maverick* ever had where a *Growler* wasn't used. He grinned and checked his Rolex. *This show should start soon.*

Duncan stroked Nazy's hand and arm. Having just returned, it was hard for Duncan to keep his hands off of his wife, but they would soon be alone. He perused the room. Everywhere he looked people were surreptitiously staring at Nazy. She was the most striking woman in the room with her smoky eyes, the face of an exotic Victoria Secrets model, and the legs of a Robert Palmer dancer.

Just because he was surrounded by the nation's highest ranking intelligence officers with their attendant security details outside the ramparts, Duncan wasn't resting on his laurels. Hunter had eluded a dozen assassination attempts and the OSS Society Dinner had been highly publicized. Nazy had been kidnapped in Algeria, the lead vehicle in her security detail had been hit with a rocket-propelled grenade, and members of the Muslim Brotherhood had been trying to kill her at least once a year for the last fifteen years. The Islamic Underground was so afraid of her it was not about to give up trying to eliminate her from the face of the earth. They knew she would be at the dinner.

The CIA had trained Duncan to be prepared to kill everyone he met, but these were senior members of the IC. They were not the *dark state* droids he had to watch for. In the ballroom, McGee was without a Secret Service personal security detail, and Director Todd was without an Agency security detail. For the evening, Duncan Hunter was assuming the job of security "inside the wire."

Duncan began reconnecting with the boys by offering an offhanded quip, "Welcome to the National Council of the American Resistance Movement, Bill McGee presiding." He got more than a few guffaws. During a string of funny comments, Nazy had to wait to catch Duncan's eye and give him their sign. Finally, he looked at her again. With lacquered cardinal-red nails, Nazy slowly tugged on her earlobe adorned with a Bentley's worth of white diamonds. That was her non-verbal way to say she loved him and missed him. Duncan received her clandestine message. He had a message of his own; with a thin smile he slowly dragged the back of his finger across his brow. *Oh, Baby! You look so good! But we have to behave.* He squeezed her hand then asked McGee in his rumbling baritone, "How are the girls?"

The comment could have been some double entendre. Nazy's bosom was covered and for a moment the men around her checked her chest. Then McGee shook his head and rolled his eyes. Eastwood and Todd's wandering eyes had recovered and were instantly amused. Bong's interest was piqued. In his deep bass with a tinge of disappointment, McGee refrained from looking at Hunter and said, "You know, *Maverick*, you are a terrible friend and horrible role model. Nicole and Kayla just finished flight training in Kingsville and are heading off to fly F-35s."

Director Todd, Eastwood, and Bong nodded *Congratulations*. *Maverick* smiled and said, "And to think I once said, 'This is the beginning of a beautiful friendship.'"

McGee smiled. Nazy said, "*Casablanca*." Todd, Eastwood, and Bong got the inside joke.

Hunter wouldn't look at the SEAL. "You're just pissed they were commissioned in the Marine Corps."

"What kind of friend does that? My girls are *Marines* because of you!" Hunter chuckled.

McGee looked at Todd, Bong, Eastwood, and Nazy and continued with feigned indignity, "You would think they would take up the uniform of their old man, but no. Duncan cheated. He taught my girls to play racquetball.... *Well.*" The proud father emphasized, "*Very* well."

Maverick interrupted, "....and now they are near world-class athletes and tournament-quality players, and Marine officers and pilots. They're not snowflakes or bums living at home. I don't see what the problem is." The table erupted in laughter. His eyes panned to Todd, who raised a hand to interrupt.

"This old fart did the same thing to my twin boys when we were at Laughlin. Taught them to play racquetball. Somehow, they got the notion they wanted to go to the Naval Academy, and they were also commissioned in the Marine Corps and went to the Navy's flight school. Do you know how embarrassing that is for an Air Force general?"

Nazy's earrings sparkled as she gently shook her head and smiled. "That is so sad." She didn't mean a word of it.

Eastwood was confused. "You mean Duncan...."

McGee said, "Yes, the dirtball recruited our kids to go in the *Marines* and flight school." He sighed the sigh of a proud father. "And they play racquetball."

Duncan looked at Nazy again. "Where they are flourishing. They are great ball-players, and they can't wait to get me on the courts again. And now they're *all off* to fly F-35s? Well, I think congratulations are in order. Admiral McGee, General Todd, it is obvious you raised some fantastic Americans. You both are great fathers!"

The table again broke out in laughter. Duncan pumped a fist then inelegantly bumped fists across the table with everyone. Bong smiled for the third time of the evening and offered his felicitations to the fathers as well.

Eastwood shook his head in wonder. That Duncan had been such an influence on McGee's and Todd's children was new information. *Well, he has known them a long time.... So the two CIA Directors' children.... Where did Hunter have time for that?* He turned his head to scan the crowd looking to see if the FBI Director had been invited.

Dory Eastwood didn't see her at any of the other tables. He knew tangentially that McGee and the FBI Director were not on speaking terms. As the CIA Director, McGee had politicked the FBI and Congress to declare the Muslim Brotherhood a terrorist organization, but the *dark state* FBI Director steadfastly refused. That gave the Democrats in Congress sufficient reason to refuse to make that declaration. At the time, Democrats had been concerned that such a designation would inflame the FBI's *Muslim Outreach* employees.

In one of Hunter's few private audiences with President Hernandez the previous year, Duncan had asked the President for some help with the FBI. The FBI believed that Director McGee had complained to President Hernandez, because shortly after Nazy delivered the President's Daily Brief, the President signed an executive order that required all members of any law enforcement or intelligence community organization that dealt with top secret information to have a polygraph. Within a month, virtually all the FBI's *Muslim Outreach* employees had been let go for refusing or failing to pass the required polygraph. Democrats on the Hill and at the Department of Justice screamed bloody murder and blamed McGee.

CHAPTER 35

July 16, 2020

While the emcee was going through prefatory administrative notes, Director Todd spoke of the day he got a call from a friend who flew F-15Cs. He had taken out the warehouse in Syria holding Iraq's weapons of mass destruction: their chemical and biological weapons programs.

Everyone around the dinner table listened to the retired general. They all had different views of what had transpired in the media, in Iraq, at the CIA, and at the White House during that time period. The IC had determined through a number of high-ranking defectors from the Iraqi army that Iraq did have the capability to create weapons of mass destruction (WMD). An in-place defector had taken photographs of the lab and equipment. The Administration had legitimate concerns over the potential of Saddam weaponizing the rod-shaped bacteria, *bacillus anthrax*, against coalition troops.

The Centers for Disease Control had determined that anthrax was not very contagious or transmissible between humans. It mostly affected livestock, and they were usually vaccinated against the disease. But the Administration was concerned that if *bacillus anthrax* had been doctored in a lab, weaponized through a gain-of-function effort as *inhalation anthrax*, it would be extremely contagious and could be fatal to humans. The Department of Defense needed to develop a vaccine and inoculate the troops, if necessary, before they were deployed to Iraq. The President authorized an experimental vaccine to be developed to protect the troops.

Maverick recalled the event with an impish grin, "Oh, I remember. I hadn't been back from the war college very long, and you gave me crap about reading everything on the school's reading list. You said you read nothing when you were at the Air War College. Yeah, you and everyone at the conference table were upbeat. Proud. It was a great day for the Air Force."

Magoo sighed, "But he called back the next day and said he had spoken out of turn, that I was to disregard everything he had said. Then the media said there were no WMD. The media and the Democrats piled on the President. They said it was *disinformation*, a lie to justify the war. The President didn't fight back for some reason."

Hunter glanced at the *Growler's* flashing light and said, "That was all propaganda."

Todd nodded. *Propaganda is like that, I suppose....*

Duncan continued, "I think it is ok to tell you, now that you're the Director, that Nazy found them. It was her intel your buddy used to take down Saddam's program." The beatific glances quickly shared by Duncan and Nazy telegraphed their mutual admiration for each other.

Hunter added, with a menacing finger directed at Eastwood, "Don't go printing that, either!" Eastwood knew the drill and gave him a thumbs up.

Bewildered, Todd shot a look at Nazy Cunningham. He asked, "You'll tell me later?" She grinned and nodded politely.

Maverick said, "The left knew the truth but used the power of the press to maintain the fiction, the narrative; another of the great lies the Democrats and the media used to beat up the President." Everyone around the table nodded in assent. Hunter then turned and asked, "Did you get to the boat this trip?"

Everyone around the table was confused. *What does that mean?*

McGee sighed, "Yes." He told the head table, "The Navy had been at me for years to fly aboard an aircraft carrier. I was always too busy. Yesterday, I was campaigning in Norfolk, and the CO of the ship got me a ride in the back seat of an F-18, which was about three dress sizes too small for my frame, but I wasn't about to say I was uncomfortable. I wanted to buy my pilot ten steak dinners. There were times the jet moved so fast that it scared the crap out of me, but I have to say, that was the most exciting thing I have ever done. Now I know what Duncan means when he said it is the most fun you can have with your clothes on." He looked at Todd and then at Hunter. "I don't know how you guys do it; I have the utmost respect for carrier pilots. What my pilot did was unbelievable, and he didn't even break a sweat."

Dinner was served.

Maverick threw his abstemious diet out the window and indulged in the filet. *Thank God — a real meal; no more junk food and water while wearing a mask. Masks…. Biohazards….* A thought entered his mind. *There was something more. Wasn't there a classified report that anthrax had been mailed to two senators trying to block the Patriot Act in 2001? And hadn't the FBI discovered that the anthrax came from the CIA lab in Fort Detrick? There were also anthrax vaccine-related side-effects, Gulf War Syndrome which the military swept under the rug, because they were using our service members as Guinea pigs. Why do I think every vaccine-related injury and boondoggle has to do with D'Angelo? I wonder where…. I have to get smarter on D'Angelo's movements.* He looked and nodded at Bong, who looked back. *I have a job for you.* Duncan withdrew a 3x5 card, scribbled a note, and handed it to Bong.

Bong nodded and returned the look. *I'll find his finances….*

After the dishes had been cleared away, the show started.

The Master of Ceremonies gripped the lectern's rails and announced that the guest of honor needed no introduction. Hunter looked at McGee as the emcee's squeaking speech struck them like Mr. Rogers' voice on crack. He said, "It is incredibly rare for such a distinguished gentleman from Special Operations Command and the CIA to be part of our festivities."

"If some of you attended the *Pumpkin Papers Irregulars Dinner* in October, the master of ceremonies there perfectly summed up the life of Rear Admiral McGee, so there will be some plagiarism. It is difficult to improve on the unique accomplishments of our recipient. He said there are some men who have made incredible history, such as Charles Lindbergh, Charles Yeager, Neil Armstrong. I would add William Donovan to this category. These men made their mark in the light of day trying to conquer something greater than themselves. But there are other men who are even more accomplished in the service of our country than Lindbergh, Yeager, and Armstrong. Their names rarely grace the pages of newspapers or are the subject of television specials or biographies. I think we would all agree this was also the case with Bill Donovan."

"These are men who on the strength of their intellect and character, *led* Americans to do incredible things. These men were continually engaged with America's enemies in the most inhospitable locations. Names you likely have never heard, like Admiral Roy Davenport and Marine General Chesty Puller, both awarded five Navy Crosses for heroism, for gallantry, for valor. Explorers like Admiral Richard E. Byrd, a Naval Aviator and the only individual to receive the Medal of Honor, the Navy Cross, the Distinguished Flying Cross, and the Silver Life Saving Medal."

"The OSS Director, William Donovan, was one of America's elite warriors and is the only person to have received all four of the United States' highest awards: the Medal of Honor, the Distinguished Service Cross, the Distinguished Service Medal, and the National Security Medal. General Donovan was also the recipient of the Silver Star and Purple Heart, as well as decorations from several other nations for his service during both World Wars."

"Tonight, the OSS Society is proud to award the William Donovan Award to an elite of the elites in the intelligence community, Rear Admiral William McGee. Admiral McGee, the distinguished son of one of the most highly decorated Tuskegee Airman, Brigadier General Charles McGee, has received the nation's highest award, the Congressional Medal of Honor, *five* Navy Crosses, *and* two Distinguished Intelligence Crosses, making him by far the most decorated man ever to wear a uniform for the United States of America. Indeed, we are blessed tonight; we may not ever see another such decorated American patriot as Admiral McGee. Rear Admiral McGee recently served as the Director of the Central Intelligence Agency and is now a candidate for President of the United States. Under his leadership at the CIA, the number of terrorists on the FBI's Most Wanted Terrorist List dropped from fifty to zero. *To. Zero.* Ladies and gentlemen, there is no one more deserving for this year's Donovan Award than Rear Admiral William McGee."

The complete assembly of men and women stood and clapped as Bill McGee took the lectern, the front was dominated by the oval gold-on-black spearhead insignia of the Office of Strategic Services. Two spotlights shot effulgent beams right to the center of the stage.

McGee paused several seconds to acknowledge the applause. He was moved by the encomium. He gripped the sides of the lectern and nodded his thanks to the members of the IC, *Thank you, let's get this show on the road!* People applauded for three minutes as McGee's baritone rumbled into the microphone, "Thank you." He waved his hands trying to get the crowd to sit down. "Thank you, thank you. Apparently, you have nothing else to do tonight. I appreciate it. Well, that's all I have. You've been a marvelous crowd! Thank you. Thank you."

The crowd laughed with salubrious approval at McGee's attempt to get off the dais. They were not having any of it. McGee had been out of the limelight for so long. Now that the OSS Society finally had a man deserving of the award, they would not let him off the stage. Warriors for America were quietly given medals and rarely heralded publicly for their accomplishments. The assembly of old school intelligence officers and their spouses clapped harder; the women shouted, and the men whistled.

McGee cast a glance at Hunter and thought, *My friend, we have helped to take down America's enemies, the worst terrorists on the planet. But you are the one responsible for eliminating the men on the Most Wanted Terrorist List, not me. I have said many times you should be the Donovan Award winner.*

When Hunter and Nazy took their seats, the rest of the dinner crowd followed their lead, but McGee said he had a request that required everyone to remain standing. He said, "If you will join me in the Pledge of Allegiance."

Maverick quietly barked the Marine Corps' grunt of approval, "*Oohrah!*"

Admiral McGee turned to the American Flag and led the assembly. "I pledge allegiance to the Flag of the United States of America, and to the Republic for which it stands, one nation under God, indivisible, with liberty and justice for all." Men and women clapped their approval as they sat down.

McGee thanked the master of ceremonies and acknowledged previous Donovan Award winners, the heads of departments, CIA Director Walter Todd, and the Director of Operations, Nazy Cunningham. McGee lastly mentioned Colonel Eastwood and Colonel Bong for their dedication to truth, and honor, and a lifetime of devoted military service to America.

Admiral McGee didn't mention the other person at the head table, Duncan Hunter. No one needed to know who he was, but there was a collective understanding regarding McGee's failure to say anything about him: the man was special. Special enough to be invited; special enough to remain anonymous.

There was polite clapping from the other tables as McGee recognized the accomplishments of the men and women at the other tables. He delivered his comments memoriter, without even a note card for reference, always making eye contact with his audience. "It's customary to start a heavy pompous speech with a joke. Have you heard the one where God went missing? In fact, God was apparently missing for six days. Eventually, Michael, the Archangel, found him, resting on the seventh day. Michael inquired, 'Oh, God. Where have you been?' God smiled deeply and proudly pointed downwards through the clouds, 'Look, Michael. Look at what I've made.' Archangel Michael looked puzzled, and said, 'Oh, God. What is it?' 'It's a planet,' replied God, and I've put life on it. I'm going to call it *Earth* and it's going to be a place to test *Balance*.' 'Balance?' inquired Michael. 'Oh, God. I'm still confused.' God explained, pointing to different parts of Earth. 'For example, this place I'll call northern Europe will be a place of great opportunity and wealth, while southern Europe is going to be poor. Over here, I've placed a continent of white people, and over there is a continent of black people. Balance in all things.' God continued pointing to different land masses. 'This one will be extremely hot, while this one will be very cold and covered in ice.' The Archangel, impressed by God's work, pointed to a land area and said, 'Oh, God. What's that one?' 'Oh, Michael. That is my greatest achievement. That is the Commonwealth of Virginia….'"

The crowd from Virginia roared its approval and applause, then quickly settled back down.

McGee smiled and continued, without notes, "'Yes, Michael, that is the Commonwealth of Virginia. It is the most glorious place on Earth. There are beautiful mountains, rivers and streams, lakes, forests, hills, and plains. The people from the Commonwealth of Virginia are going to be handsome, modest, intelligent, wealthy and humorous, and they are going to travel the world. They will be extremely sociable, hardworking, high achieving, carriers of peace, and producers of good things.' Michael gasped in wonder and admiration, but then asked, 'Oh, God. But what about Balance? God, you said there would be Balance.' That was when God smiled and said, 'Right next to Virginia is Washington D.C. Wait until you see the idiots I put there.'"

The crowd erupted in laughter.

McGee smiled. "They have a saying in San Antonio, my home town, maybe all the oil isn't in Texas, but all the dipsticks are in D.C." McGee got down to business without preamble, "On a serious note, always remember, God gave his Archangels *weapons* because he knew you can't fight evil with *tolerance* and *understanding*, and the price for ridding society of evil is always high."

"America finds itself again on the precipice of war, much as General Bill Donovan did in the 1930s. The totalitarians will not stop until they have achieved their goal of world domination."

"How many of you have seen reports of fires at large food processing plants? How about reports of train derailments, oil and chemical spills, on-airport accidents, and the record number of illegal aliens crossing our southern border? One of my personal favorites is the Air Force general who recently said in front of cameras, 'There are too many white men in the cockpits of our aircraft.' You would probably think these extraordinary unrelated dumpster-fire events are occurring in mostly Democrat-run states, and you would be correct. There is a reason."

"Americans see trains falling off rails and chicken farms ablaze and think these events are nothing more than accidents, simply isolated events. But would they ever think that these destructive events could be intentional? Those of us in this room, the leadership of the intelligence community, know exactly what these calamities are and what they mean. America is, in fact, under attack."

"Most people, and this includes many of our politicians, generals and admirals, military and intelligence analysts, mistakenly fall into the trap of thinking that unless F-22s, ICBMs, tanks, helicopters, snipers, or rocket-propelled grenades are involved, it's not war. But in this world of great prosperity, the face of war has changed. World War Two was radically different from World War One. Not only did we transition from biplanes to jets, seemingly in the blink of an eye, the Nazis gave the world a peek into the next generation of warfare with the creation of *The Ministry of Propaganda and Enlightenment*. Future wars would be fought over the mind. If the left is able to control your thoughts, there is no need for weapons, you will submit your weapons willingly, like Australia. You will become their slave in a way to make George Orwell's *1984* look like a walk in the park."

"We are in a new generation of warfare where the stakes are even greater than ever. It has been described as 'fifth-generation warfare.' This generation of warfare is not taught at our war colleges. Our adversaries have been using what we call the *silent weapons for a quiet war* since the 1940s. General William Donovan was one of the first to identify the sea-change: from guns and bombs in the hands of a trained soldier to the minds and mobs in the hands of a master manipulator. Psychological warfare."

"To counter the Nazi's Ministry of Propaganda and the KGB's counter-intelligence directorates, America created the Office of Strategic Services, which later became the Central Intelligence Agency.

The IC at home and abroad. Our coalition of free countries, our allies, English-speaking and Muslim nations are engaged in mortal combat with their home-grown terrorists. They know this next generation of warfare will be conducted primarily through non-kinetic military action, such as a radical view of religion, black propaganda, the dark side of psychology, social engineering, misinformation, cyberattacks, along with emerging technologies such as artificial intelligence, biotechnologies, and fully autonomous systems."

"Fifth-generation warfare is a war of information and perception. It will include special operations within 'the shady gray-zone,' like setting food processing plants on fire, or orchestrating train derailments to create chaos. If we want our families to live in peace, we must not fail in countering the left."

"We have done a remarkable job under President Hernandez's leadership. The United States Special Operations Command and the IC have effectively eliminated the leadership of the Islamic Underground. When President Mazibuike was in power, he did everything he could to inject radical Muslims into America's law enforcement and intelligence communities. Under his watch, there were over 200 men on the FBI's Most Wanted Terrorist List. Now there are none. The Muslim Brotherhood in America is in retreat. They are still deadly, but they are a shell of what they were a few years ago." McGee looked at Nazy. *And that's because of your work.*

The audience applauded. Nazy squeezed Duncan's hand.

"While we have made great strides against these mass murdering Islamic radicals, we still have much to do to rid the country of Marxist thought. The need for intelligence is greater than ever. The United States has been infiltrated with a host of evil organizations: communists, socialists, Marxists, radical Islamists, and a coalition of Democrat and Republican politicians. Yes, politicians who are owned by and do the bidding of anti-American interests dedicated to creating a global governance system of masters and slaves."

"This is our challenge; we must protect our Nation against our enemies with every fiber of our being. We do this service for our country, for our families, for our freedom loving friends, for Americans." As he finished his comments, McGee stepped aside.

The emcee mounted the dais, clapping until he commandeered the microphone. An older rounder woman followed him to the dais. She was vaguely familiar to McGee. After a moment passed, he remembered who she was. Then the master of ceremonies introduced her. "Presenting the William Donovan Award is Dr. Elizabeth McIntosh, General Donovan's granddaughter."

Duncan Hunter hadn't been paying much attention to the latter stages of McGee's speech. He had been admiring the profile of the lovely Nazy Cunningham. But when the words, "Dr. Elizabeth McIntosh, General Donovan's granddaughter" punctured the shell of his reverie, he slowly looked toward the dais to see a friend from his past. *Dr. McIntosh. Naval War College.* Their first encounter and subsequent interactions raced through his mind like pages of a book in a tornado. He was shocked, and his situational awareness kicked in. *I'm dead and I'm not in disguise.*

He grabbed the program from McGee's place setting and hid his face. He looked over the top of it. Hunter checked to see if it really was Dr. McIntosh. The program listed her positions in the intelligence community: Foreign Service Officer, Department of State. Aide to the Director of the CIA, Director of the National Center for Medical Intelligence, the George H. W. Bush Chair of International Intelligence. *That's Doc McIntosh but Director of the National Center for Medical Intelligence? What the hell is that?*

CHAPTER 36

July 16, 2020

McGee pulled out a step from the bottom of the lectern with his foot and adjusted the microphone for the woman. He was as inconspicuous as two bull moose fighting in the middle of the road; he tried to get between Hunter and Dr. McIntosh. She acknowledged the applause with a smile.

"I had the distinct pleasure of knowing Admiral McGee when he was a student and faculty member at the Naval War College." She looked to scan the audience as speakers and professors do at a lectern. When she got to the head table, McGee could no longer impede her view. Hunter dropped the face shield. Elizabeth locked eyes with Duncan Hunter. She stared for a long moment. She was shocked to see her star pupil very much alive.

Duncan with his eyes wide shook his head. Elizabeth got the message. *This is not the time to recognize me like you did that day at the war college.*

The unexpected pause in the award ceremony did not go without notice. Twitterings and questions rippled across the room. McGee sensed what had happened. *She heard he had died. And Duncan's not in disguise.* With a disarming smile and with the aplomb of a bulldozer, he stepped forward to accept the award in a cherry case.

Dr. McIntosh smiled at McGee whose eyes pleaded with her to finish the ceremony. The connection was clear; Duncan Hunter would remain anonymous.

Bill McGee lifted the medal as a champion would lift a trophy. He then leaned over and whispered into Elizabeth's ear, "*He's on assignment.*" The acknowledgement helped her to realize that she wasn't hallucinating. She turned back toward McGee. McGee and

McIntosh looked at the medal; the obverse showed three OSS operatives: a woman, a man, and a person in a parachute. On the reverse, it listed code words and ID numbers for the OSS and related intelligence agents and operations, along with a spearhead, the unofficial insignia of the OSS which was later adopted by SOCOM, Special Operations Command. McGee closed the case and held it up with one hand.

Dory Eastwood was there to capture the moment with several quick photographs. Before Dr. McIntosh stepped away, she whispered something into McGee's ear and clumsily handed him a thick, dark ginger-colored folder that she had somehow kept out of sight until that moment. McGee was surprised at the offering; his hands were now full, so he placed the folder on the lectern and shook her hand.

Hunter's near photographic memory kicked in. *I remember that.... I remember that color...that file! CONFIDENTIAL REPORT.*

McGee thanked Dr. McIntosh before she and the emcee walked to the edge of the dais. When he returned to the lectern, McGee said, "Dr. Stephens, members of the OSS Society, fellow members of the Intelligence Community, Dr. McIntosh, I humbly accept this award. Thank you. I will do my best to live up to the ideals of the Office of Strategic Services' Director."

Applause filled the ballroom for several minutes.

"And Dr. McIntosh; what a pleasant surprise to see you again. Dr. McIntosh and I were at the Naval War College together, what, almost twenty years ago? She was the war college's resident CIA officer, and I had returned from an assignment in Afghanistan. Doing, uh, you know what...."

The audience found another reason to clap and cheer. It was the moment Dr. McIntosh and Dr. Stephens moved to dismount the dais.

McGee watched Dr. McIntosh and the OSS Society Chairman gingerly step from the dais and said, "Dr. McIntosh, I didn't know you were General Donovan's granddaughter. Thank you. That makes this award tonight even more meaningful." McGee threw an informal salute to the old spook and the emcee. Dr. McIntosh walked to the head table and took McGee's place, next to Duncan Hunter.

She leaned into his ear and said, "Hello, Duncan Hunter 204. I heard you died."

The risible Hunter chuckled and answered her with a smile. He stuck his face into her hair where an ear would be and said, barely above a whisper, "You remembered. So, you are General Donovan's granddaughter. Still have the Mercedes?"

She nodded, smiling. They reversed positions. In his ear Elizabeth said, "I do. So, you are Greg Lynche's protégé, still Bill McGee's shadow, and are probably out of disguise. Still have the Corvette?"

Duncan switched positions. "Guilty on all counts. I think Greg's in the Caicos." He looked over to Eastwood and admonished him with another finger wag, *Not for pictures, not for publication either, colonel.* Elizabeth also looked at Eastwood and smiled at him.

Eastwood was amused at the old spook dominating the conversation no one could hear. He found her fascinating on several levels. *How could she have Duncan's ear? Do they know each other?*

Nazy found the woman's interruption interesting but not threatening. She squeezed Duncan's hand to get his attention. He swung over to her jewel decorated ear and whispered, "She knows me from Newport and thought I was in *Arlington*." Nazy understood and reached across the table. Dr. McIntosh gripped Nazy's hand for a moment as a reassurance that she was not a threat and that Duncan's identity would remain unrevealed.

McIntosh leaned back into Hunter's ear and whispered. "Before I heard you were dead, I wondered what kind of woman would capture your heart. The DO? Duncan, she's a beauty."

They switched receiving-transmitting positions. "Thank you, Dr. McIntosh."

She looked at him directly. "It's Elizabeth."

Hunter smiled and said, "Of course, it is." In a flash, he returned to her hair and asked, "What did you get your PhD in?"

She smiled at Eastwood again, who appeared to be enthralled at the activity between his friend and the woman. Elizabeth turned to Duncan's ear and said, "Microbiology."

Hunter wasn't shocked and turned back to Elizabeth's ear. Nazy, Bong, and Eastwood found the goings on at the table between McIntosh and Hunter amusing. He whispered, "Do you know Salvatore D'Angelo?"

Elizabeth looked at him for several seconds before switching ears. "He got me removed as the head of the NCMI." She pulled away and looked at Hunter. Duncan nodded and dove back into her hair and whispered, "Why did all the lab rats die during the mRNA tests? Safety and effectiveness tests."

You know that too? Her lips returned to Duncan's ear. "When all the lab rats died, it wasn't because of any safety and effectiveness test. It was because their bioweapon worked. Illegal bioweapon."

Duncan pulled away with a chilly look. She motioned for him to come back to her. Elizabeth whispered, "The labs at Ft. Detrick have a disinformation group. You were never supposed to know or suspect."

McGee was talking, but Duncan was solely focused on Dr. McIntosh.

Duncan paused and returned to her ear. "I still don't get it."

At mouth-ear reversal, "I told D'Angelo that he violated all the bioweapon test ban treaties, that he created an unregulated bioweapon that could be commercialized, and I got canned. I was — still am — on an NDA. Also, countries would pay billions for a bioweapon. A coronavirus, for example, will make you sick and is essentially harmless. It's the flu. Always remember this, it's their *patented vaccines* that kill."

Duncan returned to her ear. "Can I call you sometime?" She nodded with Duncan's face still in her hair, then she pulled herself away and extracted a business card from her clutch. Another ear exchange. "You can call anytime. If you and your wife are ever in Newport, you must visit."

Hunter smiled heartedly. He pulled out a 3x5 card from a pocket, wrote his Blackberry's number on it, and gave it to her, proving spooks don't carry calling cards. He turned to McGee's voice, rumbling from the microphone, "After defeating Nazism and fascism, Bill Donovan saw America did not have time to rest from a devastating war. Totalitarians never tire of conquest; when defeated, they reorganize and reattack with new stratagems and methods. They do whatever is necessary to infiltrate and overthrow our governments and to pass the nation's secrets to those who are not authorized to have them."

Nazy thought, *Like using children to conduct espionage….*

Duncan thought, *Like creating bioweapons to kill your adversaries.*

McGee continued, "Sometimes they are successful. They are always looking for an advantage to destroy America, enslave our citizens, and take away Americans' freedoms. Make no mistake. Today, Conservatives and Constitutionalists are under a full assault by radicals of all breeds. Criminals cannot occupy positions of trust. We are one election away from losing it all. For America to survive, elections must be fair. Forever."

Thunderous applause erupted in the ballroom.

"With the election of Mazibuike, the erosion of the Constitution and the theft of our Constitutional rights have been occurring incrementally and quietly. This is a subject no journalist has really explored. When there is no coverage, that is effectively government-sponsored censorship."

Hunter looked over to McIntosh only to find her gone. Somehow the old spook had slipped away with no one but Eastwood noticing. Hunter grinned. *I think that boy is smitten. I've said it before, that lady might be big, but she's fast… and sneaky! Typical old spook. But what a gift.*

"The IC knew President Mazibuike was the head of the Muslim Brotherhood in North America, but no one in the media or our Congress would say anything. His ascension to the White House was predicted by a curious document called *An Explanatory Memorandum: On the General Strategic Goal for the Group in North America*. This document outlined the Muslim Brotherhood's strategic plan to defeat the United States of America. But no action was taken. The media and the Democrat Party facilitated the usurper of a Nation."

Nazy nodded imperceptibly. She was on the edge of her seat. Eastwood and Bong sat in rapt attention. No one had ever talked to them like this before. Hunter was going over in his head what McIntosh had just told him.

McGee continued, "World War Three has begun and fifth generation warfare—the fight for the hearts and minds of Americans—is underway. Many did not see it coming. The other side of the political aisle is doing everything it can to bring this enemy to America as refugees, guest workers, green card workers, and foreign students and business men."

"When an unknown whistleblower released the former president's file, we learned President Mazibuike was not the man he claimed to be. The Democrats and their media friends knew he was not eligible to be president. How many in this room knew the Democrats tried eight times to amend the Constitution so he would finally be considered a natural born citizen? When that did not work, the master manipulators essentially bludgeoned Americans into submission with charges of racism. All of this is mind control. Those were *the silent weapons for a quiet war.* It's taken decades for America to realize that they were subject to psychological operations by the masters of mind control: the Democrat Party, America's newspapers, social media, and cable news networks."

Duncan looked at his wife and squeezed her hand. He turned to Bong who smiled back.

McGee continued, "Let me add, before Mazibuike was chased from office, he issued several Executive Orders approving Joseph Goebbels-like government behavioral propaganda experiments on the American public. President Hernandez rescinded them all, including the Orwellian, 'Using Behavioral Science Insights to Better Serve the American People.' Under that program, social media manipulated the thinking and preferences of Americans. The day will come when those social media giants are exposed. A billionaire should buy one of those social media platforms and expose those in government who are demanding they censor free speech."

"This is our challenge in the intelligence community, to collect, analyze, and take action. President Mazibuike set the IC back a decade by allowing the Muslim Brotherhood to infiltrate our organizations. President Hernandez has given us the funds to reverse those deleterious policies, and fight back."

The audience loudly applauded.

"Our remarkable Founders created a great country. Bill Donovan would have been right at home with them. He committed his life to maintain American freedom without the fear of being disarmed and subjugated by totalitarians. This was the purpose of the OSS; this is the purpose of the Central Intelligence Agency—protect Americans, defend America from totalitarians, domestic and abroad."

"I accept this honor knowing that it is only because of the teamwork of our incredible patriots in the Central Intelligence Agency and the intelligence community that America was able to identify, locate, and eliminate the men on the Most Wanted Terrorist List. They are pushing back the invasion that is occurring at our borders. We all have to push back these domestic enemies. Thank you again for this honor. May God Bless America. Thank you and goodnight."

After a two-minute standing ovation, McGee finally stepped from the dais and returned to the head table with the Donovan Award and the file from McIntosh in his hand. Director Todd shook his hand and said, "Well done, Bill."

Nazy shook his hand and told him, "Outstanding, Bill." He smiled back in appreciation of the comment.

McGee looked at *Maverick* for a second and allowed a smile of understanding to pass between them. McGee asked Hunter if he would hold the case containing the Donovan Award. Hunter nodded *"of course"* and said, "Damn, *Bullfrog*, you're no dryasdust; I didn't know you had that kind of moxie in ya! That's going to leave a mark…" *On Democrats, on the Muslim Brotherhood, on the propaganda arm of the Democrat Party, the media. You just declared war on all of them!*

The table erupted in laughter. Eastwood shook McGee's hand to complete the congratulatory requirements. McGee waved the massive file folder Dr. McIntosh had given him, "We have to get back to work, but I need to brief Director Todd on some things before I return to the campaign trail and you have a show to record."

McGee wanted to escape the crush of well-wishers who were lining up in droves, but he knew it was hopeless. The OSS Society members converged on him to express their appreciation. Before diving into the crowd, McGee told Hunter he would see him in the morning, leaving Hunter with Nazy, Todd, Eastwood, Bong, and the OSS Donovan Award medal. Duncan noticed the Donovan file was still in McGee's hand.

The medal's presentation case was an awkward size and shape, but Duncan slipped it into an Armani pocket that was surprisingly large enough to accommodate it. He watched McGee directing OSS Society members with the thick, dark orange file that was as thick as his forearm. The dirty folder looked as if it could have been exposed to the elements for months or hidden away in the bottom of a duffel bag.

Duncan smiled that the file was still bound with a decrepit tubular fabric-covered band that formed triangles to secure the ends. *Just as it was almost twenty years ago.*

Eastwood spoke and interrupted Hunter's thoughts which brought the old pilot back into the present. "As I understand it, the Admiral will go with you tomorrow. That will give me some time to go to New York. I'll write this up on the train and do my radio show at home instead of on the road." He hoped Todd or McGee or Hunter would offer him a lift to Washington's Union Station, but none of them got the hint. Eastwood sighed, *That means a limo or an Uber. That also means no interview with CIA Director Todd.*

Nazy was paying attention. She knew Eastwood wouldn't ask for a ride even though he always needed a ride to the train station. Bong may need a ride, as well. Nazy stepped in front of Dory and offered him and Bong one of the limos in her security detail. They would take

Eastwood to Union Station and Bong to the Airport Marriott at Reagan National. Eastwood was awestruck; Bong was grateful. Nazy texted instructions to her security detail.

Hunter retrieved the *Growler* and shut it off. He pocketed a copy of the evening's program.

McGee and Todd had wandered off to mingle with the slowly dissolving crowd of well-wishers. Nazy repositioned her silver fox and led Duncan to her Agency limo at the front of the hotel. Duncan checked to make sure his jetpack was still in the back. They drove into the heart of Washington D.C. and disembarked at the rear entrance of the Army Navy Club. He admonished the security team lead, "Don't lose that. It'll cost me a million dollars to replace."

Once in their room, Duncan deadlocked the door, withdrew the Colt, and cleared the bathroom. After he exited, Nazy wordlessly padded to the bathroom and closed the door. Duncan began his routine of checking various areas of the room for surveillance equipment or active threats, making sure they were actually alone and safe. He checked behind the doors, under the bed, and inside the box springs. Box springs are hollow and can easily hide an assassin. Intel officers overseas had found bodies and explosives in those spaces. He used the muzzle of his Colt to check behind the curtains in case someone was hiding there.

Duncan secured the room with a portable door lock and kicked a doorstop between the door and tiled floor. Hotel locks were there to give you a peace of mind, but he knew they were very easy to circumvent. Once, an agent had awakened to find the night clerk sucking on his toes. Finally, he attached an alarm to the door. It would go off if someone touched the door handle and tried to enter the room.

The first time Nazy and Duncan had stayed at a hotel, she had thought he was paranoid when he secured the room. Duncan informed her that new intelligence officers in the field do not understand how devious or clever the Muslim Brotherhood could be. "You are worth the time to ensure your safety."

Once he had finished all of his precautions, Duncan placed the Colt *Python* on the nightstand, went to lean against the door frame of the bathroom. He gently knocked on the door, one rap then two.

With her first kiss, Nazy showed Duncan how much she appreciated his efforts to ensure she would be safe. Duncan slowly undressed her and she him. Her second kiss was a reminder that not only had he been missed, but that he was loved. He held her hand and walked her to the shower—Nazy's favorite place to unwind with Duncan before bed.

•   •   •

Having relished being in a world of anonymity, Bong checked into the Airport Marriott under his own name. He had work to do. He remotely accessed the *Tailwatchers* database trying to find a cluster of jets. After ten minutes, he found what he was looking for in Aspen, Colorado. Private jets had arrived in Aspen in multiple groups. Sometimes landing at almost the same time. Some of the flights had made multiple stops and were only on the ground for 15-30 minutes. Just long enough for another person, a CEO or board member, to board.

Bong cursed himself; he should have known better. He should have looked there first. *No shit! They are all there! When there's no place else to run to, the Aspen Institute runs to Aspen.*

CHAPTER 37

July 16, 2020

Nazy's security detail was familiar with the old Marine and his Union Station destination by the Capitol Building. They asked Eastwood if he wanted to stop at a Starbucks Coffee shop for a *grande coffee frappuccino*. Eastwood flashed a $100 bill. Of course he did, and of course he bought coffees, *frappuccinos*, and fresh slices of banana bread for the crew of two. *Chicks with guns, protecting my ass, cheap fare. A sexist would say....* The security officer in the passenger seat called ahead, and their order was ready when the black Escalade pulled to a stop. In less than a minute, Eastwood was moving again and the security team pocketed Eastwood's change. He was on the lookout for protesters; D.C. always had protesters when Republicans were in the White House. Seeing none, he convinced himself it should be a quiet ride to Union Station. Dory Eastwood extracted his olive Tilley's Wanderer from his computer bag and placed it on his head. The Tilley and the tux made an odd combination. Camouflage comes in various forms. They rode in silence; Eastwood enjoyed the frozen drink.

What an incredible night! Not like the night a horde of protesters, furious that President Hernandez had won the election, practiced their anarchy skills near the White House. I couldn't get a cab, so I walked. That night, an exhausted policeman in riot gear gave me directions how to get to Union Station without being accosted, molested, beaten, or killed. I asked that cop, "Why are they protesting?" and he said, "I think they protest because they suck at life, the government isn't giving them a Ferrari, or their dad is now their mom." Oh, that was funny! The protesters were throwing bags of urine or feces at the cops; they were worse than animals in a zoo playing in their own waste.

Eastwood thanked the security agents and bid them adieu. He turned toward Union Station as his Blackberry buzzed in his pocket, signaling a text message from the news wire service: *five alarm fire at The New York Times building.* He grimaced and shook his head in wonder. *Oh great — burning building mixed with weed and trash!*

Minutes later, he had paid for his ticket and had settled on the Acela in a first-class seat. He pulled out his laptop before the train pulled away from the station and typed:

SUBMISSION
The Washington Times
By Demetrius Eastwood

In a solemn ceremony earlier today, The OSS Society dedicated a memorial at Arlington National Cemetery honoring more than 125 OSS personnel who were killed or missing in action during World War Two. Attendees included Dr. Ronald Stephens, The OSS Society's chairman, the Director of the CIA, Walter Todd III, the Director of Operations of the CIA, Nazy Cunningham, current and former Defense Intelligence Agency Directors, current and former Undersecretaries of Defense for Intelligence, the Deputy Undersecretary of Defense for Intelligence, and the National Security Advisor. The OSS Society published a booklet for the ceremony that included biographies of former OSS Society Donovan winners and of OSS personnel whose remains were never recovered.

The OSS Society was celebrating its 73rd anniversary — a remarkable milestone and a testament to General Donovan's enduring vision for the OSS and the CIA.

Tonight, more than 600 people filled the Grand Ballroom at the Ritz-Carlton Hotel for this year's OSS Society's William J. Donovan Award Dinner. The OSS Society's honorees attracted a who's who of the U.S. intelligence and military establishment. President Hernandez regarded it as "a wonderful celebration of our country at its best."

The highlight of the evening was the presentation of the Donovan Award to former U.S. Special Operations Command commander and former Director of the CIA, Rear Admiral William McGee. The presentation of the plaque and medal was made by General Donovan's granddaughter, Dr. Elizabeth McIntosh, the Provost at Salve Regina University. McGee took a hiatus from his Presidential campaign to attend the ceremony and make comments.

Short and sweet!

Eastwood had been working on Part 2 of an article for the editorial page of another newspaper. He opened the file: *Why Are Children Coming Down with Monkeypox?* He was happy with it, but read it through one more time before dispatching it to *The New York Post*.

CHAPTER 38

July 17, 2020

Nazy was fast asleep in Duncan's arms, softly snoring. He had thought he would fall asleep from utter exhaustion, but he was wide awake. The words from Dr. McIntosh and words from the former CDC Director rattled in his head like rats and rattlesnakes dropped in a boat. *The man had already been fired for threatening Bullfrog with a pandemic. Now it sounds like he hates the Nuremberg Code, and the medical community is trying to destroy Informed Consent? Why would a CDC director be involved with bioweapons unless there was...money to be made? Because of an enemy?*

No.... Elizabeth had her falling out with D'Angelo before Bill or I arrived at the war college. Would a CDC director be involved with a bioweapon because of Americans? Republicans? Maybe. But more likely there is something in the Nuremberg Code they dislike and must destroy. Code words of a totalitarian. Imagine what the left could do to a law-abiding nation without our consent? If they are able to orchestrate a pandemic, Australia would become Auschwitz with another name. Aussies who gave up their weapons would be herded into camps under the guise of a national health emergency. What fresh hell would they have in store for Americans?

There had been enough terror for one night. Duncan wanted his eyes to slam shut and let exhaustion take over, but he still had a little work to do. He slipped out of bed without a break in Nazy's breathing. He padded over to his tux pocket for a pen and paper, and under the light of a blue laser pointer crafted a short *billet-deux* to Nazy. He thanked her for waiting for him, for wearing that incredible dress, for being so incredibly beautiful and romantic, and for allowing him to be her lover and husband. Duncan looked over his work; it wasn't very original, but sometimes heartfelt didn't require original thought. He smiled at himself. *Still writing letters.* He returned the two pens to his jacket and slipped the note in her bag. He was absolutely silent in the bathroom, then he returned to bed. He gently encouraged Nazy to reposition her head until it rested on his shoulder. Duncan put his arm around her and finally fell to sleep.

•   •   •

After a short workout and a longer session in the sheets, Duncan ordered breakfast. In thick bathrobes, he and Nazy sat across from each other indulging in a standard breakfast of eggs, bacon for Nazy, Virginia ham for Duncan, hash browns and toast. They entwined their legs to maintain a level of intimate contact.

As it had been for the past twelve years when they were reunited after a lengthy separation, the *Growler* was blinking as they shared what was going on at work. Their little talks were unofficial debriefs of what was impacting the intelligence community, who was making waves, who was trying to get on the *Disposition Matrix*, who got kicked off, and other threats to the organization, the country, and to themselves. Since each of them had been targeted and escaped several assassinations attempts, and Bill McGee had rescued them both at different times in the Middle East, the information passed held a little greater significance than an old married couple simply asking, "How was your day, dear?"

Nazy said. "We are analyzing Scorpii's journals... things we suspected are coming together in sharper focus." Nazy outlined in painstaking granular detail, the weaponization of the social media networks that began after President Mazibuike vanished. She said, "His journals suggested — as we suspected — there were direct FBI portals to the social media companies. Four of the Five Eyes have hundreds of episodes where the FBI told the social media giants who and what they wanted censored. Virtually all top-tier Republicans. They call it 'canceling the discussion.'"

"So, because the government cannot censor free speech, the turds at the FBI have the social media dirtballs do it for them. Sounds like dark state actors. I take it you have names?"

"We do, and some you will not believe. The social media networks changed overnight, immediately after Mazibuike's Cairo speech, which kicked off the Muslim Brotherhood's frontal assault on the North African countries. The CEOs of social media started visiting the White House. They began using their companies like an electronic version of the East German's *Disintegration Directive.*"

"And when 3M left?" (Maxim Mohammad Mazibuike).

Nazy said, "Well, the timeline is important. It's clear that under Mazibuike, the two largest social media companies were recruited by the FBI for participation in the construct of their censoring program. This is one of the reasons 3M injected the Muslim Brotherhood into the FBI. They had an agenda to crush Jewish people. Scorpii did it; Europe social media and 3M used the FBI under his *Muslim Outreach* program to determine what was acceptable political speech and what was not. Mazibuike's VP, the Chief of Staff, the Secretary of State, SECDEF — every Democrat in his cabinet also took part. They created *disinformation bureaus.*"

Duncan said, "Dr. McIntosh said you were stunning last night, and I agree. She also said Ft. Detrick even had a disinformation directorate to kill rumors what was going on in their bioweapons labs."

Nazy smiled at the compliment and shook her head.

"When Mazibuike came along, he was so aggressive in getting his friends in the FBI, infiltration wasn't the real goal. He wanted to curtail any dissenting voice."

Nazy nodded. "On social media. It really is very insidious. After a few years of beta testing the government-corporate relationship and measuring the influence factor, things sped up. By the time Mazibuike was removed, FBI operatives had begun direct collaboration with Big Tech in constructing a neoteric surveillance and influence system for domestic rollout. By charter, there was nothing we could do."

Nazy was a bit exasperated. Duncan asked, "What else was Scorpii into?"

"Do you know about the annual Bensberg meeting in Cologne, at the Althoff Grandhotel Schloss?"

Duncan nodded, "The two security dudes who had infiltrated the European Federation and Scorpii's inner circle said that last year the elite of the elite held a coronavirus pandemic simulation." *Scorpii – like Bela Lugosi's Dracula – is body and mien. The perfect pedophile….*

"That comports with what we know…but do you know who led the simulation?"

Duncan shook his head with a grin. *That girl is always one step ahead of me….*

"Dr. D'Angelo."

Duncan rolled his eyes. "Well, there you go. Means, motive, and opportunity. Dr. McIntosh said he funded bioweapons development. I had no idea Uncle Fester had children."

I don't know who that is. He is prone to sarcasm. Nazy inhaled and asked, "The CDC Director?"

"Yes, D'Angelo. He got her canned from her Medical Intel position — which I knew nothing about. But the most amazing part was there were billions to be made from a bioweapon." *There are traitors and then there are traitors….* "Are you aware if any lab has leaked a bug?"

She paused, then continued, "Not at this time. But there has been much unusual activity in the Chinese bioweapons labs. D'Angelo recently said on the alphabet media that Monkeypox is the latest pandemic. It's supposedly out of control, which it is not, and there's no vaccine, which of course, there is."

Duncan said, "I didn't think it was that infectious. It's an STD." *The gay man's disease.*

Nazy said, "It hadn't previously triggered widespread outbreaks beyond Africa, where it is endemic in animals. But simple proper hygiene helps control the spread of the zoonotic disease. Dory released a fantastic article that said D'Angelo's pandemic is Monkeypox, that children and dogs are getting it. And our embassies in Spain and Belgium just recently reported that an outbreak occurred because of some risky sexual behavior at two recent mass events in Europe. The leading theory to explain the spread was sexual transmission among gay and bisexual men at two—what they call 'raves'—held in Spain and Belgium."

Duncan was missing something. *Nazy wants something....*

Nazy said, "You need to look into Dr. Science.... If you can."

Duncan said, "You mean his financial holdings, patents, bank transactions, offshore accounts? We collect corporate intelligence, geopolitical intelligence. Bong will run him to ground. He's a master analyst, like you."

The fatal conceit of the Democrat elites.... Nazy said, "If you can have Bong look at D'Angelo, that would be helpful. There is a Scorpii connection. D'Angelo's name is all over his journals, and not just for kids. Open-source records document D'Angelo essentially had more than $30B a year to hand out to friends and collaborators, and Scorpii looks like he negotiated billions per year for European labs in exchange for time in his hotels."

Duncan asked, "*$30 billion?*"

Nazy nodded. "A year. Looking across a 30-to-40-year career, one can easily overlook that he potentially awarded over *$1 trillion* in research grants with hardly any accountability. When he was the CDC Director, he controlled an annual research budget that was five times greater than what is needed to elect a president. Do you have any idea how much influence $30B a year can buy?"

Crap! That girl is so smart! He is a lefty, and it's not about what is in his bank account. He had government money! We will never know what he really has squirreled away, but there is no one else with his level of influence. D'Angelo could buy anything he wants. Why would he want bioweapons? So, he could threaten governments with a bug? Either play or we will withhold treatments. Duncan said, "That's pretty incredible. There's a reason D'Angelo is important to the left. The left has negated the Second Amendment. The bullets of their bioweapon is deadlier than my pistol. Not only does he represent the pinnacle moment of the dark state–top-down public policy run by an elite group of government scientists, but he has funded anything his little evil heart desired. He has a bioweapon and a patented treatment. We're screwed."

"What are you going to do?"

"For starters, I think we can look into it alarming no one." *Draining the swamp is going to be more than a one-term battle.*

Nazy said, "In the meantime, they held wargame simulations in Europe last year and this year. The premise was a fictional coronavirus passed from an animal reservoir to humans. The organizers warned of a similar pandemic in the future."

Duncan said, "I'll bet there will be remarkable similarities regarding the timing of their wargaming event and an actual or an engineered coronavirus pandemic of the kind and nature D'Angelo promised Bill will have to deal with once he becomes President. Monkeypox is an STD; not generally fatal. A coronavirus is a respiratory bug and a very malleable model. It mutates, it can probably be engineered to be lethal. But Dr. McIntosh said the vaccine for this stuff is the actual bioweapon. You said, $30 billion a year?"

"I did." Nazy got earnest as she continued, "I've been in some of the bioweapon conferences. Coronaviruses could make good bioweapons. However, every conference, every medical publication concluded that coronaviruses escape the vaccine impulse because the virus mutates too rapidly for a vaccine to be developed. Like flu, they are two or three-year events."

Duncan said, "The medical community and pharmaceutical companies know any vaccines for a coronavirus would be ineffective. A waste of time." *Unless.... Maybe they are thinking of genetically engineered vaccines?*

Nazy nodded. "If there is a pandemic in our future, there will be questions about whether the parties to the simulation had prior knowledge of it."

Duncan made a face. "The stakeholders, politicians, and businessmen who sponsored and took part in the simulation would benefit enormously from an engineered pandemic and could wield monopolistic power in pandemic response and policymaking. The world would follow any American response."

Nazy asked, "You're convinced they are going to do it — release a coronavirus? Dory's article on Monkeypox...."

Duncan half-frowned. "No, an STD isn't the stuff of pandemics. But an STD *can* start terrifying the public. Then when they release a virus, people will race to get vaccinated. These things are worth billions and every aspect of them are patented. I say whatever they have planned for us is already here."

Nazy repositioned her arms and legs; thinking.

Duncan kept thinking he was seeing something she had missed. But he realized, he only had a partial solution. He finally said, "Baby, injecting a killer virus into the population of an adversary has always been the terrorist's wet dream. Islamists would love to turn themselves into binary biological weapons. If they will drive a jet into a skyscraper for Allah, they would be more than willing to expose themselves to a bug and climb aboard dozens of jets just so they could release the seven levels of Hell. Martyr-wannabes would line up by the hundreds to punish America. They wouldn't even have to infiltrate airport security to scatter their seeds of death."

Nazy said, "They have tried."

"I know. They are just incompetent. But Democrats and their one world globalists are worse. Instead of nineteen turds flying four jets into buildings, they'll infect nineteen dudes and put them on nineteen jets to infect the world."

Nazy felt a chill. "You're convinced they'll release a virus?"

"I'm sure of it. It's a political year. When they release an engineered coronavirus, as the *patent* holders, they'll already have the treatments, the tests, and any prophylaxes. They and their disease carriers will come through it ok — but the population; well, screw them. They'll delay or withhold therapeutics or curatives by declaring them harmful. All the FDA has to say is that they are bad and they would do D'Angelo's $30 billion-a-year bidding, because big pharma would make it so. Direct payments back to him as awards. It's a money laundering scheme."

"These clowns have no compunction putting the world's population at a grave risk, as long as they can make a buck or rule some little outpost. These guys are so crooked, they'll probably intentionally release an engineered coronavirus to boost global acceptance of universal vaccination. No informed consent. Force people to be lab rats."

Nazy smiled at Duncan. "The common concern among the medical industry is, and I quote, '…that until an infectious crisis is very real, present, and at the emergency threshold, it is often largely ignored.'"

Duncan shook his head. "I will remember that. I'm certain these criminal bastards will intentionally release a coronavirus or a variant somewhere in China. It's the only thing that makes sense. Thank you, Dr. McIntosh. It's not like some billionaire becomes the mosquito king and malaria sweeps over the nation. Malaria is controlled daily with a penny-per-day dose. If it was something like malaria, then the pharmaceutical companies would have to stop making free anti-malarials and then charge them for an expensive vaccine? I don't think so."

"Bill threatens their Ponzi scheme."

Duncan concurred. "Bill knows coronaviruses are not vaccine-preventable diseases, but the public does not. They will go with what the CDC and that idiot D'Angelo, or what his replacement will say. That it is a superbug. Engineered in a lab. And the President will be convinced the government needs to create an experimental vaccine to save Americans."

"You said that was really a bioweapon?"

Duncan nodded. "When I first started thinking about this, I thought the bug was the bioweapon. Now thanks to Dr. Mac, I know it is the vaccine. They want the vaccine. Their vaccine. Bill and I stopped Iranian and the Chinese work to create a bug to kill Jews. I would not put it past Washington Democrats and the left to secretly drug Americans. Contaminate the water supply or the national blood supply. There are some bugs that can actually create mental illness in otherwise healthy humans. Unless these guys are closet totalitarians, I still cannot figure out why they want to do that. But I know the CDC needs to be wearing armbands and stormtrooper boots." Duncan looked at his Rolex. "Shit!"

Nazy knew their time was up. "Go. You don't want to be late."

Duncan stood up and brought Nazy to her feet. He unfastened her robe and let it slide off her shoulders. In his best underbreath baritone he said, "It's not like I'm meeting the President. A couple of spooks." He kissed her passionately and sucked the wind from her lungs. "I can blame security." He kissed her again. This time she sucked the wind from the heart of his soul. He didn't want to leave. "I can be a *few* minutes late...."

Nazy sensually whispered, "Maybe you can call in sick?"

Duncan whispered back, "You mean, like with a coronavirus? Could you have the boys at S&T just engineer one so I have to be quarantined with you? Maybe at home, for a month?"

"Only a month?" *We never get a month-long break.*

Nazy kissed Duncan like he wasn't coming back.

CHAPTER 39

July 17, 2020

Demetrius Eastwood still smelled smoke as he entered his apartment. Smoke from the fire from *The New York Times* hung over New York City like an orange fog. With no breeze, it wouldn't dissipate soon. Now New Yorkers had to start their day with dope smoke, rotten garbage smells, and the pungent aroma from the corpse of the old Gray Lady.

He turned off the security system and tossed his backpack in his chair, an original 1957 Herman Miller Eames lounge chair. He usually sat in it as he edited his work or napped for a couple of hours. This time a nap would have to wait. The high-speed express from Washington D.C. had gotten him home quickly enough, but he didn't have any time to relax. He moved through the 10,000 square-foot office space-apartment with purpose. His suit smelled of smoke. Dory felt a shower was mandatory, so he stripped off his clothes and entered the white marble bathroom.

Eastwood turned on the water and thought, *This shower has all the Duncan Hunter touches; huge enough to hose down a Friesian, variable water pressure from rain showers to a high pressure cutting tool, multiple shower heads....* Standing in the warm stream, he let his mind wander to what lay ahead.... He placed his hands on the wall, lowered his head, and let the steamy hot flow pour down his neck and warm his back.

There had been a time when Eastwood couldn't find work. Now he was working for Bill McGee and living in Duncan Hunter's world; it had come at him through the wet end of a fire hose. The last few days would have had been ballbusters for any journalist, more so for a man over seventy. Being the only legitimate journalist allowed inside the true inner workings of a presidential campaign made work complicated and onerous.

Once his muscles relaxed, he quickly soaped, lathered, and rinsed. He barely toweled when he saw the time on his Tudor *Black Bay*; he found clothes for his radio show.

Eastwood knew the drill like a Marine Corps Drill Instructor knows drill. Inside the recording studio, he energized five monitors, a pair of cameras, and for his on-line podcast a large microphone with an isolation shield. He donned a pair of professional studio monitor headphones, checked the output of the microphone, and got to work. He raked a comb through his hair before going live on the air. He began with his standard opening remarks then steered toward his goal of talking about *The New York Times* fire.

"As you all know, I'm honored to be covering Admiral McGee in his quest for the presidency. Are you ready to have a patriot in the White House? As many of you who listen to this podcast know, after 9/11 the SEAL Team Six Commander, Captain Bill McGee, was tasked with finding the man who had orchestrated the terrorist operation. Nineteen murderous Islamic *jihadis* hijacked jets, flew them into the World Trade Center and the Pentagon, and killed almost 3,000 innocent people, most of them American citizens. Turned New York City into a war zone."

"America learned there were terrorists whose sole goal was to infiltrate airport security so a handful of Muslim men could get weapons on board a jet to kill thousands of Americans. Complicit radical Muslim men and women in uniformed airport security positions, allowed the hijackers' weapons to pass through the x-ray machines for the sole purpose of hijacking aircraft."

"Parts of New York City and the Pentagon were in flames, and damaged buildings were collapsing all around. Now, as then, we find American cities in flames and in ruin. Cities run solely by Democrats for decades. By contrast, cities run by Republican mayors are not burning in turmoil. There is a good reason for that. Democrats foster non-stop protests over asinine topics. Their cities' populations are terrified of the anarchists, criminals, and thugs that run their cities. Residents of Democrat states and cities fear for their lives, as terrorists and Marxist Democrats push their destructive totalitarianist ideologies and radical agendas."

"It used to be that defectors from communist countries would do anything to get to freedom in the U.S. Now, residents are defecting from the communistic socialist Democrat states to the capitalistic Republican red states of freedom."

"Last night, I was honored to attend this year's OSS Society's William J. Donovan Award Dinner. More than 600 people filled the Grand Ballroom at the Ritz-Carlton Hotel in Washington, D.C. The OSS Society's honorees attracted a who's who of the U.S. intelligence and military establishment."

"The highlight of the night was the presentation of the Donovan Award to former U.S. Special Operations Command commander and former Director of the CIA, Rear Admiral William McGee. He took a hiatus from his Presidential campaign to attend the ceremony and make comments."

Eastwood talked for another hour before deep diving into politics.

"Has anyone noticed *The New York Post* article on New York's record-breaking odor complaints? It's not the stench of dirty streets now; it's the pungent weed smoke everywhere. Disgusted residents and workers say that the city has smelled worse than ever this summer. Various Manhattanites described the foul aromas as 'rancid,' 'gnarly and cadaverous,' but mostly 'like a used diaper.' I thought the air was bad in Kabul, Afghanistan, where they have been burning donkey dung for centuries to stay warm, but the trash thrown in the streets and this weed crap in New York City is ridiculous. As soon as I can, I'm out of here."

"A recent survey conducted by the *Post* ranked New York as the second dirtiest city in the world, behind Rome, Italy—the undisputed filthiest city on the planet. The ridiculous mayor of this city claims the piles of trash and rats as big as cats running wild aren't that bad. He faults merchants for not tidying up the sidewalks. Oh, that's the problem; it's the merchant's fault for generating trash which attracts vermin and causes nauseating odors exacerbated by summer heat. It certainly isn't the city's failure to haul trash out of the city. The stench isn't caused by an ineffective sanitation system or an ineffective mayor. Apparently, New Yorkers want to live and work in a dying shithole, because they keep electing these idiot Democrats who do nothing to solve the problems. Instead of solving problems for their constituents, these idiots go on meaningless crusades."

"The Big Apple's infamous habit of lining sidewalks with rodent infested piles of garbage bags may have contributed to its budding reputation as *The City That Never Sweeps*. The Democrat mayor's new solution is: we need larger trash bins. New York, you deserve these idiots."

Eastwood launched into a different subject. "Many of you know that in *The City That Never Sweeps*, with rats as big as cats, a fire totally engulfed *The New York Times* headquarters building last evening. I smelled smoke when I returned to the city. It conjured up old memories of the actions of 19 filthy terrorists two decades ago who were hellbent on meeting Allah. Reportedly, as firefighters arrived from five fire departments, the top thirty floors were a raging inferno. The New York Fire Department said that everyone was out of the building, but the fire was consuming one floor of the 52-story skyscraper every few seconds. They decided to let it burn. The building collapsed inward on itself. No one was injured, and investigators are on scene."

"For the longest time, *The Washington Post* has been losing money and readers, and none were happier than the staff at *The New York Times*. Ever since *The Washington Post* scooped *The Times* in 1971 by publishing classified material on Page One in the *Pentagon Papers* caper, the two have battled to be the *Newspaper of Record*. Now the two most liberal newspapers in the country have burned to the ground within the last six months. Some think it is poetic justice. Some will blame Republicans as soon as the shock wears off, if they haven't already."

Eastwood had been waiting for the proper moment to release something that had been near and dear to his heart for some time. Now seemed to be the time. After a few other tidbits of political news, he looked at his watch and gaged the time he had left. He found an appropriate segue and dove in.

"Ladies and gentlemen, we have late breaking news! The U.S. Supreme Court has put the kibosh on building the Mazibuike Presidential Center, what would have been former President Maxim Mohammad Mazibuike's Presidential Library. The proposed Mazibuike Presidential Center was to be built at the site of Detroit's largest mosque, but construction has been tied up in the courts. Its proposed location, the site of the largest Islamic Cultural Center in Detroit, has been causing controversy from historians and archivists for years."

"The plaintiffs, calling themselves *The Natural Born Citizen Coalition*, have repeatedly gone to court to stop the proposed Presidential Center. *The Natural Born Citizen Coalition* say the proposed Presidential Center, a complex composed of seven mosques and a 21-story minaret, would have been a monument to the Constitutionally ineligible and illegitimate President Mazibuike. And they say the location is the launching pad where the Muslim Brotherhood and the Islamic Underground began their quiet war to conquer America."

"As proposed, the Mazibuike Presidential Center would have been noteworthy; it would have been unlike any other presidential library. All other presidential libraries and museums are run by the National Archives and Records Administration. But the Mazibuike Presidential Center would have been run by the Mazibuike Foundation, a small private nonprofit organization with ties to the Muslim Brotherhood. Since the proposed Presidential Center would not have a research library, and President Mazibuike's archives and personal papers would not be housed or available on site, the Court decided it didn't comply with the law, and there was no need for its construction."

"There were those who believed that President Mazibuike didn't deserve a presidential library. He resigned in disgrace as a charlatan and an illegitimate president who fled the country in the middle of the night to avoid prosecution. The court's decision rendered that view moot."

Eastwood cautioned himself to slow down. The news from SCOTUS was incredible. "The U.S. Supreme Court tackled the unstated issue behind the controversy that led to the proposed Mazibuike Presidential Center being debated by the court. The Mazibuike Presidential Center and its proposed array of minarets, Islamic cultural center, mosques, and a madrassa was not about creating a presidential library for one of America's presidents, but was a tribute commemorating the greatest Muslim attack on America — the installation of an illegitimate Islamic president into the White House. The only thing missing from Mazibuike's White House was the green flag of the Muslim Brotherhood flying atop the building."

"There is a centuries-long history of building mosques following Muslim military victories. *The Natural Born Citizen Coalition* warned that building the President Mazibuike Presidential Library would have been seen in the same light as the Muslim conquests of Mecca, Jerusalem, and Constantinople."

Eastwood continued, "Counterterrorism officials were loath to admit that America had witnessed the improper ascension of the son of a foreign national into the top job of the federal government. Of course, the media facilitated much of Mazibuike's success in winning the White House. If they hadn't used military-grade propaganda, the election would have had a different outcome."

"Investigators, not the FBI, looking into this episode of American history have uncovered an incredible Mazibuike-Muslim Brotherhood link that engaged in culture wars meant to destroy the U.S. in order to establish a Global Islamic State. *The Natural Born Citizen Coalition* cited a document from the secret archives of the Muslim Brotherhood in America discovered during the largest counterterrorism trial in American history, the 'An Explanatory Memorandum.' The Supreme Court was very interested in the strategic goals of the Muslim Brotherhood in North America."

"It was confirmed that the actions of the Mazibuike administration had established an effective and stable Islamic Movement led by the Muslim Brotherhood. The Mazibuike administration had adopted Muslim causes domestically and globally. They had expanded the observant Muslim base, unified and directed Muslim efforts, and presented Islam as a civilization alternative. The Supremes, on a 5-to-4 vote, did not support the President Mazibuike Presidential Library, no matter where it was constructed."

"The Court found that President Mazibuike resigned from the presidency when CIA-sourced documents were released to members of Congress. They confirmed that President Mazibuike wasn't constitutionally eligible to be president, and that it was likely he and several high-ranking members of the Democrat Party had committed several treasonous crimes in order to elect him. Admiral McGee has promised a special prosecutor to investigate the Democrat Party's involvement in electing Mazibuike and to have Congress negate any laws that he passed."

"My last report comes to us from the Vincennes Police Department in Indiana. They are grappling with a rise in missing children cases. Thirty children have been reported missing within the last two weeks; a total of 66 active missing children cases in Vincennes as of mid-month. The police chief expressed concern over the rising number of disappearances among children aged 8 to 16, describing the situation as reaching 'unprecedented levels.' According to the police chief, many of the cases were likely runaways, but she feared young teenagers could also have fallen victim to predators, who could be 'wolves in sheep's clothing.' Most of the disappearances do not make the news. It's a silent crime that happens right under our noses. And it is likely happening in cities all across America."

"As are the three churches that were destroyed by fire this week. This sounds like a program. And I have a prime suspect. But it is not this guy at the FBI. A domestic terrorist investigator for the FBI has recently resigned in protest. He was notified by one of his superiors that pursuing Christian domestic terrorists was a higher priority than pursuing child pornography cases. That searching and arresting Grandma and Grandpa for entering a church was more important than pursuing the sick individuals in our society who prey on our children. Makes you wonder what is going on inside the FBI. They have lost their way. It may need to be dismantled, bulldozed, and rebuilt."

"I have time for one final story. We have a man from the Bronx who killed his roommate. When the gunman fled the scene, taking the stairs faster than his feet could keep up, his baggy trousers tripped him up. According to a detective on the case, he fell with his finger still on the trigger, discharging the weapon a final time, and blasting himself with a bullet to the neck. It was a murder-accidental suicide."

Eastwood laughed into the microphone. Once he caught his breath, he said, "That's all I have for you this evening. Thank you for tuning in. We'll be back in a few days for another episode of *Unfiltered News*. Be careful out there—the Democrats are a violent party threatening to burn down everything. That Party is an open-air lunatic asylum. Send us your EVs on fire videos. We received a great one when the battery of an electric semi-truck caught fire and ten others around it were totally burned up. These are fantastic inventions that need to go away of the dodo. Always remember, these are Democrat improvement programs."

"Remember, men do brave things every day and putting on a dress and lipstick isn't one of them. 'Semper Fi' to all of my Marine Corps brothers and sisters. And as always, I would like to close this broadcast by saluting the men and women of the military, first responders, law enforcement, the farmers and the factory workers, and all the law-abiding citizens across the fruited plain who make this country work. God Bless America. Good night. Eastwood, out."

Dory Eastwood closed up shop, locked the place, and raced out of the apartment. He had a jet to catch. To Iowa. Where the air is fresh and clean.

CHAPTER 40

July 18, 2020

Why Are Children Coming Down with Monkeypox? Part 2
The New York Post
By Demetrius Eastwood

In the land of Democrat-run states, in the world where government is sanctioning the activities of mental disorders, it is now considered normal behavior to have two gay men identify themselves as daddies. What could go wrong? With the governments' imprimatur, blue state child welfare services are increasingly placing children in the homes of gay men, à la the "German Experiment."

This isn't legitimate foster care. In legitimate foster care, foster parents are extensively vetted and will take an orphan out of the goodness of their heart. We know the system isn't perfect. No matter how hard state child services try, there are always some who take kids for the money. Government money. But state services that embrace the *German Experiment* are allowing pedophiles to take kids for sex. As in state-sponsored child sex. This is indefensible.

One of the most insidious powers the media has is the power to ignore. They find it is necessary to do so when a cultural experiment goes off the rails. The media quietly ignores or censors hospital reports or law enforcement investigations of child sexual abuse at the hands of state-approved pedophiles. There are no media mention of child abuse with pedophile involvement. It is like nothing ever happened; the media treats these cases as if they do not exist. If anyone questions the program where children are handed over to rapacious pedophiles, they are branded a homophobe or a conspiracy theorist. The creator or manager of said programs get a pass instead of jailtime. States are gutting their pedophile and child trafficking laws. California Assembly Democrats continually block bills to make child trafficking a 'serious felony.'

Is there or is there not substantial evidence of foul play, child abuse, maybe even sex trafficking of children living in the homes of pedophiles who identify as gay men? Let's look at the recently reported outbreak in America of the sexually transmitted disease, Monkeypox. The media report Monkeypox infections of children could happen for a cascade of reasons. Don't believe their nonsense; a predatory pedophile has left evidence of a child sexual assault.

Real and foster parents protect their children from the range of viruses that impact children through government tested and approved vaccinations. Gay men who identify as phony or faux parents are more preoccupied with their sexual needs than with protecting children in their homes. Monkeypox lesions on children are evidence of active pedophilia and child sexual assault. The left and their friends in the media look the other way as long as the pedophile is satiated.

Why does the present culture allow a child to have two daddies? When did this happen? We didn't have this many crazy liberals when there were lunatic asylums. The left insists a question like that is not culturally sensitive, that even asking makes one a homophobe. No, it is what makes them a pedophile. *Why Little Johnny has Two Daddies* is a propagandic book that focuses more on Johnny than his two daddies. In the book, Johnny goes from being a sad little boy to a happy one, via the help of his new parents. One reviewer posted, "As long as a child is loved and cared for, this is all that really matters."

Where is *The New Yorker's* continuing investigation on the real story of why Johnny and the dog got Monkeypox from his two daddies? Why weren't the sexual predators charged with committing an obvious sex act with a child? Weren't these the children of two daddies? Close your eyes to the cultural rot. If a hospital doesn't report the sexual assault, they are complicit. Not only are they complicit, they are choosing politics over patient care. When did that become acceptable? The disgusting corrupt media ignoring the facts are just as guilty.

Any child showing up in an emergency room with Monkeypox sores around their anus is an unnecessary travesty, an uncalled-for injury, and an obvious evidentiary crime. The dirty little secret *The New Yorker* discovered is exactly what the East German Communists found — 100% of children placed in the homes of homosexual men *by the government* are sexually abused by the pedophiles of the house. Mentally deficient liberals are directly servicing the deviant sexual needs of pedophiles.

Rational and sane people cannot be anything but outraged at this situation. Is this an illegal and immoral scheme that uses the power of government to provide children to facilitate sex between minors and adults? Maybe there is a reason the FBI, who is becoming the enforcement arm of the Democrat Party, doesn't investigate these cases.

To be accurate, at first there was one, then two. Then there was a dog. Now America has nineteen children with Monkeypox. Those are the ones we know about. And no one has been charged with a crime.

Are recent reports of a same-sex Georgia couple charged with aggravated child molestation and sexual exploitation related to reports of children coming down with monkeypox? A months-long investigation has found that the horrific story of the gay couple allegedly sexually abusing their two adopted sons may be even worse than originally reported, as it now appears the young children may have been victims of a pedophile ring.

What do the governors of red states say when their state agencies place children in the homes of acknowledged homosexuals and pedophiles? Who is going to act? Why does the Democrat Party and their media insist adults having sex with children is a normal, natural thing? Cheering for the pedophile should be a crime with consequences.

This is not bipartisan; this is your Democrat Party today. It is pure evil. Pedophiles' atrocities are being ignored by the media, the police, and the FBI. Pedophiles are being subsidized by state and federal governments in the name of progressivism.

When elected, Rear Admiral McGee intends to take action on this issue immediately after inauguration. He'll make sexual assault on a child a federal offense, a class one felony, mandating chemical castration and a life prison sentence with no chance of parole. Aggravated sexual assault on a child, infecting a child with a sexually transmitted disease, or injuring a child during a sexual assault will be subject to the death penalty. And it will become Federal law that State governments will no longer be able to place foster children or orphans in the homes of single men, gay men or pedophiles.

And finally, Rear Admiral McGee will remove the *Diagnostic and Statistical Manual of Mental Disorders* from the purview of the American Psychiatric Association. The reporting and tracking of mental disorders will become a federal government reporting program, not to be influenced by activists or special interest groups.

CHAPTER 41

July 18, 2020

Nine men exited three vehicles. They wore dark ballcaps, polo shirts, and light jackets as they walked across the tarmac at the Tolbert Field Airport. They entered a pristine Douglas DC-3 in Pan American Airways livery and found a seat. The interior smelled of aviation gasoline.

One man said, "This thing scares me. I think this deserves hazardous duty pay."

Another one said, "Nice try. How do you think this thing got so old?"

Retired four-star general and Air Force fighter pilot, CIA Director Walter Todd, call sign *Magoo*, took the copilot position and assisted Duncan Hunter, call sign *Maverick*, in the pre-start duties of the old twin radial. While the powerplants were over eighty years old, the cockpit had completely modern flat panel displays and resembled the flight deck of the newest corporate jets. In-flight internet, a satphone, and a STU-III (Secure Telephone Unit) were available in the cabin. The flight plan listed Maine as the destination. *Magoo* selected the coordinates for Portland in the GPS. *Maverick* started the engines and made the required radio calls for permission to taxi.

Magoo asked, "What do these engines run on?"

Maverick responded, "If I hadn't taken the Mazibuike administration to court, they'd be running on 87 octane, car gas. Now the Three Rivers Refinery near Hondo again produces 115/145 octane for warbird engines, especially for these radials."

"I don't understand."

Over the Bose® headset, *Maverick* explained, "You know about Jimmy Doolittle; he was still in the Army reserves when he was hired to run Shell Oil Company's aviation department. Doolittle wanted aviation fuels with octane ratings of over 100 so engine designers could make higher performance engines with higher compression ratios. The aircraft that carried these advanced engines would have stunning performance, especially at higher altitudes where the air is very cold, and where enemy aircraft had a distinct disadvantage: they could not reach them. All a function of octane."

Magoo nodded, "I didn't know that. I flew jets."

Maverick said, "Liberals hate petroleum and they really hate gasoline, but if you want to see them melt down, mention *aviation* gasoline. They hate it because it won the big one. WWII."

"Seriously?"

"It is a secret that is rarely told. The first large-scale plant dedicated to producing higher octane fuel came online in 1940, and the British were able to change their aircraft engines to use the new fuel from America for the Battle of Britain. The boosted, meaning turbocharged, engine performance of the aircraft shocked the Germans. The speed of the Spitfire increased from 340 miles per hour in 1939 to 425 miles per hour in 1944. The normal avgas used by Germany throughout WWII was what they call B-4, which had an octane rating of 91/100. The Nazis were trying to catch up with experimental fuels having octane ratings as high as 150, but the allies destroyed the Nazi's refining capability, which prevented any use of the higher-octane avgas for Axis aircraft. Now, Mazibuike was all about global warming and hated gasoline of all shades."

"Shades?"

"Yeah, aviation fuels come in colors and 115/145 is dyed purple. Jet fuel is honey-colored."

Ground Control approved the DC-3 to taxi.

Maverick encouraged *Magoo* to program the throttles forward to get the big aircraft moving. On the taxiway, *Maverick* locked the tailwheel and *Magoo* slowly taxied the ancient aircraft to the end of the runway. Once there, *Maverick* unlocked the tailwheel and helped *Magoo* to position the DC-3 to the hold short line for engine run-ups. When they were given permission to takeoff, *Maverick* helped *Magoo* during the takeoff roll.

There were no *Tailwatchers* to record the event, which was the point of the exercise. This meant Russian-sponsored *Tailwatchers* wouldn't be interested in tracking the movement of the 80-year-old DC-3. *Maverick* said, "We want to prevent any potential *Tailwatcher* with a telephoto lens from identifying you and *Bullfrog* getting on or off the aircraft." He explained, "To avoid the tracking prowess of *Tailwatchers*, we operate our Gulfstreams from Hondo and this antique from our warbird restoration business in Elmira, New York. No *Tailwatchers*."

Two men from Todd's security detail and two men from McGee's candidate security team were trying to sleep in the rear-most seats, but were having difficulties. Two mechanics from Hunter's Quiet Aero Systems company were already fast asleep under sleep masks and noise-canceling headphones. Admiral Bill McGee, call sign *Bullfrog*, had found a comfortable seat in the front row of the cabin and pulled out the Donovan documents General Donovan's granddaughter had given him. He unsnapped the elastic band, opened the folder, and reviewed the contents. Loose documents were placed in the seat beside him.

There were thirty-four, eight-by-ten, faded photographs that looked to be from a memorandum of record or personal journal. A metal clip at the corner of the photos also affixed a three-by-five card labeled:

Carl Jung
Blue Book

The half inch thick blue leather-covered notebook appeared to be an actual Carl Jung notebook, not a replica or a photographic copy. The handwriting was the same as in the photographs. An old-style paper clip held a card and several dozen loose-leaf pages that appeared to have been cut from a diary or a journal.

McGee assumed Dr. McIntosh had affixed colorful modern two-inch-square sticky papers, dashed with notes, as academics are wont to do when analyzing a reference document. The words written on one sticky note piqued McGee's interest: *Charles Lindbergh notes*. He flipped through pages of Zeppelin and Nuremberg information that did not immediately interest him, until he came upon the Journal entry of July 30, 1936.

We got a late start on the 22ⁿᵈ and flew to Germany, with Anne as co-pilot. Upon landing, we were greeted by men who clicked their heels, snapped their arms in a Nazi salute, and barked, "Heil Hitler!" Anne found the salutes silly. "This raising of the arms business adds to the complications of life," she joked later in the day when we had a private moment. "It is done so often and takes so much time and room." I was reminded of Donovan's comments on Jung and how these men were conditioned to respond in only one way. And I could see it, now that I've had some training in what to look for. When I looked for it, I saw it everywhere.

For several days, we were the guests of Generalfeldmarschall Hermann Göring. I toured German airfields and airplane factories. I spent every day with Luftwaffe pilots, who not only invited me to inspect their planes but also allowed me to fly several. On July 28, Göring hosted a formal lunch for Anne and me at his Berlin mansion. We arrived in a black Mercedes escorted by motorcycles. Emmy Göring, the general's wife, greeted us wearing a green velvet dress decorated with a swastika made of diamonds set in a field of emeralds. Anne considered it gaudy. Then a door swung open and Göring came through dressed in a bright white suit garnished with gold braid. He was inebriated, but he wasn't dysfunctional or violent.

I had studied our benefactor. Göring was the second most powerful man in Nazi Germany, serving Adolf Hitler not only as Reichsminister of aviation, but as president of the Reichstag, the minister president of Prussia, and Reichsminister of forestry and the master of a hunting lodge. I knew he had been shot in the leg during Hitler's failed 1923 "Beer Hall Putsch" and had become addicted to morphine. He had an eye for aircraft performance and production details and fancied himself an artist. He said that he had designed a range of uniforms for Nazi soldiers, including the white suit he wore at the luncheon. Göring reeked of alcohol but was the perfect host. He escorted his guests – the Americans including Major Smith and several German aviation executives – into a huge, mirror lined dining room. We feasted on courses of Black Forest ham and Nuremberg bratwurst, each accompanied by an excellent wine.

The former fighter pilot eagerly questioned me about my adventures in the air and questioned my knowledge of aviation fuels until his wife scolded him. When Göring learned that we were now living in England, he invited us to move to Germany instead. It was troubling that Göring refused to believe that Anne served as my co-pilot. He even refused to discuss my friend Amelia Earhart. His only comment was "Stalin and Der Führer cannot believe America would allow women such freedoms. They have little desire for her to succeed in her around the world flight." I was unaware Stalin and Hitler were very much interested in aviation, or followed the goings on of women in aviation. Göring was adamant that women in aviation would always be limited to noncombat roles. He considered giving women such freedoms would be the death of America.

That evening, Göring showed many facets of his personality and the scope of his intellect. I was reminded of something Colonel Donovan said, and I recalled Göring could be magnetic, intelligent, and genial one second, and the next moment he could be vainglorious, frightening and grotesque. I wondered what category of personality disorder Jung would design for him.

McGee stopped and thumbed back through several pages and realized he had probably skipped the discussion on Jung. *Maybe I'll get back to it later….*

After lunch, Göring led us on a tour of his mansion. He pointed out paintings, statues, and tapestries he had – his words, "borrowed from museums." I was sickened by that. Then he took us to his office where he introduced Augie, a lion cub he had taken from the Berlin Zoo. Except for Emmy Göring, Anne and all the other women were noticeably frightened and kept their distance. He said, "I want you to see how nice my Augie is." The lion leaped into Göring's lap and began licking the general's face. Somebody burst out laughing. Apparently, the noise frightened Augie, because the startled lion let loose a flood of yellow urine all over that snow-white uniform!

Göring shoved the lion off his lap and jumped up, his face red with anger. His blue eyes were blazing as he stormed off to change clothes. Everyone else cleared out of the office.

I was left alone in the room. Papers were scattered all over the Generalfeldmarschall's desk. Many had red ink I believed could have been secret documents. But there was a device behind his desk, in an amber-colored wooden case, which looked like a typewriter. It had a Q W E R T Z U I O keyboard between round windows and slots for round posts, but the warning on the inside cover suggested it could be something important.

Zur Beachtung!

Beachte die Gebrauchsanleitung für die Chiffriermaschine

I believed it to be a cipher machine. I removed the hidden camera from my sleeve and cycled the camera through three cycles to capture what lay before me. I returned the camera to its hiding place. I was trembling and rushed to a chair at the far side of the office near the fireplace to steady my nerves.

McGee stared at the words. He knew a little German: *For your attention. Please observe the operating instructions of the cipher machine.*

McGee glanced into the cockpit; the pilots were doing pilot things. He returned to the file and thumbed through the photographs until he found three photos, one with a paper of detailed German instructions, one with the face of the cipher machine with three different keyboard indicators, and one of the outer wooden case. *Lindbergh had photographed the Nazi's Enigma Machine? When was this? 1936? Seriously?*

McGee put the photographs down for a moment to rub his eyes. He could not believe what he was seeing in black and white. He returned the photos to the file and went back to the journal page where *Göring* had been pissed on by a lion.

When Göring returned with the entourage, he wore golf knickers and reeked of cologne. I had moved to the fireplace and warmed my hands. I was clearly the focus of his interests, for he took me aside and said we need to go hunting. He said, "The sport of elites." I was confused; hunting? I was expecting to be shown rare shotguns but that did not occur. Göring wheeled from one topic to another.

Göring returned to his desk full of papers, found a file from a corner, and shoved it at me. It was a photo album, and each page contained a picture of a different military airfield. He said, "Here are our first 70." I nodded and commented favorably on the fine aircraft I had flown during the week. He showed me each airfield and commented on its status. One picture he momentarily flashed in front of my face he called their Fuels Research Facility.

I would be remiss not to point out Göring has an affinity for trains! A fighter pilot who loved trains. After the episode with the lion cub, he took us to a large room in the palace that could have been a ballroom in the past, but it was constructed to resemble a tiny town in the Alps. It had dozens of train bridges, tiny railway stations, waterfalls, and lakes. There were steam locomotives and double-deck trains. I had never seen anything like it. It was so complicated, with multiple levels and extensions. It filled the room. I saw the largess as the mark of a fanatic.

After playing with his trains for a half hour, Göring leaned into me and quipped that if I were interested in developing the greatest aircraft designs, he would show me an aircraft design that was "out of this world." I thought his choice of words was unusual and several of Göring's subordinates vigorously cautioned him not to reveal state secrets. It reminded me of all the documents scattered about his desk. As things happened, I did not have any time to photograph them.

Prior to our saying "Auf Wiedersehen" to the Görings, which all things being equal they were marvelous hosts, the Generalfeldmarschall introduced us to Hanna Reitsch, their most celebrated test pilot. We went to the front of the mansion where she demonstrated the Focke-Wulf Fw 61 helicopter. It was a fascinating capability, and Hanna Reitsch handled the machine expertly. But I was left believing Göring and possibly Hitler saw women pilots as expendable, since experimental aircraft were prone to failures and fatalities.

Journal entry of July 31, 1936.

I was certain I had photographed something of immense importance. I will call the contraption in the orange box 'the pumpkin.' It has dominated my mind ever since I saw it. I have seen nothing like the pumpkin, before or since.

McGee lifted his head up and uttered, *"Pumpkin?" You got to be shitting me.*

I knew warplanes were being built to fill those airfields. Where? Germany is a large country. This was the information Colonel Donovan and Major Smith wanted, not some mechanical contraption. I turned the film with the pumpkin over to Major Smith. I affixed my signature to a draft report on the Nazi air force and their ongoing fuel development efforts for the War Department. Major Smith concluded, and I concurred Germany had produced as many as 70 airfields and was "forging ahead of the United States in aeronautical research and fuel production facilities." Göring called the research the wunderwaffe, the wonder weapons.

The Nazis were building powerful in-line piston engines and aircraft with aerodynamic enhancements. The U.S. was still building bi-wing aircraft with complicated and under-powered radial engines. Rotary engines from the first German war were passé. I wondered how the Nazis could have made such leaps in logic and aircraft design in such a short time. I wondered how the Germans could develop such superior aircraft and propulsion systems. I was aware there had been an intellectual diaspora with scientists and mathematicians, primarily Jews, fleeing Germany and all of Europe. I also wondered what the men who were leaving Germany and Europe knew that I did not.

McGee paged ahead until he recognized the word *Hindenburg*. He stopped flipping and read: Journal entry: May 7, 1937 7:30 a.m.

The BBC announced that the airship Hindenburg was destroyed last night during its attempt to dock with its mooring mast at Naval Air Station Lakehurst in New Jersey. I sense the Hindenburg will be the last passenger aircraft of the world's first airline. I cannot help but think of my Atlantic crossing in the Graf Zeppelin two years past. The airships were the fastest way to cross the Atlantic, and they operated as safely as they could. As much as the Germans tried to assuage the public's concerns, hydrogen gas is not safe. Had the airship been filled with helium, there would not have been a fire.

Another of Roosevelt's advisors was proven correct; do not provide Germany with helium for any reason. Yet, I cannot but wonder "why now" and could there have been another reason for the tragedy? It seems to me the timing is off-putting. I know that accidents don't occur on any set schedule. After all the Carl Jung nonsense, I now question my thoughts. Yet with the Hindenburg, I have a strong feeling that all is not as it seems.

McGee filled his lungs and repositioned his feet. The next page started out with: Journal entry: July 6, 1937 7:30 a.m.

I received a telegram that on the second, my dearest friend Amelia Earhart disappeared over the Pacific. The newspaper confirms it. The Navy is searching for her, but the Pacific is massive and unforgiving. The world is tuned to the wireless for any news. I feel as though a part of me has broken off, and a lifeless, dead hole remains. Anne comforts me, as she knows Amelia was my friend and that pilots share a special bond in the dangers of flying. I should have died several times crossing the Atlantic, but by the grace of God, I am still alive and able to fly.

Two major disasters in aviation in two months. With war looming, I again ask and wonder "why now," and could there have been another reason for this latest tragedy? Were they truly accidents? Now, I can never be sure, but I see Donovan suggesting the beginning of a pattern, that unseen hands could have been responsible. We do not have the information we need to make an informed decision. But if you take that line of reasoning, you ask how. Suddenly, there seems to be other involute explanations.

Bullfrog thumbed through more pages of Lindbergh's journal and decided some pages were out of sequence. He scanned the pages to find where Lindbergh gained a spy camera. After dozens of pages of Jung discussions, McGee thought he had found what it was looking for in Donovan's personal notes. There were pages and an entry that made him stop and mutter, "*Holy Shit!*" *Well, we've come full circle, Mr. Lindbergh.*

I debated whether to tell Lindbergh the rest of it; the rest of Jung's research. It was probably enough for the evening. I raised a wine goblet to signal our mutual understanding and partnership. Lindbergh raised his in toast.

I said, "Charles, today in America, there is a whole world operating in the clandestine. America, coming out of the great war and this Great Depression, is not prepared for any of it. Jung and Goebbels are operating at ten-thousand feet, while our politicians are stuck at sea level."

"That's very good." Lindbergh smiled at the aviation terminology.

"Goebbels fully understands the psychology of totalitarianism. Hitler understands the potential of unrestricted, unrestrained human experimentation."

"And its unlimited potential."

I paused at the pilot's insightful comment. "The Nazis and the Soviets have spies and followers in American industries and factories and drug companies, stealing American secrets for the Nazis and the Soviets. They will stop at nothing to ensure their socialist and fascist philosophies win the battle for the American mind. It may take years for the United States to develop an offensive intelligence apparatus worthy of the task. American Democrats will undermine these efforts if they notice them, and Republicans will respond too slowly to these threats. And that's why I asked your help. We are the resistance. There will be more opportunities to serve the country."

Lindbergh said he would do whatever he could.

I thanked Colonel Lindbergh. I told him he could not appreciate how much his efforts have already helped the United States. At the Port of New York, as a valet took Lindbergh's luggage, a thin man on a Western Union messenger's bicycle asked if I was Colonel Donovan. He handed me a telegram. In the distance, church bells rang midnight. It was time for The Lone Eagle to embark.

Lindbergh asked how he would be able to contact me.

I don't know what possessed me to reach into my pocket and extract the prototype Minox camera. The only one I had. I said, "You won't. We may never see each other again. I have much to do here at home, and you must be careful with your family in Europe. But I want you to take this camera. I regret I have only one film canister. Hide these for your next trip to Germany, but keep them close to you. You cannot be caught with these in your possession. This camera may be helpful if you see something you have never seen before. Not pictures of aircraft, but something incredible."

I expected the U.S. Embassy would contact him soon. Likely a military attaché, like before.

I left him on the pier. The telegram I received notified me that there had been a theft of some new technologies. Engineering drawings of a radio-controlled aircraft.

McGee closed the file and shook his head. *Damn!*

CHAPTER 42

July 18, 2020

Maverick dialed their final destination into the ancient aircraft's ultra-modern navigation system. *Magoo* was surprised and said so. *Maverick* told *Magoo* that *Bullfrog* had given it to him: the former Loring Air Force Base. Upon landing, a group of seven was driven to a hangar. The QAS mechanics stayed behind to perform maintenance on the old *Gooney Bird* and to get it ready for the return trip.

Admiral McGee carried the Donovan file.

After they deplaned the aircraft, *Magoo* said, "I haven't been here before, but I know this was an old SAC base, Strategic Air Command base."

Maverick remained mum and nodded at the information. It was new ground for him too. The Air Force seemed to have hundreds of former bases where airmen flew the most technically advanced aircraft on the planet.

To a casual observer, the hangar was unremarkable and unguarded, but to the discerning eye of those in the intelligence community, it was a very remarkable structure that was heavily guarded. A security detail of men in black battle dress fatigues and fully automatic Colt M-4s were waiting inside. Todd, McGee, and Hunter were expected, and consistent with accessing top secret facilities, their clearances and biometrics had been forwarded over the intelligence community's secure internet. Todd's and McGee's security details remained with the local security force in the hangar.

McGee quietly led the men across the hangar and through several doors requiring access cards before turning to an elevator leading to underground floors. They switched to call signs by tacit agreement.

Maverick surmised, "I guess all these old SAC bases had underground facilities." *Now I know why Bullfrog used me to get here, but exactly what am I supposed to be doing? Why am I here? I thought they would discuss transitions.*

Magoo nodded, and *Bullfrog* said, "Not like this one." *You'll see why.*

They descended five floors. The bottom of the spartan operations complex was sterile, like the hallways of an abandoned hospital after someone pulled the fire alarm. *Bullfrog* used two electronic access cards to enter the right side of a pair of unmarked doors. The sound of heavy bolts slamming against stops, signaling they were open, reverberated in the outer chamber. Once *Bullfrog* switched the lights on, *Magoo* and *Maverick* were stunned at what was in the middle of the underground hangar.

Without ceremony, *Bullfrog* handed the electronic access cards to the new CIA Director. "*Magoo*, this is all yours now."

Magoo was shellshocked. "What is it?"

"This is one of five, and *what are they* is a more appropriate question," uttered the former CIA Director. "If you were to see these airborne, you would rightfully describe them as unidentified flying objects. We believe they may have been deep space probes. Technically, because this one has vestiges of wings, it has been called the *unknown aerodyne* since the late 1930s. We have four unknown *aerodynes* here; one is in another facility nearby. Of the five, three are virtually identical. This one, like the one in another part of the complex, is unique."

Maverick was drawn to the 37-foot aerodyne resting on an unremarkable marmoreal plinth that was a quarter of the length of the object. Wide-eyed, he moved cautiously around it, taking in its full length. Gently stoking the metal, he said, "This *blue* thing, this *aerodyne*, looks like it's made of titanium, but heat-treated titanium. *Magoo*, isn't it about half the size of an F-22? I also think you may have it upside down."

Magoo nodded and raised his eyes. *Bullfrog* turned sharply and asked, "Why would you say that?"

"It's sort of like the D-21 without the engine, and it sort of resembles today's hypersonic missiles in *Aviation Week & Space Technology*. This dorsal cavity along the centerline, I suppose, would be where you would find the intake; but there is no intake. On our hypersonic missiles, the intake would be ventral, on the belly. But what do I know? An hour ago, I thought these things were just fiction."

Magoo asked, "Where did you get this?"

Bullfrog said, "We took them from the Nazis during the final days of the war. *We* as in the OSS. And, the shape of this aerodyne was found in an Egyptian hieroglyph, a Sumerian glyph, and an Aztec carving."

Maverick continued to shake his head in wonder as he walked to view the aerodyne head-on. Using fighter pilot terminology and pointing he said, "When you view this *beak-to-beak*, that is very close to the headshot of the SR-71; that whole class of jets."

Magoo cautiously nodded. Was this some sort of intricate prank? He finally said, "Hooray for our side. What are they, really?"

Bullfrog offered, "We believe they are between ten thousand and a million-year-old interstellar probes. They could be derelicts. Could be space trash. The Nazis discovered this one and others, and used them to reverse engineer advanced observable aircraft. If you recall, they started the build-up of their aircraft in 1934 after Hitler took power. At that time, no one had anything more than biplanes. By the time the war started, their engineers had developed high-speed metal aircraft. As the war was ending, their engineers increased their understanding of the mathematics of aeronautics and were able to develop jets and rockets, and flying wings, and rocket-powered aircraft."

Maverick uttered, "*Die wunderwaffe*.... The wonder weapons."

Magoo added, "I thought V-1s and 2s were the wonder weapons. Buzz-bombs."

Maverick quipped, "This was in addition to stealing art work and the gold teeth of incarcerated Jews?"

Bullfrog ignored him.

Magoo asked, "They reverse engineered aircraft *aerodynamics* from this one aerodyne?"

Maverick said, "I'm thinking it gave a thousand engineers ideas on what was in the art of the possible. What would you do after a close encounter of the third kind? This is direct contact. Of course, governments and militaries would do the same thing, if they had the capability. Dump a 1,000 engineers on a problem." *Maverick* let out a Sidney Greenstreet signature chortle.

Bullfrog ignored *Maverick* for the moment, nodded, and said, "We have the documents and the history of their efforts. Somehow, I suspect the KGB has them too. The Soviets were alerted to their existence, but was probably hearsay, there is no evidence they got to see any part of these or the Nazi's research. When we took the aerodyne, we also took their documents. We think we got all of it, but you can never be sure."

After watching *Maverick* and *Magoo* run their hands over it, *Bullfrog* said, "There were others. It was obvious they learned something from each one. Now what did you think was so funny?"

Maverick grinned and asked, "Wasn't it George Bernard Shaw who said, 'The longer I live, the more convinced I am that other planets use this planet as a lunatic asylum?'"

It was hard to strike a jocoserious tone. *Magoo* shook his head in amusement, even though he was trying to be somber.

Maverick pointed at the cavity on the aerodyne, he said, "I love winning against bad guys. But I don't see a propulsion system on this one. This cavity cannot be an intake. Maybe the motor is missing."

Bullfrog offered, "You won't find one on this one. No one has. No one has been able to detect any seam to suggest it had been assembled. We had a few engineers scrutinize every inch of what we had on hand in the forties. This thing could be a two-stage system — one stage could be what you see here, the first stage that does all the headwork, while an attachment, the second stage, provided the propulsion. There were hundreds of speculations. But what we saw is that the guys from industry were not impressed, weren't convinced. They already had hundreds of drawings of new aircraft with *conventional* designs. Not to take anything away from the geniuses at Lockheed, like Kelly Johnson and Ben Rich, but once they saw the *blue*, they realized their minds had been locked into a paradigm of conventionality."

Bullfrog continued, "The *blue* helped them shake off conventional designs and conceive what was in the art of the possible. It encouraged the aircraft designers to take chances without worrying about P&L. Profit and Loss. The basic shape of the *blue*... aerodyne could be built with enough effort, but it would also need new thinking by the engine manufacturers, because no conventional engine would have been able to power what Kelly envisioned. Kelly thought he could build a radical jet, but it would have ended up as a very large paperweight, if not for General Electric's engines."

Maverick injected some detail, "They were conventional afterburning turbojets for take-off and acceleration to Mach 2 and then used permanent compressor bleed air to the afterburner above Mach 2. No one has used that concept since."

Magoo nodded.

Maverick continued, "Engine development and manufacturing technologies often lagged the new aircraft designs. Engines are many times more complicated than airframes. But you can see the obvious lineage of the ME 163 *Komet*, the ME-262 *Schwalbe*, Lockheed's *Blackbirds*.... And the X-15. Pete Knight, test pilot, astronaut, the fastest man that ever flew. Wore a Rolex Pepsi GMT Master. I can see where this one aerodyne could have influenced Messerschmitt's jets, all of Lockheed's low-observable aircraft designs, and the Mach 6.7 X-15."

Magoo offered, "This feels smoother than anything I've touched before."

Bullfrog nodded and said, "Lockheed Martin has built a recent secret test article that looks remarkably like this blue aerodyne, but it's wider, with functional wings, and like this, no tail."

Maverick said, "You certainly don't need a tail or wings to traverse space."

Bullfrog continued, "Some contractor took pictures of it with an illegal cell phone camera as the test article came off the tower at the Helendale radar cross-section test facility." *Bullfrog* extracted a photo from the Donovan file folder and offered it to the pilots. "Like that."

Maverick smiled. "It's virtually identical to the *blue* aerodyne—if you extend the wings. But it doesn't have the titanium heat treated blue color."

Magoo's whistle echoed in the white cavernous room. "It's remarkably…*stealthy* too. Like an F-22. But that color…."

Maverick saw the question on Todd's face, and he wasn't shy. "Director Todd, when you heat treat titanium to a specific temperature, it transitions from gray to purple to blue. Then when you allow it to cool, rapidly quench it, it stays blue. Unusual reaction of the metal. I don't know of another metal with the same properties. With superfast aircraft like the SR-71, Kelly Johnson had to engineer the titanium to heat up and expand during flight, sealing the fuel tanks. That's why that jet needed to be refueled after takeoff. But high heat-treated titanium, *blue* titanium doesn't expand when heated and I thought it would be easier to work with. This blue aerodyne looks more like it has the qualities of molten glass instead of heat treated, ultra-polished metal. Metal has pores. Nazi scientists may have thought it might be a metal-glass matrix if they were able to conceive of such a thing. And it looks like it would be inherently stealthy, although it makes me wonder why any advanced entity would need to build something stealthy to crisscross the universe. Unless the shape is what we consider low-observable technology, at our level of understanding."

The men were reflecting on *Maverick's* comment when *Bullfrog* pulled a marble from his pocket and showed his friends. He said, "Watch this." McGee stepped to the *blue* aerodyne and dropped the marble on the blue metal. The marble bounced to where McGee had dropped it.

Maverick and *Magoo* were stunned at the demonstration. They knew exactly what it meant. There should have been some degradation in the bounce; but the marble acted as if there were no energy dissipation or deteriorating effect of gravity.

Maverick touched the aerodyne and said, "Oh, *that* is some weird metal! I've seen nothing so bouncy. It looks like that would bounce forever! That is hard to believe."

Magoo concurred and shook his head in disbelief.

Bullfrog handed *Magoo* the marble and said, "When we were first able to analyze it, we thought there was a thin layer of amorphous metal on top."

Magoo inspected the marble and asked, "*Amorphous* metal?"

Maverick offered, "That just means the atoms of the metal don't form a regular lattice arrangement, it's not a rigid crystalline structure like what you'd find of elements on the periodic chart. If you were to look at it under an electron microscope, the atoms look random because it is an alloy."

Bullfrog nodded. "Theoretically, you can make any metal amorphous if you can cool it down enough. But if the metal isn't an alloy, then the atoms are all the same size. They fall into a regular lattice pattern. By creating an alloy of different size atoms, it's harder for the atoms to find a regular repeating lattice pattern, meaning, you don't have to cool it down so quickly during manufacture. For this alloy to achieve this smooth surface, scientists estimated it probably required a cooling rate of about one million Kelvin per second."

Magoo had heard the term but couldn't recall what a Kelvin was. He looked at *Maverick* for clarification.

Maverick read his face and said, "That is the base unit of thermodynamic temperature, equal in magnitude to the degree Celsius. If my engineering stuff is accurate, one Kelvin corresponds to a change of thermal energy of something like 1.38 times ten to the minus 23 joules."

Bullfrog said, "That is an unimaginable rate of cooling."

Magoo said, "Other-worldly."

Bullfrog said, "Yes. Our scientists had come up with an alloy of zirconium, beryllium, titanium, copper, and nickel. And in the right proportions, that alloy approached cooling at some fraction of a Kelvin per second."

Magoo said, "From one million to a fraction…."

Bullfrog said, "Yes. That alloy still formed an amorphous metal. And from my understanding, that is how you make *metallic glass*. So, like the surface of the aerodyne here, it was probably cooled, probably at one million Kelvin per second, and our very own F-22 at one Kelvin per second."

Maverick asked, "So, what you are saying is this is *metallic glass?*"

Bullfrog said, "Yes."

Magoo asked, "And the F-22 is…."

Bullfrog said, "Yes. Like the SR-71 was made of Russian titanium, the F-22's sheet metal is made of metallic glass. It physically acts like a metal but electronically, it acts likes glass and is totally transparent to radar. Instead of the metal reflecting radar waves, the radar absorption material is behind the metal. The stealth technology is literally baked into the cake. Our enemies can take all the pictures they want and build their version of our F-22, but they will not have a stealth jet. That is why the F-22 is the ultimate stealth aircraft."

Maverick said, "That's psyops."

A smiling *Bullfrog* said, "That it is."

CHAPTER 43

July 18, 2020

Magoo's jaw had dropped onto his shoes.

Bullfrog continued, "It looks and feels like, and can be shaped like a regular metal, but electronically it is transparent to a radar beam. It was created under one of our contracts in a special glass factory near Corning. When the metal was delivered to Lockheed's assembly plant in Ft. Worth, they treated it like it was aviation-grade aluminum. Was even marked as an alloy."

Magoo thought, But it was technically glass? I suppose you really can keep a secret from a general.

Bullfrog smiled, nodded, and returned the marble to a pocket. He continued, "Before we determined the *blue* was made of metallic glass, we tried to determine its radar cross-sectional (RCS) area. It has none. I read where Kelly Johnson asked, 'Why is this 10,000-year-old aerodyne perfectly stealthy in the radio or electromagnetic spectrum? Why is there no energy loss when you bounce a marble or a ball bearing on it? How is it possible that the shell appears to be frictionless?' No one had an answer. It was only in the last fifty years scientists figured out the mathematics. How to make a crude, but effective form of metallic glass."

Maverick and *Magoo* pondered the answer. *Maverick* was missing a connection.

Magoo, a lifelong pilot, wasn't knowledgeable in the manufacturing process or the metallurgical composition of the aircraft he flew. But he figured it out and said, "And, that's why we can't have any part of the F-22 fall into enemy hands. That's why it is so special that even our closest allies wanted them, but the U.S. was adamant:

these are only for the U.S. I thought I knew that jet forward and backwards. What an idiot."

Maverick noticed *Magoo* was visibly shaken and offered, "There have been hundreds of UFO sightings...."

Bullfrog shook his head, as if he dismissed the premise, and said, "Let me answer that this way. We know its RCS is virtually zero, but it is also stealthy *thermically.* It was buried for maybe ten thousand years, so no one had ever seen this one airborne. But unlike the others, you cannot detect this one with a FLIR; it immediately assumes ambient temperature. We tried to see if any part of it had a thermal differential, but it registers like nothing is there."

Maverick said, "We can see it in the visible spectrum, but it cannot be seen in the infrared? That's crazy. Kind of like the nanotechnology paint on the *Yo-Yo.*"

Magoo said, "It's a cloaking device!"

Maverick said, "Is it even blue?"

Bullfrog continued, "Our intel says the Russians claim to have one—we call it *'the red.'* If they do have one, we assume it's an unidentified triangular aerodyne, not a *'blue'* or a submersible—and we don't believe the Chinese have any. These have been in this building almost 75 years."

"The *blue* appears to have no propulsion system, which made no sense to any of the engineers who had access to it. The Nazi's pulled a damaged triangle aerodyne out of Mongolia and tried to dismantle it. The state of technology being what it was then, the Nazis didn't have the ability to copy or reverse engineer any part of it, but there was still some *technology transfer.* Those smaller probes had tiny nuclear power plants, and over time, they killed a lot of people."

Maverick thought, *Exposure to plutonium would have been lethal....*

Magoo said, "I just cannot get over this. This one looks like an elegantly sculpted piece of blown blue glass.... Not metal."

Then the obviousness struck *Maverick* like a bolt of lightning. He blurted out, "Was this *blue* aerodyne the origin of the *Tacit Blue* program?"

Maverick knew Lockheed Martin had created the stealthiest fighter aircraft in the world, beginning with the *Have Blue* test aircraft, and Northrop had built an odd bathtub shaped test aircraft. The people who classified those things and gave them program names called it *Tacit Blue*. From a technology transfer perspective, some things were making sense. *We have the blue one.... Engineers from Lockheed and Northrop got to look at the blue to see if they could reverse engineer some of the aerodynamics, like incremental technology transfer, thinking they could achieve a near zero cross-sectional area based on its shape. Their goal was to be invisible to Soviet radars.*

Bullfrog said, "During my inbrief with Director Lynche—who had been with the Agency for forty years—we knew from Nazi records, that Hitler sent teams all over the globe under the guise of finding religious icons. But they were really looking for UFO technology. In the late 1920s and 30s, German, Austrian, and European mathematicians and physicists were discovering all sorts of things. They conceived the atomic bomb and a quantum supersolid, *metallic hydrogen....* How to make a black hole.... On paper, of course."

Maverick asked, "Like the pellets we use in *my* jetpack?"

The comment shocked Director Todd. *"You have a jetpack?" Seriously?*

Maverick grinned like an old spy with a secret. "How do you think I got to the OSS soirée from Manassas?"

Magoo asked, "I'm sorry. What else do you do besides restore or refurbish warbirds?" McGee listened.

"We—*Bullfrog* and I—our main business has been to build airport security equipment, like bomb detection equipment in an x-ray machine and anti-drone countermeasures for airports. A bunch of other stuff. I have thirty or so patents which translates to a recurring funding stream for our projects. And, we make things quiet, convert high end cars, SUVs, and trucks and up armor them for the rich and famous and executives in government. Nazy and your limos came from our company. Donated. We also bulletproof cars for foreign diplomats and corporate CEOs. We have franchised a dozen specialty shops in liberal run cities just to armor police and sheriff's vehicles, regular production cars, and install machine gun horns."

"We also have a rapid prototyping and scientific capability in Texas. I suppose our place is nothing like the metallic glass capability in Corning. It used to be an Agency shell company. It was about to be closed, but I bought it and kept a couple hundred scientists and engineers employed. They normally chase government and classified contracts, and develop things for the IC, like the jetpack and light bending materials. They also developed micro batteries, bug-sized robots, and tiny quiet drones for classified contracts. Having fully cleared, polygraphed, former CIA employees is a national treasure. Now we have a couple of thousand."

Maverick could have listed more projects that had been developed in Texas, but he was mum on the *Ravens*.

Magoo thought, *Light bending materials and tiny quiet drones? Micro batteries and bug-sized robots?*

Bullfrog said, "And *we* have a training facility in Texas."

Maverick smiled at the comment. "Had. It's *Bullfrog's*, for services rendered."

Magoo was completely confused. The men grinned. Hunter had made the retired SEAL and former Naval War College classmate a very wealthy man. Like many of the former special operations warriors, McGee had been a contract security specialist for the CIA after retiring from the Navy. After saving Nazy's life, *Maverick* gave *Bullfrog* a new opportunity as the owner-operator of a law enforcement and special operations training facility near Hondo, Texas. The facility provided the nation's best live fire and combat pistol ranges, hostage rescue team training, and urban warfare settings in the country.

Magoo asked, "What do *they* do?"

Maverick nodded and said, "The companies and the training facility? Well, the Quiet Aero Systems laboratories in Fredericksburg produce quiet specialized flying machines for the IC and law enforcement. You've seen the *Yo-Yo*, of course. They're constantly improving the aircraft and the helmet with the best demonstrated and available technologies. QAS has developed everything from the jetpack to quiet drones. They developed battery powered, silent drones with cameras and lasers as ISR platforms for an Intelligence Advanced Research Projects Agency (IARPA) contract that the Agency did not buy."

Magoo was a bit confused. "Quiet drones?"

All focus on the aerodyne shifted to Quiet Aero Systems and their products. *Maverick* said, "Yes, sir. Our scientists and engineers developed sensors and software that continually monitor the amplitude of the frequency of the rotor blades — which is just complex noise which can be countered. We developed the tech to adjust rotor speeds some 100 times a second to send a reverse amplitude signal through speakers that cancels out the frequency modulated noise of the four rotors and any audible harmonics. The result was a first-generation flying machine that could operate a few feet from anyone without them even hearing it. They could feel the wind from the rotors, but they could not hear it. There have been other contracts. We're *Quiet* Aero Systems. The drones can be fitted with the smallest thermal imagers like FLIR, night vision systems, surveillance cameras, or laser designators. They can also be used for data relay. And, if they were scaled down a bit, they could be used for other things."

"Like what?" *Magoo* suddenly wanted to take back his question. He didn't want to know, but it was too late.

Maverick said, "Oh, like delivering payloads, performing special functions. We use one with UV-C LEDs to sterilize the interior of the jet when it's configured for renditions. But they can be made lethal too, depending on the size. From a larger drone, we've shot a pistol and fired a speargun, and a suicide drone delivered explosives to terrorists holed up in a hotel, by remote control."

Bullfrog said, "That was one of mine."

Magoo was speechless.

Maverick continued, "But the best part when you're hunting terrorists is that the smallest of these drones have facial recognition,

AI (Artificial intelligence) technology, and can be programmed to find a specific terrorist."

Magoo asked, "Yes, and…."

"Our labs in Texas developed fist-sized silent drones we call *BlackWings*. Short range loitering weapons. Toss them in the air to activate them. They don't have any of the skirr you would normally associate with spinning rotors. Continuous harmonic balancing cancels out noise propagation. When the *BlackWings* are in that hunter-killer mode, they're *stochastic*; they make quick random movements and can't be swatted out of the air. They can't be stopped. The AI makes them especially relentless. When loaded with a picture of a terrorist, the facial recognition software scans the faces of people in a crowd looking for a match. Once they have a perfect match, they are programmed to strike the forehead of the terrorist. That detonates a tiny shaped charge, which trephinates the skull and blows their brains out. The AI doesn't know of the explosive charge; it thinks it is just ramming a forehead as if it is playing a game of tag."

Magoo rolled his eyes and asked, "You mean…."

"When you train AI to do something, you have to be very careful." *Maverick* then shrugged and said, "All I really do is download the photograph of a terrorist's face. AI takes over. Sometimes, when I am over a target area, the target will not step outside into the night; they know what it takes to remain protected from satellites and *Predators*. Based on the best intel, I drop *BlackWings* where I think the terrorists are or should be. The short-range loitering capability either finds the terrorist and matches his face with the facial recognition software in the databank when he steps outside, or they don't. They are programmed to wait until they get a facial match. They can land on a powerline to recharge batteries." *Maverick* and *Bullfrog* nodded and bumped fists. *Magoo* shook his head in disbelief. *Bullfrog* said, "Tell him the rest of it." *Magoo* nodded and wanted to know.

Maverick reluctantly gave the Director a Cliff Notes version of what was probably the Agency's greatest surgical strike on a group of master terrorists. "You know we have had a hell of a time finding the murderers of our citizens abroad. There was Mohammed Ali Hammadi who bombed a TWA jet in 1985. Ahmed Jibril put the bomb aboard Pan Am 103 in 1988 that killed some Agency executives and my parents."

Parents? Magoo suddenly realized the finding and killing of the terrorists who killed his parents could be the reason Duncan became involved in the Agency's special access program.

Maverick continued, "Abdullah Ahmed Abdullah built the bombs that blew up the U.S. Embassies in Tanzania and Kenya in 1998. And in 1996, Ibrahim Salih Mohammed Al-Yacoub planned the Khobar Towers bombing. The intel had them hiding out in Iran. We couldn't touch them...."

Bullfrog interjected, "With conventional means."

Magoo nodded. *So, what was so unconventional?*

Maverick reflected on just how lucky he had been that night. "An internal defector's intel suggested Hammadi, al-Yacoub, Abdullah, and Jibril would attend a wedding in Iran. Knew the location and time. A gathering of the Islamic Underground's most successful killers of Americans. We couldn't be sure they would be there. I went in, assessed the situation. I might have been able to get one with the gun but it was an impossible situation to get all four. So, I dropped *BlackWings* loaded with their photos and shaped charges over the wedding party. It was a few months later that Al Jazeera reported the deaths of the four men. There were no published photos on-line. The Iranians took some and we got them. Four powder burns in the middle of four foreheads was secondary validation the *BlackWings* worked as advertised."

Magoo was dumbstruck. After a few seconds, he said, "The Air Force trained a drone with AI to kill targets, but it attacked the operator instead."

Maverick nodded. "I'm not surprised. Let me say, we broke the code on coding killer drones. You can't teach the AI to be *kamikazes*, but you can train them to attack a target. The shaped charge is always inserted into the drone when the drone is completely deenergized. It fires on contact, without the knowledge of the AI. If the AI thought it would be destroyed, it wouldn't do it. They think they are playing tag and that their mission is complete when it hits a forehead. And for some of those guys, it was the carbuncle in the middle of their forehead."

Magoo shook his head.

Maverick continued, "I'm not in the business of giving terrorists the benefit of doubt. The Geneva Convention does not apply. I'm in the business of finding and killing terrorists. If I have to lie to a murderous drone to kill an adversary, so be it. *BlackWings* are off the grid silent weapons."

Short range silent loitering weapons…. Magoo covered his mouth with his hand for a few seconds. Suddenly he understood. "That's one reason there are no terrorists left on the *Disposition Matrix*."

Bullfrog nodded.

Maverick exclaimed, "*Bingo!*"

"Remind me not to piss you off."

Maverick saluted *Magoo*. "Duly noted, good Sir." *Magoo, Maverick*, and *Bullfrog* laughed.

Bullfrog smiled, returned their focus to the topic, and continued. "These guys were discovering new things on paper, as the state of technology wouldn't allow their development. The state of our technology coming out of the depression was virtually nil. But the European physicists and mathematicians were on a roll, and they got the interest of the Nazi leadership. A group in Germany had early access to this *blue* aerodyne when it was brought in from Turkey. They were so shaken by what they saw they wrote letters asking President Roosevelt to intervene. They could see what it meant. They had a universal message: since all aerodynamics is simply math, if Hitler were to master the math behind the engineering of UFO technology, theoretically, he could build unstoppable aircraft that were impervious to bullets. He would overpower other nations and rule the world."

Magoo said, "Like *BlackWings*."

Nodding, *Maverick* continued with another train of thought, *That's what happened at the end of the war; that's also what they said of the Nazis mastering the dark side of propaganda. God, they were busy critters, and they knew how to leverage effort and take advantage of what they found. Maverick* suddenly had an incomplete thought; he pinched his nose and rubbed his eyes, trying to make the diaphanous thought gel into something complete. *Aeronautics, propaganda.... What else? Oh, yes. Medicine.*

Magoo asked, "Do we really know how old these are?"

Bullfrog said, "No. No one knows. The *blue* is just a reminder that there may be countless more of these that have never been seen by human eyes. We have no way of knowing when this aerodyne passed through the inner solar system. With this one, there's a good chance our species did not yet exist."

"Consensus is, that whatever they are, they were attached to something. They either ran out of fuel or were shut down at the end of their mission, whatever that may have been. When the Nazi's tried to cut into it to take a sample, they were repelled across the room. Instantaneous repulsive magnetic field. We tried to analyze the composition of it with a mass spectrometer. We needed just a sample, but we couldn't scrape off enough to get a test sample. The records reflect that as many as fifty people died trying to penetrate it. Eventually we found a non-destructive way to test it."

Magoo asked, "Where was this one found? You said Turkey?"

Bullfrog said, "In a Turkish field at a place called Göbekli Tepe. Today, it's a major archaeological site. It's been dated between 9,500 and 8,000 BC, and the site comprises many structures supported by massive stone pillars. Göbekli Tepe is unique because it has the world's oldest known stone pillars and carved megaliths. They have iconography of the aerodyne carved into the megaliths which has been carbon dated for a dozen millennia."

Bullfrog continued, "The Nazis were led to Göbekli Tepe by a shepherd. They followed a miles long goat trail until they saw part of it shining in the sun. When they got closer this stub of a wing was sticking out of the ground. The Nazis dug up the site and discovered one of the oldest religious sites. They brought the *blue* back to Germany via rail. A few years later they found the bell in Angkor Wat in Cambodia—a local steered them to it. It took the Nazis a year to extract it. We don't even know if it is an aerodyne. It's not aerodynamic. Could be a marker like the flag on the moon, only it's a monster. Could be autonomous systems designed to survive even if the senders were not able to communicate with it. There are physical limitations behind each of the objects; they would require hypothetical super-fast propulsion systems."

Maverick asked, "Like metallic hydrogen?"

McGee shut him down politely with a frown. *You're jumping ahead!* "*Mav*, I will get to that in a second. One of the triangles was found on a beach in Patagonia, and one just like it was found in Antarctica. A Nazi research vessel brought them back to Germany just before the war broke out."

And with the one from Mongolia, that makes five.... Maverick asked, "How did *we* get them here?"

Bullfrog said, "The bell, *die glocke*, was so huge, heavy, and clumsy that we didn't get it out of Belgium, where the Nazis were hiding it until after the war. Unlike the others, *die glocke* had thousands of markings which are still indecipherable. NSA has tried to crack the code, using their fastest computer and AI, but they cannot. That has led others to believe it has no aerodynamic component, but is simply a marker of some kind."

Magoo uttered, "A *marker*...?"

Maverick eyes flashed. "A *marker*...! That's wild."

Bullfrog said, "Wait, it gets better."

CHAPTER 44

July 18, 2020

Bullfrog continued, "Now, there is an interesting connection. Only a few people know of it. Between 1957 and 1968, scientists in industry were investigating the processes of creating new minerals that could act as *superconductors*, another concept at the time on paper. When scientists found heideite and brezinaite in a couple of meteorites, they noticed there was an intricate relationship between the proportion of iron, vanadium, and titanium atoms. These sulfides have no natural occurrence on Earth. These same minerals in the same proportions were unexpectedly found in *die glocke*."

Magoo asked, "Are these meteoritic minerals samples of extraterrestrial technosignatures?"

Maverick said, "I suppose it's entirely possible heideite and brezinaite occur naturally somewhere, but we'll never get E.T. to phone home and explain the minerals' presence in a meteor or a single monster of an aerodyne, that may not be an aerodyne."

Bullfrog and *Magoo* nodded. McGee said, "Scientists created heideite. We think *die glocke* is a giant superconductive antenna."

E.T., phone home! Maverick then asked, "Where is the bell?"

Bullfrog said, "It is in another part of the facility. It is too much of a pain to get to and we really don't have the time. This one is inert, the one everyone wanted to touch and measure and test. You can bounce a marble on it, just don't try and poke a hole in it."

Magoo said, "It's pretty incredible."

Bullfrog continued, "Stalin knew of the aerodynes' existence through their spies in Germany. He was not happy that he didn't have a single one. Their intelligence apparatus later claimed they had one, and we thought we would find it when the Soviet Union collapsed.

We sent teams into Moscow; we took their archives and intel documents. We discerned there were no records of the mythical *red*; they were probably lying. We haven't seen it, and it hasn't been described in any of their classified literature. But we gave it a placeholder and call it the *red*. You cannot trust the Reds on anything."

Magoo asked, "Did I understand you correctly, the *blue* aerodyne and the triangles did not have etchings or markings…."

Maverick asked, "You mean something like the Voyager spacecraft's markings on gold discs…. We came in peace for all mankind."

The men laughed. *Magoo* crossed his arms again as *Bullfrog* continued, "Exactly. No markings. And except for the bell, the Nazis had stored them in an underground hangar at an airfield near Ramstein. Once we knew where they were—which is a pretty incredible story in itself—Patton ensured the Soviets would not get to Ramstein until they were extracted."

Maverick asked, "I knew there were many reports of UFO lights over Germany; you know, military encounters with UFOs in World War II. What were they called, Foo Fighters?"

Magoo agreed, "Yeah, I read those old stories as a kid."

Bullfrog concurred. "Yes, Foo Fighters. There were hundreds of sightings, and no one knew what they were. We thought they might be probes trying to find their flying brothers. The Nazis had the aerodynes, but what they had and what their aircrews experienced seemed to be two entirely different things. We know the Nazis had hundreds of engineers pouring over the triangle aerodynes while trying to dissect the Foo Fighter phenomena."

Maverick said, "But they found no connection."

"None. Göring's general belief was the technology would save Hitler, even as the country was collapsing around them."

Bullfrog continued, "They had these remarkable aerodynes, but the Nazi's state of technology didn't allow for the rapid technology transfer of aeronautics. Hitler put 50,000 men on the program, but they were about as effective as a Girl Scout troop in a calculus class. We, I mean the OSS, were credited with locating them, and Army and Naval Intelligence got them out of the country. The Brits didn't know, but they and the Soviet leadership suspected."

Maverick asked sheepishly, "Not...."

Bullfrog smiled, shook his head, and replied. "No, Captain Ortiz wasn't involved in that caper, but there were other OSS Marines involved in their extraction."

Maverick said, "How did we get these here?"

Bullfrog sighed. "The short story is they were transported under the cover of darkness to Maine in the *Surcouf*."

Maverick shook his head and crossed his arms. "I'm not familiar." He looked at Todd. *Magoo* frowned and shook his head too.

"At the time it was the largest submarine. She was French, and she carried a waterproof hangar for a floatplane aft of the sail. It was just big enough for the *blue* aerodyne. *Surcouf* had been hiding out in Dominica, avoiding the Nazis, and needing repairs. Bill Donovan used OSS funds to repair her, and she sailed to Antwerp under a heavy U.S. convoy. Immediately after delivering her cargo to Portland, she was lost enroute back to the Caribbean Sea when she collided with her American freighter escort."

Maverick nodded. *Accidental or on purpose?*

Magoo recrossed his arms and asked, "So, did I understand you to say that the security surrounding the *blue* aerodyne and others was so poor that the scientists' access in Germany was virtually unfettered? And the scientists sent letters to President Roosevelt?"

Bullfrog nodded then consulted his gold Rolex. "We probably need to go. But I have one more thing. There have been over a hundred court cases about servicemen who have been killed by UFOs. The DOD has denied their death benefits. Reportedly, most of those deaths were from a UFO that was shot down in Germany. Troops approached the glowing thing, and when they got too close, they suffered traumatic brain injuries or died. The *blue* repelled and killed those who tried to analyze it. There was a researcher who was an expert in traumatic brain injuries; DOD contracted him years ago to study these injuries. He studied their brains."

Magoo asked, "What did he find?"

Maverick asked, "So either the Germans or the Americans shot it down, and it killed troops. What did they do then? How did they get it out?"

Bullfrog said, "The Air Force used a remote-control search and rescue helicopter. A *Husky*, I believe. And I have no idea where those things went. Maybe the Air Force Research Laboratory."

Maverick nodded and said, "Kaman's other intermesher." He smiled at a faraway thought and no one noticed.

That boy knows his aircraft.... Bullfrog smiled and said, "That's right. The brains under the microscope universally looked as if some unknown energy source had burned holes in the cerebellum." He turned and walked out of the room.

Maverick thought, *Like BlackWings!*

Magoo followed *Bullfrog*; *Maverick* stole one last look over his shoulder at the *blue. I think we are consentient that the aerodynes cannot be revealed to the Marxists, the Communists, the Democrats. But they know something is out there if troops are getting their brains fried by some unknown power source. That is info that cannot be suppressed or contained.*

Once topside and out of the hangar, the men found some weather had moved into the area. It wasn't raining heavily, but the drops came down in a steady mizzle that partially soaked their clothes before they could board the DC-3. As soon as they were airborne, *Bullfrog* wedged himself in the fold-out jump seat between the pilots' seats. He wore a headset; his voice filled the headsets of *Maverick* and *Magoo* with the contents of secret documents. "The damaged aerodyne the Nazis recovered in Mongolia had a tiny nuclear power plant. The Nazis didn't know what they were dealing with, and everyone who worked on it quickly came down with radiation sickness and died. Apparently, the nuclear power plant wasn't shielded adequately, probably because it didn't need to. The Nazis didn't have the technology to reverse engineer the very compact power plants, largely because they didn't understand how to make the main radioactive element, plutonium. And they never threw enough manpower on it. They didn't understand the inherent hazards of radioactive elements; they were inept at understanding nuclear energy."

Maverick quipped, "Probably because of all the physicists who left Germany."

Magoo asked, "Half-life of plutonium?"

Maverick knew but didn't interrupt. *Bullfrog* said, "Eight times ten to the seventh power. That's years."

Magoo said, "I remember from college chemistry that pure plutonium metal is silvery gray in appearance, but it glows red in the dark because it is *pyrophoric*."

Bullfrog said, "Whatever that means."

Maverick said, "It means it is liable to ignite spontaneously when exposed to air, like laptop batteries. But eight times ten to the seventh power, that's a long time. That's why they are in a different part of the complex. Probably heavily shielded, which is why we didn't get to see them."

Bullfrog said, "10-4, G.I. Dog." *That lad is so smart!*

Maverick asked, "Didn't the U.S. build a nuclear-powered bomber; after the war of course?"

Bullfrog said, "We reverse-engineered the technology for such an aircraft."

Magoo said, "That was before my time. I understand it was a colossal flop. The powerplant took up the whole aircraft. A bomber that couldn't carry a bomb. But we learned a lot as a proof-of-concept vehicle. And we've been shrinking the size of reactors ever since." *I still have difficulty believing the concept had been derived from UFO technologies from the 1940s.*

Maverick asked, "*Bullfrog*, you said there were documents…. Letters?"

He nodded. "Yes, Einstein's 1939 letter to President Roosevelt was written in consultation with Hungarian physicists Edward Teller and Eugene Wigner. They warned Germany was so preoccupied with conquest that they might develop atomic bombs. German physicists who didn't get out of the country understood the math, and they had a device on paper which they believed could transfer the technology sufficiently. The smart guys who got out in time suggested to the President that the United States should start its own nuclear program."

Magoo asked, "Who was this Wigner—I never heard of him."

Bullfrog said, "Brilliance that approached the level of Einstein. Einstein was in a class of his own. A *three-O-plus* IQ. As the discussions were going on about atomic energy, Eugene Wigner, the mathematician and physicist, predicted on paper the mathematics behind *metallic glass* as well as creating quantum supersolids, like *metallic hydrogen*, which he considered to be a highly efficient rocket propellant, with a theoretical specific impulse of 1700 seconds…."

Maverick said, "The book of the universe is written in the language of mathematics. Our most powerful chemical rocket propellants have a specific impulse of less than 500. For frame of reference, the Space Shuttle solid rocket boosters had a specific impulse of 250-300. 1700 seconds is probably unthinkable, unless you're a theoretical mathematician."

Bullfrog said, "Correct. To make it useable as a propellant, like for your jetpack, required eighty years of intense technological development. It provides several orders of magnitude greater performance boost over current propellants."

Maverick said, "And it works. Like the rocket fuel Bill Knight needed to become the fastest man in an X-15. The early jetpack had twenty seconds of useful fuel. There are some commercial jet-engine powered jetpacks; the Royal British Marines have used them to fly between ships. I think they last about five minutes, but their real endurance might be a secret. Even five minutes is probably an entirely bogus number. I can fly mine for over an hour at several thousand feet of altitude." Duncan unconsciously looked away, back to the instrument panel. *And the penultimate time I used it, I needed every second to kill the dude who had been targeting Nazy.*

Magoo shook his head in awe. He thought, *How do these guys know so much? I guess, Welcome to the intel community when info comes at you like a runaway freight train.*

Maverick smiled at his friend, "One last thing, and I only know enough to be dangerous, not like *Magoo,* who is an expert. The ideal photonic rocket, according to Wigner in the 1930s, would be powered by a quantum supersolid, such as metallic hydrogen and could have a specific impulse of over 30,000 and maybe even 30,000,000. In other words, if you were going to power something like the *blue* aerodyne between planets, you'd probably want a supersolid like metallic hydrogen to power a photonic rocket to the edge of the speed of light."

Bullfrog thrust out a belligerent lower lip as *Magoo* concurred. *Bullfrog* continued, "But what Einstein and Teller and Wigner and others understood was not only how to generate incredible yet theoretical specific impulse but also the level of effort needed to make them possible."

Magoo asked, "Level of effort?" He thought he knew what the term was, but he was unsure of its usage in the context.

Maverick offered, "If you needed to replace a runway at a base, you can get a guy with a pickaxe and a donkey, and it may take a few hundred years. Or you can throw hundreds of workers on the project and you can remove and replace 8,000 feet of concrete runway in 17 days. To replace a runway in 24 hours sounds impossible, and it may be, but at some point, there is a theoretical level of effort. There are limits. Speed of light. Calculus is all about limits."

Maverick paused and said, "Oppenheimer understood level of effort and limits. Much becomes obvious in hindsight; it is striking how in both physics and mathematics there is a lack of proportion between the level of effort needed to understand something for the first time and the simplicity and naturalness of the solution once all the required stages have been completed."

Bullfrog nodded. "What came out of all of those discussions in the 1930s was that the Nazis and Soviets grossly underestimated the challenge of nuclear power. With every leap in the level of technology, they only threw 20 to 30,000 people on the project. Half a million scientists and engineers were required for Oppenheimer and the Manhattan Project to develop the first atomic bombs. Y-12; Oak Ridge."

Maverick said, "Einstein, Teller, and Wigner knew what it would take to build a bomb. Based on Wigner's recommendations, the Manhattan Project was broken up into manageable parts." He unconsciously stroked his chin and repeated, "Level of effort. That was Oppenheimer's gift. That's why there were multiple sites doing different requirements." Then the incomplete thought that had been dancing in the back of Hunter's mind came into focus. His mind worked to form a coherent sentence.

Magoo chimed in, "But those were the early days when we learned how to develop and use nuclear power. We were in the pickaxe and donkey days. Now we have a better understanding of it all."

Maverick imperceptibly nodded and said, "It took us eighty years to develop the technology to go from Wigner's theoretical equations on a chalkboard to the process to create supersolids, like metallic glass for *RAPTORs*, and metallic hydrogen for pencil eraser sized pellets to power a jetpack. Where does Teller come in?"

Bullfrog said, "As I understand it, Einstein was into offensive and defensive nuclear power, not peaceful nuclear power like San Onofre; he conceived the idea and ran the math, scientists helped develop the tech and engineers did the work. Wigner was into theoretical elements used for construction and propulsion. Oppenheimer was the orchestra leader. Teller, who could see the bigger picture, was into national security. These were big brain guys."

Maverick stated, "They loved the United States. Freedom." There were nods and smiles. *All the great ones did.*

Magoo asked, "Big picture?"

"Big picture stuff. Nationally, globally. After Einstein's letter, Teller was still in Europe, and he led theoretical national security efforts. He and others corresponded directly with the President via our ambassadors in Europe. Hand-delivered letters in a diplomatic pouch were the only way to communicate with the President securely. The OSS hadn't been created yet, and as you know, it wasn't until 1947 that the CIA was established. When Teller, Wigner, and the others were once again given access to the *blue* aerodyne in Maine, they met and warned subsequent presidents privately...."

Maverick was suddenly concerned and interrupted, "...but not Mazibuike...."

Magoo thought, *Whoa! What? Why not Mazibuike?*

Bullfrog acknowledged and shook his head to confirm, "No, not Mazibuike. He was never informed. All Republican presidents were briefed on Teller's letter on UFO technology. UFOs are real, because this tiny cadre of mathematicians, physicists, and engineers had seen and studied the *blue* aerodyne and other probes in Germany and later in America. But the aerodynes also implicated that there were extraterrestrials someplace in the universe. Reverse engineering their aerodynamics or metals was possibly achievable, if an appropriate level of effort could be applied."

Maverick said, "So many aspects could benefit from technology transfer. Absolutely, it would require a massive level of effort." *And the left would find ways to abuse it.*

Bullfrog continued, "Yes. The question is how bad do you want it? How fast do you want it? Everything is a function of time and money. I think Teller was in his eighties when he pitched President Reagan's Strategic Defense Initiative. The left lambasted the President for it, so it didn't get all the funding, but it moved the technological needle. Wigner was the master of metals and propellants, but in the late 40s and fifties there were too many cooks in the kitchen who thought the promise of nuclear power was absolute. Metallic glass, metallic hydrogen, black holes, and other theoretical processes were too hard to do and were shelved for speed; supersonic and hypersonic research. Scientists needed TS clearances and polys. Quantum research also continued. We pursued uranium reactors when thorium reactors were called for. Democrats didn't want us anywhere near thorium or metallic glass or hydrogen."

Magoo said, "Level of effort. How bad do you want to play?"

Bullfrog continued, "Politics and big business too. Teller saw UFO technology in the hands of our adversaries as a major national security threat. Hitler thought he could build wonder jets and rule the world with them, if only he had the technology to exploit them. But the calculated level of effort required to do so was off the scale. The state of technology and the time to develop it was not on their side. They couldn't develop or build the engineering necessary to construct the new wonder weapons. We bombed them to the point where they could never achieve their goals."

Magoo said, "Like the fuels."

Maverick said, "Exactly like the fuels. Petroleum is God's gift to humanity."

Bullfrog continued, "I need to work that into my joke. The Democrats, who suspected what was going on, would never join the Republicans and the CIA to do what was necessary to make those technologies become part of America's technological arsenal. So, the CIA created front companies, research labs, under a university or friendly millionaire's organization. Make America strong, safe, secure. The three 'esses' Democrats and liberals hate. Going all the way back to 1947, President Truman said to Bill Donovan, 'There are some things you cannot tell liberals. They are totalitarian and will use any information they have against you.' He specifically meant the aerodynes. President Truman knew the left would have sold us out to the Russians."

Maverick said, "Democrat's screech 'we need to take your weapons to protect children from guns' while they also screech 'abort them, indoctrinate them, jab them, medicate them, mutilate them, sexualize them, sexually assault them, confuse them, traffic them, sell their body parts for bucks.' Democrats in Washington are psychopaths. President Truman was a Democrat who could see where his party was taking them; right off the cliff. Mental disorders are not stable and cannot keep secrets; he knew who he could trust." *They don't like to hear it, but liberalism, like sadism and pedophilia, is just another mental disorder on the spectrum. Simply, if you support any of the mental disorders, you are a mental disorder and cannot be trusted with secrets. Scorpii understood the connection and turned blackmailing pedophiles into selling secrets into an empire in Europe.*

Bullfrog grinned and nodded, "So, America picked up the experts and technology that the Nazis started in the field of aeronautics, metallurgy, rocketry, and propulsion. We have had research teams scouring the globe for UFO vehicles under the guise of medical, archeological, and geological survey teams."

Magoo said, "Makes sense." *But why not Mazibuike? What the hell did he do? I'll ask Maverick later.*

Maverick said, "So, we chased UFO technology. What happened to the Ministry of Propaganda? Mengele's boys? *Bullfrog*, you said we were in a psychological, a propaganda war."

Bullfrog said, "I'm shocked you heard anything I said. You mentally had your tongue halfway down Nazy's throat."

Maverick chortled. *Aeronautics, psychology, and medical.... Hmmm...* He offered to *Bullfrog*, "Once it was the Soviet Union who created an industry dedicated to stealing American aviation technological secrets; now it's the Democrats, Russians, and the Chinese. The Nazis, of course, were also into medical research."

Magoo mashed his lips. Now he was seeing the left's strategy to overcome the Agency's industrial security program and level of effort necessary to safeguard the nation's secrets.

Bullfrog nodded. "There were a lot of documents floating around Washington, and the industrial security program of the late 1940s wasn't like it is today. With no polygraphs, you couldn't even get close to true security. Once we learned how to keep the Soviet Union and the Chinese from getting our secrets, they changed tactics and infiltrated or bought their way into the Democrat Party in Washington to gain access to America's secrets. Alger Hiss is their hero. Some Democrats refuse to admit they've been infiltrated."

Magoo asked, "How is that possible?"

Without looking at the men, *Maverick* interjected, "Senators, Congressmen, and their staffs are bought off with Chinese money. There's a reason congresscritters go into Congress as paupers and come out as millionaires. This group is not polygraphed. Mazibuike staffed the cabinet with his buddies and like-minded people, political appointees who didn't require polygraphs. Guys like Scorpii enticed them to work for him for sex toys. There is nothing more useful to the left than a useful idiot."

Bullfrog chuckled and continued, "Yeah. That's basically it. The Democrat Party became a major target for infiltration, beginning with the Nazis and the Communist Party. The Soviets and the Chinese did what they could to infiltrate the government, and liberal billionaires like Scorpii bought off elected Democrats until the Chinese got into the act. Once those infiltrators were fully ensconced in the Congress, the Republican-led intelligence communities worked to keep secrets from them, because the Democrat Party in Washington could not be trusted if they were given access to intel. They would sell it or feed the communists across the pond with our secrets. Documents, processes, information. What they wanted were trade secrets. They'd get invites to Scorpii's hotels as compensation."

Bullfrog reiterated, "The Russians, the Chinese, Scorpii's billions, and with 3M's assistance, the Muslim Brotherhood infiltrated every aspect of the Democrat Party in Washington, the FBI, the DHS, and the media. They turned poor unpolygraphed Democrats with access to state secrets into millionaires, as long as they passed on the Nation's secrets to Moscow, Beijing, and the Muslim Brotherhood. When Democrats got wind of some of the old secret presidential correspondence, like that from Teller and Wigner, they demanded to become involved or they would leak it to the press. Some of it was leaked, but our folks in Maine know the game and are able to counter it effectively. There were closed-door discussions on congressional surveillance concerning the UFO issue."

Maverick asked, "When was this?"

Bullfrog replied, "Let's say these discussions came to a head in the Senate in early 1956. The specific point at issue wasn't whether UFOs were real or why couldn't Democrats see them. The debate was whether Congress should establish a standing Joint Committee on UFO Intelligence, similar to the Joint Committee on Atomic Energy. The Democrats suspected what we were wanting, the CIA handling the UFO intelligence programs exclusively. They wanted access to TS info they could leak. When people with polygraphs are managing a special access program, the left knows those things will always remain a secret program, and they—Democrats, lefties, commies—will have to find other ways to get to those secrets."

Which is why Mazibuike flooded the IC with his unpolygraphed lackeys when he could. Outflank the industrial security programs that protect our secrets with an executive order. Maverick sucked a little air and said, "The left cannot be trusted on anything. When Democrats are in power, they immediately want to know about UFOs and work to repeal the Second Amendment. They want access to everything without being polygraphed. Apparently, the polygraph and the Second Amendment are the gatekeepers." *Which is what Scorpii's gay and pedophile business around NATO installations was all about. If you can't infiltrate directly, set up a hotel to catch or photograph intelligence officers in flagrante dilecto with men or minors, and then blackmail the shit out of them. The left always finds a way. And we always must protect America from them. Our domestic enemies.*

Magoo's head was being whipsawed around. *They speak as if Democrats are evil; their polar opposite. There is no benefit of doubt. If you look at it that way, their way, things make sense.*

Bullfrog said, "True. They were terrified of the Agency and the polygraph and, of course, the Second Amendment, then and now. You see what happened when the President required the FBI to take polygraphs. None of their *Muslim Outreach* infiltrators could pass it. Mazibuike misused the power of his office to give them workarounds to avoid the polygraph. He called it *Muslim Outreach* instead of what it was: *Direct Islamic infiltration.* This created an avenue, if not a free pass, into the inner workings of the IC and the nation's secrets."

Maverick said, "When he was there.... I stopped that nonsense."

Magoo snapped his head to focus on *Maverick.*

Bullfrog smiled, nodded, and said, "You did, *Mav*. You struck a blow for freedom. That was the day you became a hero for the *Resistance*. I would have given you a medal."

Oh, wait! I did!

CHAPTER 45

July 18, 2020

Magoo was about to question McGee's assertion but held on. *Maverick stopped what? Maverick is a hero for the resistance? Why would Bullfrog give Maverick a medal? For what, exactly? Did I understand correctly, he stopped Mazibuike? As in….*

Bullfrog offered, "There are six things that Democrats have a visceral loathing for—the First and Second Amendments, the CIA's polygraph program, the *Diagnostic and Statistical Manual of Mental Disorders*, the Nuremberg Code, and the Natural Born Citizen clause of the Constitution. Some of these are unbreachable walls which prevent radical Dems from getting the keys to the kingdom. With Mazibuike, they thought they had overcome the Natural Born Citizen clause. They want foreigners running the country, but Alexander Hamilton nixed that idea. What they can't prohibit, they want to make mandatory. What is mandatory, they want to prohibit."

Maverick said, "Like the Nazis."

Bullfrog continued, "For years, Mazibuike allowed his hand-picked, politically appointed people to ignore the polygraph and get into the CIA. They didn't gain direct access to America's secrets, but it was a start. The communist left, the Islamic Underground, the Muslim Brotherhood are all big on incrementalism. The Democrats knew that if they could get their toe in the door, over time, they would get full access. They demeaned the effectiveness of the polygraph and generated nonsensical studies saying the polygraph was ineffective."

Maverick said, "Like the left generated nonsensical opinions saying the natural born citizen clause was discriminatory or invalid because it wasn't defined in the Constitution."

Bullfrog and *Magoo* said, "Exactly."

Maverick said to *Magoo*, "*Bullfrog* polygraphed the shit out of them."

Bullfrog smiled and said, "And let's not forget, Nazy was the secret weapon. The left ran spies to infiltrate the CIA or steal the contents of documents."

Maverick said, "*A la* Alger Hiss."

Magoo thought, *There it is again.* He still didn't know who Hiss was.

"But she knew who was bad, and who wasn't. One look and she knew if they were a patriot or a spy; a good guy or a domestic enemy. It was like she could see an evil aura about them."

Maverick said, "Like a magician who can tell instantly who can be hypnotized and who can't. That's my girl."

Magoo thought, *So Mazibuike allowed people access to the IC by simply making them unpolygraphable political appointees? Now I'm realizing, and Nazy had a sense who was an infiltrator and who was a patriot. Bullfrog, this is an incredible brief.*

Maverick continued, "So, there was a scission, but not formally. Republicans were the gatekeepers, and the Democrats were the foreigners the Founders warned us about: the domestic enemies, the dark state, the globalists. Or as God would say, *A place of balance.*"

They all laughed.

Magoo said, "I can see the CIA asserting that UFO intelligence and technologies be treated as double top secret so as not to allow any of the Democrats to have knowledge of it. I can see the left trying to make the UFO technology an unclassified program." Then he added, "Because Moscow would also have it."

Bullfrog replied, "And Beijing, and Al-Qaeda, and the Muslim Brotherhood. Thankfully they were stopped, at least for the moment. CIA and DOD argued we should not let our enemies know we possess those advanced technologies, and the CIA became the gatekeepers of the technology."

Bullfrog pointed at *Magoo* and said, "The Chinese have dutifully copied your F-22 from thousands of photographs...."

Maverick said, "Raw technology transfer, but no trade secrets. Their jet is a cardboard 3-D printed copy of the outside; not what's inside. They can run it across their radar test cell and never be able to figure it out."

Magoo acknowledged, recrossed his arms, and said, "Agreed. They do not have the intel on the materials or the processes used to make the jet unless they got it from the Russians. Even I didn't know what the jet was made of until today. I only knew it was a fifth-generation aircraft. With hundreds of advantages over last generation aircraft: stealth, sensors, survivability, and connectivity. It skipped two generations. There is nothing else like it on the planet. Now I know it's actually a *seventh-generation* aircraft—forty years ahead of anything because of aerodyne metallurgy perfected over the decades."

Bullfrog smiled, "So, we are using fragments of alien technology in our F-22s, and your boys in blue have no clue."

Magoo shook his head. *That is so true. Our job was to fly them. We did not need to know how the CIA intervened to make them.*

Holy shit! Did Mazibuike know the F-22 was a product of alien technology? *Maverick* shook his head and said, "Didn't the Air Force want to replace all F-15s with F-22s? That would have given us total worldwide air dominance with a snap of the fingers. We could have sent F-22s to destroy air bases in Moscow and Beijing, and there wouldn't have been anything they could do about it, but...."

Magoo whispered, "Mazibuike canceled the contract. We have fewer than two hundred."

Maverick commented, "Probably enough for us to protect the homeland. F-22s could have freed the billions under commie rule, but with only 200, that isn't possible. Level of effort equation."

Bullfrog and *Magoo* mashed their lips together. *So true!*

Magoo thought, *The Nazis thought they could dominate the air with UFO technology; now we have it. Our Air Force was poised to achieve total air dominance, but Mazibuike stopped production of the F-22 that would have given us that edge. Forever. Edward Teller would have said that guy was not on our side.*

Maverick smiled and said, "And he forced the Air Force to make plans to retire that jet. And he canceled the Space Shuttle contract and the replacement Presidential Helicopter contract. Unmanned *K-MAX* won awards from *Popular Science* and *Aviation Week & Space Technology*, but Mazibuike slowed us down to let the others catch up. Capitalism was on the march. We could have easily defeated the commies and the Islamic Underground, but he didn't want the U.S. to have any advantage over our enemies. Direct interference. True psychological operations from a master manipulator."

Magoo thought, *The Space Shuttle? Unmanned K-MAX? Stop production and early retire the F-22? Now I get it.*

Bullfrog said, "The Deputy Director of Plans, Richard Bissell, thought there should be a follow-on to the U-2, that there should be one more round of *Blackbird* aircraft before satellites made aircraft reconnaissance obsolete. The Agency created a dummy corporation to buy titanium from the Soviet Union so we could build the A-12 and SR-71. We didn't have sufficient quantities of Ti, so we tricked the *Reds* into selling theirs. We are still several generations ahead of anyone else in aircraft technology, and I'd like us to keep it that way."

Maverick said, "Their guys are trying to steal secrets for their industry." *We were able to collapse the Soviet economy and their aero industry. Maybe that set the Russians back decades. Maybe not.*

Magoo asked, "Is there a specific line item for the CIA's UFO intelligence budget?"

Bullfrog said, "No. That budget is concealed within various government departments, mainly Defense and DARPA. The average member of Congress does not know the size and scope of CIA UFO operations, which don't exist officially. But…."

Magoo asked, "But?"

Bullfrog said, "By adding an amendment to this year's defense bill, the Democratic House voted last week to fund the creation of a government system for reporting UFOs. The amendment would compel current and former defense and intelligence officials to reveal information about UAP reports. It's a backdoor way for Democrats to discover CIA UFO operations through DOD's budget."

Maverick playfully asked, "So, we have CIA UFO *operations?*"

Bullfrog, said, "Well, someone has to pay the rent on those buildings at Loring and Area 51."

The men laughed.

Bullfrog added, "*Magoo*, you'll see in the passdown book in your office safe that there is an executive special access program. All the appointing letters from Republican presidents are there. The Agency has a crew operating out of Loring who investigate UFO or UAP, unidentified aerial phenomena sightings, kind of like what Operation *Blue Book* did. They also provide disinformation to the public and Democrats in Congress on the existence of UFOs and UAPs. Standard stuff. Sometimes when we thought something was a UFO, the decision was made to disinform locally, inform headquarters, and censor any information for Democrats in Congress."

Magoo was startled, "Extraterrestrials?"

Bullfrog said, "I am not aware of any walking the planet. Einstein, Teller, and Wigner extrapolated their existence from the evidence they saw, the 10,000-year-old *uninhabited* aerodynes. We were able to keep them quiet by giving them money to research this stuff. Generally, those guys were not interested in politics."

Maverick said, "I know Operation *Paperclip* brought German scientists into the country. How was the technology brought in?"

Bullfrog said, "Fair question. But it is a two-parter. The Nazi's aeronautical documents flowed to the Air Documents Division T-2, Wright Field, Ohio. T-2 was the air technical intelligence division which later morphed into Air Branch."

Magoo said, "So these ancient probes from extinct civilizations are stored at Loring, but they work on the technology in Nevada?"

Bullfrog said, "That's really it. The CIA has investigating crews...." He made a gesture toward *Maverick*.

Maverick said, "Performing like aircraft accident investigators...."

Bullfrog said, "Exactly. We have polygraphed psyops crews whose sole job is to discredit sightings and disinform the public and Congress, if they have to. They investigate reported crashes and tracked down unidentified aerodyne incidents, even when they hide underwater. Nothing has actually popped up for years, but we maintain the capability. So, that is a unique special unit... just like the reverse engineering crews in Nevada, or Lockheed Martin *Skunk Works* in California, and Northrop too."

Magoo asked, "When you say 'discredit' do you mean like the characters in *Men in Black*?"

Bullfrog smiled and said, "Exactly, but not with the flashy thing. The basic premise is the same. Basic psyops. What is not widely known is that while the left has been able to dominate the social media companies, we've been able to infiltrate the executive offices of those same social media companies. Mazibuike got his lackeys in social media; our guys are in key positions. Now there are many social media executives who are former IC executives, SIS, department heads. Most are on our side, but there are still some who go rogue, censoring free speech. They are the latent lefties who become contributors for *Covert Action Magazine*, for example."

Bullfrog continued, "So, when there's been an event seen by many, our guys in Maine are trained to collect intelligence and information. They are masters of disguises and propaganda. They come into a suspected area secretly. They do not flash badges or credentials. The vast majority of sightings are still jets on final into a distant airport, murmurations of starlings, or tricksters flying kites or four-rotor drones with pen lasers. There hasn't been a triangle aerodyne seen in flight since the early forties. You and *Maverick* are two of only a handful of people who have seen them and know these relics exist."

Magoo squinted a bit. *How about the triangle shot down over Germany in the 70s? It was all over NATO. Was that real? Was that squelched?*

Maverick asked, "*Bullfrog*, I can understand briefing *Magoo*, but why me, why now?"

Bullfrog grinned, "I told you, *Maverick*, I plan to win this election, and you're going to be my National Security Advisor. There is no Plan B. By President Eisenhower's executive order, the NSA has to be briefed on all the capabilities of the country. I had to brief *Magoo* as the new CIA Director. And I briefed you as the future NSA. Kill two birds with one stone."

Magoo turned to *Maverick* and said with a huge grin, "I think I know what your next job is."

Bullfrog smiled. "One of the greatest challenges a president has is to nominate his staff. *Maverick's* recommendations were the best; President Hernandez said so. The think tank and party leaders' nominee recommendations to President Hernandez were horrible. Duncan has a gift of choosing well."

Maverick chuckled in a self-deprecating way, while *Magoo* smiled and nodded at the comment. *Yeah, that's right. I'm only in this job because of Maverick. I still feel like a duck out of water.*

Hunter was a known, thoughtful, trusted patriot and a member of the resistance. Lynche, McGee, Todd. All winners and patriots. The founding members of the new resistance who knew who was the domestic enemy of the country. The country benefitted from those assignments. The think tanks, which were actually Democrat Party front organizations, lost their power to influence the Executive Branch with the election of President Hernandez.

Maverick smiled at the inevitability of working for Bill. *I'll be out of the cockpit. How shallow I was to think the CIA just cleaned up when the shit hits the political fan, like it did with President Kennedy's girlfriend, what was her name? Mary Pinchot Meyer. Ah yes, she was murdered by the KGB to punish Kennedy's foray into the Bay of Pigs. The National Clandestine Service Director broke into her house, took her diary, and instructed the press to report the woman's death as an accident. Clean up and recovery. Additional duties of the senior intelligence service. I don't think this is the same CIA General Donovan expected it to be…but then again, maybe it is. I think he assumed patriots would always run the CIA; he probably never considered the Democrats in Washington were just undercover domestic terrorists with diagnosed and undiagnosed mental disorders.*

Magoo said, "And we're not Washington Democrats. I'm shocked at the number of scientists who knew about the UFO artifacts and metallic hydrogen that *Maverick* uses in his jetpack. *And that is what we know at our level.* I'm a little shocked we've been able to keep it away from the other side for so long. Who else knows?"

Bullfrog smirked and said, "Bill Donovan knew; Charles Lindbergh knew."

Maverick and *Magoo* were stunned, and looked at each other.

"And, Lindy took pictures of the *blue and* the Enigma machine in Göring's office."

Maverick and *Magoo* exclaimed simultaneously, *"What!?"*

Bullfrog chuckled, "Wait a second. It gets better. Not only did the *Lone Eagle* take pictures of the Enigma machine in Göring's office, he photographed *the operating instructions.* Donovan quietly fed the information to the Brits and Polish codebreakers who were able to help reverse engineer Enigma decryption techniques and equipment."

Maverick asked, incredulously, *"The Lone Eagle?"*

Bullfrog said, *"The Lone Eagle."*

Magoo asked, "How was that possible?"

Bullfrog said, "He used Donovan's personal Minox prototype camera."

Maverick said, "You know, that makes Lindy the greatest spy who wasn't a spy. Hundreds of people died trying to get that info.'

Magoo said, *"The Lone Eagle."*

Bullfrog nodded and said, "Charles Lindbergh."

CHAPTER 46

July 18, 2020

Bullfrog smiled and explained, "So, the other night when Donovan's granddaughter gave me that file, it was papers from the general's safe; an incredible treasure trove of intel history."

Maverick asked, "Like?"

"There were pages of journal entries from Charles Lindbergh's diary. A book of research notes from Carl Jung. Stuff the General wanted to keep under lock and key. It was too weird to share in the 30s and 40s."

Maverick had a way of cutting to the chase and asked, "*Seriously? Are you saying Donovan ran Lindbergh* before there was an OSS?"

Bullfrog asked, "Didn't Greg Lynche essentially run you when you were on active duty? Then later as a Border Patrol and Air Force civilian? Even before he got the *Wraith* contract?"

Magoo was instantly shocked.

Maverick smiled, heaved a sigh of acknowledgment, and nodded.

Magoo asked, "How, pray, tell?"

Bullfrog said, "You met Dory. Colonel Eastwood. *Maverick*, correct me if I'm wrong. When Eastwood was on active duty and working for the NSA out of the White House, someone from Langley asked him if he knew anyone who played racquetball." McGee gestured at *Maverick*. "I guess you were a general's aide at the time, and I suppose that whenever you came to Washington, you played racquetball at the POAC, the Pentagon Officer's Athletic Club. The word was that you beat the snot out of everyone when you were there. Eastwood had seen you, so he said he knew of some Marine who could fit the bill nicely. He found out who you were, F-4 pilot and multiple All Marine racquetball champ. Come to find out that Greg Lynche already had his eye on you, so when your name came up for a counternarcotics operation, Lynche gave the green light to use you instead of an Agency asset who could barely spell racquetball. You were a much better fit. Someone in the DO's office had heard that Pablo Escobar, the cocaine drug lord, loved to play racquetball, but he wasn't very good. The counterdrug taskforce wanted to see if they could get a tracking device on Escobar. I never heard what happened, but I think it was after a couple months had passed that Escobar was found and killed. *Mav*, you were just like Lindy; you had a special skillset the Agency needed for a special mission."

Maverick quipped, "How many guys can say they beat Pablo Escobar and lived to talk about it?"

Magoo asked, "How did you do it?"

"I got orders to represent the U.S. Racquetball team at the Pan Am games in Havana. My general was pissed—I guess someone at CMC told him the details. Before the games started, I was in a court by myself practicing when Pablo barged in and said, 'We have to play.' Long story, he said his name was Emilio, which I found out was actually his middle name. I showed him how to make his game better. He offered to buy everything in my bag, right down to my shoes. I said, no thank you. After the Pan Am games concluded, his men stopped me from getting on the plane, took my bag, and gave me $10,000 cash. Like the magic was in my bag, not from thousands of hours getting my ass beat. The tracking devices were in the bag or a ball or racquet—I never knew. Something S&T had come up with that they never shared with me. I had signed an NDA; I read about Escobar being killed after I retired. My general knew and gave me a medal before I left."

Bullfrog smiled. *Magoo* smiled and said, "That's simply amazing. *Mav*." The old general turned to *Bullfrog* and asked, "So, Donovan ran Lindbergh before there was an OSS?"

"Apparently."

"And he had pictures of the aerodyne and Göring's personal Enigma machine?"

Bullfrog pulled the old photographs of the aerodyne and the Enigma machine. "There's one reference of Göring getting pissed on by a lion cub and everyone rushing out of his office. Lindy was left alone in his office and snapped some pictures of it; as you can see, the case was open. There's no mention of how he got the pictures of the aerodyne, only that he was blindfolded until he saw it."

Magoo and *Maverick* found the story and the photographs incredibly interesting. They passed them back and forth to each other.

Bullfrog continued, "Hermann Göring tried multiple times to entice Lindbergh to come over to the Nazis. He promised to make Lindy part of the German air force high command. The Donovan file has documents which show Göring had visions of making Lindbergh either head of the German research and technical institute in order to develop a synthetic fuel that could withstand the higher compression ratios at high altitudes, or making him the head of German aircraft industry."

Bullfrog read the passage from Donovan's papers where he gave Lindbergh the camera prototype.

Magoo and *Maverick* just smiled.

Maverick said, "I read somewhere that Lindbergh had been to Germany a few times and had seen the Luftwaffe's planes fly with fuel-injected engines. They really didn't have the right fuels to defeat the U.S. and British aircraft."

Magoo nodded.

Bullfrog continued, "Lindbergh's journal details Göring blindfolded Lindy and took him on a circuitous route to a remote location where he showed Lindy the *blue* aerodyne. Göring claimed that only the Nazis possessed this 10,000-year-old UFO technology, and they were going to use it to dominate the skies over America and Britain. They would vanquish their enemies' ground forces. Blitzkrieg the planet. Hitler took the *blue* aerodyne as a sign that whoever built it was not only from a superior race, but that they were blonde hair, blue-eyed spacemen. The Aryan race were their descendants. Which was complete BS but made for great propaganda."

Maverick said, "And somehow, Lindy got the *blue's* picture."

Bullfrog said, "I know — it's incredible. And it looks remarkably like the photo of the Lockheed test article."

Maverick and *Magoo* shook their heads.

Bullfrog said, "To entice Lindbergh and his family to crossdeck to the winning side, Göring promised him a special position in the Luftwaffe. Lindbergh could develop new fuels, explore new aircraft designs; he could write his own ticket. Göring allowed Lindy to fly just about every cutting-edge airplane in the Luftwaffe's inventory, except for the wonder weapons. He gave Lindy medals and watches and paintings. Göring even proposed giving Lindbergh a huge villa and turning him on to *Ambrosia*. All the Nazi leadership were on *Ambrosia*."

Maverick smiled the smile of an old guy with an old secret.

Magoo was shocked. *Nazy just briefed me on Scorpii's business supplying the elites in Europe and American businessmen and politicians with Ambrosia!*

Already aware of the Nazi's and Scorpii's propensity for *Ambrosia,* *Maverick* said, "But in the end, the *Lone Eagle* rejected the killing of children, like his own, and chose America."

Bullfrog thought it was a poignant comment.

Still somewhat in shock, *Magoo* nodded.

Bullfrog also nodded and said, "In reality, Lindbergh was a pilot, not a scientist. He had been hurt badly when his child was kidnapped. R&D was not his bag, baby, and neither was the German's offer of *Ambrosia*. When the Germans gave him their best and final offer, he chose America. In the end, despite all of Göring's machinations to prevent its discovery, Lindbergh's sense of direction — even blindfolded — was so good that he knew where the *blue* aerodyne was hidden and got a picture of the *blue* on a plinth. He got the information and apparently the film canister to Donovan or most likely, the military attaché at the embassy, who then, years later, got the information to Patton. Patton kept the *Reds* at bay while his troops got the aerodynes off the continent. The OSS helped, but the Nazi's advanced technologies program was huge. Well advanced. Among others."

Maverick didn't like the way McGee said, "Among others." He recognized there were implied other advanced technologies programs. "Others, like what, exactly?"

Bullfrog answered, "Biology, medicine, and psychology. Donovan detailed they had 38,000 doctors working on biotechnologies, although they weren't called that then. Mengele's work. Goebbels was in charge of the Ministry of Propaganda. Probably another 30,000 psychologists. Now Dr. McIntosh had read and analyzed the file for years, likely as a lark, since intel has a shelf life. Lindbergh discovered, and McIntosh discerned, the root of the Nazi's ability to create troops who were virtual warrior machines. Seems Goebbels provided dead women…."

Maverick got it immediately and said, "It was an initiation rite. It completely *reprogrammed* their minds to do exactly what Hitler wanted."

Bullfrog said, "*Bingo.*"

Maverick said, "The Muslim Brotherhood does the same thing. Boko Haram. Nazy used that fleck of knowledge to interrogate al-Qaeda and the Taliban at GITMO. Shamed them to the point of despair and suicide. They knew they would not go to Paradise because of what they did to the dead. They were told that when they died, they would be buried with pigs and pig's blood. She was the ultimate bad cop; she broke them spiritually. Then the good cops came in to get whatever information was in their heads. After Nazy got through with them, they talked to cleanse their souls. We no longer needed to waterboard them. Intel is not a pretty game."

Magoo considered the information and said, "I'll bet Donovan was pleased with Lindy."

Bullfrog nodded and intoned, "But Lindbergh infuriated Roosevelt."

Now *Magoo* was confused. "Why was that?"

Bullfrog said, "He felt Charles Lindbergh could have been America's greatest imbedded spy at a time when America needed intelligence on the strides being made by the Nazi air force. The Nazi's, and Göring, the number two guy in Naziland, wanted credibility. Göring believed having Lindbergh on their side would give the Nazi's the credibility they sought on the world stage, without having to use propaganda to bludgeon their way across Europe. Propaganda can be very effective, but there is a limit to what it can do."

Bullfrog continued, "Roosevelt believed Lindbergh should have emigrated to Germany, renounced his citizenship, and continued to spy for us. Lindbergh refused to be an imbedded asset and Roosevelt never forgave him for walking away. Roosevelt perceived Lindbergh had a unique responsibility and solemn duty as an officer, especially in the lead up to war. Lindbergh viewed the request as an illegal order; FDR thought the *Lone Eagle* had turned chicken. But I believe Donovan knew how to play the president; he knew Lindbergh was a patriot and had been extremely effective as a spy, even though he hadn't expected him to be such a great spy. But there are limits to what can be achieved."

Maverick asked, "Like the time it takes to remove and replace a runway?" *Magoo* nodded.

"Donovan learned things he never dreamed of. He got the picture of the Enigma and the *blue*. Roosevelt didn't interfere with Donovan's schemes, so Donovan continued to run Lindy out of his own pocket. The man owned a Duesenberg during the Depression! Apparently, he did not share everything with Roosevelt."

Like the Nazi's other advanced technologies programs — biology, medicine, psychology, and propaganda. Maverick checked his thoughts and said, "Whatever Donovan had Lindy do, he had to know it was done for the good of the country." *Unlike that idiot D'Angelo, thinking Americans should give up their freedom for the good of the country. He did what he had to do to advance his agenda, not what was best for Americans. I really despise that guy.*

Magoo nodded and *Bullfrog* said, "Yes, sir. Like the number of aerodynes and where the Nazi's had hidden them. Göring's conclusion was the aerodynes were simply ancient unmanned probes. Donovan held on to that photo like a talisman. Hitler was convinced they could conquer the world with the technology they contained. Donovan didn't tell the President what Charles Lindbergh had done for America. Donovan considered Lindy one of the greatest spies for America."

Maverick was quicker than *Magoo*. "No shit!"

Bullfrog looked at the men and said, "He deserves a star on the wall." *Maverick* and *Magoo* agreed.

Magoo asked, "Is there more? It seems there has to be more to this story."

Bullfrog said, "There is more. Because we have the records, we know. It is a matter of history that there were several times over the years when the Nazis publicly and privately tried to recruit Lindbergh. Göring would show him their newest aircraft with some new UFO aeronautical technology derivative. He would put Lindbergh in the cockpit of some of them, like Messerschmitt's ME 163 *Komet*, which he sat in but did not fly. Lindbergh, who could barely maintain altitude and airspeed over the Atlantic, observed the aircraft's performance telemetry and had difficulty fathoming the ability and the speed of the rocket-powered aircraft. The *blue* probably shattered his paradigms."

"From what I saw in some of those special pages from Lindbergh's journal, there were moments. Moments where Göring was unguarded with Lindbergh. Moments when Göring tried to gain his total confidence. As a former fighter pilot, there were moments when Göring tried to impress Lindy, the most famous pilot at the time. Moments that show Göring and the Nazis were into everything. Göring thought he almost had Lindy's commitment. He bragged to Lindbergh that he had his own intelligence apparatus for all things aviation, and that the Luftwaffe conducted extensive intelligence operations against the Soviet Union and by extension, the United States."

Maverick inhaled and held his breath. *That's new! It's also obvious. I should have known that.*

Magoo asked, "Such as?"

Bullfrog sucked a lungful of air. "For starters, the official history is that the *Hindenburg* disaster was an accident, but according to Göring it was brought down by a drone. Göring's spies in Russia reported that Nikolai Ivanovich Yazhov, the head of the Soviet secret police, met with a group of Communist Party of America members who were visiting Moscow. One of them worked at a military testing field conducting aviation experiments in Dayton, Ohio...."

Maverick said, "Wright-Pat." *An early version of a BlackWing. Incredible.*

"... and he was able to steal the plans for the first small remote-control airplane and its controller, which looked like a rotary phone."

A rotary telephone. Oh yes. Now, I remember. Maverick asked sarcastically, "Mommy, what's that?"

Bullfrog dismissed the comment and continued, "Armed with the intel from Lindbergh, Donovan visited the military research facility at Wright Patterson, the Technical Data Laboratory. Its primary goal was to ensure the prevention of strategic, tactical, or technological surprise from any source. That's a quote."

Maverick repeated, "...or technological surprise from any source."

Bullfrog smiled. "I know what you're thinking, but I think this was before Donovan knew about any of the UFO improvements Lindbergh was seeing during his flights in new Nazi aircraft. Donovan may have suspected something. But when Lindy got the photos out of Germany, it was obvious then the Nazi's had UFO technologies on which to model their new generation of aircraft. But we don't have a good timeline and Donovan's file is not helpful in that area. Lindy dated his journal entries. Donovan did not."

"The folks at Wright Patterson did not know of those things yet. It is very likely they could not conceive of those things then. But they confirmed their security had been penetrated, that indeed Communists had stolen the designs for a remote-control airplane. Many of the component's schematics for the controller had also been stolen. Probably a more accurate assessment is that they were copied."

Magoo, said, "Why spend money and effort on R&D when you can just steal what you need?"

Maverick said, "The unofficial motto of the Russians and Chinese. That's also what Alger Hiss—KGB code name ABEL—did. He was a copy machine before there was Xerox."

Magoo nodded. *Now, I remember….*

Nodding, *Bullfrog* continued, "But as the Commies quietly celebrated the theft of the designs and schematics and their ability to build and test it, a member of the Communist Party of America in New Jersey flew the drone into the side of the *Hindenburg*. The drone penetrated the outer cover and set it on fire. That brought the zeppelin down. The little drone was consumed in the fire. For stealing the plans, for attacking the *Hindenburg*, for leaving no trace of the crime, for getting away without being discovered, and for staining the reputation of America, Stalin gave the thieving infiltrators awards for heroism."

Maverick said, "First generation *BlackWing*. And Stalin let them live." *Maverick* already knew the technicalities. *The drone was painted silver to match the color of the zeppelin. Göring knew, Lindbergh knew and recorded it, and Donovan researched the breach in security. That was new.*

Magoo was speechless. He knew the basics of the *Hindenburg* disaster from books and movies. He had seen the video archives but couldn't remember seeing another aircraft, however small, near the great zeppelin. But the zeppelin took up so much of the camera's viewfinder that something small could have easily slipped in behind the *Hindenburg's* programmed and well publicized clockwise turn so the swastikas on the airship's rudders would not be seen by non-European spectators on the ground. The airship's turns were predictable. Then a drone destroyed it.

Magoo vaguely remembered the reports that unexpectedly strong headwinds had put the airship hours behind schedule. Its landing at the U.S. Navy's largest airship facility in Lakehurst, New Jersey was expected to be delayed even further because of afternoon thunderstorms in the area. Advised of the poor, yet temporary weather at Lakehurst, the airship's captain diverted the *Hindenburg* over Manhattan Island to demonstrate the power and glory of the Nazi Party, making counterclockwise turns to emphasize the swastika on the tail, while waiting for the weather to clear at Lakehurst.

A Communist Party cell in New Jersey had received the plans for the remote-controlled airplane from another Communist Party cell in Ohio. Plans for the aircraft, plans for the electrical servos, plans for the remote controller. They built a working model, tested it, painted it silver, and on command, the tiny aircraft flew into the *Hindenburg* as it attempted to dock.

Magoo said, "I didn't know remote control airplanes were available or operational in 1937."

Bullfrog added, "Many didn't know. Part of General Donovan's papers contained sources reporting the first remote controlled airplane out of Wright-Pat flew in the early 1930s. They were carrying cameras three years later. The Army put explosives on some, making them the first cruise missiles. Hobby groups all along the Eastern seaboard began to spring up in the mid-to-late thirties. The first RC built in the U.S., the same type of unmanned aircraft that was used to bring down the *Hindenburg*, is on display at the Air Force Museum in Dayton, Ohio."

Maverick said, "I know. I've seen it. It's a little red aircraft. You can't miss it. I've seen it several times, and I've finally figured out why they painted it red."

Magoo stuttered, *"Red aircraft?"*

Maverick said, "To remind us a commie airplane achieved a kill over America. A red Communist *tool*. A silent weapon in a quiet war. Several years ago, Nazy learned all of this through another source. The Lindbergh-Donovan link is new. It is a secondary confirmation that the intel is absolutely true."

Against the hum and low vibration of the old airplane, *Magoo* asked, "What else was in those journal entries? Is that all of it?"

Director McGee shook his head and said, "According to Lindbergh's diary, Göring stated that Yazhov bragged he was actually the brains behind the effort to frame the United States for the destruction of the *Hindenburg* over American soil, and that fellow communists in the United States facilitated it all. Yazhov said Stalin also directed the Soviet Navy to bring down Amelia Earhart."

Chapter 47

July 18, 2020

Magoo slammed his eyes shut, mashed his brows together, and asked, "How was that possible?" He looked at *Maverick* for confirmation. *Maverick*'s frown and nod confirmed that he already knew. *Magoo* transitioned from astonished to perplexed.

Bullfrog said, "Göring's spy in the Soviet Union's secret police claimed that on orders from Stalin himself, a submarine was dispatched from Vladivostok to the South Pacific. It waited for the American aviatrix to resume her around the world record flight. It was publicized internationally that the U.S. Navy had established a runway and an omni-directional homing beacon on Howland Island, and that they provisioned the island with food and water, fuel and oil. The Navy didn't know when she would land and need the provisions, but they never expected problems in that remote part of the ocean. Apparently, a Soviet submarine landed at Howland at night, and Soviet Marines disabled the homing beacon. The sub moved away and got into position between her departure point of Papua, New Guinea, and her intended point of landing, Howland Island. The Soviet sub transmitted a bogus direction finding (DF) homing signal."

Of course! Magoo whispered, "They *spoofed* the signal! Now it all makes sense. Amelia didn't get lost; she was purposely taken off course…."

Maverick said, "Exactly, and in that part of the ocean south of Howland Island, there is nothing." *It was not the time to relate the rest of the story, that I found her flying boots in a harem in the Middle East, suggesting Amelia survived her ordeal at sea but did not survive being a white sex slave. Amelia and Lindy were close friends, and that might have turned*

Lindbergh from renouncing his U.S. citizenship. You just don't know about these things.

For the fourth time that evening, *Magoo* was speechless. He shook his head in disbelief. *How long has Maverick known this? Nazy?*

Bullfrog said, "There was much more in Donovan's papers. One of the most interesting stories was from Carl Jung. He recorded his thoughts to establish and record a baseline of basic psychological experiments. Jung recorded his 'visions', or 'fantasies,' or 'imaginations,' terms used by Jung, to describe his dark psychotic mental activities in black journals. It was him thinking the unthinkable. It was a blue leather-bound folio manuscript that recounted his psychological experiments, mind control experiments on individuals in groups. Those with behavioral and sexual disorders. Through his human experiments, he knew that there were several ways to control the masses using psychology. To induce a psychosis in a group, he would make them fearful. Once they were afraid of their position in life, Jung was able to get them to do incredible things, up to attempted murder. The personality disorders responded a certain way; the sexual disorders responded in a completely different way, every time. It was these group experiments on the normal and the mentally disturbed that worried Jung and reportedly frightened his friends. Donovan's file contained Jung's blue journal."

Maverick said, "I guess he stole it!"

Bullfrog nodded and concluded, "This is the prime reason Bill Donovan encouraged the OSS and subsequent CIA Directors to explore psychological experiments on groups. Basically, they continued Jung's secret work. And Jung also wanted to conduct ethical, open and transparent human experiments with biologicals. Donovan and the Agency couldn't do that, because we did not have the Nazi's biological research. But we could do research in the area of the psychology of groups."

Maverick snapped his fingers. His thought had been answered. "There it is. Validation. We don't have their biological research. And you don't have Mengele's papers on secret human experiments, but the CDC and the Army does."

Magoo asked, "What do you mean we don't have them?"

Bullfrog continued, "Here's what I know. We have — had — some, but the bulk of the Nazi's biomedical research became the purview of the Army when the OSS became the CIA. That's also when the CDC came into being. Originally the CDC was the Communicable Disease Center; now it's the Centers for Disease Control and Prevention. The Army had its own bioweapons labs, so all the Nazi's biological warfare and vaccine development research was transferred to them. And they probably had Nazi and Japanese scientists who continued their research."

Maverick said, "Dr. McIntosh said they did."

Magoo asked, "*Bullfrog*, you said we had some. Do we know what is in those? Did you say there were Nazi and Japanese scientists brought in?"

They were interrupted by a call from air traffic control directing *Maverick* to a lower altitude. He retarded the throttles, and the DC-3 descended. They'd be on the deck in a half-hour. He was busy in the cockpit, trimming the flight controls and the throttles. *Maverick* finally said, "What you are really talking about is the *Nuremberg Code*."

Bullfrog and *Magoo* looked at him for more.

Maverick rolled into professor mode. "Doctors were prescribing new treatments and therapeutics without testing, all to make a buck. Even today, testing and approval processes for safety and efficacy are lengthy and expensive. In response to the criticism of the *unethical* human experimentation that was going on in Germany, the Weimar Republic, that is Germany's government from 1919 to 1933, issued '*Guidelines for New Therapy and Human Experimentation.*' Those guidelines were based on noneconomic gain, of beneficence and nonmaleficence, and the legal doctrine of *informed consent*. They clearly distinguished the difference between therapeutic and nontherapeutic research. For therapeutic purposes, the guidelines allowed administration without consent only in dire situations. For nontherapeutic purposes, *human experimentation*, any administration of experimental drugs or procedures without consent was strictly forbidden. No one could conduct human experiments without attaining *voluntary informed consent.*"

Bullfrog said, "Nuremberg Code…. But that didn't happen until the war ended."

Maverick said, "Yes, but now you're jumping ahead. I think this is worth the wait. Dr. McIntosh was simply great. So, the guidelines for New Therapies and Human Experimentation passed by the Weimar Republic were immediately negated by Adolf Hitler in 1933 when he came into power. And I mean, the first hour of the first day he became chancellor, they were gone."

Maverick looked out the windscreen and continued monitoring the aircraft on autopilot. "I read that by 1942, the Nazi Party had over 38,000 German physicians carrying out human experiments, such as the Sterilization Law on incarcerated prisoners—meaning Jews, gypsies, Africans, communists, homosexuals, and an assortment of other undesirables under the Third Reich including the crippled, the old. They also used mental cases like trannies, transgenders, and pedophiles. Let me say here, Mengele created the first diagnostic and statistical database, which the Army found. The Army tracked mental and sexual disorders in the country for thirty-forty years, until they were forced to turn that research over to the nascent American Psychological Association. They collected stats in the *Diagnostic and Statistical Manual of Mental Disorders.*"

Bullfrog asked, "Seriously?"

Still looking forward, *Maverick* nodded and said, "Seriously. Forceable sterilizations was the most publicized procedure, but that was just a tiny part of their research."

Bullfrog said, "Of course, there were others."

Maverick said, "Remember level of effort? The Nazis had 38,000 doctors conducting unrestrained human experiments on six million test subjects. The Japanese had 10,000 docs conducting experiments on a million Chinese."

Unrestrained experiments on humans? Magoo said, "I don't need to know the specifics."

Bullfrog said, "So, you are saying there were official '*Guidelines for New Therapy and Human Experimentation*' until Hitler negated them. After the war, the Nuremberg trials of 1947 reinstituted ethical guidelines for human experimentation as elements of the Nuremberg Code? Okay, what am I missing? Are you saying the left today has negated the Nuremberg Code?"

Maverick said, "Today's left, yes, good sir. That's exactly what I'm saying. You can see it in what these idiots are doing. Look at the history of the left protesting the DSM; they started with homosexuals and now trying to normalize pedophilia. At what point does a homosexual become a pedophile? They couldn't protest the DSM when it was under the Army's control, but under the APA, the sexual activists could go wild and did. Now they are coming for children; they are conducting psychological warfare to groom children for sex with adults and worse. Child sex changes without parental consent. Negating parental rights. There are hundreds of examples in America of the left ignoring the *Nuremberg Code* and conducting human experiments in secret or without parents' consent."

Magoo said, "You're saying they have effectively negated the Nuremberg Code."

Maverick nodded.

Bullfrog said, "In the folder, Donovan had a tiny notebook. It looks to be private thoughts, but it could be he had heard of things and didn't have the documents. What he gained is probably a small fraction of what was going on. Anyway, there were three items. First, the Nazis had plans to achieve eternal life by continuously injecting the blood of children into themselves. But they didn't want the blood of Jews, so they stole non-Jewish children across Europe and harvested their blood and their organs. For research, for food for their elites. It was probably the first organized child trafficking program before Scorpii."

Magoo turned to McGee and mouthed, "*Seriously?*"

Bullfrog nodded. *Maverick* wasn't shocked. *Bullfrog* said, "Nazi researchers discovered that if they injected young blood into older mice, it had a massive rejuvenating effect. It seems Nazi leaders rejected the inevitability of death, so child sex trafficking wasn't only for sex, but for their blood." *And their organs…. And their flesh….*

Maverick asked, "What were the other things?"

Bullfrog said, "He summarized some of Jung's findings. Jung said populations break out into roughly three groups, about thirty percent each. One group can be easily hypnotized, the other group basically goes along with the hypnotized group. That's called *social policy*. The third group is indifferent. So, if you can hypnotize the one group with your BS you essentially have a majority when the middle third flows with the crowd."

Maverick asked, "That's ninety percent. What about the other ten?"

Bullfrog said, "I knew you would pick up on that. The other ten percent are leaders; left and right, about equally. Half are solid citizens, honest and trustworthy. The other half are crooked and dishonest; you couldn't trust them to watch your dog. Jung said the guys on the right make up a movement to promote community and family, while the left seeks to destroy them. Resistance versus totalitarians. See, you really are part of the *Resistance*."

Maverick said, "Which is why we are always at war with them. I can see it. And the last thing?"

Bullfrog looked at *Maverick* and said, "You won't believe it. On a single card Donovan jotted: *they are using silent weapons for a quiet war*."

Maverick snapped his head to *Bullfrog,* then returned his focus to piloting, scanning the instrument panel, shaking his head.

Magoo was confused. "What's that? I don't think I have ever heard of that before."

Bullfrog said, "I barely mentioned it at the OSS Society Dinner. *Maverick*, this is your area."

Magoo listened better this time.

Maverick exchanged a worrying glance with McGee. Then he nodded and said, "We have some time. My flying partner, when he was in the FBI, worked on translating the Muslim Brotherhood's *An Explanatory Memorandum.* That was their strategic plan to conquer the U.S.A. and North America, also known as Mazibuike's handbook on how to steal an election. Link Coffey came across an Arabic pamphlet entitled *Silent Weapons for Quiet Wars.* It was a former secret pamphlet, Army document, about social engineering or the automation of society on a national or worldwide scale. A German version with the same title was one of the documents Captain Peter Ortiz of the OSS brought back from Goebbels' Ministry of Propaganda."

Magoo said, "Okay…."

Maverick continued, "Most Americans have heard of Pavlov's dog. The dog was trained to respond to the sound of a bell that presaged the delivery of food. The dog was being conditioned to salivate on command. That's a mind control experiment. The different ways or specific words to control or manipulate the mind are *silent weapons.*"

Bullfrog said, "Even though Donovan found out about the psychological experiments, he probably didn't know they had been used for over a century. They were called the *silent weapons for quiet wars* by shrinks like Freud and Jung. Shrinks explored the use of specific words as tools to alter the mind or change one's way of thinking. For the left these tools were also weapons."

Maverick continued, "Which is one of the reasons AI is so dangerous, through the selection and manipulation of some words, people will kill themselves. Anyway, the silent weapons are the tools of propaganda or persuasions needed to conduct a political war. All of our adversaries know the United States cannot be defeated militarily, but through propaganda the U.S. can be destroyed culturally. It's the left's counterweight to a thousand F-22s. Once the foundations of American culture is demolished, the cohesive culture of our wonderful military will collapse. Then, when there is no one left to protect the sheep, the wolves will attack the flock. Remember, Mazibuike signed an executive order which allowed transgenders and transvestites into the military. When President Hernandez was sworn in, he immediately reversed Mazibuike's edict. The President knew exactly what he was doing."

Magoo said, "Yes, I remember that. I just thought it was the prerogatives of the executive. Democrats are into social engineering."

Maverick said, "Set them back decades. Democrats went thermonuclear. No one has ever asked why they are hellbent on these social engineering efforts. Do you really think they are benevolent? *Silent Weapons for Quiet Wars* is about social engineering on a national or worldwide scale. There's a reason they are called culture wars. That is their nirvana. This is where we are in the age of social media."

Bullfrog interrupted, "Greg Lynche and I had the Agency's security officer give a brief on the East German's *Disintegration Directive* for everyone with a blue or green badge. Social media is just an electronic form of the *Disintegration Directive*."

Maverick added, "Remember these guys still want to move your mind in another direction in order to control it. That is the essence of Orwell's *1984*. In the case of the East Germans, it was to compel the unbelievers to accept communism or die. If they lived, they could still be milked for taxes. If you're dead, nothing. The Democrats use the word *racism* or *racist* because they are the most effective of the silent weapons. But they also use another silent weapon against their enemies. In Europe, where there are few blacks, they use unfounded charges of pedophilia. With just a word, racist or pedophile, people recoil and run away. Physically, mentally."

Magoo said, "Three years in Europe, I can attest to that."

Bullfrog said, "Being labeled a racist today by the left in America is much like being labeled a witch during the Middle Ages. No evidence is required."

Maverick added, "They want to control you. That is why when the left couldn't make Mazibuike an eligible legitimate candidate for president, they and the media were forced to engage in dark psyops to get 3M elected."

Bullfrog continued, "The belligerent liberal mob."

BLM? Sure. Maverick said, "Always remember, you can't reason with these people; they have mental disorders." *But why do they have mental disorders? Hmmm….*

Bullfrog said, "Anyway, the social media giants are simply a Democrat propaganda tool to censor free speech. The government cannot do it legally, so social media does it for the left, in their disguise as a free service. There's your answer to the Democrat Party's Ministry of Propaganda — it's the social media giants and their media."

Maverick said, "Now, look at President Mazibuike's executive order allowing the government to 'help Americans make better decisions.' That's nothing more than saying, 'Trust us; allow us to do the thinking for you.' Psychological operations disguised as caring concern. There is so much more to this."

Magoo said, "That is hard to believe. A traitorous president."

Maverick said, "President Hernandez forced Europe to dismantle their clandestine pedophile infrastructure. The FBI, as a tool for the Democrat Party, protects child sex trafficking and pedophilia in America, and the Democrats protect the FBI, a compromised FBI."

Bullfrog said, "That will change when I'm President. President Hernandez set Europe's child sex trade back fifty years. I will crush it in America."

Maverick said, "Scorpii had built his empire on all forms of the child sex trade, catering to gay men from the aristocracy to…."

Suddenly aware of his place in history as the former SACEUR, *Magoo* cut him off. "That's why NATO's Secretary General committed suicide."

Maverick and *Bullfrog* were quiet for over a minute. McGee offered, "You should know by now that Nazy has Scorpii's library of videos."

Magoo said, "Yes. She briefed me."

Bullfrog continued, "If those videos were released to, say *Whistleblowers*, I think you'd see that some of the high and mighty aren't so high and mighty when they start jumping out of buildings."

Maverick said, "Those videos are like the *blue* aerodyne. Only a few people can be trusted to protect national secrets, even the ugly secrets.

President Hernandez was right to have Nazy keep those videos under lock and key. At some point they can be used as leverage. I suppose if a Democrat Attorney General ever became aware of them and got his hands on them, those videos would disappear. Leverage disappears. And the crazies on the left would be right back at it. Assaulting kids. But if we were to release them, there would be murder in the streets. As long as we have them, we have leverage."

Maverick said with a smile, "We *are* in the business of blackmail, just not officially."

Magoo shook his head and said, "Another silent weapon for the *Resistance*."

Maverick said, "It's not my call to release some of those tapes to *Whistleblowers*. Scorpii made thousands of tapes. Kept them in a vault."

Bullfrog said, "I certainly would, but *Magoo*, that's the President's and your call."

After scanning the instruments and adjusting pitch trim, *Maverick* nodded and said, "Then, look at how the left attacks the *Diagnostic and Statistical Manual of Mental Disorders* as the sick musings of demented psychiatrists who classify innocent people, stigmatizing them for no reason. That's one of the Big Lies. They don't think the DSM should be government policy, because to them it is nothing more than a research document, a spreadsheet and definitions of mental disorders, which they view as totally arbitrary. The left was able to terrorize the membership of the American Psychiatric Association into removing homosexuality in 1994...."

Magoo said, "Under the Arkansas president's reign of terror."

Maverick continued, "...and transvestitism and transgenderism were removed in 2012...."

Bullfrog said, "Under Mazibuike's reign of terror."

Maverick nodded. "And now these sick people who are no longer classified in the DSM declare themselves normal. They are the torpedo that is coming back around to kill us all. In other words, the left freed America's mental and sexual disorders to wreak ruin on the country. These people don't breed; they recruit, starting with kids."

Magoo said, "I can see how the *Nuremberg Code* flipped the lever from Nazi craziness back to the rational and ethical behavior. I don't understand…."

Maverick waved his hand. "It was never made a law or an amendment to the constitution. The *Nuremberg Code* was policy, and it was good policy until the left crashed the DSM."

Bullfrog said, "*Maverick,* are you suggesting the CDC and the FDA are leveraging their hatred of the *Nuremberg Code* to bypass it? That they will force Americans to submit to experimental drugs or sex changes without their consent, or in the case of children, their parent's consent? On the first hour of my first day, I'll make the *Nuremberg Code* an Executive Order and Congress will make it law. Maybe an amendment to the Constitution."

Maverick grinned. "I think you are almost there. It's not just experimental drugs or sex changes. It used to be against the law for pedophiles to be anywhere near a school. Now schools are hiring them, and teachers are grooming students to have sex with adults. Trannies or some other pedophilic sexual disorder are grooming kids to feel that they are trapped in another person's body, so they need surgical reassignment without parental consent. It is out of control. These mental cases are like terrorists; you cannot reason with them. The DSM needs to be a federal program, so sexual activists cannot manipulate favorable outcomes."

Magoo said, "You're saying it's not just people being forced to…."

Maverick paused long and hard. Another chord had been struck. He said, "Lefties here and abroad have effectively negated the *Nuremberg Code* and *parental consent.* Their goal is to legalize pedophilia. And probably necrophilia. The United Nations is laying the groundwork for defining pedophilia as a human right. They have used the silent weapons to great effect; they think they are very close to declaring victory in the culture wars. And, then they want to force experimental vaccines on us to control or kill us."

Bullfrog thought, *Gene therapy! The Iranians targeted vaccines to destroy Israel. Targeted vaccines to kill white and black men. I can't say that but I realize it is obvious to Duncan.*

Maverick said, "Remember, Iran tried to develop an ethnically cleansing bioweapon to use against Israel."

Magoo interrupted, "...teachers are grooming kids in school for pedophiles; trannies are claiming parents are hostile to kids who pretend to be *T. rex* or a dragon, or boys who want to play with dolls, or girls who want to throw a baseball. They convince them, they separate them from their parents, and they help them change their gender. All that crap. Holy crap. I never looked at it that way."

Maverick said, "The madness is spreading."

Bullfrog uttered, "Because of the death of the *Nuremberg Code*, I have a new topic for the campaign trail. We'll get the law changed."

Maverick said, "*Bullfrog*, you have to fix that."

"We, Kemosabe."

Maverick nodded and responded to another radio call. He added, "Also remember, many Democrat states are drastically reducing the penalties for illegal contact with minors. *The same process* will deny parental rights, thus allowing children to have gender affirming surgeries and have sex with adults. Eastwood highlighted that more kids are showing up in emergency rooms with Monkeypox. That is, at the very least, a symptom, and maybe evidence that government officials are providing children for gay men. Men who were taken off the DSM and as pedophiles should be in a cell."

Suddenly, *Bullfrog* and *Magoo* could see what *Maverick* saw. *Implications.*

Maverick said, "There is a vigorous debate in the medical establishment whether *informed consent* is an ethical obligation or a legal compulsion. The left's position is to deny both. Our stance is informed consent should be a federal law or a Constitutional amendment, just like the First and Second Amendments. I think, the government has to take the position of freedom; *informed consent* is freedom."

Bullfrog said, "You mentioned they want to force experimental vaccines on us to control or kill us."

Maverick caught his breath. "They need an excuse to say we are ill or have a virus and we have to get jabbed or we have a mental illness and can't be trusted to own a gun. D'Angelo ain't Willy Wonka. Dr. McIntosh said Dr. Science created vaccines that were bioweapons for viruses that didn't exist. President Hernandez fired D'Angelo when he told the people at the CDC, 'There is a strong likelihood that a coronavirus pandemic will strike the United States and crush the candidacy or the presidency of Bill McGee if he is elected.' D'Angelo was also heard to say, 'I guarantee it.'"

Magoo added, "Salvatore D'Angelo is also on record and on camera declaring Americans should give up individual freedom for the greater good of society."

Bullfrog said, "We are part of the herd they need to cull. But nothing is immediate. Starting with giving up parental rights for the greater good. The media never challenges these ridiculous statements."

Maverick said, "Yeah, well, the media ignored Dr. D'Angelo's other remarks that the *Right to informed consent is a dangerous idea that risks going viral and infecting the masses, so it must be disposed of carefully like all other hazardous materials.*"

Magoo said, "*Bullfrog*, I think you got the right guy for National Security Advisor."

Bullfrog said, "Even a blind squirrel finds a nut every once in a while."

"I resemble that remark!" *Maverick* always left them laughing.

They laughed at each other.

CHAPTER 48

July 18, 2020

Maverick said, "*Bullfrog*, while you were on the campaign trail and *Magoo* was being nominated to replace you, I heard something interesting. When your infiltrators on the personal security team for Scorpii and I flew out of Germany, they said the main event of the annual econ meeting in Cologne was a coronavirus pandemic simulation. Horst and Blohm were the heads of security for the hotel, and they knew what was going on. Key points, the specifics of the meeting were not shared on social media."

Magoo asked, "And…?"

Bullfrog said, "The Global Economic Forum and its backers seek to impose an extremely authoritarian agenda upon humans, under the guise of healing the planet from climate change. So, they ran a coronavirus pandemic simulation. *Maverick*, I hate it when you are right."

"You're welcome, Boss."

Bullfrog sighed, "We can't do anything about that now, but there were a couple of curious things in the Donovan file."

Maverick banked the aircraft until the runway was in sight. He lowered the flaps and landing gear and trimmed the aircraft for approach. He said, "We'll be on deck in three. We need to hurry."

Bullfrog said, "Donovan wrote that if they developed an intelligence agency, they would need the finest people in it. To create the best and most effective intelligence gathering apparatus in the free world, hiring would need to be extremely discriminating—spies and Democrats have no place in that work. Donovan knew of Jung's findings, so he knew that the people at any new intelligence agency could not possess mental or sexual disorders, that you would need the absolute fittest minds."

Maverick said, "Democrats oppose using 'merit' in federal personnel decisions; they want race-based decisions."

Bullfrog continued, "I'll kill that bullshit too. There has to be some kind of in-depth screening for mental disorders; selections should be based on merit. These people are ridiculous. Donovan said he couldn't let spies in, because an intel agency is where all the nation's secrets are. They would need comprehensive background investigations."

Maverick said, "And polys. We developed ways to identify the mental disorders at the Pentagon without polys because they didn't have access to classified info. And we kept them out of the militaries until Democratic presidents let them in. Russia and China don't have mental and sexual disorders in their militaries. The military is a meritocracy, not a mental institute—which is exactly what they are trying to make it. One of the reasons for tough training is that the mental disorders quit. Until *Don't Ask, Don't Tell*. They were poisoning DOD until President Hernandez repealed 3M's executive order. *Bullfrog*, you'll be busy on inauguration day."

Bullfrog smiled, "We will."

Maverick grinned knowing as the NSA, he would be busy too.

Bullfrog continued, "So, what do you think the Dems plan to do?"

Maverick said, "Led by Scorpii, the Global Economic Forum conducted a coronavirus pandemic simulation when you announced you were running for office. I think if their bug isn't already here, it will be soon. The media won't report on kids with Monkeypox, and they sure as hell won't report when an influenza-like bug comes across our shores, just in time for the election. My bet is that if they cannot wound, cripple, or kill you politically before the election, then they will go full on nuclear after you are elected. Maybe assault you with multiple pandemics. A tripledemic or more. They've tried to make Monkeypox a national pandemic."

Magoo turned and asked, "With what? How?"

Maverick said, "D'Angelo, Mr. Science, the infectious disease expert on HIV and AIDS. I'm sure he hates Bill with a passion."

Bullfrog was offended, "But I'm so loveable! Maybe I'm the wrong color."

Maverick deadpanned, "The problem is you're not *red!*"

Magoo grinned and said, "You have a point. *Maverick,* how will they do it?"

Maverick inhaled fully. "One minute. The FDA recently declared HIV men can start giving blood. In other words, contaminate the national blood supply."

Bullfrog said, "No way!"

Maverick said, "It's a fact, Jack. Look at the national crisis that would occur if everyone got vaccinated, let's say against a coronavirus, but the vax gave them HIV. Everyone would get AIDS. The vax was a bioweapon. The problem Dr. McIntosh found was that D'Angelo may have created a smorgasbord of bioweapons."

Magoo asked, "Are you serious?"

Washington Center gave *Maverick* approach instructions and a new frequency. *Magoo* dialed in the new frequency, and *Maverick* made the radio calls. He received clearance to land.

After contacting the airport's control tower, nothing more was said as *Maverick* expertly landed the old *Gooney Bird.*

On roll out, *Maverick* continued, "Americans believe their government is benign, that it is benevolent no matter which political party is in power. But they can be manipulated with targeted disinformation. Government offices lying to control the narrative. Americans are familiar with *inactivated* vaccines which are used for polio and influenza. They inactivate the germ, but it retains its ability to produce antibodies to fight future infections. Then there are the *attenuated* vaccines like those used for measles, mumps and rubella, as well as Monkeypox and chickenpox. They contain a weakened version of the virus to boost antibodies. Then there are the *viral vector* vaccines used for the really nasty ones like Ebola, which can only exist in certain locations, like the jungles of Sub-Saharan Africa. Those vaccines take a modified version of a different harmless virus to smuggle genetic instructions to the body's cells to make antibodies necessary to keep the Ebola virus from infecting people."

Looking through the windscreen *Magoo* couldn't see a thing and wondered how *Maverick* kept them on the runway. If *Maverick* wasn't concerned, he wouldn't be.

Bullfrog said, "Okay...."

Maverick said, "I was aware of an experimental vaccine technology with a twenty-year failure in the lab, but D'Angelo wants to use it on the upcoming pandemic. It's *gene therapy* that's called messenger RNA, or mRNA. It was supposed to deliver instructions to build the spike protein of a coronavirus to evoke antibodies. Dr. McIntosh said it is actually a bioweapon."

Magoo asked, "A bioweapon?"

Bullfrog was suddenly concerned. "In theory?"

Maverick continued, "Yeah, in theory, on paper, open-source, it was marketed as being great. Dr. McIntosh said D'Angelo actually created a bioweapon and hid it from regulators. Had a university patent it. The literature said that in over twenty years of testing, it killed all the lab animals. From mice to monkeys. They've spent billions on it. The FDA would never give approval to anything that acted as a bioweapon."

Bullfrog asked, "It killed *all* the lab rats?"

Maverick said, "The CDC leaked a bogus failure rate. Ft. Detrick has a disinformation directorate. Dr. McIntosh said killing all the lab animals is what bioweapons are supposed to do. I know some of it but not all of it. Dr. McIntosh was all over it and was shitcanned by D'Angelo for calling him out on it. I think we need her to talk to the President or something."

When *Maverick* turned off onto a taxiway, *Bullfrog* and *Magoo* acknowledged the perfect landing and *Maverick's* analysis with nods. The control tower told *Maverick* to hold his position on the turnoff until a departing aircraft passed, then to contact Ground Control.

"Ground Control, Pan Am one-one-seven antique, clear of the active."

A moment passed when *Magoo* turned over his shoulder, looked the sleeping men in the rear, and asked, "*Bullfrog*, Did we actually kill Kennedy?"

CHAPTER 49

July 18, 2020

Maverick looked at the CIA Director incredulously.

There was an increasing crescendo to the former CIA Director's nodding until McGee found the right words. "Yeah, but not in the way it's been portrayed. It's a long story."

Maverick spoke into the radio, "Tower, Pan Am one-one-seven antique request to hold position. I'll call when I can taxi."

"Pan Am one-one-seven antique, are you experiencing difficulties?"

"Tower, Pan Am one-one-seven antique, we're checking a couple of things out — I don't want to FOD your taxiway unnecessarily."

"Roger, Pan Am one-one-seven antique, there is no traffic, hold and advise when you are ready."

Maverick completely shut off the radio, turned to McGee and said, "We're listening."

Bullfrog said, "You know Nazy has Scorpii's papers, and we can now show that Scorpii was one of the kids Goebbels tried to program to kill FDR, Churchill, and Stalin."

Magoo asked, "Like the *Manchurian Candidate*?"

"Kinda, but not exactly. No matter how much propaganda and programming the Nazis used on those kids, they couldn't find the magic words to turn one into an assassin. Enter Donovan's papers regarding Jung and Mengele's 38,000 Nazi doctors conducting human experiments on incarcerated Jews. Experimental inoculations. The Germans found one of their viruses showed the ability to alter a mouse's behavior. Their labs refined the virus so that it could turn a normal person into a mental disorder in a very short period."

Maverick and *Magoo* sat quietly as *Bullfrog* continued. "It was called *T-gondi*. *Toxoplasma gondi* is a parasite that altered behavior in ways that increased an infected rodent's chances of being preyed upon. The Nazis infected thousands at Buchenwald."

Where the Army liberated thousands of political prisoners, mentally ill, and sexual deviants who were human guinea pigs. Maverick asked, "When was this?"

Bullfrog continued, "Supposedly, about a year before the war ended."

Maverick said, "They could have been part of the experiments."

Bullfrog continued, "Yeah. And you know in July 1946, the Communicable Disease Center opened its doors in Atlanta, and the CIA was created as a part of the National Security Act of 1947. They virtually overlapped."

Magoo asked, "Why Atlanta?"

Bullfrog said, "Supposedly there weren't any offices available in Washington because of the war effort, but there were those in Congress who said any Communicable Disease Center had to be placed in another state. They didn't want a commie to bomb the place and potentially kill everyone in Washington with a bioweapon."

Magoo said, "Makes sense." *Maverick* made a hurry up motion to McGee. He wanted to get back on the radio.

Bullfrog said, "Most of the Nazi's biological research was captured by the Army and was sent to the new Communicable Disease Center. We received very little at McLean. But we started some psychological experiments using Goebbels' propaganda research coupled with Mengele's *T-gondi* research, which was actually Jung's research on ways to control groups that Jung described as noteworthy because *T-gondi* altered the mind, making some crazy and schizophrenic, but also making some recipients more susceptible to programming. It began as a covert funding mechanism for research and development of behavioral modification techniques. By the late 1950s, we thought we could turn a special operation soldier and make him, through infection, inoculation, and psychology, an assassin of the kind in the

Manchurian Candidate. To be an assassin but not really. Just to prove it could be done."

Maverick said, "Ok...."

Bullfrog continued, "Oswald was stationed at the Naval Air Facility Atsugi in 1957. The base had a facility where the Agency conducted psychedelic drug research. Many of the classified documents from the facility prove Oswald and others were subjects in the Agency's experiments."

Magoo asked incredulously, "You mean like easier to hypnotize?"

Bullfrog continued, "Exactly. So, the only man of the eight candidates to show a propensity for programming to become an assassin, was Oswald. Instead of just being a test subject, he was chosen to kill Castro. All new game. SAP. He had gone to Russia and married a Russian girl, all part of the cover in the plan to assassinate Castro. Then something went wrong; we lost contact with him. In the game of ultimate spycraft, the KGB snatched Oswald, fully *reprogrammed* him, and he was sent to go after Kennedy. A defector provided the details because the Agency didn't have a clue what had happened to him."

Maverick said, "He was that torpedo that was launched, but came back around and killed the crew that sent it out." The men nodded; they were familiar with one of the most dramatic scenes from *The Hunt for Red October*.

Bullfrog continued, "It was another way of saying Americans had a long way to go in the business of programming people with mind-altering viruses, vaccines that were actually bioweapons, and propaganda. Dem presidents shouldn't try to assassinate their competitors. They gave him a parasite that could have been controlled with anti-parasitics but their vaccine turbocharged his behaviors. *Politics is war by other means*. You can turn the radio back on."

Magoo was quiet. *Maverick* complied, said "Clausewitz" to his friends, squeezed the transmit key, and called Ground Control, "Ground, Pan Am one-one-seven antique, request taxi to the transient ramp." The men knew of Clausewitz's axiom from their military PME. (Professional Military Education).

"Pan Am one-one-seven antique, as requested, approved."

Maverick said into the microphone, "One-one-seven antique, roger." Once they were headed down the taxiway, *Maverick* locked the tailwheel. The twin-engine antique airplane slowly ambled straight down the taxiway with some light differential braking from *Maverick*, keeping the aircraft tracking down the middle of the taxiway's centerline that he could not see.

Maverick thought, *Nazy had briefed me on Oswald. They programmed an assassin, and that is probably why the rest of those docs will never be declassified. Means and methods that programmed Oswald to be a shooter. Of Castro! Of course, they were protecting him, just like Lynche and McGee have worked tirelessly to protect me from the domestic enemies who wish to expose the program and the guy who eliminates their terrorists overseas; whatever it takes to paint the Agency and the President in a good light. Oswald should not have been chosen as a lab rat. The CIA or any one of the Kennedys should not have tried to kill Castro.* Hunter shook his head. *It was a different period.*

As the DC-3 trundled slowly down the taxiway, *Maverick* finished his train of thought that the Donovan papers and Democrat sponsored bioweapons had hopefully run their course. When they approached the airport's parking area, he unlocked the tail wheel and slowed the aircraft's ground speed, anticipating the need to taxi the Pan Am bird through other parked aircraft to a location close to the line of government vehicles waiting for them. Directors' vehicles. But Ground Control intervened and asked *Maverick* to hold for a follow-me truck. Maverick responded, "Ground, Pan Am one-one-seven antique, off the taxiway and holding present position for a follow-me."

While waiting for Ground Control to dispatch someone to guide the fairly large ancient twin to its parking spot, *Maverick* asked *Bullfrog*, "Was there any information in Donovan's papers on vaccinating Nazis?"

Bullfrog asked, "Yes, why?"

Maverick said, "I'm thinking they might have infected the troops with *T-gondi* or a variant, inoculated them, and then programmed the range of personality disorders—paranoid, schizoid, borderline, histrionic, antisocial, avoidant, abusive, obsessive-compulsive—to be warriors."

The follow-me truck took them to the location on the Tolbert Field Airport where the black government limousines awaited. *Maverick* shut down the engines. The door opened, and all the men deplaned the *Gooney Bird*. Black Suburbans and Escalades repositioned a car length away and perpendicular from the wingtip of the DC-3.

The QAS mechanics noted the black vehicles and began securing the DC-3. They inserted landing gear pins on long red REMOVE BEFORE FLIGHT streamers, intake and pitot covers, and installed battens to protect the flight controls from being tossed about if there was any wind later. They buttoned-up the DC-3 for the night.

Maverick's Blackberry buzzed. A text message from Nazy. She was running late. Hunter's thoughts and focus were interrupted when *Bullfrog* tried to give him something.

Bill McGee finally got *Maverick's* attention and handed the Donovan file to him. He told *Maverick* to check out the top page before giving the complete file to Nazy. "I didn't have time to digest all of it. It's all fairly incredible. I saved the best for last."

Maverick thought, *There's more than just photos of the blue and the Enigma machine? T-gondi? Must ask Dr. McIntosh.*

Bullfrog and his security team turned and walked to the vehicles that would take McGee to Washington's National Airport, where one of *Maverick's* large corporate jets was waiting at the Signature executive terminal. The G-900 was the newest Gulfstream from the Savannah factory, powered by the latest generation of Rolls Royce BR750 turbofans. It had blue and gold stripes running down the length of the fuselage to reflect McGee's Naval service. It had once been the private aircraft of the world's richest man, Rho Schwartz Scorpii, until *Maverick* took it from him.

From National, *Tailwatchers* could track the Presidential candidate all they wanted.

CHAPTER 50

July 18, 2020

After McGee departed the airport, but before CIA Director Todd and *Maverick* could say their own goodbyes, their Blackberries buzzed with the ferocity of a dozen hornets. *Magoo* checked his classified email and motioned to *Maverick* to come closer, to compare notes, as the messages were received with some measure of synchronicity. Both devices shared the subject line: NOIWON ALERT. *Magoo* and *Maverick* looked at each other, then their eyes followed McGee as he and his campaign and security teams passed through the airport's security fence. The CIA Director opened the attached file on the Blackberry.

Maverick was tangentially familiar with the NOIWON (National Operational Intelligence Watch Officer's Network). It was a hotline that allowed the several WAOCs (Washington Area Operations Center) 24-hour alert centers to discuss things that go bump in the night. The CIA's Ops Center or Air Branch forwarded the message to Todd; as Director he got a copy of all the potentially HOT messages as a courtesy.

According to U.S. Central Command (CENTCOM), increased concerns about a potential Iranian attack against U.S. partners in the region necessitated the deployment of Alaska-based F-22 RAPTORs to the Middle East. During nighttime inflight refueling, one RAPTOR reportedly diverted to South Korea with mechanical problems. It was not heard from again. A letter to the Chief of Staff of the Air Force suggests the jet may have been diverted on purpose, and the aircraft may be in the hands of N. Korea, Russia, or China.

Maverick plunged a hand into his pocket and turned on his *Growler*. Just in case. *Recovering stolen jets—not my forte; not my problem. Not my job!* But he got that *feeling.* He saw nothing on *Magoo's* Blackberry screen that suggested he would be needed for another mission. A missing jet was an Air Force problem.

The text was just simple advisory intel from the Ops Center.

Hunter tried to convince himself, *I don't work the Orient. All my terrorists are in Africa, the Middle East and South America.* He wanted to get back to Nazy's message, but he didn't want to be rude. Maybe someone had just ruined Director Todd's day.

Hunter ruminated a bit. *It is a radical bit of news. It wasn't a question of who would steal an F-22, but who the hell would defect with an F-22! Oh yes! Shades of Viktor Belenko! Stole a FOXBAT, a MiG-25. The Soviet's newest jet used to intercept SR-71s. Landed in Japan. We took it apart. I'm sure the CIA was there. But an F-22? An American defector? A closet liberal Democrat? I won't say that's impossible…but that probably has to be an error. Lost his radios or something.* Then *Maverick* reconsidered: *the Air Force may have the greatest jets in the inventory, but they also have more than their share of leftist fruit loops. They even had a radical racist three-star who hated white men. Maybe he's a dark state defector.* He said, half-jokingly, "Maybe it's the *Red October*, only in reverse."

The Director of the CIA didn't immediately respond; he was deep in thought. Todd had seen these types of informative intel dispatches that originated from NOIWON when he was the head of SACEUR at NATO. *Foreign stations…embassies… often produce information on US citizens attempting to contact Russian and Chinese embassies while in foreign countries. Occasionally they are able to apprehend and return military personnel attempting to defect. Was this one of those? One that got away? With a jet!? An F-22? Jesus!* He frowned. "I assume we will provide all required support to the Pentagon." *I don't see this impacting us, but I need to talk to the DO and the Deputy; I need to get back to HQ. What capabilities do we have that could help? But first….* "*Maverick*, what did *Bullfrog* mean when he said you *stopped* Mazibuike?"

Maverick sighed; he looked to his left and right, stuffed his hands in his coat pockets, disconnected and deposited the cellphone, and withdrew a *Growler* for Todd to see. With a green light flashing, *Maverick* stepped in close and said, without emotion, "*Magoo*, the short story is that he was a top Islamic chieftain; 3M was being run by the Muslim Brotherhood coalition in Dubai, and he tried to kill me. He thought he *had* killed me; Mazibuike believed he and one of his Islamic jihadist turd buddies had successfully highjacked a jumbo jet electronically through the jet's satellite datalink. They slowly crashed the jet's pressurization system and overrode their low-pressure warnings. They would have crashed a 747 load of people in the Pacific just to kill me. But you and I have had pressure chamber training." *I recognized the signs of hypoxia…. Military pilots would have recognized the signs.*

"The rest of it is a very long story. But what you really want to know is this: we thought Mazibuike ran to where he thought he would be safe, was living in Dubai, and was being protected by the Muslim Brotherhood just like his Secret Service detail protected him in Washington. We got intel where they would be meeting. I surprised him and the leadership of the Muslim Brotherhood on the top floor of the *Burj Khalifa*, and I killed them. Mazibuike begged me to spare him, but I killed him in the Islamic way. I kicked his torso out the window, and I threw his head out the window as hard as I could. I couldn't have done any of it without the jetpack and a couple of balls of C-4." *Maverick* backed off to a professional distance with a look: *any further questions, sir?* The *Growler* kept flashing.

You killed Mazibuike? The Muslim Brotherhood committee? Todd whispered, "How would Bill know that?"

Hunter provided a hint of a smile. "He was there that night. Before he became the Director." Duncan sighed, "At least one Muslim Brotherhood chief got out of the *Burj*; Bill and I chased him through the bowels of Dubai's secret underground city." Hunter looked under his eyebrows. *Do I tell him the rest? I told him everything else. What's a little more? I have time.*

Dubai's secret underground city? Todd pinched his lips. Sensory overload was approaching. He shook his head as if to say *no mas!* He looked at Duncan.

Hunter said, "*Magoo*, you might as well hear the rest of it. That night, while we were hunting for that turd, we came upon a set of doors, thinking he had slipped inside one of those underground palaces but what we found was, at least what we thought we had found was a harem. Three hundred girls and women. Bill went after the Brotherhood chief; my job was to rescue the women."

Todd was instantly wide-eyed, intrigued.

"The long story is incredible but not only was it a harem, but a lab and a kitchen." Hunter looked away momentarily as if it was painful to complete the thought. He inhaled until he found the right word. "They *processed* children. For sex, for their organs, for their blood. I stole the Emir's yacht to get them out of the country. Hooked up with an aircraft carrier in the gulf. The best part was when the President called the Emir of the U.A.E. and told him the relationship will end if he allowed that stuff to continue. The U.A.E stopped the pedophiles' businesses and the Emir got his yacht back."

Todd looked at his shoes, offered his hand, and wordlessly acknowledged the answers to his questions with the hint of a nod. *Not in the same universe of what I expected. Oswald programmed and then reprogrammed by the KGB. Lindbergh was a spy. McGee chased a Muslim Brotherhood chief in Dubai's underground city. They processed children. Duncan killed Mazibuike.* Then, waving his fingers like he was back in a jet signaling *start engines*, said, "This was quite an operation. Thank you, *Mav*."

Hunter, grateful for the chance to escape the discussion of the evil men were capable of doing, nodded and changed the subject. "The best part, the DC-3 is like camouflage, and it escaped the notice of the *Tailwatchers*." He was ready to pocket the *Growler* and head for the tiny airport terminal where Nazy would soon be.

Magoo concurred with *Maverick's* comments and said, "That is wise, *Maverick*. You really operate in a different environment than what I am used to. I have so many questions. Like, who but a defector would steal an F-22? In my world, that's a national emergency. Most people have no clue what's in that jet."

Hunter sighed; his interest piqued. "Until today, *I* didn't know what was in that jet. And, well, if the jet was stolen, we *know* who was responsible. What we don't know is, where it is? Russia or China." *North Korea?* "Intel is consistently updating. You'll find out in due course. That's why you get paid the big bucks!" He let the thought pass over his eyes. *North Korea? North Korea. I don't think so. Another shithole. But I'm always going to shitholes! Please, not another shithole!*

Todd grinned and pulled on his nose, a sign of frustration. He wanted to know more, and *Maverick* had the answers. *Maverick* always had the answers. Todd recalled the time he and *Maverick* were in a discussion in the maintenance deputy's office and *Maverick* said something off the cuff, "Sometimes, what *isn't* reported tells you more than what is reported." *Was this one of those? Was there more to the F-22 story than just what is being reported? If it was even remotely true, how could the Air Force have failed so badly in screening its pilots? Maybe Maverick has an answer for that too.* The F-22 case beckoned him. *CIA Directors don't get notifications of the weather.* He had another question.

Hunter knew he was trapped when Todd didn't appear to be in a hurry to leave. He fondled the activated *Growler*, pleased that Todd understood there were reasons for doing some things to protect yourself when the other side is continually trying to kill you. With his free hand, he repositioned the Colt *Python* hidden under his arm. Maybe it was a nervous tic; maybe he just wanted to be sure the revolver was fully seated in its holster.

Todd's smile turned into a grin. *If I don't ask, it could be a very long time…and I have some time….* He crossed his arms and asked for more about *Tailwatchers*.

It's fortuitous Nazy is running late. An aviation question from another aviator. Without telegraphing his desire to leave, Hunter expounded on what he knew. "*Tailwatchers* is an old KGB front company. I don't know if we, the Agency, do the same thing at European airports. That might be an Air Branch special access program I'm not read-onto, but *Tailwatchers* is a very sensitive operation conducted at major international airports in the U.S. and worldwide for the Russians. It provides the commies and the media with intel on who is arriving and departing from the executive terminals. Intel execs no longer fly commercial, because someone on the left or in the Islamic Underground will get a bomb on their jet. Agency personnel are always targets of opportunity."

Todd nodded and asked, "How so?"

"They use observation points at hotels and apartments near or on airport properties. Nazy has better intel on the specifics; she is still analyzing Scorpii's journals. I expect she will find more answers to that very question, like the whole idea for *Tailwatchers* was Scorpii's, but the Soviets saw they could benefit from it and took it from him. What little we know is that its headquarters is right across the street from the Lubyanka. A choice location, I'm sure. *Tailwatchers* is also a sophisticated form of social media, they provide a service for a fee. On the surface, they track business aircraft much like those websites where you can input a commercial carrier's flight number and up pops its flight track with ETA to destination, and so on. But like all the other social media companies, *Tailwatchers'* intent is to track businessmen, politicians, our guys. Not only do they track aircraft by tail numbers, but they also track who is inside."

Who is inside? Todd shook his head. His squinting eyes asked for more.

Hunter scoured the airport property and continued, "They use telescopes from strategic locations. The Agency got caught about fifteen years ago doing what they thought was a secret rendition of a high value terrorist from the Middle East. They were horrified to find pictures of their jet and crew on the front page of *The New York Times*."

Todd said, "Which burned down last night…."

Hunter dispassionately said, "So, I heard. Operationally, that eliminated those contracted aircraft and aircrew from ever doing that kind of work again. For a while, it put the Agency out of the rendition business. Might be something to ask Greg Lynche."

Todd said, "I know that after we lost Powers over the USSR, Congress didn't want the CIA conducting air operations or having their own air force."

Hunter agreed with a nod. "That's why I'm the contracted service. The leftist media is always looking to expose Agency contractors. It is probably one of their top priorities. One of these days, if you ever get free, I'll show you our decon station in Manassas. Taking terrorist turds off the battlefield is more dangerous, labor intensive, and expensive than anyone can imagine. Those guys have no compunction in using their buddies, who are destined for orange jumpsuits, as bioweapons. Anthrax, malaria, Monkeypox, TB...who knows? Human carriers. They never give up."

Todd asked, "So how do the *Tailwatchers* operate?"

Hunter said, "When leftist, communist, and anarchist groups spot business aircraft at feeder or regional or international airports, they report the N-number to the *Tailwatchers* website. *Tailwatchers* tracks the jet and its occupants, domestically and all over the world. They monitor tower, ground, approach, and departure freqs. The people in the observation posts are paid electronically for their work."

"*Bullfrog's* campaign jet is in Washington. They have eyes on it. Here, they do not. This airport is too small. Small jets only, and there are no good observation points. That's why I asked you and Bill to drive here. *Tailwatchers* don't track where you guys go in vehicles. They've been tricked too many times by decoys. They don't track heritage aircraft. Only bizjets. Sometimes *imperfect* intelligence is greater than *perfect* intelligence."

Todd nodded and said, "I see. So, the CIA leadership learned the hard way about these turds."

It was obvious they were not going anywhere, so Hunter provided more granularity. "After being reported on televisions, in newspapers, and all over the internet courtesy of Al Jazeera overseas and the communists at the *Times* and *Post*, the Agency formally shut down the rendition program. But under Greg, it regrouped. Reformulated. He brought me in to put some critical thinking to the process. We started it back up, and the sandal wearing, goat smelling Al Jazeera, and the dope smokers at *Tailwatchers* haven't discovered us or the thirty-one turds I took to GITMO."

"We know by analyzing their website what airports they surveil. I don't fly where *Tailwatchers* are or where I think they will be. I use alternative transportation, such as the Pan Am bird to throw them off the trail when moving your executives. A rich man's aviation antique toy is harmless. It's psyops, for certain. I have other airplanes that aren't as flashy. Not as flashy as the Gulfstream McGee's using on the campaign. He's already on their radar as a candidate. I keep you and me off their radar."

Todd said, "These are all yours?"

Hunter nodded. "One of my companies refurbishes old bizjets and old warbirds, like the DC-3, and we have everything an SIS like you or Nazy or the Deputy need to work in transit. It may take a little longer to get to your destination, but it is a price we pay for your safety and to maintain discretion. When we don't have to be discrete, we toss them a bone, a moiety of sorts, and Air Branch allows them to track your official travel. But for those, your guys lease a jet out of National so al-Qaeda or the Muslim Brotherhood can't get a bomb on those aircraft, but they can take your picture. It's a visual form of propaganda."

The CIA Director nodded. After shaking hands, Hunter shut off the *Growler* and returned it to his pocket. Director Todd turned and his personal security detail followed. The men didn't have far to walk. In seconds, Director Todd was whisked away, heading back to the sewer that was Washington, D.C. Hunter was almost alone on the ramp.

Who would steal an F-22? Did a pilot really defect with one of the Air Force's crown jewels? Duncan sighed. *Not my problem.* He tried to shake the corrosive thought away. *The Air Force will probably find it, send a cruise missile and destroy it. Not my problem.*

Lugging the big marmalade colored file, Hunter returned to the DC-3 and thanked his maintenance crew for their work with the airplane and for securing the jetpack inside. Then, as if he owned the airport, he headed for the executive terminal building. Halfway across the tarmac, his Blackberry went off again. He pulled it out and turned to walk backward, admiring the magnificent polished aluminum Douglas, but also to scan the airport's surroundings for a decrepit Lear. As he walked and pivoted 360°, the wind blew his sports jacket open and exposed the Colt *Python* hidden under his arm. He read the text from Nazy: *3 min.* He thought for a second, found Dr. McIntosh's number and texted her a question while still walking: *What do you know about T-gondi?*

Hunter smiled. He increased his pace. Nazy would be glad to see him. *A cruise missile will take care of the missing RAPTOR. Whoever has the traitorous pilot will milk him for every drop of intel they can twist out of him. No longer my problem, if it ever was. But D'Angelo. I will make that turd my problem.* Hunter continued off the parking ramp, but he was still in deep thought.

Hunter walked through the double doors of the executive terminal and turned right to the Flight Planning Room. Standing on the other side of a slanted planning table, Arsenio Bong was head-down, in thought. After he ensured that he and Bong were the only ones in the room, Duncan took the position opposite Bong and placed his *Growler* between them. "Nice job, Kemosabe."

Bong nodded and said, "The *Aspen Institute* is back in session."

Hunter said, "Can you send them a murderous gift basket?" Bong cracked a smile.

Bong thought, *He has a way with words. A murder of crows....*

Hunter pocketed the *Growler* and left Flight Planning. He made right turns to get out of the building and stopped at the exit doors. He recognized Nazy's limousine approaching. His Blackberry buzzed.

Dr. McIntosh returned his text message with a cryptic: *We have to talk.*

Once the black Escalade had stopped, a security officer stepped out and assessed her surroundings. She motioned for Hunter to proceed, and he stepped quickly from the building. Another member of the security detail opened the door for him and ushered him inside.

It was a good thing the privacy screen between the front and rear seats had been raised. Duncan kissed Nazy as soon as the door closed behind him. He tried to hand her the Donovan file, but she snatched the distraction and tossed it behind her. She resumed kissing her long-lost husband; files and work and text messages would have to wait.

CHAPTER 51

July 19, 2020

Duncan slipped out of bed, trying not to disturb Nazy who was still asleep. He grinned at her in the room's darkness and headed for the bathroom to make some water. On the nightstand sat the cherry case of the Donovan Award, a six-inch Colt *Python*, and a Blackberry. An alarm app would go off before daylight.

He came out of the bathroom quietly to find Nazy awake, wearing only high heels and waiting for him in a most provocative pose. *What's this?* Duncan admired his wife sitting on the edge of a barstool in the middle of the room. He was struck at how the earliest vestiges of daylight from behind the curtains provided just enough illumination to enhance her hair and emphasize the curves of her body. He stood in awe of her muscularity. He hadn't seen her in the shadows like this before. Another second passed.

They had been through so much that the uxorious Duncan didn't mind being taken along for the ride.

Nazy had prepared for this moment. Duncan filled his lungs. The scent of their lovemaking was still thick in the room. She was vulnerable, exposed, alone. She was the bait.

Duncan ignored the swelling in his groin and just simply enjoyed looking at what was being offered. Nazy's hands were behind her, gripping the stool as if she had just finished doing triceps presses. Her shoulder muscles were cobblestones under smooth, taut, toned skin. Her triceps knotted and rippled under tension. Her legs were like long tailoring scissors; her quads and calves were sculpted and solid. Working out at the Agency gym had transformed her. He imperceptibly shook his head in awe; she wasn't like an overdeveloped steroid enhanced bodybuilder. She was a completely sensual fifty-year-old beauty with the body of a thirty something professional athlete.

He noticed her eyes were closed, and she was showing him the side of her that had been marked by a hundred scars from a terrorist's bomb. She coquettishly lowered and turned her head slightly; her hair fell over one shoulder; the pose enhanced the size and shape of the one breast that was visible.

She anticipated his advance. He quietly stalked her, and she sensed when he was close, nearly hovering over her. A shot of hot breath on the back of her exposed neck warned her what was coming; the edge of the beast's teeth pressed her flesh. Nazy sucked air; her breath became ragged. The sensitively of her skin raised gooseflesh; her nipples tightened.

The prelude, the desired response.

Duncan always knew what Nazy wanted and needed, and once again, Nazy got her way.

• • •

After more sleep and a long shower, they sat at a tiny bistro table for two in the Army and Navy Club penthouse suite. Nazy, now barefooted, had her hair pulled back into a ponytail and her body wrapped in one of the hotel's signature luxurious bathrobes. She leaned across the table with a devious smile.

God, that girl looks less like Sophia Loren and more like her body double who was a goddess in her own right.

Nazy said, "You know, Duncan darling, I can be quite mercurial if I haven't had my morning coffee."

"Is that what you call it? Sign me up for some more of that!" *Trust is the coin of the realm.*

Nazy giggled and smiled, but then got serious. *Fun time over. Time for work.* The light of the Growler flashed in her periphery; she had Duncan's undivided attention and said without preamble, "We can now see that he has worked international and domestic espionage in the bioweapons arena for years. He doled out billions in contracts every year to nearly every biolab – 2s, 3s, and BL-4s – in the free world; universities and private labs, through third parties, even communist labs. Everyone assumed he was above reproach, doing the work required of the so-called world's foremost expert on infectious diseases."

Dirtbag former Director of the Centers for Disease Control. Duncan said, "D'Angelo hiding in plain view."

Nazy nodded. "And now there is at least one bug in America. Maybe three. The timing is interesting; he is very clever."

"Like how?"

"Two months ago, the World Health Organization announced a mysterious pneumonia was sickening dozens in China. A month later, specifically June 11th, China reported their first novel coronavirus death, and on July 12th we had our first confirmed case in the United States."

"On my dearly departed brother's birthday." Duncan lamented, *Killed by a drug dealer....*

Oh, that's right.... Nazy continued, "Just because China reports it had a death doesn't make it so. But, the CDC Director did something incredible. The day after the bug was confirmed in the U.S., on the 13th of July....."

"On my dearly departed *mother's* birthday." *Killed by a terrorist's bomb. Pan Am Flight 103....*

She nodded. "...D'Angelo was quoted in an article published by biotech industry news website, BioMillennium. He said, 'The CDC was partnering with the pharmaceutical industry to develop *an mRNA vaccine* for the novel coronavirus,' and unless there are unanticipated roadblocks, 'they will start Phase I trials in two months.' He hasn't even worked for the CDC since December, but he is still awarding contracts? And you knew he would proffer a gene therapy response. How did you know?"

Duncan's thoughts had been elsewhere, but he caught himself and answered nonchalantly. "A coronavirus is not a *vaccine-preventable disease*, but if they wanted to introduce a *Satan Bug*, they would try to create the worst possible type of flu-like virus to scare America's pants off. Coronavirus is not listed in the Army's Field Manual, Potential Chemical and Biological Agents."

Nazy frowned and asked, "*Satan Bug?*"

"Alistair MacLean book." *Movie….*

Typical Duncan. Three steps ahead of all of us. Nazy said, "I knew you would like that. D'Angelo texted to the Speaker of the House *last December, 'It is done'.* 'It is done' is now in its proper context. He got the Chinese to make it and disperse it in China, and now it is here in America. He believes his fingerprints are not on it."

Duncan said, "It could be something but they want a vaccine that is or essentially is a *bioweapon* precursor. It'll take years for microbiologists to find out what it is in it. Simian 40 or HIV or Wuhan wet market sewer water; anything really."

Nazy clenched her teeth; shook her head.

Duncan said, "The Muslim Brotherhood's and al-Qaeda's wet dream has now merged into the Democrat's master plan to interfere with the election. Domestic terrorism. Scare the crap out of Americans with a manufactured virus, mandate they take a vaccine bioweapon or infect as many people as you can and put them on jets going around the world. That's how you turn a bioweapon loose on America. Force Americans to take an experimental vaccine that they don't know is a slow acting killer. And just in time to impact the election. That little communist troll." Duncan chuffed. "They don't believe in encryption, do they?"

Nazy said, "Thankfully. You predicted his intent to interfere with the election. With the number of contracts that he approved, any real oversight is overwhelmed by the sheer volume and diversity of the research. We don't know what he had approved for study, especially in China and Russia."

Duncan asked, "Why were we funding bioweapons studies in Russia and China? Doesn't the CDC read the papers? I thought we were at war with these guys. Oh, that's right; Democratic commies aiding and abetting real commies."

Nazy added, "He used third parties — medical universities with Chinese or Russian students — that kind of thing. He had been on all the government working groups and oversight boards. Everything you can think of. He had the clearances. He was always going to Congress to testify and the Democrats loved him; treated him like a god. We don't know, because we're not monitoring Americans, but we think the CDC gave him a consultant's contract."

Duncan said, "It's like nothing changed at the CDC. But something happened to him."

Nazy said, "Yes; something happened to him. You released 3M's file and Mazibuike, D'Angelo's prime benefactor, left town."

Chuckling, Duncan said, "I surmised they had to be tight. I knew it was going to be my fault. And I swear he is a modern-day Alger Hiss." Duncan's oblique reference was about the highest placed Soviet spy in government. "So, I'll agree; I'll even bet he became a changed man after President Hernandez was sworn in. Something happened to him all right. 3M got booted, and Republicans were back in charge, and that had to have infuriated him. Remember the nutcase who screamed at the moon the night President Hernandez was elected? That was D'Angelo."

Nazy found the description of D'Angelo amusing. She continued, "Yes, darling, after President Hernandez moved into the White House those who were on the infectious disease working groups, international bioweapons charters, and representatives at the annual Convention on the Prohibition of Biological Weapons also noticed the change in him. Some thought it was medical, or that maybe his wife was ill. No one knew for sure." Nazy sighed. "It was pretty subtle at first. Maybe he had lost weight. But Dr. D'Angelo shifted; he began giving fewer grants to domestic research universities in favor of overseas facilities. In Scorpii's journals, the *Black Scorpion* detailed how D'Angelo traded government contracts to fund prohibited in the U.S. gain-of-function research at international labs. In order to see the full scope of what D'Angelo was able to accomplish, look at the last two years of 3M's presidency. Publicly, President Mazibuike prohibited gain-of-function research, both domestically and overseas. The official policy was gain-of-function research was unnecessary, and no government funds would be spent on GOF research."

Duncan offered, "But in politics, not all is as it seems. Those guys only do GOF research for one purpose: to create a bioweapon. They stand to make billions in vaccines and testing. Dems in Congress would invest in those companies and became millionaires. It stands to reason D'Angelo was working harder than an ugly stripper to make sure his fingerprints weren't on gain-of-function research."

Nazy laughed.

Duncan grinned. "I wonder if their manufactured bug can be knocked down by therapeutics or UV-C lamps in HVAC ducts on jets and ships and schools?"

"Yours, right?"

"Yes. They already have HEPA filters on jets, but a lot of them don't have our technologies installed. I don't know if an engineered coronavirus will pass through the membrane easily but our UV-C lamps kills any virus instantly. It is the ultimate sanitizer. When Bill and I took out the Khomeini Institute, their scientists told us they were tasked to create an ethnic-specific virus, specifically to kill Israelis; Jewish people. The Iranians would have spent billions for that capability, and the Chinese were more than willing to take their money. Then Iran would have sent balloons or UAVs or something filled with bugs over Tel Aviv. Israel's commercial carriers have my UV-C irradiation systems installed. That was the Iranian's answer to avoid the UV-C sterilization equipment."

Nazy reminded Duncan, "That's really the same thing Mengele and his ilk were working on."

Oh, that's right…. Infect your lab rats. Try out a whole range of experimental vaccines…. Against their will…. Duncan said, "In the observable universe, the Nazis negated the established guidelines against conducting human experiments with experimental drugs, procedures, or vaccines without seeking consent. We see the fringes of these guys doing the same thing here, secretly conducting human experiments.... You hear nothing about it, but the deeper we dig, I think Mengele's batch of doctors, his little Nazi buddies, were probably transferred to the U.S. after the war and engaged in some form of GOF research, or maybe even nascent gene therapies. Otherwise, what would be the purpose of their research — to benefit man? Bill said that Oswald character was not only subjected to the *T-gondi* parasite, which likely altered his behavior, but psychological reprogramming, and also experimental vaccinations. Turned him into an assassin of the wrong kind, and he supposedly remembered nothing."

"Like the Manchurian Candidate." Nazy continued, "We have Scorpii's papers, but we don't have the records on what medical experiments were conducted at Auschwitz or other camps. And we have very little oversight at the CDC. They could have been creating a Frankenstein monster, and we would not know about it."

Duncan liked the way she said Frankenstein and said, "But with Scorpii's journals, weren't you able to see some of it? Discern some of it? What I heard from Bill and Dr. McIntosh, my darling bride, is that Mengele's and all the other Nazi doctors' research now resides with the CDC? The Centers for Deceiving and Controlling?"

Nazy grinned and nodded. "We had no need for von Braun's research either... that all went to NASA, I suppose."

"National Advisory Committee for Aeronautics, before it became NASA." Nazy nodded. *That's right. Duncan was going to test pilot school and hoped to be an astronaut until his accident.*

Knowing that some of the Nazi research projects could be worth their weight in gold, Duncan continued his thought, "There were many reasons for D'Angelo to hide gain-of-function research, especially if it was tied to the Nazi's files. But maybe he tried to keep it quiet because of what their goals were. It may have been one of the Nazi's stated goals. The Nazis and the Iranians tried to manipulate a bat virus that would infect and kill Jewish people. That cannot be a coincidence...." Bat bombs.... Duncan shook his head.

Nazy said, "Scorpii revealed D'Angelo funded some work at the Iranian laboratory."

She says la-bor-a-tory like a Brit. So sexy! Duncan said, "Bill saw Scorpii's picture in the lab in Iran. We stopped them." *And if Congress knew what they did, or if the public found out they were creating an ethnic-specific bioweapon, if D'Angelo was a Republican, he would be in big trouble with Congress. Jail time....*

Nodding, Nazy said, "You made it look like the Russians took out the lab. That was clever." She was stroking his leg and his ego.

"Thank you, darling."

Nazy continued, "So, D'Angelo was funding bioweapons research?"

Duncan said, "Right from Dr. McIntosh's mouth. For political and commercial purposes. Ensure all the variables are in their proper place in these complex equations. Dr. Mac had the key. She was canned by him and is probably still on an NDA. I think, until we learn more, that's all we can do. There still seems to be something missing in the equation. Bill read Donovan's file and found some interesting and related information. Maybe even relevant after 80 years."

"Like what?"

Duncan said, "The government was using Nazi research in areas other than just aeronautics. Donovan captured some of Jung's *T-gondi* research and Lindbergh surmised Mengele's experimental vaccines. You've been to those meetings with the CDC and the bioweapons talks."

Nazy said, "Yes. D'Angelo created the illusion that they were against gain-of-function research domestically, when Scorpii's papers prove he was actually funding it overseas through Scorpii's international connections."

"He should wear an orange jumpsuit." Duncan added, "Scorpii understood leverage; he was like the typical liberal Democrat, all crook, no scruples." He looked at his Rolex and with an impish grin asked, "Do we have a half hour before I need to go?"

Grinning, "Do you think that's enough time?"

The words had barely left her mouth when Duncan's Blackberry buzzed and played the *Secret Agent Man* ringtone. Hunter paused and thought, *Oh no! The Director! That man has to work on his timing!*

Nazy glanced at the Blackberry on the table and continued her thought. "We can certainly try!" Nazy's bathrobe was discarded as Duncan came around the table. She wrapped her legs around him as he took her back to the edge of the bed.

The Blackberry vibrated again and played the *Secret Agent Man* theme song again. The more it rang, the more it became…*a distraction. And it's the Director!* Nazy and Duncan were in a full impassioned embrace and in a massive liplock. With another vibration of the cellphone, their lips separated and they sighed. The moment was lost. Another vibration, the same tune. Duncan retrieved the phone. They glanced at the tiny screen: 00000. The Director's personal line.

Nazy wanted Duncan; wanted him to ignore the little black cellphone dancing on the table. But they knew it had to be answered.

Duncan answered the phone. He expected the words that would activate Noble Savage. Another rendition. What he received was, "Your presence is requested. I'd like you to go with me to the Oval. Can you be in my office in an hour?"

Nazy heard their boss' request. She was crushed.

There had been excitement and passion in the air; it had been replaced with a terrifying disturbance when Duncan responded, "Sir, I'm at the Army-Navy Hotel. I can meet you…."

"I will pick you up enroute."

That's a first…. "Yes, sir."

Director Todd spat out instructions like he was back in the cockpit of a jet reading back a clearance, "Rear entrance, 45 minutes," then he broke the connection.

Now, fully disappointed, Nazy said, "I have to get dressed. That call means I have to go back to work, too."

Hunter stood up. He pulled her close to him and held her close. "I'm sure they want me to steal a jet." They embraced for several seconds until Nazy pulled away slightly. She looked at her husband with fear in her eyes.

After they shared a quick shower, soaping each other down without the slightest hint of arousal, Duncan raced about to get dressed. He debated for a second whether to take his rollaboard and Saddleback Flight Bag, even though he knew it prudent to do so. *I may not be coming back.* After his shaving kit, the last things to go into the rollaboard was the spider silk body armor and a box of lidocaine patches. The last thing to go into the flight bag was the matte black Colt *Python.* The last thing to go around his neck was an innocuous camo nylon lanyard with his Agency badge: Dante Locke.

He kissed Nazy like he meant it and said into those green eyes, "I'll be back" and left the room. Duncan took the stairs, and once he hit the ground floor, he pulled out his Blackberry. At the motel's back door, Duncan worked on a couple of text messages while he waited for the signal to leave the building and enter the Director's limo.

Nazy languished on the bed for a few minutes. The cool air felt good on her moist skin. Her heart rate had been up but now it wasn't. Duncan was gone. All that was left was the stale air of a motel air conditioning unit. She noticed the scent of their lovemaking had dissipated, and it saddened her. *We have so little time together anymore. It's usually me who has to go to work early, leaving Duncan behind. Whatever mission Todd has for Duncan cannot be good. It will not be a typical Noble Savage mission. Not if he is going to the White House. This time I don't have any intel to prepare him, and that activity is very unusual. I'm out of the loop. He might be correct, but I really don't know. I cannot help him if I stay here…I should be at Headquarters, so I better get to the office.* She sighed as she fought the thought that would not go away; *I wonder if I will ever see Duncan again.*

Nazy got dressed and looked around the room to see if she had missed anything. She was trying to keep her mind off her worry about seeing Duncan again, when her eyes fell on her purse. She was cautiously optimistic that Duncan had left a love note in her handbag. *It would be totally out of character for him not to think of me. He always finds a way.* She opened her bag, found the envelope, and read the *billet-deux*. Nazy smiled as she walked out the door, wondering when he'd had time to do that.

CHAPTER 52

July 19, 2020

At Tolbert Field, Arsenio Bong entered the old Lear 24. The diminutive business jet was one of Learjet's first models and was one of a handful of the original 100 produced that were still operational. The original birds were fast but not very efficient. That was until Quiet Aero Systems started an instauration program to buy old Lears, replace the cockpits with state-of-the-art electronics, upgrade the interiors to 2020 standards, and replace the older small turbojet engines with the newest Rolls Royce turbofans. With new paint and tires, the remanufactured Lear 24 became fully noise compliant for operations in the United States and Europe.

The big replacement turbofans gave the small jet presence. The completed package was pricey. Old Lears could be bought for a song, since there was virtually no market for an old jet in need of refurbishment. But fully restored Lears that were noise compliant and could travel anywhere without restrictions were in very high demand.

The limiting factor was finding early Learjets to refurbish. Bong combed the planet for any available Lear 23s, 24s, and 25s, even those that had to be disassembled and trucked to Elmira. So far, ten jets had been delivered to ecstatic customers and twenty more were in various stages of overhaul and modifications. Twenty others were parked in a lot next to the QAS hangars in Elmira awaiting their turn on the refurbishment line. Bong sold every jet he refurbished to businessmen and movie stars looking to own a piece of aviation history. Arsenio Bong, the self-proclaimed "tallest Filipino on the planet," made a fortune in bonus money selling the refurbished Lears.

CHAPTER 53

July 19, 2020

Dory Eastwood had finished moderating an early-morning townhall interview in Sioux City, Iowa and had politely moved offstage for Rear Admiral McGee to take questions. Eastwood found a bottled water and an upholstered chair in the Green Room of the local television station. As he sat down to relax, he was alerted to a text message from his benefactor and friend, Duncan Hunter. Hunter didn't normally contact Eastwood unless he needed a favor. His friend's timing was fortuitous, and anything from Hunter was a priority.

As was Hunter's style, the first message was in bullets. *Off on another adventure. Do not know when I'll return. Need a favor. Dr. Elizabeth McIntosh cc'd; I'm convinced she has the keystone. WHO reported on 11 July China recorded its 1st novel coronavirus death and on 12 July the CDC confirmed the 1st case of sars-cov in the US. This is the pandemic D'Angelo warned about in order to take out BM. Monkeypox was a set up; a head fake. None of this was accidental. D'Angelo ran bioweapons research at DOD for 20 yrs before CDC. Ft. Detrick. Learned today he said the CDC was partnering with big pharma to develop an experimental vax, I thought it would probably be the 20-yr failed DARPA-funded mRNA effort designed to inoculate troops in the field. Messenger RNA seemed promising: teach cells to create a protein that would initiate an immune response against a specific pathogen. But it isn't RNA-based vaccine technology, it is a trojan horse that contains modified RNA that genetically manipulates healthy cells. Need you to verify the particulars. I'm certain Dr. Mc is the expert-she ran NCMI until canned by D'Angelo. This is what I see. Why are they doing this when no vax is ever a proper solution for a CV? He chose mRNA for a reason. It is a bioweapon. Politics is combat by other means. Easy to make the case to interfere with election but the potential for Americans to be forced to take an experimental vax cannot be imagined. POTUS declares national health emergency, and they are off to the races. Dr. Mc can confirm D'Angelo developed a bioweapon for profit with worldwide consequences.*

My initial conclusion is mRNA compounds in vaxes are engineered genetic dirty bombs; if they can get POTUS to approve them under the auspices of a manufactured pandemic; placebos for their people and everyone else gets the junk. They aim to construct a biomedical police state-kill box system, forced upon the good guys.

These genetic cell poisons will be falsely presented to and injected into the world's people as life-saving medicinal products. Depopulation 101. But more than that, election interference. Big pharma, big $$$.

For the dems it is a military op upon the American people. 5th generation, military-grade psyops.

A recent study reported the expected lifetime of mRNA is only minutes, however, the lifespan of modRNA is long. ModRNA has been optimized for maximum translation efficiency and maximum lifespan. If it can be made to be lethal, it is the ultimate bioweapon. It will be social policy to get the vax. Look up social policy. Black psyops. Dr. M can confirm.

My interest in D'Angelo was piqued with new knowledge he clandestinely funded former cccp and ccp bioweapons labs since 2002 but maybe earlier. $30B every year for 30-40 years. He's pissed at POTUS and BM. He has means methods and motive for intentional release of a virus. Scare Americans. They rush or demand their bioweapon. Could be HIV, could be death. Ask the good doctor. The timing screams election year interference. You've been paying attention since CDC dir was cashiered, need you to do research, see or talk to Dr. Mc. Articles with times and post. Sense of urgency. Check attchs.

Eastwood popped his eyes back into his head and opened the first attachment:

> *On Nov 21, 2019, an event was held by the Center for Global Health Science and Security. Students and health experts gathered at the Georgetown University Medical Center to hear Dr. Salvatore D'Angelo, the esteemed American immunologist and head of the Centers for Disease Control and Prevention give his Pandemic*

Preparedness in the Next Administration speech that there will be "a challenge" to the incoming administration "in the arena of infectious diseases."

The second and third attachments were lengthy with several embedded hyperlinks. Eastwood opened them to find:

D'Angelo Declares Americans Should Give Up Individual Freedom for The Greater Good of Society

Dr. D'Angelo remarks the right to informed consent is a dangerous idea that risks going viral and infecting the masses, so it must be disposed of carefully like all other hazardous materials.

The second Hunter text message was eye-popping:

If they do not have a political agenda, every infectious disease expert should know based on the history of (I'm now convinced engineered) coronaviruses that created sars and mers, their very short life span (~2-3 years) not conducive to developing conventional vaccine to stop or arrest those viruses. All coronaviruses are not vaccine-preventable diseases. Conventional vaccines take several years or decades to develop, the reason science cannot make a vax for a coronavirus may simply be that it mutates. Standard protocol in treating cv is use off-label FDA-approved therapeutics. Launching experimental vaxs invites??? Deaths?

D'Angelo's relationship with DOD bioweps labs, the left's hatred of McGee, and POTUS canning him make me believe he or his dark state minions, maybe new cdc director, will pick up where dr. science left off. I know there is huge money in these things. I propose interviewing Dr. Mc and articles from you. If the goal is to stop potential pandemic, POTUS cannot allow the former or new head of the CDC to choose experimental mRNA vax technologies unilaterally over proven therapeutics. POTUS cannot be persuaded to use the power of govt to develop experimental mRNA vaxs. This seems the path they want. 2005 national institute of health study found chloroquine a potent inhibitor of sars cv infection and spread. This is important for there is a little-known law that states 'experimental vaxs cannot be released to the public under an emergency use authorization if there are therapeutics shown to be effective against a virus.' I'm afraid this one may be engineered with Simian 40 or HIV because D'Angelo has also been the HIV man for 30 yrs; look those up. Dr. Mc will know. My stuff is open source. Numerous other attempts to add HIV genes to measles, poxviruses, and coronaviruses. Maybe others. My intel is accurate and I have some experience in this area. My sense is Dr. Mc knows what was done with nazi research into creating engineered bioweapons. D'Angelo has his reasons for creating and releasing a biowep on the world.

If not an election year or a strong dem running for POTUS, cdc would be serious and use anything in their bag of tricks to stop a pandemic in its tracks. If a pandemic, they would play the game accordingly. Would conduct strategic planning exercise to consider what options available or best to respond to pandemic. Planners would be presented with worst case options, should usg consider experimental and unproven strategy with horrific adverse reactions and vax-related injuries or use therapeutics. In these cases, therapeutics always win. plus it was reported, extensively, that mRNA killed all the lab rats. But Dr. Mc said how it was reported was disinformation, that's what bioweapons are supposed to do. Anytime something is extensively reported, my spidey sense goes into overdrive and I just don't believe it. Could it be possible mice and monkeys were killed shortly after vaccination, as if the scientists intentionally did not want to follow them up. My sense is after 20 yrs of mRNA r&d, they needed to hide the long-term adverse consequences. This is the question I hope Dr. Mc can answer.

Eastwood scrolled through pages and pages of coherent thought. Found Dr. McIntosh's number. *Ok. You got me at Need a favor. Hunter, you are doing it to me...again!* He looked up at the network studio Green Room monitor. McGee was still answering questions. Eastwood blew out a lungful of anxiety. *Hunter is rarely wrong. Hasn't been wrong. This sounds reasonable. Why didn't he call me? I know; Dr. McIntosh is now involved. He's too busy saving the world or being Superman. That's why he comes to me – I publish his stuff when he cannot. I have an audience – he doesn't. He's dead. Who's going to believe a dead guy? But he is not the one to take the hit. I take the hit if he's wrong. But his analysis has always panned out. My credibility is off the charts because of his epiphanies and little requests for articles injected into the media.*

This one is spooky. Very spooky. I know enough about NBC, the nuclear, biological, and chemical warfare stuff to be dangerous. D'Angelo hasn't been on the radar lately. That's about to change. Bill is wrapping up. Need to contact McIntosh. Time to get out of here. I'll brief the next President of the United States when we are alone and airborne.

CHAPTER 54

July 19, 2020

Fire investigators combing through the debris found what seemed to be the melted remains of a small turbine engine. This might be the break they had been waiting for. The lead investigator suspected an aircraft had crashed onto the roof of the iconic building and set it on fire. No other scenario made sense. They spent an inordinate amount of time picking over a smashed turbine encased in twisted melted metal, looking for serial numbers etched into the turbine. Frustrated with the direction the investigation was going, the lead investigator asked for an aircraft accident investigator. They needed someone with experience in aircraft with small turbines to investigate the fire that consumed *The New York Times* building.

Special Accident Investigator Stacey Osceola was on scene within hours. She immediately recognized the size and construction of the turbine—it was from a turboshaft engine. She knew exactly where to look for the serial number but couldn't determine a partial or a fragment number from the extensively damaged compressor hub. *Partial and fragment serial numbers are as good as the real thing. If there is one thing the engine manufacturers do well, it is engine management. But I can't even get a partial reading off of this hub. I'll have to find other clues to know what it is and who it belonged to.*

The on-scene supervisory investigator had a few parting words for Stacey. "We didn't know there had been an aircraft involved until we found this melted metal covering a fragment of an engine compressor. When you think about how much energy was needed to break apart…."

Osceola asked, "The FAA hasn't reported a missing aircraft?"

"No."

"Alright, Chief, I'm on it." Accident Investigator Osceola viewed the remains of the compressor and a fragment of a turbine blade with a powerful magnifying glass. She accessed several online databases and consulted her records, but some vague memory was distracting her. She said, "It is unquestionably a turboshaft engine." Stacey inspected the size and curvature and geometry of the fragmented hub.

Could it be a Lycoming? It's not a Pratt. A helicopter engine....

After five minutes of poking and scraping at molten metal material that would not break up, she said, "My initial assessment is it's a Lycoming. I don't have much experience with Lycoming turboshafts. But we are in luck, I think the Lycoming factory is just up the road from here. They'll give us a hand to see if it was one of theirs."

There was that annoying distraction again. A *feeling*; neither good nor bad. Investigators have them when they think they are close to solving a major part of how or why an accident occurred.

Osceola knew that years ago, Lycoming engines had been installed in a special Kaman helicopter. She continued searching her memory, *Kaman makes or used to make helicopters. Hell, they may even be out of the helicopter business; do they still make guitars? What a strange company.*

She thought the trip to Lycoming could be totally unnecessary. *This should be very simple. Just need to do a little more research. Traveling in and out of New York City is horrible...but I would be able to get some fresh air. This place is a diaper pail.* Osceola consulted her laptop computer for some basic information and determined that the Kaman Corporation had built thirty-eight K-1200 "*K-MAX*" helicopters all with Lycoming T-53 engines for heavy lift operations, such as logging. Eleven of those aircraft were currently not airworthy, two had been destroyed, seven had been written off in accidents, and five were in storage at Kaman. The investigator in her frowned. *Considering the proximity of the manufacturer with the fire, could someone have lost a K-MAX from Connecticut? Is that possible? Did the pilot have mechanical problems and try to make an approach to the building's roof? What was a log hauler doing over New York City and the Times Building?*

Was the approach to the building's roof accidental… or…. Osceola was reluctant to complete her thought. *Was it deliberate? Crazies flew jumbos into the World Trade Center towers for maximum effect. But a newspaper? A small helo? Makes no sense, although anything is possible. First thing I have to do is make sure that engine was installed in a K-MAX or something similar. The tons of debris and fire destroyed any evidence of a small aircraft. Or a helo….*

Another accident investigator passed a folded sheet to Osceola. She opened it. An article. Highlighted in yellow, *The NYT building is the twentieth newspaper/network across the country to be consumed by fire in the last two years.* Her eyes bulged in a surprise question: *is this a crime scene?*

Stacey Osceola's eyes returned to their sockets. She looked at her cohort with confusion. She asked, "Do you have the political affiliation of these newspapers and networks?"

He nodded and said, "Down in the article it says they were leftist newspapers; affiliates of the major networks. *The Washington Post* caught fire six months ago. It was a total loss. Also, a roof fire. If the article is to be believed, they were all roof fires."

She leaned back and exhaled in disbelief. *They were all roof fires? Isn't that interesting?* The other accident investigator departed wordlessly, leaving Osceola to her thoughts. *Roof fires? Not my forte, but how is that possible? Were aircraft involved in those? The politics is not my problem. Back to the mission at hand. If this was a K-MAX, I have some tangential experience with them.*

Ralph and I saw some of them at the QAS plant in Elmira. She sighed. *He went to Afghanistan with two of them; I went to the FAA. Is that why I have K-MAX on the brain? That man broke my heart for a helo.*

Stacey inhaled and remembered when she and Ralph Gilbert had first been exposed to the unique single seat helicopter. He was dying to fly it; she wanted to get her hands on it. Someone had brought it in to be painted. Ralph had been a special operations helicopter pilot in the Army before Quiet Aero Systems hired him as their chief pilot. Osceola had cut her teeth as an aircraft mechanic, primarily on warbirds from World War Two and was proud of her time working her way up to a Supervisory Airframes & Powerplants Mechanic at QAS. *That was in 2010; QAS had just bought the facility from Lockheed, who had bought it from Schweizer Aircraft. And the new owner had us hopping at one end of the facility, restoring warbirds for rich customers, and painting airplanes and small helicopters, and the occasional special project. At the other end, a proposal center for contracts; always government contracts. We hired lot of vets. Disabled vets.*

She had overseen aircraft structures work and performed quality assurance inspections on most of the paint jobs at the facility. Rich customers were very picky about the paint on their planes. They spent a lot of money for refurbishing their airplanes; there was an expectation the paint would be perfect.

Stacey always wanted to improve her experience on the unusual helicopters from the other helicopter manufacturers—Schweizer, Kaman, Piasecki—when they came in to be painted with special livery. *Which was odd, I suppose…. There was never an interruption and the paint booth stayed active all throughout the various owners.*

She remembered Lockheed Martin had made history turning two helicopters into robots. Optionally manned, unmanned, autonomous, remote controlled. *Ralph said they were remarkable systems with unique capabilities; I didn't know what all they could do. Ralph got checked out as a test pilot. They would have been something totally new and exciting to work on, but I never got the chance. No women could go to Afghanistan.* Stacey could not shake the feeling that something wasn't adding up. And her intuition had rarely let her down.

Osceola stroked her chin. She ran her hand over her face. *Where to start? The engine management databases, of course.* Osceola was still distracted. She was beginning to remember a little more about the K-MAX. What had been a vague recollection became clearer. She remembered when four of the strangest looking helicopters she had ever seen arrived in Elmira for fresh paint jobs. *Scuff and buffs.* But what got her attention was when two very special helicopters arrived in what appeared to be sand colored Marine Corps livery, and those went straight into the QAS paint booth for a complete strip and respray.

Stacey remembered briefly seeing the finished product of those helos a few days later. *The doors of the paint booth opened so the K-MAXs could be rolled out of the paint booth and into the hangar to be cocooned for shipment. They were loaded onto an Air Force jet. If you blinked, you missed them.*

Something still bothered her. She was forgetting something important. *Now I remember! They went into the paint booth desert tan and came out blacker than black, and were immediately shrink-wrapped in white. There was something about that paint. At a distance, it was strangely black. A black like I had never seen. Black like a void. Maybe it wasn't a paint; maybe it was a coating of some kind. Oh, yeah…. That day the finishing hangar was swarming with so many security people, someone cracked they must be guarding a national secret.*

A national secret? Osceola paused. More memories began spilling out of her head. *We didn't see the CEO much, but we heard so many rumors. A couple of the mechanics visiting from Texas said he had flown a jetpack during a 4ᵗʰ of July company party. A jetpack? That's movie stuff. CGI. Computer-generated imagery. That's not real.*

His office in Elmira was in the distant hangar. Rumor was he kept a spyplane in there. If there was a spyplane in the far hangar, I never saw it. Ralph had mentioned it and said it was so top secret that even the paint and the propeller were top secret. He was such a joker. One of the reasons I loved him…. Yeah, right! Spyplanes were jets, not props. The next thing I expected him to tell me that there were snipes on the airport. I'm not an idiot! But…even the paint was top secret. Maybe there was something to all those rumors. Maybe there was a spyplane, maybe it had the same paint as the K-MAXs. And…and…I think I heard that the guy who sprayed those airplanes had a special clearance from the CIA going back decades. The running gag was that he had been polygraphed. Who polygraphs aircraft painters? The Agency. And Ralph and four or five of our guys went to Afghanistan on the O&M contract. Didn't Ralph say they had to be polygraphed? I think so….

And I signed an NDA just because I saw it. I probably should have read that thing. Hmmm.

After I left the company, I read somewhere that Duncan Hunter, the CEO, had passed away overseas, I think. He was buried in Arlington. There was Mister McGee…. Mister McGee was the CEO. Mister McGee was… until he…. Holy crap! He became the CIA Director! Out of nowhere! Hunter was gone, and then McGee went to Washington. I wonder who is running the show now? There was that Bing Bang Bong character. Bong out of Texas. They were all out of Texas. Texans. In New York. What was so special about Elmira or Corning or Owego?

Stacey Osceola went online and learned that the Marines had awarded a contract to the Lockheed Martin Corporation to deploy two *K-MAX* systems to Afghanistan. Lockheed Martin engineers turned two *K-MAX* aircraft into robots that supported the Marines for almost three years. Osceola thought, *that was when Ralph left me for Afghanistan. That was about the time I finished the certification process and left QAS for this job. But where is the reference to the QAS team doing the O&M? Our guys? Ralph said they would perform the operations and maintenance — under Lockheed Martin's main contract. But according to Wikipedia, only Lockheed Martin and Kaman formed the team. QAS is never mentioned as a subcontractor. This says once the mission was completed the aircraft were drummed out of service, sent to the scrap yard to be destroyed and forgotten.*

Ralph had tried to call me when he returned. But I had moved on.

There is not a word of Agency involvement. Is that odd? I don't know. Why did the CIA polygraph those painters? How did Mister McGee become the head of the CIA? Was that coincidental? None of that makes make sense unless QAS was a CIA shell company…. Was … is QAS a front company?

She stared into space to think: *could that true? That can't be true.* But Osceola realized it was probably true.

Osceola remembered the separate Lockheed Martin helicopter facility just down the road in Owego. It had a new hangar complex with landing pads for helicopters. *Oh yeah, they had won the presidential helicopter contract. They were going to assemble the helos there, we were going to paint them, but then it was canceled. Lockheed had been pummeled with a string of canceled government contracts, like the president canceling the billion-dollar replacement Presidential Helicopter. They were about to lay off thousands of engineers until someone suggested replacing the dozens of supply vehicles and hundreds of troops that made up replenishment convoys in Afghanistan with a robot. A robotic helo.*

Oh yeah…. That's right. More rumor mill stuff that Lockheed's wunderkind was Duncan Hunter, the owner of QAS. At that time, was he really on contract with them? Osceola remembered hearing the old CEO took a lot of interest in the paint job of Lockheed's little helicopters. *Why would any CEO even care about a paint job?*

What was the deal with that paint? Why was it so special?

The Lockheed Martin engineers poured their hearts and souls into the *K-MAX* project; turning it into an unmanned robot. It wasn't a billion-dollar contract, but it kept a lot of them employed. Two of the very specialized, single-seat, heavy-lift helicopters had been quietly taken from logging camps in Canada and brought to the Lockheed facility in Owego. They were outfitted with countless electronic systems and converted to fly autonomously, without a pilot. They were programmed and tested to deliver supplies. Supply troops in Afghanistan no longer had to run the al-Qaeda gauntlet of IEDs and Taliban snipers. Troops wouldn't have to die getting supplies to their buddies in the field and in the mountains of Afghanistan.

And Ralph on a classified contract in harm's way….

Osceola read on the screen that each of the unmanned *K-MAX* aircraft was programed to deliver over two tons of supplies—fuel, food, ammunition—each night in the mountains of the Tora Bora; whatever the Marines needed. She continued to read in bullets: up to 15,000 feet of altitude. Thousands of pounds of cargo. Unmanned. Deaths and injuries of supply and security personnel performing replenishment activities fell to zero.

Why was it black? Because they were only flown at night.

Then it struck Stacey Osceola. *Did the K-MAX carry secret stuff along with the regular cargo? I was just getting started at the FAA, but I heard those helos won several awards. Ralph must have been doing a great job. Was that why the aircraft were treated as a national secret? Were the Marines cover for some CIA operation?*

The online encyclopedia provided additional insight. With the successful delivery of thousands of pounds of supplies, Special Operations Commanders became interested in the Marines' *K-MAX*. They had people in the mountains, and deliveries were made to them too. President Mazibuike learned of the novel rotorcraft that was changing the game in Afghanistan through the Secretary of Defense and the Chairman of the Joint Chiefs. *So, the K-MAX not only sustained combat operations in the mountains, but it allowed Special Operations troops to advance rapidly. I read somewhere the most challenging aspect of mountain fighting in Afghanistan was the cave system the Afghanis built over the centuries. That it was impossible to dislodge the Taliban or al-Qaeda or Osama bin Laden from the Tora Bora....*

Our troops couldn't fight an entrenched enemy.

Did the K-MAX carry special robots...secret...robots to eradicate the enemy from the mountains?

Stacey Osceola took a deep breath. *That had to be it, or something really close to that. Did the autonomous helicopters deliver autonomous ground robots to clean out the caves?*

If they were so effective, why were there only two of the helicopters converted? Maybe that was all that was necessary? But...but...why were they removed from the battlefield?

Stacey paused her research and sat back. She subconsciously squinted to make the picture in her mind come into better focus. Here and there, word on Lockheed's unmanned *K-MAX* would drift through the FAA's Aircraft Accident Investigations Office. It would remind her that Ralph Gilbert had left her for a helicopter. She heard how Marines and Special Operations warriors and presumably others would be so excited when the robotic helicopters flew in.

Stacey remembered the rest of the story: *but they wouldn't have been able to see it! They were painted a very special black. I guess they knew it was coming because they could hear it. Wait! QAS was Quiet Aero Systems!*

Lockheed made K-MAX autonomous; QAS made them quiet. Silent. The Marines knew what time it would be there. I am such a dolt.

Osceola touched her lips. Her office occasionally received Lockheed Martin publications, and there was one tiny article; some reporter was allowed a limited report. She recalled, *The troops had expected the unmanned K-MAX to be a spectacular sight, but in its special camouflage paint, it could not be seen, even with a cloudy background. And because it had an intermesher rotor system, no tail rotor and quiet wooden rotor blades, the K-MAX was virtually impossible to hear. Some troops who thought they had glimpsed the aircraft against an overcast sky said it resembled a skinny black praying mantis on a stick. A long wire from the airframe connected to the four-position carousel assembly underneath which carried four payloads. The helicopter didn't even have to land.*

There were sensors and switches which precisely lowered the cargo to a spot on the ground. The delivery program sensed when the load was safely on the ground, and the weight-on sensor automatically disconnected the load from the carousel. They didn't want the cargo released fifty feet above the landing zone.

Stacey Osceola harumphed. She thought she had figured it out. *That special black paint and the quiet rotors allowed them to safety deliver the cargo! And maybe other things.* Stacey vaguely remembered that there were a multitude of antennas. *And maybe some odd cowling.* She assumed the antennas were an enhanced differential global positioning system for pinpoint cargo delivery.

We weren't allowed to really see those helicopters. We only got a glimpse. We were incidental. We got NDA'd.

She nodded to herself, pleased that she had figured it out. Knowing what technology was likely employed for the Marines' K-MAX was both thrilling and sobering.

Maybe Ralph couldn't tell me....

Osceola narrowed her brows; *If this fire was caused by a K-MAX, why would that level of technology be flying around in commercial, civilian airspace? Was that on purpose? Did an unmanned K-MAX try to land on the roof of the newspaper building, or was there a pilot at the controls?* She continued her mental gymnastics. It was part of the process of being an investigator, but some of it was simply her curiosity.

Was that really what happened? Twenty newspaper companies have been destroyed across the country, but a K-MAX doesn't have the range. Did it have enough range to fly from Elmira to New York City? Why try to land on The New York Times?

I have to stop! Now we are getting crazy.

Stacey purged her thoughts on the *K-MAX*. She went to the internet for more information from the engine manufacturers' databases, but the *K-MAX* was still fascinating her. She hadn't thought about the helos since Ralph left for Afghanistan. Now she was very interested, borderline obsessed.

Again, she thought the unthinkable: *Maybe Ralph couldn't tell me....*

She learned that after almost three years of accident-free flying, an accomplishment so rare with unmanned rotorcraft that it bordered on the technically impossible, the commanders in the field had received cease and desist orders directly from the White House. President Mazibuike prohibited further unmanned *K-MAX* flights. The systems were to be removed from Afghanistan immediately. Osceola thought, *were they needed somewhere else? Or was there something else?* She continued reading, a few months later President Mazibuike resigned from the presidency and left the country.

Osceola analyzed the Wikipedia entry and ascertained that the combatant commanders, the Joint Chiefs of Staff (JCS), and Defense Department leaders *slow rolled* the White House decision to evacuate the unmanned *K-MAX* system for a few months. *K-MAX was so effective, why would the president do that? According to Wikipedia, there was no discussion on the presidential decision; there was no discussion that IED deaths would resume unnecessarily. With no explanation offered, it was as if the president wanted those casualties. That can't be right; that would be criminal. Whose side was he on, anyway? But wait, there was a reason he resigned. Someone dropped some documents that proved he was a bogus president; he wasn't even eligible to be president. And wasn't he a Muslim? That was the rumor.*

She read the final paragraph that said thirty-two months after beginning autonomous replenishment operations in Afghanistan, the two unmanned *K-MAX* aircraft were quietly brought home. Once they were stateside, they were disposed of. *Not shoved into the back of a hangar? Why not a museum? Why would you destroy a system that won awards? Was it because of the paint? Or the quiet technology? Or was it because there were more missions for the little black helo?*

It doesn't say where…. Hmmm…. So, after its missions with the Marines, official paperwork attested to the destruction of the unmanned K-MAX systems. They were scrapped.

What are the chances the serial number of the engine ties back to one of the Marine black birds that was… supposedly destroyed? Oh, that would be wild. If I could only find it.

Before perpending the ramifications of such an action, Stacey again reminded herself she had to get back to work. It worked for a few seconds. But then she focused on that Mazibuike decision to shut down the *K-MAX*.

They probably still had that special black camo covering. And if they were using secret equipment to purge the Taliban and al-Qaeda from the mountains…. I no longer wonder why…. I think I know…. Someone on that program was pissed. Pissed that they had something that was working against the enemy, something that gave them the edge. But the president…. Osceola considered the unthinkable. *Was it possible the president didn't want our troops to gain an upper hand against the al-Qaeda? Was he trying to protect someone? Bin Laden reportedly got away. Was that the reason? That's crazy.*

So, was the pissed off person on the K-MAX program the same pissed off person who crashed a supposedly destroyed unmanned K-MAX on top of The New York Times building to set it on fire?

Stacey, get a grip!

But why The New York Times? That does not make sense. The New York Times is a newspaper. I don't think it could be the same person. But…but what about Duncan Hunter? He died overseas some years ago. So, if that serial number is from an aircraft supposedly destroyed, am I supposed to believe that Duncan Hunter is really dead? When Mr. McGee was the CIA

Director? They play a game we are not familiar with. I sure as hell will not believe it!

Stacey read the Wikipedia entry's conclusion: *politicians from both sides of the aisle wondered why the White House, especially President Mazibuike, demanded that the lifesaving unmanned K-MAX aircraft were to be removed from Afghanistan and demolished.*

Osceola thought she had it. She narrowed her brows and said out loud the words she had been told earlier, "Why *The New York Times* and others? They were leftist newspapers. *The Washington Post* was a roof fire and a total loss. *The New York Times* was a roof fire and a total loss." She thought, *One fire is a data point, two fires are interesting, and three fires are a trend. Twenty fires is a program. Did someone declare war on the Democrat Party?* She blurted out an uncharacteristic, *"Shit!"*

Stacey Osceola looked up from her computer screen and said aloud, "Houston, I think we have a problem. While investigating one problem, I think we may have discovered another!" Stacey inhaled audibly. *I have more questions and suddenly Ralph can fix them. But I can't call him. He's out of my life.*

She found herself breathing hard. Stacey had thought about calling him ever since he returned from Afghanistan but never came close to connecting. He was still in her speed dial.

Ralph has his life and I have mine.

But the *K-MAX* had suddenly become a millstone around her neck. Stacey needed a simple answer, and then she could continue on with her investigation. She didn't want to make the trip when a call would do. She swallowed her pride. Stacey pulled out her smartphone, touched 1 and maintained pressure. In three rings, Ralph Gilbert answered the phone without looking to see who had called.

"Ralph, it's Stacey."

Long pause. "Hey Stace. It has been a long time."

"I know. Ralph, I have a technical question. I'm investigating the fire at *The New York Times* and I need to know if QAS has those two K-MAXs you worked on in Afghanistan."

We haven't talked in three years and this is what you call me for? "Yes. They're in the far hangar of the business. Preserved. I put them there myself." *What is she investigating?*

Stacey asked, "Are you sure?"

"What? You want me to go physically check?" He inserted a Bluetooth device into his ear and it connected automatically.

"Could you? It's important."

"Ok; for you, I'll do it. Let me get a golf cart and run down to the other end. Do you want to hold or have me call you back?"

"I can ride with you, if that's ok?"

They chatted about Afghanistan and returning home to New York as he drove the length of the QAS restoration business and the storage hangar where the CEO's office was located. Ralph thought she was being silly and had looked for an excuse for calling him. He maintained a friendly running commentary. "I'm entering the building. It takes two key cards. And I'm in. Through the double doors. I might lose you the deeper I get into the hangar. And there we go. Two *K-MAXs* in plastic. Wait a second while I send you pictures." He pushed a couple of icons on the smartphone and took the photographs of the two mechanical war heroes in white plastic.

Stacey asked, "Ralph, are you sure those are the aircraft you worked on?"

What an odd question. He shook his head in mild frustration. He said, "For you, I'll cut the cover and show you the black. Remember how black they were when they came out of the paint booth?"

"I do."

Gilbert flipped open a Buck pocketknife and cut two ten-inch lines forming a 90° angle. When he peeled back the thick plastic, he was instantly shocked and stared mutely at what he saw. He expected the strange black coating he had become familiar with in Afghanistan but found only red. Scarlet red; the same color the company had painted some firefighting helicopters years before. *WTFO? That cannot be!*

Stacey expected an answer but silence filled the connection. Either the connection had been severed or Ralph quit talking. "Ralph, can you hear me?"

Ralph was in shock and could say nothing. He stared at the red wedge under white plastic. He mechanically moved to the other *K-MAX* and cut a similar flap: there was the expected black coating. He found his tongue. Ralph whispered, "Stacey, what are you really looking for?" He looked over the white plastic of the red aircraft and noticed there were issues.

"Ralph; what happened? What did you see?"

"I have one black and one red *K-MAX*."

Stacey asked for clarification. "Not two black birds?"

"No. Just one. I don't…know…why there is a red bird in plastic. And it isn't an unmanned bird. This one is missing the GPS antennas and the loudspeakers on top."

Ralph was stupefied and began scrutinizing the covering of the red helicopter. "Ok, Stacey, what does it mean?"

"Ralph, don't do anything. Don't say anything. I'm in New York City. I can be there in a few hours. This I have to see for myself."

"Dinner?"

Stacey smiled, "It's on me. I'm on per diem. I'll see you soon. And thanks, Ralph. I'm looking forward to seeing you again."

"Me too." She signed off leaving him standing between the two *K-MAX* helicopters. With both hands, he felt the covering of the red one and found a clue. When he looked closely, he found the covering had been expertly cut amidships, into two pieces, and retaped to look as if it had never been tampered with. *What happened to the black K-MAX? I know we haven't painted either of these or any helicopter since we returned from Afghanistan.* Ralph looked closer, focusing on the antennas. The black one covered in plastic still had all the satellite data link antennas and loudspeakers used to kill rotor noise, but the red one did not have those. *What is going on?*

•   •   •

Ralph Gilbert brought Stacey into the hangar with the two *K-MAX* helos. He was intrigued how she was able to discern a black *K-MAX* explained the differences between the unmanned *K-MAX* and the manned version. She was a little bigger but still very good looking. Before he could ask the questions, Stacey said, "I have a sense Duncan Hunter is still alive."

Man, that girl is sharp! Ralph nodded. "He is but no one is supposed to know about it. He flew a DC-3 out of here a few days ago."

"I think he's CIA; Mister McGee was the CIA Director. I think it is all CIA. I don't know why."

Ralph said, "For the cover. QAS now has a firefighting group with a couple of surplus C-130s and flying boats, and helicopters. Like the *K-MAX*. Special crews on the QAS LM-100J from Texas work on the spyplane."

"There's a *spyplane?*"

Ralph nodded and said, "Everyone here — polygraphed. When you were here, it was just the painters. Now everyone is."

"What's it all mean?"

"First, I'll need you to sign an NDA stating you will not divulge what you have seen."

"And then?"

"Welcome to one of the Agency's special access programs."

•　　•　　•

Over a pizza, Stacey said, "I've been thinking about leaving the FAA."

Ralph asked, "What do you want to do?"

"There's too much death. At first it was interesting but it isn't for me."

"Want to come back here?" He grinned a bit.

"I think so."

"Maybe pick up where we left off?"

"I think I like that."

Stacey told Ralph about the newspapers. "They were all liberal newspapers. I want to work for a good company."

Ralph said, "The most interesting work is in federal service or supporting federal service."

"Like QAS?"

"Yeah. Sign me up."

CHAPTER 55

July 19, 2020

When President Mazibuike abandoned the United States, the Democrat Party was suddenly without a leader. With no charismatic leader of the stature of Mazibuike anywhere in the Democrat Party, the Democrat leadership, whose median age was in their seventies, were forced to host a handful of lengthy private meetings with groups of next-generation House Democrats. The early sessions featured dozens of new lawmakers, but there wasn't anyone of the caliber of the young Mazibuike.

Before President Maxim Mazibuike splashed onto the scene, the Democrat Speaker and the Senate Majority Leader barely took much of an interest in developing and counseling new Democrats. They rarely stumped each year for new lawmakers because the former president shooed the elders away and did all that. Overshadowing the development of new blood for the Democrat Party in Washington was Mazibuike's fixation on his *Muslim Outreach* programs. Mazibuike really wasn't interested in getting Democrats elected to office, but he used every trick of his office to inject radical Muslims in government offices. His first program under Executive Order was to demand federal contractors show they had a diversity hiring program in order to compete for government contracts. Instead of fighting the obvious discriminatory hiring policy, government contractors' hiring would now be based on how one looked instead of one's qualifications. Fear of being blackballed from government contracts if they complained, government contractors complied up to the moment President Mazibuike resigned from office. President Hernandez rescinded the Executive Order.

The moment Mazibuike resigned from office, never to be seen again in public, the Democrat Party in Washington found themselves in utter disarray. They had been unable to stop the Speaker of the House of Representatives, Javier Hernandez, from being sworn in as President, and they failed to stop his election. And the Republicans' next candidate was a political party juggernaut; Bill McGee was an African American and a war hero. He was beholden to no one, and Americans from both parties loved him.

The Speaker and the Senate Majority Leader knew they would soon be eradicated as a political party if Admiral McGee were to be elected. Whereas Republicans were the Party that went along to get along, McGee understood leadership and combat, and that *politics is combat by other means*. Democrats were experts in the political game of which typical Washington Republicans were unfamiliar. McGee was also familiar with treachery and evil, and had made his mark in uniform fighting them with every ounce of his being. If Democrats stood any chance to defeat McGee, they would have to use every dirty trick in the book up to and including destroying the electoral process to ensure McGee would not be elected. They called it the *nuclear option*.

After *The Washington Post* and *The New York Times* buildings had been turned into smoking piles of rubble, Aspen was the perfect place for a retreat and an emergency meeting of the minds of the *Aspen Institute*. Media moguls, a couple of industry and Wall Street billionaires, Democrat Party leaders, a pharmaceutical company billionaire CEO, and a representative of the Muslim Brotherhood joined the group for a series of meetings.

Dr. D'Angelo's five-year-old strategy had significant merit. Create a panic before the election, create a solution, and create fear that any Republican—even a distinguished war hero—didn't know how to save Americans from an invisible enemy. An infectious disease expert would come in with a solution and save the day, and create a win for the candidate who promised to protect all Americans.

The *Monkeypox* pandemic didn't generate the crisis they had hoped for. Its failure forced the CDC to speed up their next manufactured crisis. A weaponized virus purportedly escaped from a Chinese weapons laboratory had the CDC hyperventilating on camera that it had the potential to kill billions. It would take a special man, one who had fought infectious diseases all his life, to lead America to safety.

The former head of the Center for Disease Control, Dr. Salvatore D'Angelo, was the man of the hour. He wasn't the leader of the *Aspen Institute,* but he was one of the critical *Gatekeepers* of the Democrat Party. He would drive the charrette's agenda for the next two days in one of the nation's most stunning venues.

Privacy, serenity and elegance accurately described *Aspen House,* the most expensive home in Colorado. It was an extraordinary multi-acre estate, one of several owned by a software billionaire who provided the venue but was not in attendance for the meeting. The gated estate offered stunning views of Aspen's four mountains from its location just five minutes walking distance from downtown Aspen. The timeless and sophisticated architecture welcomed the natural beauty of the outdoors into every one of the lodge's fifteen bedrooms.

Highly collectable artwork from around the globe adorned the walls of living spaces, halls, and the sleeping quarters. Each room featured a different artist's pedophilic vision, typically faceless, nude, muscular adults with bound childlike figures. A painting of Muhammad bedding his child bride, Ayesha, hung over the mantle. An oil painting of former U.S. President Maxim Mohammad Mazibuike lounging in a chair wearing nothing but red heels, with a bound child between his legs, was displayed in the master bedroom. The Prime Ministers of France, Canada, Germany, Great Britain and other European elites possessed similar examples of the pornographic artwork in their homes. But *Aspen House* proudly distinguished itself in having the greatest and most diverse collection of pedophilic art in the country. *Aspen House* was not open to the public.

It was also the perfect place to hold a conference for the progressive elite in America. A series of French doors on the ground level opened to a gracious stone terrace for indoor/outdoor entertaining and allowed the mountain air to flow through all living areas. The multi-story, log lodge provided all the accommodations the decision makers, a baker's dozen of the left's most influential men and women, required for an emergency strategy meeting.

The *Aspen Institute* was in emergency session.

The CEOs of two of the nation's largest banks wondered aloud if their companies would be the next to go up in flames.

All but two of the members were terrified. Dr. Salvatore D'Angelo was frantic. Inwardly, so was Sheikh Zaid Jebriel. During the early hours of their meeting, there was an unspoken understanding not to mention Bill McGee.

First the *Post* and then the *Times* had been destroyed. Their billionaire owners were in attendance, one from Albuquerque the other from Seattle. They were livid and let it be known that it would take years to re-establish their newspapers and their social media operations to their former glory as the Democrat Party's main propaganda arm. Everyone around the conference table knew what had created this crisis. It was impossible to believe.

There must be a resistance movement within the Republican Party. Surprisingly, they were not playing by the rules. It was as if the buildings in Joseph Goebbels' Ministry of Propaganda and Public Enlightenment had been torched by the French resistance.

The U.S. government was not in the business of censorship, due to the First Amendment. The newspapers and the growing influence of the social media giants had been transformed by President Mazibuike's leadership to make it easier for the Democrat Party to censor political thought they did not agree with. They also spread misinformation, disinformation, and conspiracy theories to manage the narrative and to influence the voting masses, as necessary. Everyone trusted *The Times* and *The Post* not only for their news but for the truth. But now they were gone and the other newspapers of the left weren't convinced their turn in the volcano wasn't around the corner.

The American media companies had been successful in modeling themselves on the highly effective East German secret police policy used to control anti-communist activities, the Stasi's *Disintegration Directive*. They had been reaching their goals under a Democrat president, but after eight years of President Hernandez, they were now being strangled with their own unscrupulous reporters' behaviors and lies. They were hemorrhaging money and customers at a prodigious rate. The truth was getting out; their control of the narrative was being cleverly torched. They could not allow any more successes to the *Resistance*.

The American war correspondent, Demetrius Eastwood, had written several exposés on the fallacy and illegitimacy of the Monkeypox pandemic and the death of the world's richest man, Rho Schwartz Scorpii. Scorpii had been the prime financier of social media outlets and the mastermind of international child sex trafficking in Europe. The revered old man of the left had been obsessed with destroying America. Eastwood's television specials in the U.S. and Europe seemed to accelerate the collapse of European social media and significantly affected America's legacy and social media networks. His Monkeypox articles provided clarity and were anti-propagandistic, and garnered an ever increasing following.

Activities designed to impede or stop the left's media from controlling the narrative were every bit as effective as American military leaders running the *Maquis*, the French Resistance against the Nazis. It was obvious to the men and women of the *Aspen Institute* that there was a *resistance* movement in the U.S.

All but one of those in attendance at the mountain hideaway were American Democrats. The exception was a senior member of the Muslim Brotherhood, a Sheikh from the House of Saud. Sheikh Jebriel loathed the Muhammad and Mazibuike paintings in the house. He avoided traditional garb when stateside, favoring Saville Row while still anointed in the unguents of cinnamon and vanilla. He had been extended an invitation as a major donor, but he was ready to abandon his investments in America.

Sheikh Jebriel was the only surviving member of the original Muslim Brotherhood leadership council, which also had included the former American President Mazibuike. They had been a group of leaders from a dozen countries in the Middle East. Some of the dead were easily replaced. Internecine war broke out among the rest.

Because of a mechanical problem with his personal business jet, Sheikh Jebriel had run late for the strategy meeting at the top of the *Burj Khalifa* in Dubai in 2014. Being late had saved his life. When building security responded to the top-most habitable floor, they had found the bodies of all the other leaders of the Muslim Brotherhood scattered about with their brains blown out. The floor was awash in blood and glass; the conference room had been destroyed. Security cameras designed for passive surveillance were obliterated in the blast. Security had also found a blood smear leading from a pool of blood in the center of the lobby to the blown-out window. There were footprints in the blood smears.

At first glance, the carnage 2,000 feet above ground level had all the appearances of a surgical missile strike because the men's bodies had been shredded by flying glass. However, bullet entry wounds to the back of their heads told another tale. Every member of the council had been executed, and the former American president's body was missing. Dubai's secret police suggested Mazibuike might have been the target of the attack and may had been kidnapped. But when Mazibuike's crushed head and splattered torso were found at the base of the *Burj Khalifa*, the Dubai secret police rushed to control the crime scene and the narrative. It had been a precise decapitation strike on the Muslim Brotherhood's leaders.

Footprints in the blood were evidence that a single assassin had somehow gained access to the floor and systematically destroyed the Muslim Brotherhood elders. There had been nothing recorded on any surveillance camera. The only member of the council to have lost his head was the former American president.

With the controversial election of Mazibuike, America had been on its way to becoming part of the Muslim ummah. But a martyr who lost his head to the sword could never lead an insurrection, even in spirit. The assassin left his calling card: bootprints in the blood of an

American President. America was not surrendering her freedoms easily. Whenever the Muslim Brotherhood had the good fortune to place a *Brother* in the American government, some unseen hand eventually removed him.

Sheikh Jebriel was concerned he would be the next to vanish. "We have come so close to defeating your Republicans. The American Constitution was invalidated with the election of Maxim Mohammad Mazibuike as President of the United States, but we have not been able to maintain the momentum of that great day. We have become complacent, celebrating the victory of the *quiet war*, the victory of the Muslim Brotherhood in America, and the worldwide Islamic movement. We were so busy patting ourselves on the back and thinking our win had been total and all-encompassing, believing it was time to erect a monument to our successes that we forgot our enemies had not yet been vanquished. We now know America possesses weapons of unknown capabilities, and the evidence suggests they are using those weapons to fight back. Those bloody prints were made by U.S. military flying boots."

D'Angelo said, "You're saying an American killed Mazibuike."

Everyone around the conference table nodded. What was left unsaid was the *Resistance* was more organized and powerful than the *Aspen Institute* had believed possible.

Sheikh Jebriel continued speaking about their devastating defeat at the hands of unknown interlopers, the *Resistance*. "We still do not know how Brother Mazibuike was exposed. We know that since the day, the evil *Cee ah a* has purged every Muslim Brother that Mazibuike placed into the FBI."

"We don't know who at the *Cee ah a* is responsible. Our Brothers in Dubai cannot conceive a Muslima could have been at the heart of murdering Brother Mazibuike. To my Brothers, the evidence that an American organization could be responsible is not totally compelling. But the evidence of bloody footprints and your newspapers being destroyed by fire suggests one organization is responsible."

The software company chairman asked, "If it isn't CIA or McGee, then who?"

The Sheikh paused and looked around the room. *I don't believe any of these people are on the side of the Cee ah a. They are too dedicated to the cause of defeating the devil Republicans.* "One who we know is likely involved is the *Cee ah a's* Director of Operations, Marwa Kamal."

"Nazy Cunningham," spat the Speaker of the House of Representatives.

"We know who she is. She renounced Islam; she wears a Christian cross. She's an *apostate.* Her rapid ascension to the Director of Operations and the Director of their National Counter Terrorism Center was never expected."

The Senate Majority Leader said, "Or foreseen."

The CEO of a social media company interrupted, "Was that because she was assigned to Operations and not Administration? Seems like someone trusted her."

The Speaker of the House of Representatives immediately hissed, "She wears a *cross.*"

Sheikh Jebriel considered the question for several seconds. He said, "The *Cee ah a* has never had a Muslima in Operations before. We received reports there had been a green-eyed Muslima in Cuba, interrogating our al-Qaeda and Taliban Brethren who had been kidnapped from Afghanistan and Iraq. Cunningham has the green eyes of the devil Shah. Green eyes was very effective."

Quiet murmuring and nodding oozed from the assembly of men and women. They refocused their attention to Sheikh Jebriel.

"Since she arrived at the *Cee ah a* with an Americanized name, she has worked diligently to eradicate Muslims. The Cunningham woman was uniquely positioned to know how the Mazibuike documents were collected, and likely spirited them from their headquarters. We should not be surprised this Cunningham had agents who released those documents in the manner that they did."

Someone killed one of our Brothers and used his credit card to duplicate and distribute copies of Mazibuike's documents to the American Congress and alternate media. Our hubris was our downfall. We dismissed any Muslima in Operations at the Cee ah a as a myth. No Muslima would do those things she was reportedly doing. But we didn't have complete visibility over her when she was a junior intel officer. She was protected by unseen hands. She is the only one who could have done it. It had to be that Cunningham bitch. She knew that a Muslima in their Resistance movement would be an especial affront to Allah.

"The beheading of Mazibuike in Dubai…. That is not the work of a Muslima. But that was a signal. From their *Resistance*. Are we listening?"

There was another wave of murmuring and nodding from the *Aspen Institute* before the assembly broke up for the afternoon meal. They agreed that the Sheikh's analysis was on target. Nazy Cunningham's rise as the prime counterterrorism and anti-terrorism senior intelligence officer likely ensured the CIA could detect and eliminate the Muslims that Mazibuike had forced into the CIA administrative offices under presidential edict. Under the leadership of the *Black Shadow*, McGee and the illegal Republican president who replaced Mazibuike, the purge of Muslims from the Agency had been completed. Mazibuike had been defeated from within.

Before going to lunch, some of the *Aspen Institute* leaders met in a small lobby outside their rooms, wringing their hands. The discussions they were having now were the most important discussions of their lives. The right, the hated Republicans, and the CIA, were not only fighting back, but were attacking the very foundations of the Democrat Party: *The New York Times*, *The Washington Post*, the banks, the social media giants, and the pharmaceutical and software companies. *And that was illegal!*

The *Resistance* was using fire, the great cleanser. It was becoming a great problem, and the *Aspen Institute* had to make some decisions about the future of their Democrat Party. If they failed, the Republicans, led by the war hero Bill McGee, would destroy the Democrat Party, the counter-patriots conservative media called *dark state*, and everything they had worked so hard to achieve.

Their earlier discussions had been depressing. It was obvious the Republicans, despite the propaganda, were effectively countering Democrat Party initiatives. The wind had been in the Democrat's favor with the election of Mazibuike. Few people in America had been able to discern how the Democrat Party had facilitated the destruction of the *Nuremberg Code* and voluntary informed consent, and the emasculation of the American Psychiatric Association and their DSM. By advancing the rise of social media networks, they had been able to attack the Department of Defense, Christianity, and the CIA with charges of discrimination, racism, white supremacy, homophobia and Islamophobia. Now, there was blowback.

The Speaker of the House of Representatives spoke through her tremors, "We were drinking our own bathwater. We thought if we shouted racism every minute and demanded gun control and white supremacy investigations, we could achieve the downfall of the Republicans. We did not see an effective social media countercampaign, and when they brought down the newspapers...."

The Senate leader concurred. He said, "You'll never be able to convince me the CIA didn't kill Scorpii...."

The CEO of the world's largest pharmaceutical company dismissed the charge. "Viktoria, Ellis, he was in hospice and was taken to Houston's Anderson Cancer Center. It was a mercy flight and all above board. If someone wanted to kill him, they would have offed him in Germany."

The Speaker of the House of Representatives said, "Scorpii's personal guards are still missing, and his number two man was found immolated in an electric car."

Sheikh Jebriel had an off-handed comment, "Those *things* will kill you.... Was it an accident? I will never believe it was. No, I'm certain he was executed by the *Cee ah a*, and his car was set on fire to *cleanse* the scene. If there is fire, the *Cee ah a* is behind it, whatever it may look like. Do not doubt me."

A social media CEO said, "Classic contract CIA hit. In Europe? I don't know. They must use surrogates for things like that."

Viktoria pointed an eighty-year-old bony finger at the newspaper chairman and the media moguls, "*It is your job to tell them what to think!*"

Dr. D'Angelo added, "Free speech, informed consent, and their silly infatuation with assault weapons are dangerous ideas that need to be eliminated from the minds of Americans. You have to force behaviors. Like you did with Mazibuike, leverage propaganda and psychology in order to elect the next president."

The social media billionaire said, "Without the *Times* and the *Post*? We can only do so much. Good luck with that."

Sheikh Jebriel said, "The *Resistance* is becoming more effective than we imagined. The Republicans are not entertaining your arguments any longer."

The software chairman nodded concurrence with the outburst and offered a question, "Didn't the authorities recover all of Scorpii's wealth?"

The Speaker of the House jumped up and yelled, "*But not Scorpii's diaries; not the videos!*"

The Sheikh bluntly stated, "Hernandez has them."

A bank CEO turned and asked, "*President* Hernandez?"

The social media CEO who refused to wear a tie said, "Hernandez, CIA. Sameo, sameo."

The Speaker, Viktoria Bugliosi, sat down and said, "If the FBI had gotten to them first, I could have had them destroyed."

Sheikh Jebriel said, "It seems the *Cee ah a* was ahead of you. Suddenly it seems they have become more active. There is an element within that's functioning like the *Resistance*. You assumed Scorpii could not be taken or killed. You assumed he was protected."

The Speaker of the House said, "You assumed Mazibuike was protected."

Sheikh Jebriel thought, *What a Khazarian witch.* He turned his head away.

Dr. D'Angelo said, "Which is why this *Resistance* has to be stopped through unconventional means." *Like mosquitoes infected with T-gondi.*

"Mandate vaccines. It will turn them into sheep. I have done my part. It will take some time for you to find and defeat the *Resistance*. I said five years ago, we cannot let McGee win the White House. If he becomes president, he will destroy all of us."

The Speaker of the House of Representatives said, "It seems the only source of infection are the coastal states...."

Dr. D'Angelo said, "That's not correct. Half the country has been exposed to *T-gondi*. It's taking a little more time for symptoms to appear."

The bank CEO said, "Someone just needs to kill him."

Sheikh Jebriel said, "We thought he had been killed in Texas. But miraculously, he changed jets and escaped an American *Stinger*. Do you know the cost of that failure? Fifteen *mosques*."

The Speaker of the House had calmed down, "We all knew what Scorpii was doing to get intel out of NATO."

The *Times* chairman finally said something. "I didn't think he would record us! He betrayed us."

"Maybe Mazibuike jumped," said one of the social media CEOs.

Everyone looked at the man from the Muslim Brotherhood.

Sheikh Jebriel said, "That's wishful thinking, my friend. Someone cut off his head." *In the Islamic tradition.* "Beheading is done to make a statement. There are one or two seconds of consciousness after decapitation." The man from the Muslim Brotherhood placed his hands in his lap. "Someone is coming after us. We were once fifty; now we are but fifteen. They are effectively dismembering us just like they did Brother Mazibuike. We once had over a hundred active cells, but mosques across America are also being firebombed. Like your newspapers."

The Speaker of the House spat, "Now there is no one on the FBI Most Wanted Terrorist list. How can you recruit when the leaders are...."

Sheikh Jebriel asked, "... being decapitated?"

Vikoria Bugliosi said, "That is unprecedented."

Sheikh Jebriel said, "That is their *Resistance* at work."

The owner of the *Times* said, "I thought they all died naturally!"

The owner of the *Post* turned to the owner of the *Times* and said, "Get a clue. We might not report the truth, but we know the truth. It seems you are the only one who cannot believe they are systematically hunting down our surrogates and us."

The Senate Majority Leader said, "It would help us if we knew who they are."

The social media CEO offered, "CIA. It's always been the CIA."

Sheikh Jebriel said, "That doesn't tell us anything. If there was someone responsible at the FBI, my people who were there would have known it, but we have no visibility at the *Cee ah a* or the FBI anymore. Of course, it's them. And except for their Muslima and McGee, we do not know who is their leader."

The owner of the *Times* said, "Except for Mazibuike's death, Al-Jazeera reported many of the others appeared to have died of natural causes."

Sheikh Jebriel said, "We control them, and they report what we tell them. The reality is the men on the list died with holes in their chests or tiny drones blew their brains out. Please accept, some were made to look like accidents. But they were all assassinated. At night. They let their guard down. Do not let your guard down. If you have the correct capability, it is easy. Even Al-Jazeera is subject to disinformation."

Turning his head to the software company chairman, the chairman of the *Times* said, "I agree. The military on scene reported the villagers stopped them."

"But the Boko Haram units vanished as if they had been fed to lions. Scorpii's man, I understand his EV stopped, caught on fire, and trapped him inside. The doors wouldn't unlock. An incredible accident in Belgium. No one has that kind of intel and range."

The Speaker of the House whispered, "The CIA does."

"What if Sperry, Gertz, Whittle, Duran, and Murphy were actually killed? You're suggesting their deaths were made to look like accidents."

The pharmaceutical CEO said, "We've taken billions...."

The social media CEO with the tie said, "Not lately…."

The newspaper mogul who had been quiet for much of the discussion offered, "An unexpected interruption."

The Senate Majority Leaders said, "You can't do anything with it if you're dead."

The Speaker of the House said, "Regardless, we are no longer able to control the narrative. We can no longer count on or use media to influence people's decisions and attitudes. Even transgenders have suddenly realized they have been used, and they have turned on us. Same for the Hispanics and the African Americans."

She wagged a bony finger at D'Angelo. "You may think your vaccine will save us, but I am not convinced."

D'Angelo said, "These things take time. But they are very effective."

Viktoria Bugliosi looked defeated. She said, "You are going to get your billions and McGee is going to win. And when he does, he'll have them come after us."

The owner of *The New York Times* said, "Then it is obvious. It is time to decamp and move to a less hostile climate. I understand Dubai is marvelous this time of year."

The software company chairman barked, "What? And hope they don't come for us there?"

Sheikh Zaid Jebriel "Mazibuike tried to run, and they still found him and killed him in Dubai. No one could envision someone entering the *Burj* from the outside."

The Senate Majority Leader spat, "Arrogance killed him. He thought he discovered who outed him, who drove him from office…."

The Speaker of the House decried, "And the VP killed himself? *In his house*? *That* was impossible, unless the Secret Service was in on it."

The owner of the *Times* said, "And ever since Hernandez became President, we have been on the defensive."

The group looked at the man from the Muslim Brotherhood. He didn't disappoint.

Sheikh Jebriel said, "We found him, the *Cee ah a* operative. We paid the fatwa on him. He died in an aircraft accident. The President and the *Cee ah a* director presided over his burial at your Arlington Cemetery."

The owner of the *Washington Post* noted, "But the men on the FBI's Most Wanted Terrorist List continued to be found and purged."

"Are you are suggesting whoever this person is, he isn't dead?"

Admitting defeat was not his forte. His fingertips formed a teepee. Sheikh Jebriel nodded saying nothing. "We may have been led to believe the military funeral was real when it was an illusion." *A grand illusion. The president and the CIA director walked in the rain! They wouldn't walk in the rain to maintain an illusion, would they? That would mean Hernandez is Resistance!* Exasperation overcame him. "They continue to use our methods against us. They are coming after us."

After another audible exhalation, Sheikh Zaid Jebriel lowered his head, closed his eyes, and then said, "We must do whatever it takes; McGee cannot become president. I will redouble our efforts to destroy him. If he is able to live, he will change the trajectory of government and the governments of the world. He will reverse everything Mazibuike accomplished. All of our work will have been for naught. We will be eradicated. We may not even be safe here."

The Speaker of the House said, "Many of us threatened to leave the country if Hernandez was reelected; if McGee is elected, he will turn the dogs of war on us. I concur, we are not safe. We must go. Let us meet in Europe."

"Dubai," said the Sheikh. "We have an underground city." *Although… the same night my Brothers were killed atop the Burj, our inventory escaped and the emir's yacht was stolen. 300 children…. Gone…. They know of that too.*

Dr. Salvatore D'Angelo turned toward the pedophilic artwork and interrupted the deafening silence. "I must visit Cologne."

CHAPTER 56

July 20, 2020

Twelve hours after he had last seen Duncan Hunter, Director Todd welcomed Hunter into his Escalade limo with a frown. They remained silent until they entered the White House grounds.

Hunter and Todd passed through security by flashing blue badges annotating their Cat One *Yankee White* clearances. Hunter's badge identified him as covert asset, Dante Locke. They left their Blackberries in the limo.

They walked side by side, in step, directly to the Situation Room. As they approached the special conference room, Hunter ran his hand through his Cary Grant-like, perfectly gray, Hollywood hair. He was glad he had worn his good suit. It fit him well and was one of Nazy's favorites. It usually made her smile, but the impromptu meeting with the Director changed the atmosphere and presaged trouble.

As the men were escorted into the Situation Room, Director Todd asked for Duncan to sit next to him. "They may have place cards." Once inside, they saw men and women in suits and uniforms standing along the walls; two empty seats beckoned, and they sat down. President Hernandez occupied the seat at the head of the table and said in command voice, "Now we can get started."

Hunter took stock of who was in the Situation Room. It was filled to the brim with people he mostly did not know. A pair of Air Force generals with visitor badges had seats around the table. Having seats meant you were someone important, like the Joint Chiefs of Staff. There were old guys in suits with blue badges. Hunter thought, *Probably NRO…NSA?* There were no introductions – probably for his benefit. He sighed. *Why do I feel like I'm about to be shot?*

The White House Chief of Staff spun his fingers. To the retired Air Force general running the CIA, it was the signal to start the brief.

Hunter's eyes panned to the projector screen on the wall opposite the President. There were no briefing materials.

The Director of the CIA began, "The following information is Top Secret and contains SCI information. The banner markings for this slide is TOP SECRET// HCS/ TALENT KEYHOLE/ IMCON// SPECIAL ACCESS REQUIRED// NOT RELEASABLE TO FOREIGN NATIONALS. There are no handouts."

When President Hernandez eyes shifted to the man at mid-table, all eyes turned to the uniformed Air Force four-star general.

The Air Combat Command (ACC) Commander began, "About 12 hours ago, one of our F-22s enroute to Okinawa left formation after aerial refueling off the coast of South Korea and disappeared."

Director Todd said, "Slide. IMCON satellite imagery placed the aircraft on a trajectory for a fighter base in North Korea; as you can see, it is on the ground at Toksan Air Base. Slide. We believe it was towed into a bunker. We believe those bunkers are well protected from JDAMs, Joint Direct Attack Munitions, by twenty feet of reinforced concrete. Slide. There is only one hangar that is now guarded with gun emplacements and reinforcements."

The Air Combat Commander said to the President, "It could be dismantled already."

Hunter interrupted, "Unlikely. But you have a quickly closing window of opportunity to get it back before they start taking it apart."

That was the moment the CIA Director and everyone else in the room panned their eyes toward the man with the Dante Locke badge.

Hunter continued, "When Belenko took the FOXBAT to Japan in 1977, it took several days before we got the right guys into Japan to look at it and take pictures. The real problem is whether they have taken action to disable it from flying. This is not Hollywood, Clint Eastwood, and FIREFOX. It will be impossible to get it out of there if they disable it in the simplest of ways, like deflating a single tire. You want it back. Have we contacted them to acknowledge one of our officers diverted to the closest runway because he had an emergency? Say it was an accident? Offer a thousand *gomennasais* or *joesonghamnidas*. Have we offered the little dude in Pyongyang a reward for taking care of our pilot and aircraft in the interim, like a new Gulfstream? Anything to buy some time to keep the Chinese and the Russians away from it?"

President Hernandez said, "I concur with the Chairman that we make all efforts to recover the jet, or if that is impossible, destroy it. You make a good point. We haven't contacted them. That has its challenges because they are not talking to us or anyone. What is the status of North Korea's missile program?"

The Director of the Defense Intelligence Agency, a Marine Corps Lieutenant General said, "North Korea test fired four long-range cruise missiles off its eastern coast today. Pyongyang's official Korean Central News Agency said the launches, which were confirmed by South Korea's military, were intended to verify the reliability of the missiles and the rapid response capabilities of the unit that operate those weapons."

President Hernandez said, "Or to send us a message. Try nothing."

"Yes, Sir. The North Korean state media said the missiles flew for nearly three hours after being launched from the northeastern coast and showed they can hit targets 2,000 kilometers away."

Reference to the "northeastern coast" got everyone's attention. Heads turned to the screen. The Lt. General continued, "It also test-fired an intercontinental ballistic missile yesterday. But the Korean Central News Agency implied a pair of short-range missiles were launched last week to proclaim a dual ability to conduct nuclear strikes on South Korea and the U.S. mainland. South Korea, Japan, and the U.S. cannot verify the accuracy of those statements."

The White House Chief of Staff scribbled some notes.

Director Todd nodded and said, "Slide."

President Hernandez continued, "The National Security Council knows that a conventional response for recovery would require multiple aircraft and hundreds of personnel. This is not Osama bin

Laden's compound in Abbottabad. This is a base with about a thousand troops, maybe more."

"I believe we need to hear from a neoteric — not only someone who can bring in fresh ideas, but someone who has done this kind of, ah, *work*. We don't have time to study the problem like the bin Laden raid. We don't have time to build models or recreate compounds. If we are going to recapture the *RAPTOR*, we need a different approach. I asked Director Todd if we could hear from one of his special assets."

Hunter said to the Air Force General, "You have an unconventional problem; you require an unconventional response."

Most of the men and women around the Situation Room wondered, *Who the hell is this arrogant sixty-something superannuated spook?*

All eyes switched from Hunter to the President; when the President cleared his throat Hunter turned his focus on the President.

President Hernandez said, "I do not want to start a war over a missing jet. If we cannot resolve this quickly or peacefully, if we have any hope of resolving this crisis in our favor, I believe *Noble Savage* assets are necessary. *Maverick*, I know what you have done in the past; is this something you can do?"

There was a collective, nearly inaudible gasp from the men and women around the conference table, as they collectively thought: *what can one guy do?*

The SOCOM Commander was taken aback. *Maverick? Wait, is this that Maverick? Nigerian Queen? Rescued 6-700 passengers from terrorists who hijacked the jet? Killed the heads of Islamic terrorist across the Middle East and Africa? How many times have we been given credit for missions on the other side of the planet, that were impossible and that we did not do? This dude must have a RENEGADE airplane. Very hush hush. What else has this guy done?*

Hunter heard the thought pounding in his head, *This could be a suicide mission. It depends on what I find there. I feel like I'm between Scylla and Charybdis. This could be undoable.* He turned his eyes from the satellite image to Todd and the ACC Commander and asked, "Do

*RAPTOR*s have *cart-start*? Does it have a battery, or does it require external power to start it?" His gaze returned to the overhead. *If I can't start it, I can't get it out of there.*

For the first time that day, the Air Combat Commander and the CIA Director smiled. The general nodded and Todd answered, "Yes, on the *cart-start*. It requires two cartridges and it takes about a minute to load them."

Maverick pressed the issue. "Soviet military aircraft do not use a standard AN external power receptacle and jets typically don't have batteries."

The ACC Commander looked at *Maverick* hard. "We have a battery pack for engine start emergencies. A battery control unit. A BCU which fits into the auxiliary power receptacle."

Maverick responded, "Just like a BCU for a *Stinger*. Where is the receptacle located?"

The SOCOM Commander thought, *A pilot that knows about Stingers? Firsthand?*

The ACC Commander replied, "Left wheel well. The BCU is the size of a motorcycle battery and allows a pilot to have power specifically for the engine ignitors to start the engine when external power is not available. Once the engine has fired off, you'll be able to bring the generator on line to fire the other engine ignitors to start the other engine."

Hunter said, "So, just so we are all aware, if we are able to neutralize the North Koreans, and if it hasn't been disabled, and if I'm able to start it, then Mr. President, I might be able to get our *RAPTOR* out of there." He returned to scrutinize the satellite image still on the projector screen. *I can get in; the trick will be not to get killed.*

The men and women in the Situation Room were incredulous. *How is that even remotely possible?*

Hunter's scrutiny of the target airbase was interrupted when the ACC Commander said, "*Maverick*, we can show you how to load them. It takes an APG a minute. The BCU clips into place."

The President asked, "APG?"

Hunter took his focus off of the satellite image of the Tokson, North Korean air base. "Mr. President, that is an Airplane General. An aircraft mechanic. So, if I can land with no one shooting me, and if they haven't disabled the aircraft where I cannot fly it, I'll load the *cart-start* canisters and the BCU to start it. Those bunkers are constructed for protection from JDAMs, so any aircraft can taxi into and out of them. The level of effort and the time required to extract the jet for flight is already in the realm of the undoable for one person. I'm going to need help."

The SOCOM Commander at the far end of the table accused Hunter, "You're *Maverick*. You disabled a dozen hijackers who took *The Nigerian Queen* a few years ago. It would have taken us days to get into position...." He offered any of his troops or equipment.

Hunter shook his head. "Sir, thank you." He almost shrugged. "That night; I was, uh, *in the area*. For this, mission success will require *both* of my airplanes." *And Chain. And cart-starts, and a battery. And there's only so much I can carry.* He inhaled and exhaled, and said, "To be clear and manage expectations, if the 22 hasn't been disabled, and I can start it, then we have a chance. I'll need a checkout of the cockpit. After that, we need a fast ride into theater. I can't get the *RAPTOR* out of there if they drained the fuel tanks, flattened the tires, removed some necessary-for-flight panels, or it just won't start, something like that. If I can't start it, you will want me to destroy the jet, correct?" There were nods around the table.

The Chairman of the Joint Chiefs asked, "You think you can get on the ground without being detected?"

Hunter said, "Sir, I can get there and I can get on the ground. The problem becomes infinitely more difficult when I am on the deck." He mentally double checked what he would need: *I have cloaking material.... Firestarters to turn the jet into a flaming unusable mess. I'll need my spider vest, one or two AeroDogs. If I can start it and get it to the runway, I'll program the Yo-Yo to return to Osan. We just have to incapacitate a thousand? Well, we have the technology and should have the element of surprise. The North Koreans are notorious for not conducting night ops. But that's an awful lot of chances for unexpected variables. Every second I'm on the ground makes it more difficult to survive.*

Chain will just have to get them to look up. That means flares, and we have those. For those who don't want to play, those that don't look up, an AeroDog on wheels should incapacitate any protection the Koreans have deployed on the ground. And if that doesn't work, I guess I'll blast our way out of there. Any way you look at it, I'll be a sitting duck on the ground. Maverick turned to the sound of a voice and found a general talking to him.

"We can give you a check out at Langley." The ACC Commander remained incredulous and asked, "Have you flown fighters?"

Maverick said, "F-4s. TOPGUN. LATT. (Low Altitude Tactical Training). My helmet is tuned for my aircraft and is not compatible, I'll need to carry one of yours with an O2 mask. I'll also want a skullcap, G-suit, and a torso harness. No LPU." (Life Preserver Unit).

Life Preserver? Must be a Navy pilot. For your aircraft? What the hell aircraft are we talking about? The SOCOM Commander interrupted. "I cannot see how a pilot can recover this asset."

President Hernandez turned to the CIA Director. Todd said, "*Maverick* has unique capabilities."

President Hernandez gave Director Todd a thumbs up. *I don't want to tell them Hunter has been doing this much longer than I've been President.* He said, "I have the utmost trust and confidence in *Maverick's* ability to recover your jet, if it hasn't been disabled." *I'm not confident SOCOM can.*

The four stars around the table nodded. *Meaning, the Agency will use some secret capability that only the Agency may have.* The ACC Commander said, "We will provide you with flight equipment. Anything else?"

"Thank you, sir. Whatever else I need, we have in our container. Flares, chaff, *TROJANS*, ammo." *Maverick* suddenly smiled and said, "*Stuff.*"

The attendees' ears and the corner of their mouths perked up when *Maverick* said, "*Stuff.*"

He thinks he can do this? Does he think he can just walk in?

Maverick looked at Todd, "Success is a function of multiple facts, can I start it, and is it flyable. I won't know that until I'm on the deck. My playmate will provide cover overhead."

Director Todd nodded and said, "We need as small a footprint as possible, and I'm very comfortable with *Maverick* attempting to recover the *RAPTOR*."

Maverick nodded as President Hernandez said, "I wouldn't put *Maverick's* life in undue danger if he hasn't gained *some experience* in these types of scenarios. He has proven himself to be unusually adept and has solved very complex problems on the fly."

The SOCOM Commander interjected, "Like parachuting onto the back of a jumbo jet, getting in, then neutralizing a dozen hijackers to rescue hundreds of passengers. Within an hour of their landing."

President Hernandez divulged to those in the Situation Room a national secret, "That's *rescues* times three…." Attendees were stolid but taken aback. Hunter remained indifferent, scanning the map projected on the wall. Thinking.

President Hernandez continued, "The other option is to let them keep it. I don't want to blow it up, but I don't want them to think they can keep it. I want to give *Maverick* the best chance for success."

Maverick smiled at the vote of confidence.

Director Todd asked, "Mr. President, everyone, is that all?"

Duncan Hunter turned to the generals and asked, without the slightest hint of a drawl, "Who took your jet?"

The Air Force Chief of Staff was prepared. "Darius Laskin was born on 31 August, 1993, and spent his infancy in Berkely, California. His parents were Daniel Laskin and Daria Laskin. These are actually Russian names. His mother and father were professors at the University of California at Berkeley; his father taught constitutional law and his mother had a PhD in jurisprudence and social policy. Professor Daniel Laskin is a frequent contributor to the California Law Review. Both professors were members of the Communist Party USA and were lifelong subscribers to *The Economist, The Eastern*, and *The*

Socialist Review, as well as contributors to *Covert Action Quarterly* and *Covert Action Magazine.* They remain active and committed communists. Laskin' younger brother, Melor Laskin, committed suicide shortly after he withdrew from UC Berkeley at age 22. Laskin's youngest brother, Sasha died as a child, cause of death, unknown. Also, the name Melor means a 'member of the communist party.'"

The vice president asked, "Good God, how many warning signs did you need....".

The Air Force Chief of Staff pinched his lips and continued, "Laskin cited his parent's dedication to the Communist Party USA and his brothers' fate as the many reasons he *rejected* Communism. He commented that he 'had been surrounded by this evil ideology all his life and wanted nothing to do with it.' The investigator didn't perceive him as a threat, and with no other adverse findings to his character, recommended he be given a clearance. However, just recently we learned that while at UC Berkeley, Darius Laskin wrote about Communism in a Marxist theory class. He wrote, 'It offered me what nothing else in the dying world had power to offer at the same intensity, faith and vision; something for which to live, and something for which to die.'"

The General inhaled after the caustic words and continued, "UC Berkeley had a 'Great Books' series of Marxist and Communist authors, and Laskin's term paper was on Vladimir Lenin's *Soviets at Work.* The instructor remarked he was deeply affected by it. This is all new information. His background investigation, obviously, wasn't performed properly. Neighbors, friends, and classmates were dedicated fellow travelers."

President Hernandez remained silent as he pinched his lips tight. The vice president said, "He fooled a lot of people."

Maverick asked, "How did he come to the Air Force?"

"Cal Berkely has an Air Force ROTC (Reserve Officers' Training Corps) and he majored in Aerospace Studies. His background investigator was impressed that he had separated himself from his parents. But now that we know the rest of his story, it may have been a ruse to gain access to the ROTC and Air Force's secrets."

Hunter thought, *You think!?*

"Also at UC Berkeley, his undergraduate peers and friends included a Who's Who of Marxist activists, many of whom went into the Soviet underground after the USSR's dissolution in 1991 and were active in socialist causes. Darius Laskin is not mentioned in any Communist Party USA literature."

Maverick looked up from under his eyebrows and asked, "Sexuality? Did he like girls?"

The Air Force Chief of Staff didn't like the question or the implication. "Under the *Don't Ask, Don't Tell* law we've been prohibited from asking."

Maverick glared at the generals and said, "In other words, a gay white man took your jet. Let me make you aware that in 1987, *homosexuality* was struck from the *Diagnostic and Statistical Manual of Mental Disorders* by a majority vote of the American Psychiatric Association. When a Democrat president was elected in 1992, sexual activists lobbied him to allow gays in the military. That president leaned on the JCS for support of gays in the military and fired enough of them until he found some who would capitulate. *Don't Ask, Don't Tell* was the DOD policy from 1993 to 2011, when it was repealed by Congress. So, since World War Two, the JCS had been the bulwark against Communist and Democrat Party attacks on destroying the good working order of the Pentagon and the discipline of DOD troops. But since 1993, the JCS has shown no leadership or bravery against the left's culture war. Instead of rejecting it, they allowed the Democrat policy of *Don't Ask, Don't Tell* to become the law of the land. Prior to that law, physicians screened recruits and cadets with *sexual* and *mental* disorders from penetrating DOD. *Don't Ask, Don't Tell* prohibited physicians screening recruits with *sexual* and *mental* disorders, and the military's leaders offered no resistance. Now crazies have infiltrated the DOD. Now we have an acknowledged Communist, raised by UC Berkely Communists, likely a gay man who took one of your wonder jets to a hard Communist country. Is anyone surprised? This did not have to happen. For almost forty years, JCS had multiple opportunities to stop rogue Democrat presidents from implementing policies that undermined DOD and adversely affected the warrior culture that is essential to win America's wars. JCS allowed the infiltration of Communist and socialist thought into DOD. Russians and the Chinese do not allow gays in their military, and there is a reason. Your predecessors showed no leadership in protecting the country against domestic enemies; your peers chose their careers over their country."

The Situation Room was totally silent. The outburst was wholly unexpected.

Maverick took a deep breath and pointed a finger at the Chief of Staff of the Air Force. "Sir, if I run into the turd who took your jet, what do you want me to do with him?"

The ACC Commander recovered from *Maverick's* soliloquy. He was astounded at the question and the man's confidence and the fire in his eyes. His eyes never left Hunter's. *He is absolutely right.* The ACC Commander interrupted, "Send a signal." *You can kill that traitor for all I care.*

Maverick touched his fingers to his brow in an informal salute and said, "10-4, sir. I need some pictures of him."

The ACC Commander nodded and thought, *I don't know why you would want his picture...I guess it wouldn't hurt.*

The vice president asked, "Can we maintain a media blackout until *Maverick* retrogrades the area?"

President Hernandez said, "Make it so."

The Director of the National Reconnaissance Office asked, "*Maverick*, will you be detected crossing the border?"

President Hernandez warned, "Any comments made in this room stay in this room. Continue."

Hunter looked at Todd and the President, then turned to the man in the dark suit and dull tie. *Maverick* addressed him directly. "Sir, to my knowledge, I haven't in the past. The airplane is coated with the latest in nanotechnologies, and its stealth characteristics were validated at Helendale to have the RCS of a BB, but that's head on. It has been proven to be undetectable by conventional means, meaning Soviet-era anti-missile defenses, but our *countermeasures* have not been tested against space-based assets…." *Because there has been no need over the Middle East and Africa. Maverick* continued, "We have no data that a space-based radar could pick up the planforms of our aircraft. Against a backscatter radar? I have no data, sir. Is that your real question?"

The man from the NRO nodded and said, "Mr. President, we may be able to *neutralize red assets* for the period *Maverick* and his playmate are on their run, without disclosing means and methods, if the weather cooperates."

President Hernandez nodded his assent. He thought, *In other words, you'll use a laser to blind Chinese or Russian satellites. Maverick uses lasers in a similar capacity to incapacitate terrorists. He saved those SEALs in Syria. Got the defector out of Iran. But will he really be able to do this on an industrial scale?*

Hunter thought, *The NRO Director used "playmate" in the context of a fighter pilot's vernacular. This guy's a player.*

President Hernandez said, "I expect all of you will help in any way you can. Thank you, Director Bose."

The NRO Director said, "We'll maintain liaison with Director Todd; flight following *Maverick's* progress."

Maverick smiled and added, "Thank you, sir."

Director Todd paused and thought, *Maverick acts as if the word fail doesn't even exist. His confidence is incredible. He's acts as if he knows exactly what needs to be done; he can see it. He probably knew he would get the call. Like McGee on 9-11. The President can see it. I regret, I don't. I can see why his capabilities are Presidential Eyes-Only material. And the President has nothing but confidence in him.*

The President allowed Maverick to tear into the pompous generals for their lack of leadership without comment. He did the same thing at Laughlin. The man is fearless. There's really nothing more to say. Time to get this show on the road. Director Todd said, "There is to be no further discussion of this mission for any reason. Divulging special access program information can get our people killed. Maintain a media blackout for as long as possible. After recovery, we can reconvene at my place or the Pentagon for a hotwash, if necessary."

President Hernandez nodded and stood up, signaling the meeting was over. *We'll know if Duncan was successful. I won't need to know the minutiae.* The military men stood when the President stood. President Hernandez walked over to Duncan Hunter, shook his hand, and placed his other hand on *Maverick's* shoulder. "God Speed, *Maverick*." Then the President turned on his heels. He and his staff departed, leaving the remaining men and women in the Situation Room to line up to shake *Maverick's* hand and offer their support. The final two people in the handshaking queue were Todd and the ACC Commander. Todd told Hunter, "I'll let the DO know what you're doing."

Maverick took Todd's hand and said, "Thanks, Boss. I know she's worked with STRATCOM to coordinate special lifts."

From behind him, the STRATCOM Commander said over *Maverick's* shoulder, "Director Todd, we'll get with the DO for anything *Maverick* requires." *Maverick* turned and thanked the general.

Then the ACC Commander gripped Hunter's hand and pulled him close, "*Maverick*, we're burning daylight."

Director Todd pulled the Air Force Chief of Staff aside and whispered into his ear, "When I deliver your jet, you'll transfer what UAP assets you have to me. (Unidentified aerial phenomena). *Capiche?*"

The general was shocked but nodded. *We allowed a commie to take our jet. Magoo is probably correct; we probably can't protect the UAP we have.*

CHAPTER 57

July 20, 2020

During the six hours immediately after the meeting at the White House adjourned, a C-17 *Globemaster III* was tasked for a top secret mission and positioned at Andrews Air Force Base. General officers were all over the place. Both of the *Noble Savage* program aircraft had been loaded aboard the massive cargo jet. The CIA Director of Operations, Nazy Cunningham, had contacted the special access program's current and former mechanics for the special tasking, and the men rendezvoused at the Baltimore-Washington International Airport. Agency vehicles provided the bulk of transportation to Andrews.

One of the YO-3A's oldest mechanics should not have been available. He lived in an arcadian paradise in a cabin he had built along the Yukon River. But he was south in the 48 contiguous, visiting a granddaughter who had completed Army flight training at Fort Rucker, Alabama. When the CIA's DO called, Bob Jones was standing in "the Vault" of the U.S. Army Aviation Museum Restorations Division. He was telling his family the history of the three experimental aircraft in the room that led up to the development of the YO-3A. Jones promised Nazy he would be on the first jet out of Dothan heading to Baltimore.

• • •

On a VC-37B, a militarized version of a Gulfstream G-550, the ACC Commander and two instructor pilots gave *Maverick* a crash course in the nuances of flying an unarmed F-22 *RAPTOR*. Upon their arrival at Langley Air Force Base, *Maverick* and the instructor pilots were ushered into a full-motion simulator. They familiarized the old pilot with the cockpit layout, switches, and multi-function displays. Proper switchology to drop external tanks. *Maverick* practiced start, taxi, takeoff and landing procedures until he memorized them. Then he received on-ramp, hands on training on accessing and loading the *"cart-start"* cartridges, and how to attach the Battery Control Unit. The Air Force wouldn't allow a failed ladder hatch to get sucked into an intake and destroy a $50 million engine, therefore, the *RAPTOR* was not equipped with an internal boarding ladder. *Maverick* learned how to raise the canopy and how to gain entry to the cockpit without a boarding ladder.

Since he had upgraded the YO-3A's ancient analog indicators to the latest electronic displays of an F-18 cockpit, *Maverick's* familiarity with upgraded cockpits enabled him to get checked out quickly. The positioning of the throttles, ignition switches, speed brakes, landing gear and flap handles were the same as they had been since aircraft first rolled off WWII assembly lines in Canada and the U.S. Normal equipment — landing gear handle, speed brakes, throttles — on the left; emergency handles — tail hook, RAT, canopy jettison — on the right side of the cockpit. Ejection seat handle always between the legs to protect the boys.

•   •   •

Back at Andrews AFB, Duncan Hunter met up with the other YO-3A pilot, Link Coffey, call sign *Chain*, and the *Yo-Yo* support crew. Joe Thompson, Tom Barraclough, Bob Jones, and Bob Smith met *Maverick* and *Chain* in the Base Operations building for last-minute head calls and a hot meal from the flight kitchen. Bob Jones and Bob Smith — both U.S. Army veterans who had cared for the two QT-2 *Prize Crew* and later the YO-3As, when the aircraft were in Vietnam — had served as Hunter's support crew from the earliest days of the Agency's special access programs. They had served under *Wraith* when the aircraft only had a FLIR, and under *Weedbusters* with the installation of the UV-C laser aerial eradication system, and finally under *Noble Savage* with the installation of the Terminator Sniper System and multiple laser designators.

Bob Jones was still as tall and thin as he had been in those early days. But his bushy, shoulder length gray hair that had always been pulled back into a ponytail at the start of the program was gone. Bob Smith was still heavy, still bald, and still sported a long, thin, ZZ Top beard. For the better part of fifteen years, Bob and Bob had kept the *Wraiths* in better than pristine condition. Joe Thompson and Tom Barraclough, the newest members of the *Noble Savage* team, reminded *Maverick* and *Chain*, both former Marine Corps pilots, that once again the Army was helping the Marines do their missions. *Maverick* inquired how Bob and Bob got the word, and Jones told him, "Nazy called and said she needed us. You know we cannot tell that woman, 'No.'"

Maverick smiled and erupted, "Tell me about it!" *What did Nazy have to promise them to get them out of their retirement cabins in Montana and Alaska? Jones had to have been in the States when Nazy called him. He couldn't have traveled from Alaska. I'm just glad he is here. I'm sure we will need him.*

Maverick thought, *the players are all here. Now we're gonna need a lot of luck.*

CHAPTER 58

July 21, 2020

During the first two hours aloft of the sixteen-hour flight, *Maverick* briefed his vision of the mission to *Chain* Coffey and the maintenance crew. The men were surprised to be going to South Korea. ETA 2100 local. No further details of the *need-to-know* operation were provided to the maintenance men. *Maverick* discussed which aircraft would be loaded with what special equipment. *Maverick's* aircraft would be loaded with flares, and *Chain's* aircraft would be loaded with chaff, flares, and TROJANS—air launched decoys. Both *Yo-Yos* would be provisioned with incendiary bullets; 100 for *Chain's* TS2; twenty for *Maverick's*.

Maverick said he would need as many *Firestarters* with timers as they could fit in his backpack. A 9MM Heckler & Koch (H&K) SP5K-PDW semi-automatic, close-quarters pistol would be in the front cockpit of both aircraft. "Bob, when we are done here, please show *Chain* how the H&K is mounted."

Maverick continued briefing aloud. "Five 30-round magazines, 100 incendiaries for *Chain*, two mags for me. I don't need the extra weight. When we hit the ground, my *Yo-Yo* will be the first out of the cargo bay to be assembled." The implication that *Chain's Yo-Yo* would follow was understood, as was the fact the pilots would fly from the rear seat so they could to access the TS2's magazine housing. *Maverick* spoke in the military Brevity Code they had been taught as fighter pilots decades ago. "Ingress, *Maverick* lead; *Chain* takeoff, ten second delay." Link nodded. The maintenance crew left *en masse* to the other side of the cargo jet to prepare the YO-3As for their mission.

Maverick continued, "From what I saw on the overheads, the route I have planned will not take us over any towns or buildings as we ingress to the base. However, we will overfly an S-400 *Triumf* anti-aircraft battery. They have them everywhere. The coating on the *Yo-Yo* makes us invisible to radar, so even if they are *AWAKE,* it shouldn't be a factor. The Koreans don't fly at night, so we shouldn't have to deal with any *BANDITS.* If either of us experience an engine or gearbox problem enroute and have to bail out, the mission is officially scrubbed. Then it becomes a rescue mission. Deploy the IR beacon; whoever is airborne will scan the area for unfriendlies and will find the other with FLIR. We will use the LD (laser designator) to *SPARKLE* directions to the pickup area where the rescue will land."

"If I cannot get the jet after an extended period on the ground, if they have made rescuing the jet impossible, we abort. If the jet is kaput, I'll shoot the fuel tank and set *Firestarters* to immolate it in place. That will make noise. You cover my escape."

"If we have no problems ingressing, you become the *EYEBALL* and the *SHOOTER.* Once over the target, we *SPIN* it 180° for separation; you go left, I'll go right. FLIR out both jets. You deploy *Weedbusters,* the TS2 and the LDs. We check for thermals generally; you monitor thermal activity over my position. We'll use the discrete encrypted channel for comms. The overheads suggest there are two new machine gun emplacements with bodies north and south of the *RAPTOR* bunker. Probably two and two. Alert me if there is another one taking a piss where I cannot see him."

"*WILCO.*"

"A guard walks the perimeter of the armory. We need to check to ensure there are no hidden surprises in the other bunkers or guard towers, which are too far away to intervene effectively. If that is what we find in the FLIR, I'll clean up the airplane, cut the motor and land. You're my *EYEBALL* while I'm on the ground. I'll have two radios in case one goes *TANGO UNIFORM.*" (Tits Up.)

Chain gave *Maverick* a thumbs up.

"You're in orbit; maintain *SA* (situational awareness). Talk to me on any deviations, such as the changing of the guard at the armory. As the *EYEBALL* you have complete visibility of the battlespace; use

Weedbusters as appropriate, and you're the *SHOOTER* at your discretion. We do not want to announce our presence until engine start. I'll make the call *GO,* and then you're *CLEARED HOT* to hit transformers to knock out their power and their antenna for good measure. Take out the back-up generators and target the fuel lines to them. *CONTINUE* the attack; do not let up. Create as much confusion as possible. Men coming out to investigate are *Weedbusters* targets of opportunity. Pop a flare; hit them with the laser."

Chain nodded. *Get them to look up.*

"I should be able to get to the jet and disable the men north and south of the bunker. I'll need some time to determine if the *RAPTOR* can fly. At that point, the only active thermals you should have are the armory watch, the guards in the guard tower, and the guards in the sandbags where the 22 is located."

"If the *RAPTOR* is incapacitated, I should know in a heartbeat. I'll say *ABORT.* If we have to go, we have plenty of gas; *BINGO* fuel is not an issue." The execution of the mission went on for another thirty minutes.

Maverick had moved to a critical phase of the operation. Egressing. "If you think I need to get the hell out of there for whatever reason — reinforcements coming over the hill, mobile SAM launchers racing to the air base, hordes of Chinese, whatever — call '*SCRAM*' three times. I'll get back to the *Yo-Yo,* and we'll *BUGOUT. SMACK* them with everything you have to interrupt their advance until I can get airborne. *SMACK* their jets. *SMACK* any *SQUIRTERS* or *STRANGERS* or *SUSPECTS* until *WINCHESTER.* (Out of ammo). We don't want anyone coming after us. You *RESUME* the outbound GPS track at two-o; but *BUMP* me ten knots until I can rendezvous on you. *BUSTER* to the beach. You are the flight lead as we *RETROGRADE.*"

"On the *RETROGRADE* leg, if one of us has problems and has to jump, we have to do what we can to survive. Basic *SERE* training. So, depending on where the emergency arises.... I had an engine chip light right after I targeted al-Zawahiri in Yemen and had to return to Djibouti. It was a stressful period crossing the Red Sea thinking the engine could shit the bed at any moment, and there was no place to land. So, depending on how much actual night time is left, if one of us cannot land safely under cover of darkness and get the other out of there, then the mission becomes a rescue mission for the next day."

Chain asked, "Deploy the IR beacon?"

Maverick shook his head. "Not yet. The pilot aloft becomes the mission commander. If we suffer an emergency during ingress, we will scan the area for unfriendlies and thermals of buildings, vehicles, people. If necessary, pop off a flare to blind them but if there is *DARK STAR*, try again to incapacitate them."

"*DARK STAR?*"

"It's an illumination round or a flare that fails to ignite. If that happens, pop off another one. We have the ability to select singles. Our survival depends on our ability to stop them, blind them *en masse* with *Weedbusters*. We are on our own, we will not have any air support."

Chain gave *Maverick* another thumbs up. *Message received.*

Maverick continued, "If able, provide directions via the LD. If there is time, attempt a pick-up. These places are remote; we will have to hunker down until the following night. We will plan for an extraction at midnight."

Chain repeated, "Midnight."

"The most dangerous phase of an extraction is determining if the place is overrun by unfriendlies. So, at midnight, the person airborne will be able to see the thermal image of the one on the ground. If on the ground, select NVGs in your helmet and look up for the shade differential and find the outline of the Yo-Yo. This would be the time to deploy the IR beacon."

"Got it."

"There's an extra battery for our helmets in our helmet bag to keep the helmet FLIR and NVG systems fully energized, for about six hours. Besides the IR beacon and some extra batteries, there are some pen flares, a couple of *Firestarters*, the cloaking sheet, and the magazines for the H&K. Questions?"

Chain said, "Not at this time."

Maverick nodded and continued, "So, *ROLEX* for pickup, midnight, plus or minus ten minutes. In the case of a *DEADEYE*, the LD stops working, flash the landing light and get the hell out of Dodge. The autopilot has a memory that tracks our GPS route and position over the ground, so whoever is on the rescue trip, program the autopilot to cover the same ground. *SKINNY* rules apply; log the coordinates of the downed pilot. We will try to stay in the area where we go down for as long as we can. If we have visitors in the night, use the cloaking sheet for camo. There's jerky in our helmet bags."

"I have a question. Cloaking sheet?"

Maverick pulled the material from his helmet bag. "The lab boys call it *light-bending material*. It's the next generation of camouflage; a couple of other companies are experimenting with the technology. Ours is a better solution. It's lighter, foldable, and completely assumes the image of what's around it with little loss of clarity. There is a slight shade differential, but at a distance you can't tell."

Chain asked, "What's it made of?" as he touched the material, which felt like tiny smooth glass beads under his fingertips.

"It's also *nanotech*. When our lab rats, the guys in Fredericksburg, started developing this, they also stumbled on a combination of materials that block IR. That stuff *with* the nanotechnology was very heavy, but there was absolutely no heat transfer. They haven't been able to amalgamate the two technologies into one lightweight material yet, but even individually, both are radical leaps in camouflage. I carry the light-bending material whenever I fly a mission."

"This is the craziest stuff...."

Maverick said, "Yes, it is. Even saved my life when I had to jump out of number seven over Algeria. So, it works. Field-tested."

"*Mav*, I don't think you told me you had to jump out of a *Yo-Yo* before. How?" *And how many planes have you trashed on this program?*

"MANPADS." (Man-Portable Air Defense System). "Long story, different SAP to stop...well, the U.S. was paying a terrorist an annual ransom of $100 million in gold coin not to shoot down our commercial jets. The turd knocked down TWA's Flight 800 in 1996 with a

MANPADS and warned the president at the time that if he didn't pony up the gold, more jets would get shot out of the sky. It took years of intel work to find the dude and his missiles, which were probably bought or stolen from Gaddafi's cache. Fast forward. McGee was hired on as an Agency contractor; he had seen the cache in Libya. The turd who had them, had over a thousand of them in an underground bunker. The CIA was trying to buy them when the Muslim Brotherhood attacked the consulate in Libya. 9-11-12."

"Seriously?"

Maverick yawned and nodded. "I got knocked down. The sheet saved me from two *TANGOES*. It gave me enough concealment that I was able to survive an encounter with two Muslim SEAL wannabees and counterattack. That was quite an evening. Bottom line, that night in Algeria we recovered $3 billion of the ransom the U.S. had paid in gold. The MANPADS cache in Libya was destroyed, and I killed the asshole who shot me down. I even took his jet to get off the continent...." *And that was the night McGee rescued Nazy from the troglodytes from hell.* "So, while we are on the subject, we don't know if they have MANPADS, but we always assume they do. We make left turns to keep the heat of the mufflers away from an IR seeker head."

"It will take them some time to figure out that a low-level aircraft of some kind is creating havoc. They will assume something unmanned. But they'll know immediately we are after the *RAPTOR,* and we can expect increased resistance on the ground. We want to be able to get overhead and on the ground without announcing our presence. I think we can assume that if any MANPADS are on the base, they will be in the armory. I can't imagine any scenario where a *Stinger* or a *Blowpipe* or a Chinese FN-6 is bunked with a Korean trooper. So, if they have any, they will be in the armory...."

Chain said, "Which has a guard."

Maverick nodded and pointed to the location of the armory on the satellite image and continued, "At engine start, I say *GO*, and you attack. It will take time for them to get out of bed, organize their thoughts, analyze the situation correctly. It will take time for someone in authority to make a decision and take corrective action. Create chaos continually; keep them hunkered down. Knock out the armory guard. Targets of opportunity."

"If you see someone heading to the armory from the barracks, here and here, or the operations complex, here, it's time to signal the situation may cascade into something we cannot recover from. Notify me it is time to leave."

"WILCO."

"I was in Algeria and I thought I could tangle with a guy with a *Stinger* and lost. I used chaff and flares. With three mufflers and tons of insulation surrounding the engine, my thermal signature was still sufficient for a heat-seeker, and was shot down. That missile did not hit the engine, but it chased a flare and blew my wing off. It may have had a defective proximity fuse, or maybe it just wasn't my time to die. But it was not fun. If you can't stop a horde with *Weedbusters*, it's time to go."

Chain nodded.

Maverick remembered the phases of the moon and added, "A couple of more things. The Moon phase when we are over the target will be a Waxing Crescent phase."

"And that is....?"

"That is the phase where the moon becomes visible again after the New Moon. I try to fly when it's a New Moon Phase. No moon benefits us. Moonshine used to reflect off the Yo-Yo's wings, but since we have the black coating, it doesn't any more. Someone on the ground might have been able to get a glimpse of Waxing Crescent moonlight off the canopy but, you may not have noticed, we've coated the transparency with a million tiny dots of the *black*; it doesn't interfere with our vision, but it knocks down any glint and helps reduce our RCS." (Radar cross section).

Chain said, "That's nifty."

Maverick concluded, "The time I was shot down was during the plenilune. The full moon. There was enough moonlight and clear sky to discern the outline of an aircraft flying in the night sky, masking and unmasking stars."

"I expect more information to come through while we are asleep, maybe an update on the jet's SATPHONE. Forecasted weather, winds. I'm ready for some shuteye. You?"

Chain said, "I'm ready. It's been a hell of a day."

Before the pilots crawled into sleeping bags and spread out across the jet's troop seats, they washed down some jet lag pills the Air Force Medical Group at Langley had provided *Maverick* before he had returned to Joint Base Andrews. *Maverick* lagged behind Coffey's preparation for sleep. When *Chain* pulled a sleep mask over his eyes and noise-canceling headsets over his ears, *Maverick* pulled his laptop, a tiny portable scanner, and two *BlackWings* from his flight bag. He scanned three pictures into his computer, connected a USB cable to each of the *BlackWings*, and downloaded the photos into the drones' facial recognition program. In five minutes, *Maverick* completed his task. He put his computer and scanner away, and placed the *BlackWings* into his helmet bag. Sleep came easy.

The men of *Noble Savage* slept all the way to Osan Air Force Base.

On arrival, the *Noble Savage* maintenance crews assembled the two YO-3As. *Maverick* and *Chain* departed to the east, in echelon, over the Sea of Japan. Forecasted cloud cover and headwinds were greater than expected. Expected *feet dry* into North Korea: midnight.

CHAPTER 59

July 21, 2020

The Defense Intelligence Agency had briefed that the North Korean coastline was protected every five miles by an export version of the Russian made S-400 *Triumf* anti-aircraft battery. *Maverick* was surprised that the DIA's intel could be so wrong; *Maverick* and *Chain* didn't fly over a legacy S-400 anti-aircraft battery. They flew over the unmistakable thermal image of Russia's newest deployable *Tor-M2* surface-to-air missile system. The *Tor-M2* was an all-weather, short-range, surface-to-air missile system designed to destroy airplanes, guided missiles, drones, and other aerial targets. It had a range of about 7.5 miles and could simultaneously engage up to 48 processed targets and 10 tracked targets.

Before leaving Andrews, *Maverick* had specifically asked if he would face the *Tor-M2* or the S-400. The briefer from DIA said Russia touted the *Tor-M2* missile system as one of its most prized weapons. The *Tor-M2* was for domestic defense only, and it was not exportable.

Yet here it is…. Can't turn away. Hold on! Maverick and *Chain* were committed. They held their breath as they overflew the *Tor-M2* in a tight echelon, quickly entering the radar's *cone of silence* and departing. *Maverick* was poised to launch flares and chaff at the first suggestion they had been detected. *Maverick* thought he was probably too close to the *Tor-M2* for his flares and chaff to be effective.

The missile warning systems in their cockpit remained quiet, signaling the YO-3As had not been detected by radar. With the *Tor-M2* anti-aircraft battery safely behind them, they knew they had dodged a bullet. There was a sigh of relief in both cockpits and no further threats to their underwear.

Flying at the optimum altitude and airspeed for quiet flight, *Maverick* knew it was still another hour to the Toksan Air Base. He thought about loading some music from a flash drive but decided against it. *Too much going on….*

•   •   •

Arriving overhead a few minutes ahead of schedule, *Maverick* and *Chain* confirmed the location of the main electrical power transformers and secondary diesel generators with the FLIR. As briefed, *Chain* lowered the Terminator Sniper System and deployed the *Weedbusters* UV-C aerial eradication system into the airstream. The FLIR showed the thermal imagery of a single soldier walking around the armory and troops in the guard towers along the perimeter of the airbase fence. They would be able to hear the YO-3A's engine exhaust during landing.

Maverick set up for landing and shut down the motor. He silently greased the landing, and rollout of the glider-like *Yo-Yo* on battery power was uneventful. He was on the brakes immediately, and the *Wraith* stopped quickly astride the runway's centerline. He raised the canopy and programmed the YO-3A's automatic takeoff and landing system, ATLS, from one of the airplane's three multifunction panels. Once he was out of the aft cockpit and standing on the wing, he removed his YO-3A helmet and replaced it with a four-tube, panoramic NVG-FLIR system with the SCBA. He had a 15-minute supply of Aviator's Breathing Oxygen (ABO) and hoped to be airborne before half of his external air supply was exhausted.

Maverick removed the *AeroDog* from the front seat. He tossed it in the air, and like its cousin *BlackWings*, it sensed it was falling and the rotor-wheels immediately activated, folded outward, and stabilized in a silent hover. The positive-pressure regulator was working as advertised as *Maverick* removed two *BlackWings* from his helmet bag and placed them in his backpack. He secured his YO-3A helmet in his helmet bag in the aft seat, so that it could not possibly lodge in the flight controls. He clipped the F-22 helmet to his backpack.

The final weapon to come out of the front seat was a silenced Heckler & Koch (H&K) SP5K-PDW. He pressed the button to activate the red laser aiming pointer and slung the fully loaded weapon over his shoulder.

Before stepping off the wing, *Maverick* placed the ATLS on STANDBY and lowered and locked the canopy. He turned toward the target; he had counted fifteen individual bunkers in the satellite photo and knew each one had a jet inside. There were no lights on anywhere. An overcast sky with no stars or moon made it pitch black in all directions. It was so dark that without NVGs, no one would have been able to discern if anything was inside the aircraft bunkers. All that was needed was some fog rolling in to provide a completely eldritch atmosphere to freak out the hardiest spy trying to evade men with guns on a North Korean air base.

Maverick had the advantage. *Chain* confirmed no one knew he was on the base, and as the EYEBALL he had eyes on the whole air base. If anyone emerged from the buildings, *Chain* would be able to see them. As long as the battery supplied power to the four-tube NVG-FLIR system, he would have sight in the infrared. Through the helmet's night observation systems, in shades of white-blue, yellow, and red, he saw the distinctive vertical tails of a Sukhoi Su-27, designated *Flanker* by NATO, sitting deep in the bunkers. It did not calm *Maverick* for the moment. *Jets, no bodies nearby…. But those are not the jets I expected. The only Russian fighter never to have been shot down….* He ran to the edge of the nearest bunker. The intel said to expect single-tail MiG-21 *Fishbeds*, but the twin tails proved the best Russian fighters were there instead. He continued to jog toward destiny, thinking, *The intel was wrong or it hadn't been updated. What else did the DIA get wrong? Was the F-22 even there?* He wouldn't let a few incidentals bother him; however, the exertion made his mask cloud.

Finally, about 100 yards away, he saw the thermal image of the distinctive cranked dihedral tails of the F-22. He also saw the thermals of two men in the south machine gun emplacement. He was on the correct course. *This is why you plan…. Thank you for the overheads. Maverick* continued jogging with the *AeroDog* silently following in quadcopter mode.

As he approached the next bunker with a Su-27 inside, there were no thermal images of men. *No threat; move to the next one.* He filled his lungs with ABO and exhaled. He was grateful the mask wasn't getting any cloudier.

The bunkers were widely distributed and he was carrying a lot of weight, starter cartridges and a battery in a backpack, the F-22 helmet, and three weapons.

That jet's a long way off! No thermal images of anyone in or near this bunker. Don't get cocky! Off to the RAPTOR and men with weapons.

The protection of the F-22 bunker was unique. It was the only one delimited by two outside sandbag emplacements on opposite corners, north and south. *Maverick* approached the opening of the bunker with the *RAPTOR* inside with great caution. *AeroDog's* sensors picked up the change in *Maverick's* movements, landed and converted into a four-wheeled robot and silently followed, ready to flood the area with UV. He had expected to find more men in the emplacements during his pass overhead, and was grateful there were only two.

Chain took up an orbit over the F-22 bunker and confirmed two men were in each machine gun emplacement.

Maverick monitored the men's movements in the infrared for a minute. He had made a living observing and predicting the movement of men at night. They acted more like they were asleep than on guard duty.

Maverick approached silently and placed the red pointer of the silenced H&K on the backs of their necks. He killed the sleeping men one by one. *Maverick* moved inside the bunker. No thermals of humans or rats or cats inside. He peeked around the other end and killed another group of men in the machine gun emplacement immediately outside the bunker. He double checked the outside of the bunker with FLIR.

The radio crackled in his ears and interrupted his work as *Chain* transmitted, *"Clear."*

With a swipe on the screen of his Blackberry, he guided the *AeroDog* to wheel to a position about fifty yards away, between bunkers to flood the area with UV.

Led by the laser pointer on his H&K, he again scanned the inky black interior of the concrete bunker for life. He was breathing hard into his mask. No one was home. Now came the hard part. He would have to turn his back on the unknown.

Inside the bunker, *Maverick* found cool shades of white-blues and the silver American jet. No reds or moving thermals. His heartrate was off the chart. He ran around the jet and checked the hangar. It was not outfitted with a fire extinguishing system, no HALON. Then he checked the condition of the jet. *Tires look inflated. No panels had been removed. Nothing in the engine intakes but fan blades. Canopy down. Time to open it. Here we go!*

Over his nanotechnology flight suit, *Maverick* wore the essential flight equipment necessary to fly the *RAPTOR*, a G-suit and torso harness. He gently sloughed off his backpack. He activated two *BlackWings* and tossed them into the air; they flew out of the bunker in search of a powerline. He moved to the nose wheel well.

He found and activated the canopy open switch. It wasn't a job he could do standing up, so *Maverick* dropped to his knees. He emerged from the wheel well to check that the pneumatic system had raised the canopy fully. He kicked away the chocks on the nose wheel and kicked the tire on his way to his backpack. *Not underinflated! Another potential showstopper down. Now the BCU and load the cart-starts.*

Maverick crab walked to the left wheel well, trying not to bang his four-tube helmet into the wing, the drop tanks, the landing gear, or the door. *Maverick* crawled underneath the aircraft, sat on the concrete, and affixed the BCU to the emergency power receptacle. He extracted the thermos-sized starting cartridges from the backpack. It took a full minute to open the breeches and load the cartridges. He ensured they were seated properly, and then secured their covers. *Maverick* round-housed his boot and kicked the tire. *Good inflation!*

Now I need to get inside. Moment of truth! Maverick called out, "Update!"

•   •   •

Chain replied, "Still quiet."

•   •   •

"Two minutes." *Maverick* tossed the backpack onto the wing and moved to the stabilator, which was not parallel to the deck but wasn't vertical either. He ran as fast as he could and threw himself on the trailing edge of the *RAPTOR's* stabilator. He clawed his way up until his whole torso was fully aboard. The leather on his flight gloves and rubber-soled boots aided his traction. He rested on his back; his face mask clouded with the exertion. ABO filled heaving lungs. Thankfully, the angled stabilator did not move.

Maverick rolled over on his belly and scampered to his feet. He retrieved the backpack from the wing and ran up the spine of the jet. Holding the edge of the canopy for balance, he worked his feet to the cockpit sill. *Maverick* placed one foot into the seat pan, then the other foot. He ducked under the canopy bow and turned to step to the floor. He was in the cockpit. But it wasn't time to call *GO!*

He sat down and hoped the battery worked. He inhaled and selected AVIONICS MASTER to ON. Electrical power energized some of the cockpit warning and caution lights. Then ENGINE MASTER SWITCHES to ON, then ENGINE START to ON. That discharged the starter cartridge on the number one engine with a bang. The explosive charge's expanding gases impinged the compressor blades.

The engine spooled up, filling the bunker with the sound of a starting turbine. Over his helmet radio, *Maverick* called, "*GO!*"

Still on battery power from the BCU, the center MFD indicated 10% RPM. He depressed the right IGNITION button and moved the throttle half-way up the quadrant, then snapped it back to IDLE. Light-off occurred at 16%. *Maverick* released the IGNITION button with the sudden rise in EGT. (Engine Gas Temperature). As the engine RPMs quickly spooled up, *Maverick*, connected his lap belt, G-suit hose, and the upper torso fittings and lowered the canopy. At 45% RPM, he returned the ENGINE START switch to the neutral position. Oil pressure came up. He selected the right GENERATOR to ON. No longer was just the center MFD energized, all MFDs were fully activated and the cockpit was awash with lights. He pushed buttons on the multifunction panels like a lab rat on amphetamines. *Maverick* checked the walls of the bunker for reflections to ensure all external lights were off.

While programming the throttle of the number one engine forward to get the jet moving, *Maverick* selected ENGINE START to ON, which discharged the other cart-start. He depressed the left IGNITION button, pushed the throttle halfway up the quadrant, then snapped it back to IDLE to get fuel into the engine. The #2 engine lit off and was spooling up just as the F-22 emerged from the bunker.

•   •   •

Chain was incredulous as the thermal image of the *RAPTOR's* exhaust clearly showed thermal activity and then the nose poked out of the bunker. *Fight's on!* He transmitted, "*SCRAMBLE!* You're clear to the taxiway!" He yelled inside his cockpit, "*Let's go, let's go, let's go!*" *Chain* launched several incendiary laser designated bullets into the largest of the electrical power transformers and riddled the Chinese made emergency generators' diesel feed lines and electrical control panels with the heavy spent uranium bullets. The incendiaries were far more effective than standard bullets, because they would ignite fuel or volatile chemicals when they came into contact with a fuel tank or an electrical transformer.

Immediately after puncturing the transformers, the incendiary bullets caused the transformers to explode which extinguished the few lights that were on in the buildings at the air base. With the diesel generators out of action, all the buildings on the base were plunged into total darkness.

Chain overflew the operations and maintenance facilities and aircraft bunkers and ejected a pair of flares from the *Yo-Yo's* countermeasures system. *Chain* lowered his altitude to make the altitude sensitive *Weedbusters'* laser more effective. He set the autopilot to orbit over the field, in a left turning racetrack pattern, while hawking the FLIR's scope for thermal imagery.

•   •   •

Maverick used differential braking to steer the jet straight out of the bunker, then eschewing nose wheel steering, depressed the right toe brake to turn the *RAPTOR's* nose wheel to track over the taxiway centerline. Engine exhaust blew the *AeroDog* across the tarmac where it rolled violently over the concrete and disintegrated into a hundred pieces.

•   •   •

With the power cut to the base, the sound of a jet's turbine and flares overhead brought out the inquisitive. Men poured out of buildings and guard towers. Upon seeing the flares, the soldiers looked up in a coordinated synchronized move. *Chain* mashed the *Weedbusters* firing button on his control stick, and the hundreds of eyeballs scanning the sky were hit with the powerful, low-altitude UV-C laser. Every soldier looking up was instantly blinded by the radiation. Darkness transitioned to a white-hot pain, as if their eyes had been caught wide open by an arc welder's torch. *Chain* took out two refueling trucks with the laser-guided incendiary bullets, setting them on fire. He circled overhead monitoring the FLIR for additional thermals and continued flooding the base with UV. In seconds, *Chain* had disabled the base's armory guard, the tower guards, and the standing army, or had intimidated it into staying indoors.

He was overwhelmed that in an instant, the virile and active soldiers had been disabled, had fallen to the ground, and were crawling for shelter. *The know they are helpless and easy targets for killing. But not today, G.I. Dog.*

• • •

Maverick jazzed the throttles to taxi as quickly as he dared. He still had not felt the full power of the jet and was cautious when making turns. Engine response was instantaneous and what power he had defied his senses. *Thirty years ago, the F-4 was not this strong....* The simulator at Langley didn't even come close to this. *This thing is going to kill me!* Well before he got to the end of the taxiway, he asked, "Bogeys?

• • •

Suddenly, *Chain's* helmet was awash with the thermal images of men with weapons pouring from two buildings the satellite photos had identified as barracks. He launched another flare, which popped and ignited and stopped the men instantly. They looked toward the heavens at the flare. *Chain* mashed the *Weedbusters* button to irradiate their eyes. Images of armed men running to the airfield were replaced by images of men falling to their knees or scrambling around on the ground aimlessly. Most men dropped their weapons and covered their damaged eyes with their hands or forearms. In the FLIR it was obvious the men were shrieking or writhing in pain or stumbling around in fear.

Chain continued to monitor the wounded men on the ground when he radioed *Maverick*, "Two *TANGOES* with NODS moving your way, and two more are moving toward the armory."

•   •   •

Maverick saw that half of the air base was on fire. He was emphatic, "Take them out." *You don't need permission, Chain.*

•   •   •

As if he was discussing the potential for rain, *Chain* responded with a phatic double click of the transmit key.

The men rushing toward the bunker with the defector's prized aircraft didn't realize they were being *tracked*. It took only a few seconds for *Chain* to *acquire* the two men's backs with the TS2 radar system and have the computer laser-designate them. Another second and the targeting program of the Terminator Sniper System took over.

As long as *Chain* could keep the laser designator on the target, even as the men were at a dead run, the targeting computer constantly calculated, at twenty times per second, where the laser-designated target would be. *Chain* eliminated the dual threat moving toward *Maverick* and the *RAPTOR*.

As the armory guard writhed on the ground, two other North Korean soldiers entered the perimeter fence of the armory. They fumbled with a ring of keys to access the base's special weapons inside.

Those remaining in their barracks heard the heavy thumps of the .70 caliber rounds and saw the conflagration of refueling vehicles outside. They were under attack and refused to leave the safety of their buildings to investigate.

• • •

Chain had eliminated the potential direct threat to *Maverick,* but he lost situational awareness of the men running to the armory. He cursed himself for allowing them to get to the building.

• • •

Maverick approach the taxiway. In seconds he would be airborne, and it would be time to leave. He radioed, "I'm going to take the taxiway. Check six! Let's get out of here!" He aligned the jet on the centerline of the taxiway and stopped.

With his feet on the brakes, *Maverick* took his Blackberry out of his chest pocket, selected the ATLS icon, and engaged the takeoff system to return the YO-3A to Osan. He ignored the windsock, looked over to the YO-3A, and saw the thermal image of the prop turn.

Maverick switched helmets. He connected the O2 mask and felt the positive pressure ram air down his throat. Standing still on the taxiway that paralleled the runway, he felt exposed, but he was beginning to believe he was going to make it. *Maverick* selected half-flaps, took his feet off the brakes and ran the throttles to MIL. He moved the throttles into the afterburner detent and smoothly advanced the throttles to MAX power.

The engines in *blower* pressed him hard into the seat. Just like on his first flight in the F-4, *Maverick* shouted, "*Holy shit!*" He used the rudder pedals and the landing light to guide him down the centerline. The old habit from flying fighters, he automatically called out the jet's airspeed, "*50, 80, 120, 150, 180… gear … 220… flaps… 250… three-o!*" *Maverick* turned hard to port at 6Gs and felt the G-suit inflate; the first hard application of Gs in decades. He leveled his wings, checked his heading and accelerated straight for the Sea of Japan at low level. Favonian tailwinds expedited his departure. His back muscles tightened.

Now we just have to blow the doors off a Tor-M2 to escape. I don't need a missile up my tailpipe. They'll have their antenna pointing for enemies coming from the sea, not approaching from their rear. My back is still in one piece. Advantage, Maverick!

CHAPTER 60

July 22, 2020

Maverick jettisoned the external fuel tanks and pushed the *RAPTOR* to the design limits of the aircraft. It was the first time he had been supersonic since his accident. The familiar encased-in-concrete feeling of supersonic flight returned; there was no maneuvering the jet at that speed. *Maverick* trimmed as necessary and would be just along for the ride until he took the throttles out of *blower.*

A supersonic shock wave that would have broken windows at five miles in altitude, obliterated the *Tor-M2* when it passed five feet over the anti-aircraft truck. The next second, *Maverick* was over the Sea of Japan. He programmed the throttles out of afterburner for subsonic flight. He was tossed gently into the shoulder straps during deceleration.

Who knew that all that LATT training would be useful thirty years later and at night? Parallel rooster tails streamed from behind the speeding *RAPTOR* as *Maverick* kept the jet low over the water to decelerate in the thicker air. When he entered South Korean airspace, he pulled the RAPTOR into the vertical at 6Gs, rolled the jet at 20,000 feet, and leveled off. *Never get the chance to do that again. My back is going to be screaming at me for patches!*

Maverick selected the frequency for Osan and made the radio call, "Osan Approach, *RESCUE ONE.*"

• • •

Pandemonium erupted from men and women who had been standing quietly in the RAPCON, hoping to see history made. The radar approach controller wiped a spontaneous tear from her face with the

back of her hand: "*RESCUE ONE, TESLA* squawk 7777 INDENT."
Maverick repeated the directions as *quad sevens*, selected the four-digit
Mode 5 IFF code and toggled the IDENT switch for ATC. (Identify
Friend or Foe, Air Traffic Control.)

"*RESCUE ONE*, radar contact! Turn heading 240, altimeter 30.11.
I'll give you vectors to the field."

Even with oxygen being forced into his mask, the deep rumbling
Texas accent came through the radio, "Much obliged, Approach."

•   •   •

After an uneventful landing on the centerline that would have made
an Air Force pilot proud, *Maverick* taxied the *RAPTOR* to Base
Operations at the base of the control tower. He followed the directions
of the transient alert (TA) man in his Mickey Mouse sound suppressors
and lighted wands. When the TA man crossed the wands over his
head, *Maverick* mashed the brakes and stopped. He threw the throttles
to OFF, shutting both engines down simultaneously, and raised the
canopy. He took a moment to breathe one last shot of ABO before he
dropped the O2 mask and removed his helmet. The flight equipment
troops at Langley hadn't had time to make him a form-fitted helmet.
Gratefully, the one they had provided him hadn't given him a hot spot.
Getting out of the cockpit was going to be a challenge.

*I should have had Chain put lidocaine patches on my back. Can't
remember everything.*

Bob Jones found the wing commander and reminded the brigadier
general there were to be no pictures of the pilot. At 0330, the growing
crowd had little doubt what had transpired. They assumed anyone
dressed in black from head to toe was not Air Force, but maybe an
Agency type. The directive "No Photos" was passed quickly, without
question.

TA chocked the *RAPTOR*'s nose tire. All was quiet on the flight
line again.

It seemed like half the troops on the base had organized a welcoming committee. Seeing an F-22 bathed in ramp lighting with a man in a nonstandard black flight suit sitting in the cockpit drove some to the edge of celebration. *Maverick* disconnected the upper torso fittings and the lap belt connectors as more people lined up along an imaginary DO NOT CROSS line. He didn't care if his cover was likely blown; it was the cost of doing business. But he needed someone to bring a real set of stairs so he could get out of the jet. *Maybe 6Gs was too much. And I'm too old to jump off this thing!*

A two-man transient alert crew rolled towable boarding stairs into position; they were careful not to allow any metal to touch the fuselage. When the stairs' wheels were locked, one TA tech raced up the stairs and helped the pilot in black get out of the cockpit. Several dozen people watched from afar as *Maverick* fidgeted with the gun in the black holster. They had never seen an Air Force pilot wear a sidearm in such a fashion, and they had never seen any pilot with a black flight suit, especially one that just didn't look real. *Maverick* remembered, *The flight suit needed a warning label.* He told the TA man whose eyes were being drawn to the black void, "Don't look at the material; it will screw with your equilibrium." *Maverick* handed him a backpack with the four-tube NVGs, the F-22 helmet, and the O2 mask separately. He removed the thin skullcap and stuffed it into a chest pocket. He ran a hand through wet hair.

"Thanks for the warning, sir." It was still difficult for the TA man to keep his eyes off the flight suit that seemed to suck light. It was also difficult not to notice the gun and black holster slung under the pilot's arm.

Maverick asked the TA technician in a tired raspy baritone, "Could you please disconnect the green battery control unit in the external power receptacle? I need to return that. Thank you."

Stunned, the man ran down the stairs and retrieved the BCU; he was amazed how warm and heavy the thing was. He had never seen one before, but knew intuitively what it had been used for.

The escape in the jet and the expenditure of energy, the 6G pulls, and adrenaline stiffened *Maverick*. It took work for him to get out of the jet. He finally climbed out of the *RAPTOR*, went down the stairs slowly until his feet hit *terra firma*. He was immediately surrounded by Air Force brass, led by a brigadier general in a flight suit, and the *Noble Savage* crew. After congratulations, the crowd hushed and watched *Maverick* in his crazy flight suit shed the torso harness and unzip the G-suit. He handed them to Tom Barraclough. The *Noble Savage* crew followed him and the Air Force officers into the Base Operations building.

To Bob Jones, it was obvious *Maverick* was laboring, but his mobility seemed to improve with every step. *What did that lad do? He knows he's not supposed to pull any Gs. Every time he does, he's out of action for a week.*

Inside the lobby of Base Ops, *Maverick* asked about the status of his playmate. An officer at the duty desk made a call to radar approach of ATC; RAPCON reported they did not have any aircraft on radar.

Maverick thought, *No shit, Sherlock. Maybe later when Link throws out the gun to get some radar reflectivity.*

Ground-based radar was never able to detect the nanotube technology coating of the YO-3As, and the *Yo-Yo's* level of stealthiness would preclude an air traffic controller from detecting it. When programmed for autonomous operation, the automatic takeoff and landing system would deploy the TS2 weapons system to provide ATC radar approach some reflective metal so a ground-based radar system could detect the aircraft.

No aircraft? Maverick you're an idiot. I BUGGED OUT supersonically. Chain wouldn't even be feet wet yet. Maybe another couple of hours. Maverick took a deep breath. *Stand down until you know more.*

A telephone rang from behind the Ops counter. The Operations Duty Officer (ODO) tried to get the attention of the wing commander with no success. He gave up, went around the counter, and approached the general. The general followed the ODO to the land line.

Maverick could not think of anything else. The experience of extracting the *RAPTOR* was now a memory; that mission was complete. But he had a new one. He needed a hot tub, a massage, and patches. *You couldn't just help yourself. Now you will pay. But, we have to wait. A couple of hours and then we can worry where Chain and my Yo-Yo are. No airplanes now mean nothing. It took a couple of hours to get in.*

We briefed hunker down, use that old SERE training and all the toys we provided to survive. I'll go for him tomorrow if my Yo-Yo ever returns. I hope Link is ok. A flood of additional bad thoughts dominated his head. *What if they shot him down? What if he crashed...died? What if I can't get him?*

Time will give us an answer.

They are going to be as mad as a kicked fire ant mound. If something happened to him and they know he is down, they will send out thousands to find him. And there will be no Weedbusters to stop them.

The one-star wing commander approached *Maverick* just as the blaring tocsin of an air-raid siren went off. The general said, "The North just launched seven missiles toward the Sea of Japan, and the North Korean state media are reporting an invisible UFO attacked and destroyed one of their airbases. We need to take shelter."

Maverick started moving away from the general and said, "Sir, not until that *RAPTOR* is in a shelter." *Maverick* jogged out of the Base Ops building on stiff legs to the flight line where the F-22 was parked and said to the *Noble Savage* crew, "We have to get this into a shelter, even if I have to drive it there. I don't want all of my work going for naught." Outside Base Ops people with and without uniforms were running with celerity from the Base Operations building for shelter. Apparently, the TA techs had abandoned the *RAPTOR* for the safety of an unseen air raid shelter.

Like they had been able to read each other's minds, part of *Maverick's* crew converged on the Transient Alert office. Joe Thompson commandeered a tug and towbar and Tom Barraclough rode beside him; they drove to the nose of the F-22 while Bob Smith waited to hook up the towbar. Bob Jones moved to disconnect the grounding wire and removed the wheel chocks. He waited until *Maverick* hobbled up the movable stairs and stepped into the cockpit before he moved the stairs out of the path of the jet. Bob Smith placed the towbar's pins into the nose wheel hub and tightened the chain. *Maverick*, riding brakes, hollered at the general over the peal of the siren, "Where do you want this thing?"

The general stood there, abandoned by his troops while people he did not know were ready to move hundreds of millions of dollars of America's precious property to a shelter. He was pissed, but he understood instantly why each group did what they did. The Air Force had sent him troops; the Agency had sent him patriots.

• • •

Still under darkness, an unmanned YO-3A arrived two hours later, landing astride the runway centerline, braking to a stop, and cutting fuel to the engine as programmed. It was as *Maverick* thought; worst-case scenario. Where's *Chain?*

The wing commander said, "I know what you're thinking. You cannot go. You cannot go back to get him out. You don't know if he is alive."

"Yes, sir. I know. But I must try. I can get in. I promised him I would come for him if anything happened to him. But tonight is not the right time. We briefed, if one of us went down, the other would return."

The general simply stood there facing the man in the black flight suit; the material made him uneasy when he looked at it. Sirens were still blaring.

Maverick sighed and said, "We are glad we were able to return the *RAPTOR*. The reds have never had one of our wonder jets in their possession; I don't think they have the moxie to try it again. I'd put the jet on jacks and remove the nose tire until it is ready to continue its journey."

"I'll see to it."

"We still have work to do. I may or may not have lost a comrade; that does not need to be mentioned except as a FLASH message to the White House. You can tell them the asset was recovered and we are awaiting our playmate. I'd still give it a half an hour. I need to either plan to get him out of there, or if I must, leave him behind. I will go in tomorrow night. I need as much sleep as I can get before then. Please do what you can to take care of your aircraft and people. We must prepare for tomorrow."

"We'll get you and your men a room."

Maverick outstretched his hand. The general took it. "Thank you, sir."

Barraclough shouted, "*Look!*"

The ghostly shadow of a noiseless YO-3A crossed the landing threshold and landed.

The Osan Wing Commander smiled wide, double-pumped *Maverick's* hand, and bid the Agency's crew *adieu*. *Maverick* asked the general, "Sir, could I trouble you for one more thing? Could you send a CRITIC FLASH message precedence that *RESCUE ONE* is MC and RTB?" (Critical Intelligence, Mission Complete, Return to Base.)

"*WILCO.*"

The men watched the black *Yo-Yo* spin around in the middle of the runway and taxi to the tail of the C-17 and shutdown.

Maverick walked as the crew trotted to the C-17 where they greeted Link Coffey climbing out of the aircraft. The mechanics collaborated to get the YO-3A disassembled and loaded aboard the C-17. *Maverick* went straight for his seat.

Inside of twenty minutes, the C-17 took the runway. And, then they were gone and the flight line was silent again.

CHAPTER 61

July 21, 2020
Washington, D.C.
3:00 pm

President Hernandez was sitting behind the Resolute Desk and Director Todd was standing when the secretary informed the Chief Executive the expected FLASH message had been received in the Situation Room. When the *RAPTOR* had touched down, the Oson Wing Commander had called on an encrypted line to an eagerly awaiting group in the White House Situation Room to announce its arrival.

"Congratulations are in order, Walter. You'll have to find something appropriate to reward him." Todd nodded, took his leave, and headed back to the Situation Room where an ebullient bunch were celebrating the victory over communist ideology and socialist machinations.

Across the room, the CIA Director and the Air Force Chief of Staff exchanged looks. There was still some unfinished business between them.

They had known about each other a long time as colonels and generals. Both were fighter pilots, assigned on opposite coasts, and never assigned together. In a few social settings they had been courteous, not overly friendly, but they hadn't been enemies either. They were survivors of the Mazibuike purges, and during President Hernandez's two terms in office, both men had flourished with choice operational assignments that kept them out of the political spotlight, away from the Pentagon, away from Congress, and away from the media. They had worked hard to be seen as a politically agnostic nonthreat under a radical liberal president who looked for any excuse to remove a potential competitor from the ideological playing field. Under President Hernandez, they were able to get some work done. Todd reached for his hand and asked, "Did he ever know?"

The Chief of Staff said nothing; he shook his head.

Director Todd asked, "Where do I pick up your package?"

●   ●   ●

July 22, 2020
South Korea

Maverick and *Chain* remained mum and played a version of *eye footsie* until they were airborne. *Maverick* had questions and *Chain* knew *Maverick* was dying to know what took him so long to return to S. Korea. About an hour into the flight home, they were alone. The maintenance men had retired to their side of the cargo jet for sleep. *Maverick* turned to *Chain* and asked, "Could you put lidocaine patches on my back and tell me what the hell happened back there?"

After he applied the sixth patch on *Maverick's* back, *Chain* said, "I had plenty of ammo left over, and I wanted to take out the rest of the Su-27s. You were in blower on your takeoff roll when I saw the lights of a convoy approaching the base. You turned to port; I flew out to meet them—they had a *Tor-M2* that was just coming to a halt, and I was certain they would target you. Your afterburners lit you up nicely for a heat seeker or a radar missile if they could have gotten their system up. So, the gun was already out and I engaged them at five miles. They were just coming to a stop when I took out the launcher and I hit one missile, which cooked off the warhead. It exploded and destroyed their truck and the other missiles. That was when I felt you could make your escape without having a SAM chasing you from the rear. You were gone but I felt the job wasn't done."

You felt the job wasn't done?

"*Weedbusters* and the TS2 incapacitated most of the convoy and they were in disarray. I headed back when I saw this, probably half million-gallon fuel tank, just sitting there. No berm. I could tell in the FLIR where the fuel level was—it was at least two-thirds full—so I wondered if I could get it to go, too."

Maverick remained mum and wondered exactly how *Chain* planned to do that. The TS2 rounds were spent uranium and could put a hole in nearly anything, but they had a crystal seeker head, and would have been ineffective as an armor-piercing round. He said, "I've engaged nothing harder than an engine radiator and block." *The steel plating of a fuel tank? Would a TS2 round with a glass eye poke a hole in it? What a great idea....*

Chain continued, "I still had *Weedbusters* out and I remembered something you said; the beam was altitude sensitive, and that Lynche almost had to fly in the weeds to get close enough to shred a sniper's eyes. I wondered if I got close enough to the fuel tank with the laser, could I poke a hole in the tank, or could I get the metal hot enough for a TS2 round to penetrate the tank. I had little success with the armory door, but I didn't heat it up."

"And?"

"So, I programmed *Weedbusters* to focus on where the feed line comes out of the tank to the main shutoff valve. I circled for four minutes at fifty feet, focused *Weedbusters* at max power on a spot just above the feed line, then turned the gun on that spot which was white hot in the FLIR and hit it three times; the third time punctured the tank. Fuel poured out the hole, but it didn't amount to much in the FLIR."

Maverick's eyes got wide....

"I thought the tiny puncture was going to ruin my plan, but it ended up being a *felix culpa* as the crack widened and more fuel began spilling out." *Chain* grinned and nodded. "More fuel was pouring out of the tank, but I wished it had been a more vigorous stream. The resolution of the FLIR is incredible. Anyway, I climbed and turned the *Yo-Yo* hard, nearly a 90° turn and ejected some of the flares from the countermeasures can to where I thought the fuel had spread. I don't recommend doing that. The fuel and the tank exploded. Jet fuel went everywhere. The explosion nearly swatted me out of the sky. There might have been a half-million gallons of flaming jet fuel flooding the base. In seconds, flaming fuel reached all the buildings and they were ablaze. The troops with good eyes ran for their lives. On my way out, I killed the rest of the *Flankers* for good measure, and here I am."

What are the chances he vaporized the BlackWings? Oh well, the best laid plans…. Maverick frowned for a second, shook his head, and asked, "Circuitous route?"

"Circuitous route."

Maverick said, "Link, I was about to go nuts. When my bird landed and you were not in trail, I thought you were down, and I would not be able to get you until tomorrow. But, if roles were reversed, I would have prioritized a perceived threat to you and done the same thing. I like the idea about focusing the laser on the tank and launching flares to set the place on fire. That was brilliant. Good job."

"Fire has a cleansing effect."

"That it does."

It was time for the sack and *Chain* was exhausted. He was asleep in minutes.

Maverick had one more thing to do before turning in. He retrieved his bullhide computer bag, placed it on his lap, and smiled. The company who made it had advertised, *They'll fight over it when you're dead. Maverick* opened the bag and took a moment to reflect. He knew the *Saddleback* story. *The owner was living in Rwanda, a white dude with a hot wife, two sons, and a dog when a crooked federale was sent to kill them all. Some locals got them out. The left is always trying to kill good people. Tonight, I cheated death once again…. Maverick* removed thirty $50 Gold Eagles from the saddle-colored bag, moved to the cockpit, and handed each crew member two coins in appreciation for their service. He said, "I know the Air Force is into challenge coins. These are *my* challenge coins. Don't tell the IRS. Thank you for your help in this endeavor and for your service. And let's keep this little excursion just between us girls."

Maverick returned to his sleeping bag and slept all the way home.

CHAPTER 62

July 21, 2020

Dory Eastwood finally got Dr. Elizabeth McIntosh to answer her phone. She had expected him to call but her schedule didn't allow for frivolous calls. She had read the lengthy text message that Duncan Hunter had sent both of them. She assumed Duncan was "on assignment again" and couldn't be disturbed to make his own calls, for whatever reason. Dr. McIntosh entertained Eastwood's nontechnical questions until he asked about Dr. Salvatore D'Angelo.

"My office at the National Center for Medical Intelligence was vehemently attacked by the CDC Director on several topics, primarily for not going along with the AIDS narrative promoted by the medical establishment. We found the inexpensive generic drug Bactrim effectively treated AIDS-related *pneumocystis carinii pneumonia*, which was frequently fatal. This drug was withheld from those who would have benefitted from it. Instead, D'Angelo insisted AIDS patients be treated with AZT, a horrendously toxic and expensive cancer drug that was never proven to work, and which killed about 300,000 AIDS patients, most of them gay men. But I always thought his attacks on me were for something else I had said to him."

"What's that?"

"I accused him of circumventing the law, bioweapons convention and biowarfare law. Specifically, should Europe adopt the U.S. policy on the patents of biologically derived materials? He was awarding contracts to European biolabs and American universities which essentially weaponized biologically derived materials."

Eastwood said, "Dr. McIntosh, please stop right there. I think I now understand what Duncan knows or suspects. You need to share your story and I think I know how to get that done. Are you willing to come to Washington and make a presentation?"

"To whom?"

Eastwood's answer chilled her but she said she would do it if he could make the arrangements. *I'll do it for Duncan.*

•   •   •

July 21, 2020
Washington, D.C.
5:00 pm

President Hernandez left the Situation Room with several staff members in trail. Osan Air Force Base reported North Korea had stopped launching missiles into the Sea of Japan. The Secretary of State wanted to issue a press release. The Chairman of the Joint Chiefs offered, "Inform the South Korean media there is a battalion of Marines from Okinawa deployed for war games."

President Hernandez said, "That should be sufficient."

•   •   •

Back in his office with the Director of Operations, Director Todd asked Nazy, "What can we do to reward *Maverick* for this?"

There wasn't a second's delay. "Some time off with me?"

Todd was shocked at the temerity of his Director of Operations. He smiled and nodded, "*Two for one?* Ok; whatever it takes. Make it a surprise. He'll be home on Friday?"

"Yes, sir."

"Take as much time off as you need, but I will have you for the rest of the week?"

She nodded. "Thank you, Director Todd."

CHAPTER 63

July 21, 2020

The *Aspen Institute* adjourned without a plan. Some members stayed a few more days in the spectacular home overlooking Aspen's breathtaking mountains; some decided they would leave. Sheikh Jebriel, Dr. D'Angelo, a pharma CEO, and the two senior members of Congress were driven to the airport where their private jets awaited.

Aircrews checked the weather and filed flight plans. The *Aspen Institute* members boarded three white Gulfstream jets. The Speaker of the House of Representatives and the Senate Majority Leader boarded a militarized version of a Gulfstream G-550. Dr. D'Angelo and a pharmaceutical billionaire boarded his company's G-600. Sheikh Jebriel was alone in the spacious cabin of a new extra-long-range G-700.

• • •

At the far edge of the Aspen/Pitkin County Airport parking ramp, Arsenio Bong stepped inside the Lear 24 and put away the camera with the motor drive and telephoto lens. He had acted like any camera buff who was surrounded by breathtaking vistas and majestic mountains in the Aspen valley. He took a lot of pictures of the green manicured ski trails and the massive homes that dotted the surrounding mountains.

There were three Gulfstreams on the airport, and they were parked beside each other in a row adjacent to the terminal. The aircraft noses pointed slightly to the west. At the north end of the parking ramp, behind the wing of the Lear, he took a few photographs of a group of four men and a woman who arrived by limousine. They separated and walked to their respective brilliant white Gulfstreams. The aircrafts' aircrews took baggage from the limo's trunk and placed it in the cargo holds of each jet.

Through the telephoto lens, Bong recognized the Speaker of the House of Representatives, the Senate Majority Leader, and Dr. D'Angelo. He did not recognize the man walking with Dr. D'Angelo and assumed the man in the suit was a professional colleague, possibly a pharmaceutical executive. But the man who had exited the limo last caught Bong off guard. He was unexpectedly different in several ways; a swarthy Middle Eastern man who looked more comfortable in business attire than the traditional flowing robes of a Saudi prince. The man did not offer goodbyes but just climbed the airstairs of the most distant Gulfstream.

Bong had barely got the man's headshot before he turned in profile and marched directly to the G-700. Once he was done sightseeing, he turned to determine the wind direction from the windsock at the north end of the field: about nine knots running mostly south. Satisfied with himself, he placed the camera inside the Lear and closed the door.

The day before, he had stopped his rental car at the north end of the airport to take some pictures of Owl Creek. He had removed seven round black bundles from his backpack and haphazardly placed them in the grass. If anyone stopped to scrutinize the bundles, they would have seen they were simply dead ravens. Bong had continued to snap pictures of his surroundings and had departed for his motel, the *Inn at Aspen*.

Aspen Ground Control approved the three large corporate jets to taxi south to the hold short line of the active runway 33 for a northerly departure. Ground gave them surface winds and altimeter settings. The jets formed a line as they trundled down the taxiway at two hundred-foot intervals. The pilot of the lead Gulfstream didn't immediately acknowledge but noticed a trio of dark spots approaching from the south. He pointed in the general direction and finally uttered, "What's that?"

Seconds later, the approaching spots became more defined as large black birds. He was startled as one flew over the cockpit windscreen and into the left engine intake; the subsequent compressor stall caused an internal explosion. Failed turbine blades shot out of the intake, and pieces of molten metal exited the exhaust. The ENGINE FIRE light illuminated.

A second bird flew into the intake of the jet following the lead Gulfstream. The engine immediately flamed out. From inside the cabin the noise from the engine sounded like a thousand ball bearings had been dumped into a commercial blender. The ENGINE FIRE light illuminated.

A third bird struck the engine of the third jet on the taxiway and the engine exploded into flames. The ENGINE FIRE light illuminated.

Each engine fire warning light was followed by warning lights, caution lights, and audio alarms; engines instruments confirmed the engine failures. The copilots of the three corporate jets pulled the emergency fire handles per the manufacturer's published emergency procedures.

The engine failure was heard and felt inside the VC-37B; the Speaker of the House of Representatives screamed in terror, and the Senate Majority Leader recoiled from the sound of the engine destroying itself.

The pilots of each of the three Gulfstreams reported to Ground Control that they just had a crow or raven fly into the intakes of their jets resulting in engine failures. They were shutting down and evacuating the aircraft. Ground Control dispatched Crash Fire Rescue trucks and a van.

Crash, Fire, and Rescue emergency trucks raced to the three stopped Gulfstreams on the airport taxiway. Dark and thick smoke roiled from the damaged engines. Each jet's door was open and the airstairs deployed. All the passengers and aircrew stood in the grass off of the taxiway's concrete to get out of the CFR trucks' way.

The airport was closed temporarily until the mishap aircraft could be towed back to the main ramp of the executive terminal.

A limousine service returned the members of the *Aspen Institute* to *Aspen House*.

The aircrews were adamant. It was crows or ravens that had flown into the intakes of their jets.

·   ·   ·

Aircrews were told replacement engines could take days to a month to arrive; replacement aircraft and aircrews from their respective aircraft operations were dispatched to Colorado.

Aspen Air Traffic Control issued a NOTAM, a Notice to Airmen, and cautioned there was unusually high bird activity in the area.

No one could recall a crow or a raven ever being involved in a bird strike at the Aspen/Pitkin County Airport.

A local news correspondent was informed that three jets at the Aspen/Pitkin County Airport preparing for takeoff had experienced devastating engine failures. A flock of blackbirds had flown into their engine intakes. The journalist discovered the Speaker of the House of Representatives and the Senate Majority Leader had been aboard one of the afflicted corporate jets. The Pentagon had dispatched another aircraft to return the Congressional members to Washington, D.C. The wire service reported the strange event nationally.

·   ·   ·

Several hours later, Arsenio Bong departed the Aspen/Pitkin County Airport to the north using the published Standard Instrument Departure. He held a 360° heading until he was two miles from the airport. Passing 15,000 MSL, he turned starboard and flew via direct to Texas.

·   ·   ·

Demetrius Eastwood received a text message notification from his wire service that three jets in Aspen, Colorado had been disabled when three black birds flew into the engine intakes of a government, private, and a corporate jet aircraft. *Well, that's strange….*

The Admiral said to go. I have to get to Washington. I have a feeling this is going to be wild.

•   •   •

The members of the *Aspen Institute* were forced to return to *Aspen House* and convened an emergency meeting. An hour after the aircraft incident with the purported black birds, the Speaker of the House of Representatives was still visibly shaken. She could not hold a drink in her hands, and she shouted, "I need one more than ever!"

Dr. Salvatore D'Angelo had been sitting close to the engine engaged in conversation with the pharma CEO, when the engine failed. The sudden sound of grinding metal pieces slamming into the engine intake case startled him and caused him to jump; he wet himself from the suddenness of the engine failure.

The Senate Majority Leader was still speechless.

Sheikh Zaid Jebriel was still quietly shaking, as were the others. He could still not hold a glass of water without water flying out of the goblet. *I have had experienced bird strikes before… and yes, those engines failed, but never catastrophically. The engine sounded like it was coming apart! Three failed engines. All failed catastrophically. How was that possible? That's not only improbable. That's impossible. Unless those were not birds. Unless it was planned.* People were talking in the background, consoling the others. He could hear them but could not understand them. A voice in his head said, *Yes, that is impossible. You must think the unthinkable. You have become too lackadaisical. It was planned. They have found you and targeted you. They have sent a message.*

Jebriel heaved a sigh of angst. He blurted out his final thought, "We are no longer safe. They have found us. We are being hunted." *And before I take my last breath on this Earth for Allah, I will kill the man responsible for murdering Brother Mazibuike and denying our victory over America.*

·   ·   ·

Four ravens appeared to come alive, flapping wings until they were airborne. From the bank of Owl Creek, they climbed and circled as if they were a flock, and then in a diamond formation, headed toward the ski resort of Aspen.

CHAPTER 64

July 24, 2020
National Press Club
Washington, D.C.

Demetrius Eastwood and Dr. Elizabeth McIntosh walked into one of the smaller briefing rooms and waited for their cue to mount the dais. Eastwood was surprised most of the White House Press Corps was in attendance, instead of returning to the White House after finishing lunch in the dining room. He knew some of them personally and shook some hands.

When he took the lectern, Eastwood introduced himself, and began his prepared remarks, "Our speaker today is Dr. Elizabeth McIntosh, currently the Provost at Salve Regina University in Newport, Rhode Island. After receiving her PhD in Microbiology, she graduated from the Walsh School of Foreign Service and served as a Foreign Service Officer at the United States Department of State. Dr. McIntosh was assigned as a medical intelligence analyst at the Central Intelligence Agency and in 1985, she became the Director of the National Center of Medical Intelligence. She held the George H. W. Bush Chair of International Intelligence at the Naval War College where she received a master's in National Security and Strategic Policy. Ladies and gentlemen, please give a warm welcome to Dr. Elizabeth McIntosh."

There was a smattering of polite applause from the White House press pool. They couldn't stay long; they had to return to the White House for the President's press conference. Dr. McIntosh mounted the dais, stepped up on a stool, and took a position behind the microphone. She thanked Colonel Eastwood for the introduction.

"For my topic today, I must acknowledge my last assignment before I became a staff member at the Naval War College in Newport, Rhode Island. I was the Director of the National Center for Medical Intelligence at Fort Detrick, Frederick, Maryland. The NCMI is largely unknown outside the Washington Beltway. It is a component of the Defense Intelligence Agency. As Director, I was responsible for the production of medical intelligence and all-source intelligence on foreign health threats and other medical issues to protect U.S. interests worldwide. The center provides finished intelligence products to the Department of Defense, U.S. Intelligence Community, Five Eyes, NATO, our allies and partners, as well as international health organizations and NGOs. My comments will be from the time I spent there."

"During the time I was the NCMI Director, Dr. Salvatore D'Angelo was the Director of the Centers for Disease Control, and we interfaced frequently. One day in mid-2001, we were in conference where the topic was whether Europe should adopt the U.S. policy on the patents of biologically derived materials. I argued against the proposed policy with its innocuous title and urged Dr. D'Angelo to provide full transparency on their proposed policy, which was actually the weaponization of biologically derived materials. This policy would have dire consequences against humanity. Although it was an esoteric conversation about biological patents, Dr. D'Angelo did not care to provide transparency or accountability. No one around the conference table cared to challenge Dr. D'Angelo. Being aware of the full scope of what was being discussed during these conversations, I cared about them greatly."

"Let's place this in the proper context. Today, Dr. D'Angelo is warning Americans of a future coronavirus pandemic that he suggests will strike the United States. What pandemic? The genesis of Dr. D'Angelo's pandemic did not happen recently. This did not come in the last three or four years. Or five or six years. No, this has been an ongoing question since the early 1900s. By 1913-1914 this conversation took place in central Europe. Germany took the lead, that is the

Weimar Republic, Germany's government from 1919 to 1933. They issued *'Guidelines for New Therapy and Human Experimentation.'* This is open-source material that anyone with a cellphone and a modicum of interest can find."

"A coronavirus, as a model of a pathogen, was secretly isolated in the latter days of the war in 1945. In those waning days of Nazi Germany, coronavirus was identified by one of Dr. Josef Mengele's units as one of the first virus variants that could be *spiked* to extinguish life. Let me repeat, *spiked* to extinguish life. It was isolated from and associated with the common cold. How did this happen?"

"The U.S. government brought hundreds of formerly Nazi bioweapons researchers to the United States. In secret Nazi labs in 1945 Germany, and later in Army bioweapons labs until 1965, these microbiologists found something unexpected: coronavirus was a pathogen which could be altered for a whole host of purposes."

"These references from 1965 and forward are open-source, public domain, published materials; please use those references."

Members of the White House Press Corps exchanged glances and concerns. Eastwood stood with his arms crossed.

"In 1966, the very first post-Mengele COV, or coronavirus model, was used by the U.S. Army bioweapons labs as a transatlantic biological experiment infecting humans between the U.S. and the U.K. Allies sharing non-lethal bioweapons. 1966. This was not an overnight thing. In 1967, they did the first human trials inoculating people with an early-modified coronavirus vaccine. The biological warfare community celebrated the success, replicating the Nazi's findings. They were not Nazis, but they were in violation of biological and chemical weapons treaties. Where were we as a human civilization that we thought it was acceptable to make a pathogen that could infect the world? Where was that conversation? That conversation was not had."

"I tried to have that conversation with Dr. D'Angelo in 2001. For asking 'where is the law that allows you to create your very own bioweapon,' I was removed from my position as the Director of NCMI by the end of the day. It was rumored I had lost my mind and I was given a position far away from the NCMI and Dr. D'Angelo. I warned my leaders at the CIA what was coming if Dr. D'Angelo was able to achieve his dreams and goals."

"More history. Ironically, the common cold was turned into a chimera in the 1970s. In 1975, 1976, 1977 biolabs started to figure out how to modify coronavirus by putting it into different animals. Pigs and dogs. Not surprisingly, by 1990, they found out with the help from our Nazi friends from Germany, that coronavirus as an infectious agent was an industrial problem for two primary industries. Dogs and pigs. Dog breeders and hog farms found coronavirus created gastrointestinal problems. That became the basis for one of the pharmaceutical giants' first spike protein vaccine patents filed in 1990. The first spike protein vaccine for coronavirus."

"The recently cashiered Dr. D'Angelo and the new CDC Director are telling you that the spike protein is a new thing, and the government needs to rush an experimental vaccine to protect you from this coming coronavirus pandemic. Do not believe them."

"We didn't just find out about the spike protein. The first patents were filed in 1990 for the spike proteins of coronavirus. But in 1990, the pharmaceutical companies conducting the research found there was a problem with vaccines for coronavirus. They didn't work."

"Why didn't they work?"

"The Nazi researchers discovered and the U.S. bioweapons teams confirmed coronavirus is a very malleable model. Over time, it mutates. In fact, every publication on vaccines for coronavirus from 1990 to 2018, every single publication for vaccines, concluded that coronavirus *escapes the vaccine impulse*. It mutates too quickly for vaccines to be effective. Documented. Open-source, peer-reviewed material."

"Every publication on vaccines from 1990 to 2018. That is the published science, ladies and gentlemen. That's following the science."

"Dr. D'Angelo says his researchers are following the science. That is actually a self-indictment, because the science shows that their coronavirus vaccine programs don't work. It is an illegitimate use of an experimental vaccine."

"There are thousands of publications to that effect, and they were not paid for by the pharmaceutical companies. These are publications from independent scientific research that show unequivocally, including the chimera modifications made by research labs in the U.S., that vaccines do not work on coronavirus. That's the science. And that science has never been disputed. It isn't esoteric, but it is simple. You can look it up." Dr. McIntosh raised a thick sheaf of papers to illustrate her point.

"However, we had an interesting development in 2001. This date is most important. This was right before I was fired from my position as the Director of the National Center for Medical Intelligence. With grants from the CDC, the University of North Carolina at Chapel Hill patented, and I quote, 'an infectious replication defective clone of coronavirus.' What does *infectious replication defective* actually mean? For those of you not familiar with the vernacular, let me unpack it for you. Infectious replication defective means *a weapon*. It means something to target an individual, with no collateral damage to other individuals. That's what *infectious replication defective* means."

"Now in English. University of North Carolina at Chapel Hill patented an ethnic-specific bioweapon."

"When I found out, I strenuously objected to Dr. D'Angelo for using the UNC at Chapel Hill to bypass bioweapons labs and bioweapons treaties to patent an *infectious replication defective clone* of coronavirus. A bioweapon that attacks a group *who share common DNA*. Not just any bioweapon, but an illegal *commercial ethnic* bioweapon. By the end of the day, I had been removed from my position. I was reassigned to the George H. W. Bush Chair of International Intelligence at the Naval War College to Newport, Rhode Island."

"Let me make this clear. The record will reflect that patent was filed in 2001 by the University of North Carolina at Chapel Hill on research conducted from 1999 to 2001 which was funded by the National Institute of Allergy and Infectious Diseases (NIAID). Mysteriously, one month later there was the SARS 1.0 outbreak."

"SARS 1.0, the Severe Acute Respiratory Syndrome coronavirus caused the 2001–2004 SARS outbreak. Am I suggesting SARS 1.0 came from a laboratory? No. It is a fact that the University of North Carolina at Chapel Hill created it. The question is, who released it in China, Hong Kong, and Taiwan?"

"Under Dr. D'Angelo, American bioweapons labs engineered SARS. SARS is not a naturally occurring phenomenon. The naturally occurring phenomenon is called the common cold. It's called influenza-like illness. That is the naturally occurring coronavirus. SARS is the research developed by humans weaponizing a life-system model to actually attack human beings and, in this case, Chinese. And Dr. D'Angelo oversaw its patent in 2001."

"And then, surprise, the CDC filed a patent on coronavirus isolated from humans in violation of biological and chemical weapons treaties and the laws of the United States. When Dr. D'Angelo's CDC filed a patent in 2001 on SARS isolated from humans, what did they do? They downloaded a SARS sequence from China and filed a patent in the United States. Anyone with knowledge of biological weapons treaties knows that is a violation. That is a crime. And the U.S. Patent Office rejected that patent on two occasions until the CDC bribed the patent office to override the patent examiner and ultimately issue the patent in 2007 on SARS coronavirus."

"The RT-PCR, the reverse transcription polymerase chain reaction test, is the test allegedly to be used for the upcoming and alleged coronavirus pandemic. Industry is already gearing up to make it. However, the commercially produced RT-PCR test was actually identified as a *bioterrorism threat* by me in the European Union-sponsored pandemic simulation events in early 2001. Before I was dismissed from the NCMI."

"In 2005, this RT-PCR test was specifically labeled as *bioterrorism and bioweapon platform technology* and was described as such. Not my terminology. Since 2005 it has been officially classified as a *biowarfare enabling agent*. Biowarfare enabling technology. This isn't public health. This is not medicine. This is not a test."

"Disguised and marketed as a test for infection, this is a weapon designed to take out humanity. At least the humanity that Dr. D'Angelo or one of his customers does not like. Create a pandemic, offer a test. Iran could take out Israel, and as unintended consequences, maybe wipe out all the Middle East."

"We've been lured into believing DARPA and the pharmaceutical companies and all these organizations, like the UNC at Chapel Hill are benevolent. We should point to, but have been specifically forced to ignore the facts. Nazi and Japanese bioweapons researchers advanced U.S. bioweapons technology by decades. Over $100B has been funneled to black operations and special access programs through the grant-awarding checkbook of Salvatore D'Angelo. Half of the budget is hidden in bioweapons grants. No one talks about that. The media doesn't know and Congress is not told. I know for a fact the CIA does not know that this has been going on since 1995. Why? How? The CDC and Ft. Detrick have inhouse disinformation review boards. A federal publication they create tells the reader all is well."

"We now come to what it all means. The gain-of-function moratorium was supposed to freeze any R&D, any efforts to do gain-of-function research. Conveniently in the fall of 2001, a letter from the CDC to UNC at Chapel Hill said that while the gain-of-function research on coronavirus *in vivo* should be suspended, their grants had already been funded so they were receiving an exemption."

"A biological lab at the UNC at Chapel Hill received an exemption from the gain-of-function moratoriums going back to 2001. It is ok for you to continue to develop and patent a bioweapon. Signed Dr. Salvatore D'Angelo. In 2016, the CDC published a journal article that said, SARS coronavirus is poised for human emergence. That's 2016."

"What was the coronavirus poised for human emergence? Open-source materials. It was WIV1 — Wuhan Institute of Virology virus one. A peer-reviewed paper stating coronavirus was poised for human emergence was presented at the National Academy of Sciences in 2016. By the time we get to 2017-2018, the following phrase enters into common parlance among the community: There is going to be an accidental or intentional release of a respiratory pathogen. The operative word in that phrase is *release*. Does that sound like a leak? Does that sound like a bat and a pangolin went into a bar at the Wuhan wet market, hung out, had kinky sex, and, lo and behold, we got SARS coronavirus? No. *Accidental or intentional release of a respiratory pathogen* was the terminology used."

"In April of 2019, seven months before the allegation of patient number one, four vaccine patent applications were modified to include the term 'accidental or intentional release of a respiratory pathogen.' This was done as justification to make a vaccine for a thing that did not exist."

"Let me repeat that. Make a vaccine for a thing that did not exist. Not the other way around; for decades we derived a vaccine from a virus found in nature."

"In September of 2019 the world was informed, by no less of an authority than Dr. Salvatore D'Angelo, that '…we are going to have an accidental or intentional release of a respiratory pathogen. So, by September 2020, days before the election, there will be a worldwide fear of a coronavirus; there will be worldwide acceptance of a universal vaccine template.' Those are Dr. D'Angelo's words."

"His intent was to use the President of the United States to declare a health emergency and order an experimental coronavirus vaccine that would cause the world to accept the mRNA platform as a universal vaccine template."

"Dr. D'Angelo said just the other day, and I quote, 'Until an infectious disease crisis is very real, present, and at the emergency threshold, it is often ignored. To sustain the funding base beyond the crisis, we need to increase public understanding for the need of medical countermeasures such as a pan-influenza or pan-coronavirus vaccine. The media is a key driver. The economics will follow the hype. We need to use that hype to our advantage to get to the real issues. Investors will respond if they see profit at the end of the process.' Closed quote."

"Does that sound like public health?"

"Does that sound like the best of humanity?"

"No, ladies and gentlemen. This was premeditated domestic terrorism presented at the proceedings of the National Academy of Sciences, published in front of them. This is an act of biological and chemical warfare perpetrated on the human race. Dr. D'Angelo admitted in his own words and in writing that it was a financial heist, a financial fraud: investors will respond if they see profit at the end of the process."

"For the more than forty years that he was the CDC Director, Dr. D'Angelo awarded billions in contracts to overseas biolabs. In the 1990s, the Chinese, the Iranians, the Iraqis, the Libyans, and others were spending billions of dollars developing ethnic bioweapons with a targeted 50% infection fatality rate. Targeting people by race. By their DNA."

"In 1945, Nazi researchers had created the first ethnic bioweapon that targeted the Jewish people. They collected the first DNA from their incarcerated Jewish prisoners. They were stopped from doing any further research and were not able to deploy their ethnic cleansing bioweapon because the war ended and we got the Nuremberg Code of ethics. When Dr. D'Angelo awarded billions of dollars to biolabs across Europe, China, and Iran, it set off a new arms race, of sorts. The Chinese collected Islamic and Russian DNA; the Russians collected Chinese DNA. Europeans and Iran collected Jewish DNA. Countries couldn't afford nuclear weapons, but unscrupulous infectious disease and bioweapons experts were gladly trading their knowledge for cash. So, countries developed an arsenal of bioweapons and cures to attack their enemies or protect themselves from their enemies. Targeted ethnic bioweapons are the poor country's nuclear weapons."

"In conclusion, nature was hijacked. This all started in 1945. It was resurrected in 1965 when we decided to hijack a natural model and manipulate it."

"Science was hijacked. The only questions to be asked were questions authorized under the patent protection of the CDC, the FDA, the NIH, and their equivalent organizations around the world. We didn't have independent science. We had hijacked science."

"There was no moral oversight. This was a violation of all the codes we stand for. No independent, financially disinterested review board was ever empaneled around coronavirus. Not once. Not since 1965. There has never been a single independent review board empaneled around coronavirus. Do you know why? Coronavirus is the common cold and so tame that it isn't even listed in the Army's Field Manual of Potential Chemical and Biological Agents. But manufactured and patented coronavirus *clones* have the potential to be biological Trojan horses where vaccines made in a laboratory and patented can decimate and even eradicate any population a tyrant deems unworthy."

"Morality was suspended. Ultimately, humanity will be lost. Bioweapons to the highest bidder granted by an unelected bureaucrat. We allowed it to happen."

"Mr. President. You must stop gain-of-function research. Period. No more weaponization of nature. Period. No more commercialization of bioweapons. And most importantly, no more corporate patronage of science for corporate's own self-interests, unless they assume 100% product liability for every injury or death."

"Mr. President, do not allow yourself to be manipulated by people who do not have America's or the world's best interests in heart. Reject their siren song of a national health emergency to gain approval of experimental vaccines. It is documented; for twenty years they have been hiding the immediate and long-term adverse consequences of mRNA technology. They were making a vaccine for something that did not exist, but these vaccines have the potential to eradicate an ethnic group of people. Bioweapons should not be available to the highest bidder. Instruct the White House *Pandemic Response Office* to investigate and approve off-label FDA-Approved therapeutics that have been shown for fifty years to be effective against a coronavirus. Thank you."

Demetrius Eastwood clapped and grinned from ear to ear. He shouted, "Dr. McIntosh, you're the bomb!" as she left the dais. He said, "You were incredible!" *That was incredible! That's why Duncan wanted her, what she had in her head.*

The White House Press Corps was in shock.d

Dr. McIntosh was excited about the speech. She tried not to scream as she said, "My knees are shaking! I need to get out of here."

He tried to shake her hand to congratulate her but wound up holding her hand. She really was trembling. *What a performance!* Eastwood was still holding her hand when he said, "We can get out of here. Are you able to eat?"

Elizabeth nodded. "Will that get to the White House?"

Eastwood was still holding her hand. "I think so. I hope so. Eventually. Could be a couple of days."

"Suddenly, food sounds good."

He asked, "What are you in the mood for?"

"I don't care. What did you have in mind?"

Eastwood asked, "Ever been to the Capital Grill?"

"Best steaks on the planet."

He smiled. "And Key lime pie."

Elizabeth squeezed his hand and finally let go. "Lets!"

•   •   •

President Hernandez had gotten up to leave the Oval Office with the Joint Chiefs of Staff, the Chief of Staff, and the Vice President, the team he had assembled to meet with the *Pandemic Response Office* when he heard a voice from the television say, "...There is going to be an accidental or intentional release of a respiratory pathogen." There was an image of a portly woman at a lectern with the National Press Club sign in the background. He stopped.

At that moment, the Chief of Staff turned off the TV, sparking a sharp rebuke of the President: "*Turn that back on!*"

It took more than a few seconds for the Chief of Staff to find the correct buttons on the remote to reboot the TV. Questions flew around the room.

"What was that?"

"Who was that?"

"Was that the National Press Club?"

They moved to the television. The JCS and White House regulars filled in around President Hernandez. He turned up the volume, and the group watched, transfixed.

The unknown woman concluded, "Mr. President, do not allow yourself to be manipulated by people who do not have the America's or the world's best interests in heart. Reject their siren song of a national health emergency to gain approval of experimental vaccines. It is documented; for twenty years they have been hiding the immediate and long-term adverse consequences of mRNA technology. They were making a vaccine for something that did not exist, but these vaccines have the potential to eradicate an ethnic group of people. Bioweapons should not be available to the highest bidder. Instruct the White House *Pandemic Response Office* to investigate and approve off-label FDA-Approved therapeutics that have been shown for fifty years to be effective against a coronavirus. Thank you."

President Hernandez turned off the television. He turned to the Vice President and the Chief of Staff and said, "That was live from the National Press Club. Find her. Don't let that woman to leave the club. Get the Secret Service to bring her here; I want to talk to her. If she isn't at the Club, just find her."

•   •   •

Alone in the Oval, President Hernandez called the CIA Director, who was in conference with his staff. Todd cleared the room except for the Deputy and the DO. President Hernandez was direct. "Walter, I'd like you to release the *pumpkin* to Interpol. The DO knows what they are and who they need to go to."

Todd looked across the table at Nazy. "Consider it done, Mister President."

The President asked, "Did you see who was on at the National Press Club?"

Todd wasn't sure what the question meant but knew the answer was, "No, sir."

"See if you can get a transcript. I want a full debrief tomorrow. And Todd, I'm going to need to send you to China as soon as possible."

Director Todd was stunned. *China?*

"I want you to carry a message for me. I'll tell you in the morning. Bring Nazy. *Capiche?*"

"Yes, Mr. President." The line went dead. Todd looked at Nazy questioning what he had just heard. He said, "He wants us at the White House tomorrow. He is sending me to China. To deliver a message."

"A message?"

The two Agency executives looked at each other. Nazy said, "Maybe tomorrow will provide some insight into what the President wants."

"Let's hope. I don't even know what to pack."

•　　•　　•

There are things that are physically impossible, like a speeding car outrunning a police radio. In Washington, D.C., when the radios of the Secret Service Special Agents on the east side of the White House compound crackled to life directing agents to converge on the National Press Club, a dozen of America's finest executive protection special agents determined it was faster to sprint the one block than to drive it. In less than thirty seconds, the Secret Service were on scene. The radio continued to spit out directions and descriptions. In less than a New York minute, when Dr. McIntosh and Demetrius Eastwood approached the entrance, they were surrounded by men and women in black battle dress uniforms and gold SECRET SERVICE letters emblazoned on their backs, with guns drawn.

Dr. McIntosh grinned as she said to Eastwood, "So you think it could take a couple of days?" Eastwood smiled and shook his head.

The White House Press Corps had followed McIntosh and Eastwood out of the building. They were stunned at what they saw.

It took longer for McIntosh and Eastwood to get onto the White House grounds and through the building than it did for the Secret Service to find them. They had been stopped before they had even stepped out of the National Press Club building.

At the White House, identities were checked and backgrounds verified. They were frisked, and their belongings were confiscated while they remained in an outer office. Two minutes later, Dr. McIntosh and Eastwood were ushered into the Oval Office and greeted by the President of the United States.

Guiding them to a sofa, President Hernandez said, "Dr. McIntosh, Colonel Eastwood, please...." When they were seated, the President asked, "Dr. McIntosh, you have a message for me?"

"Yes, Mr. President, I do. You walked in the rain behind Duncan Hunter's caisson to protect his identity. He asked me to deliver a message to you...."

Wow! That was unexpected! "He's on... *assignment*...." The President smiled, giving away a national secret.

Elizabeth smiled back, "Mr. President, he's *always* on assignment. I surmise, he's a national treasure." Dr. McIntosh talked for twelve minutes without interruption, summarizing her speech at the National Press Club. She ended with, "Mr. President, throughout history, powerful individuals have sought to eliminate certain races or ethnicities, and current-day bioweapons give them the ability to do that very efficiently. For this reason, gain-of-function research and bioweapons development must be guided by robust regulations and oversight. America cannot allow an unelected individual to usurp the authority of this office."

When she finished, President Hernandez was quiet for full minute. Then he pinched his lips, nodded, and said, "Dr. McIntosh, it's a national scandal what happened to you. D'Angelo compromised the CDC. He took the CDC which was the gold standard for scientific research and abandoned the mission of protecting Americans, what makes them sick, and adopted a new mission, which was to develop things to kill Americans. He got millions in perks and royalties for doling out billions in government research contracts."

Dr. McIntosh and Eastwood nodded.

President Hernandez said, "D'Angelo rose to the top of the infectious disease agencies and remained there for fifty years. He's there for one reason—because he knows how to serve the political ambitions of the Democrat Party. Elizabeth, you are a great American. I'll take it from here. Thank you for your bravery, your courage, and your service to our nation. Colonel Eastwood, take care of her and Admiral McGee. And yourself. I thank you for coming on such short notice."

The three of them stood; the impromptu meeting was over. President Hernandez asked, "Where were you off to before I, uh, I interrupted your plans?"

Eastwood finally had a speaking part. "Mr. President, we were off to the Capital Grill."

President Hernandez smiled wide. "Okay! Dinner is on me." He walked to the door where his secretary sat. The President pointed to the head of the White House Secret Service and said, "Take Dr. McIntosh and Colonel Eastwood to the Capital Grill; whatever they want it is on the White House."

CHAPTER 65

July 24, 2020

An 18-wheeler with OVERSIZED banners fore and aft was guided into one of the abandoned aircraft hangars at the former Loring Air Force Base. A very large forklift with twelve-foot-long forks lifted the forty-foot by eleven-foot wooden crate and allowed the driver to depart the hangar before setting the crate on the ground. On the hangar floor, the crate rested within an eighty-foot square, marked by yellow and black diagonal painted lines on the concrete.

Once the tractor-trailer and forklift had departed the hangar, and the hangar doors had been closed, the crate was slowly lowered by a massive elevator in the middle of the hangar. The elevatorman notified the Security Chief by the Agency's secure internet, "The Director's package has been delivered."

•   •   •

Dr. Salvatore D'Angelo was halfway through his massage at the spa at the Althoff Grandhotel Schloss when his smartphone chimed; he had an incoming call. The male masseuse stopped rubbing high on his inner thigh to provoke a response and asked in perfect English, "Would you like me to get that for you?" D'Angelo said yes and turned over on his back. One of the pharmaceutical chief executive officers he had traveled with extensively had forwarded a video. He shouted to no one, *"I don't have time for this!"* He handed the phone back to his masseuse when several more chimes announcing text messages had come through to the device. *You just got hammered at the National Press Club!*

D'Angelo stared at the screen as more new messages came through. *What does that mean? Why would I get hammered at the National Press Club?*

His erection dissolved as he watched the tiny video.

•   •   •

Reuters News Flash
London

The secretive online organization *Whistleblowers* reported they are in possession of and have delivered the first tranche of thousands of high-quality videos showing primarily European men engaged in child sexual assault and other crimes against children. Much of the cache of videos is believed to be surveillance video taken from the many European hotels of the world's richest man and Auschwitz survivor, Rho Schwartz Scorpii, before he died in America seeking cancer treatment. Led by Interpol, European countries' top law enforcement organizations are scrambling to identify the perpetrators in the videos and bring them to justice. Senior officials at *Interpol* believe the videos were used in blackmailing men of means or those with access to national secrets.

This is a fast-moving story and updates will be provided continuously.

•   •   •

Associated Press Newswire
Aspen, Colorado

The magnificent multi-acre estate owned by a software billionaire known as *Aspen House* was declared a total loss today. The cause of the fire is still under investigation; however, the garage at *Aspen House* housed several electric vehicles. All the EVs and millions of dollars in one-of-a-kind collectible artwork were also lost.

The gated estate prevented the local fire department from limiting the damage to the fifteen-bedroom lodge. The raging fire spilled out of the compound and set half of the mountain on fire. No other multi-million-dollar homes were affected. That only *Aspen House* was lost was a tribute to the speedy reaction of the Aspen Fire Department.

CHAPTER 66

July 25, 2020
0800

The four-man Marine Corps Color Guard marched through the Original Headquarters Building lobby toward the Memorial Wall. Two Marines carried chromed M-14 rifles on opposite shoulders and silently moved to Present Arms. The flag bearer rendered Honors by lowering the light blue flag of the Central Intelligence Agency while the American Flag remained ramrod straight.

The National Anthem played over the loudspeaker system. When the music ceased, the color guard retired the colors and marched out of the lobby.

In a navy suit, Nazy Cunningham stepped behind a lectern off to the side of the Memorial Wall. Her voice was strong and clear. The acoustics of the lobby did not interfere with her words.

"Good afternoon, ladies and gentlemen. Behind me there are 135 stars mounted on white Alabama marble." Beneath the stars of the Memorial Wall, a black Moroccan goatskin-bound book rested in a steel frame.

"Each star represents a fallen hero of the Central Intelligence Agency or the Office of Strategic Services. Today, we shall add another star to the Memorial Wall. Some of the identities of those who served their country in the field of intelligence will remain unknown forever. Their names will live in memoriam within the Book of Honor."

Nazy said, "We gather to honor the accomplishments of an intelligence officer who truly performed above and beyond in the performance of his duty. The identity of today's honoree has been added to the Book of Honor and will remain secret."

150 people from the intelligence community had filled the lobby and each was silent for the somber occasion. Dr. Elizabeth McIntosh was accompanied by family members of servicemembers who had been assigned to the Office of Strategic Services.

The Director of Operations continued, "Our honoree is awarded the Distinguished Intelligence Cross posthumously for uncommon and extraordinary acts of heroism and valor. His unwavering courage and steadfast devotion to country reflected great credit upon himself. Like those before him, he upheld the highest traditions of the Office of Strategic Services. Signed this twenty-fifth day of July, 2020."

Nazy and Director Todd turned as a Marine approached the Memorial Wall with a black star resting upon a light blue pillow. Todd stepped forward, lifted the star from the pillow, and pressed it onto the marble face.

The Director of Operations continued, "America will never know of the courage and heroism or the accomplishments of our honoree as he gave his life to our National Security and Defense. On behalf of a great Nation, please accept our deepest appreciation and gratitude. We will forever be in your debt." Nazy raised her eyes and her voice. "Ladies and gentlemen, that concludes our ceremony. Thank you for coming."

Each three-dimensional star measured $2\frac{1}{4}$ inches tall by $2\frac{1}{4}$ inches wide and was a half an inch deep. Every star was spaced six inches apart from the others. Every row was also six inches apart from the other rows. Newer stars were black, the older stars had faded to gray.

Director Todd shook Nazy's and the Deputy's hands. He was out the door to catch a military jet for a meeting with the Premier of the State Council of the People's Republic of China.

•   •   •

The QAS Chief Executive Officer, Arsenio Bong, was in the office on a Saturday to oversee the delivery of a restored warbird to its owner. After the acceptance inspection and engine run had been completed, he returned to his office. He greeted Stacey Osceola with a smile and a hearty handshake, and a promotion as chief inspector.

She and Ralph Gilbert took a golf cart back to the Quiet Aero Systems main office. An Agency polygrapher interviewed Stacey for an hour, announced she had passed, and that she would pass the information on to the Security Manager.

Believing they had stumbled on to a Central Intelligence Agency special access program, she and Ralph agreed to never discuss the white cocooned *K-MAXs* in the far hangar of Quiet Aero Systems or the unmanned *K-MAX* program ever again.

CHAPTER 67

August 3, 2020
Salve Regina University
Newport, Rhode Island

Dr. Elizabeth McIntosh had exited the front door of her home only to find a man with a thick cigar in his mouth operating the controls of a *Tracy's Wrecker Service* truck. A 1957, robin-blue Mercedes 300 SL roadster sat atop the bed of the wrecker and the bed was moving. She rushed directly to the truck. "May I help you?" she asked.

The wrecker driver didn't hear her as he was busy getting the bed of the wrecker off the back of the truck and onto the ground.

She was aghast and yelled, "*What are you doing?*"

"If you are Dr. Elizabeth McIntosh, I'm delivering your car, lady."

Elizabeth waved her arms in exasperation. There had to be a mistake. "*My car?* That's not my car." She pointed at the tired worn out formerly cream-colored 1965 Mercedes 280SL in the driveway and said, "*That,* is my car."

"Yeah. That's right. I'm to drop this *blue* thing off to Dr. Elizabeth McIntosh, which is you, at this address, and return that…*tired-ass thing* you call a Mercedes to Texas."

Texas? "But, but…?"

The cigar rolled to the other side of the man's mouth as if by magic. He handed her an envelope. "Where do you want this?"

Shocked, she fumbled to open the A2 envelope. It was embossed in gold leaf with the Marine Corps emblem. The card inside said:

Dear Elizabeth,

I wasn't able to thank you appropriately for your time speaking at the National Press Club. I can assure you, you saved countless number of lives with your words.

I'm offering you a deal of a lifetime, please accept this 1957 Mercedes 300 SL as a token of our gratitude and esteem in trade for your 280SL. My plan is to restore the 280SL back to its glory days.

If you want to keep the 300 SL it is yours; if you want to keep your restored 280SL, just let the driver of the truck know the 300 SL is just a loaner. He'll bring your car back better than new.

Thank you again, Elizabeth. We'll talk soon.

Best,

Hunter 204

P.S. The 300SL is a better deal, IMHO.

She shouted at the man, "*I can't drive a million-dollar car to school!*"

The cigar made the trip to the other side of his mouth. "Not my problem, *Doc*. Sign here."

CHAPTER 68

August 10, 2020

"Thank you for tuning into this episode of *Unfiltered News* and what is likely to be our last broadcast until the election. We are still free from the pharmaceutical companies' influence—no big pharma sponsorship like the networks and newspapers. We usually open this show saying there is no difference between the communist message and the Democrat Party's message, and that we can report accurately the Democrat's propaganda arm is at it again and we have the video! Turns out *Interpol*, the International Criminal Police Organization, actually has the videos."

"We must get right to the news because there is so much of it and this will be my last show for what could be several weeks. Freedom makes this radio program and on-line telecast possible from coast to coast. I've got much to discuss. This is Demetrius Eastwood. Let's get your *Unfiltered News* rolling!"

"Every year, thousands of Shia worshippers take part in the ceremonies performed to mourn the death of Husayn ibn Ali, a grandson of the Prophet Muhammad. They did so again on Friday, July 31st as Muslims took to the streets *in London* for the 'Ashura Day Procession.' In a show of force, Muslims held a public procession that began in front of the iconic Marble Arch and marched towards the Islamic Universal Association, Holland Park. Muslims even waved the Iraqi flag on top of the Marble Arch, celebrating their victory over London. Victory over London? Isn't that what Muslims tried to do in Detroit with the Mazibuike Presidential Center; a tribute commemorating the greatest Muslim attack on America when their illegitimate Islamic president moved into the White House? The only thing he didn't do was raise the green flag of the Muslim Brotherhood over the White House."

"Now to our special report. The Hungarian-based, international non-profit organization, *Whistleblowers*, has gained what seems to be secret video recordings of what could be tens of thousands of European men sexually assaulting children and other related crimes. This is a quickly moving report out of Europe that American media has shown no interest in. What we are learning from European sources is that *Whistleblowers* has turned over these videos to *Interpol*. For our liberal friends listening, that's the International Criminal Police Organization and they acknowledge the videos are authentic, that the artwork prominently displayed in the videos matches the unique artwork found primarily at the Althoff Grandhotel Schloss in Germany, as well as other hotels in major cities throughout Europe. This hotel and apparently the others shown in the *Whistleblower* videos, once belonged to the world's richest man, the late Rho Schwartz Scorpii, the greatest liberal philanthropist to emerge from World War Two. Reportedly, he lived at the Althoff Grandhotel Schloss in Cologne. Authorities at *Interpol* and law enforcement agencies throughout Europe and Great Britain, are trying to unpack Scorpii's business holdings and reach."

"We hear little in the way from Rho Schwartz Scorpii in America other than he was a supporter of progressive and liberal political causes. Few know he dispensed billions in donations through his *Ostgut* Foundation. *Ostgut* was the name of the former railway depot from which Scorpii and his family boarded a train for the Nazi concentration camps. Reportedly, he had donated over $10 billion in America alone to various philanthropic causes through the *Ostgut* Foundation, 'to reduce poverty and increase transparency, and for scholarships and universities around the world.' That all sounds peachy, but if there are tens of thousands of men on video assaulting children in his hotels, the *Whistleblowers'* tapes may prove to *Interpol* and law enforcement authorities that they are just the tip of the iceberg of what the billionaire and his foundation were actually doing. The investigations are ongoing, but it seems for now that Scorpii might not have been the philanthropist many thought he was."

"In other news, likely related to the release of the Scorpii videos, as we are calling them now, men from across Europe have suddenly started jumping out of buildings or jumping in front of trains, buses, or trucks—lories as they are called over there. Law enforcement has taken notice that men are killing themselves at a prodigious rate before the perpetrators of the sex crimes caught on video can be brought to justice. Since the release of those videos, dozens of men: royalty, military men, officials, legislators, CEOs, men of means and status are committing suicide every day. As more videos are released from *Whistleblowers*, and as more men are identified in the videos by Interpol, can we expect more suicides from these—let's call them for what they are, criminal pedophiles?"

"Break, break, new topic. Here at home, President Hernandez has invoked the Defense Production Act, forcing businesses to produce a range of mass-produced drugs, such as FDA-Approved anti-malarials and anti-parasitics. China has monopolized their manufacture for decades. This may be in response to the CDC's insistence that a pandemic will strike a devastating blow to America so Americans will need to be vaccinated against the unseen pathogen. However, since Dr. McIntosh's speech at the National Press Club, vaccine manufacturers have pulled *all the*ir proposed experimental vaccines from consideration. Defense Production Act contracts will not go to the pharmaceutical giants but to small pharmaceutical businesses in the industry. There are many questions swirling around the oncoming pandemic, if and when it gets here. We'll stay on top of this one as well."

Eastwood spoke for two hours about how the McGee campaign was awash in the news that nationwide polling had him, on average, 25 points higher than the Democrat Party contender. "If the polling is accurate, Admiral McGee will win forty-eight of the fifty states. New York and California may be the only states for Senator Neil Burgess."

"On the Pentagon front, the Secretary of the Air Force announced their secretive and highly classified *Next Generation Air Dominance* fighter program has started its crucial engineering and manufacturing development phase. The Air Force has completed early development of key technologies needed for the production program and experimental prototyping on what is essentially an X-plane program. Designed to reduce risk and cost, and the new fighter will use the same metallurgy as the jet it replaces, the F-22 *RAPTOR*. The order will be for 1,500 jets. Longtime listeners know President Mazibuike canceled the F-22 contract for 1,000 jets, and the Air Force received less than 200. I don't think a President McGee will allow our magnificent Air Force to be weakened like it was under President Mazibuike."

"And a final note, President Hernandez issued an emergency executive order, countermanding the FDA's decision that would have allowed HIV men to give blood. In other words, the FDA was going to endanger Americans and contaminate the national blood supply. The President said, 'Not on my watch. It's time to investigate the CDC and the FDA, and the NIAID. They seem to have lost their way. The mission is to protect Americans and not worry about hurting someone's feelings.' All I can say is Wow! So much for being a lame duck President."

"As we close shop until the election, a final word. Admiral McGee's courageous taking on of the satanic cult of Mazibuikism and their perpetual war on Christianity is the biggest poke in the eye a presidential candidate could ever give the Democrats. It says Admiral McGee is not going away, that America is worth fighting for. Admiral McGee is telling the world that God's children cannot be bought and sold, that parents have rights and America will protect its women, and that as President, America will do everything it can to stop child sex trafficking across the globe."

"Well, that is it for now my great and loyal audience. Thank you for dropping in. Get out and vote. It is more important now than ever before. Please remember and offer prayer for our service members who are *the tip of the spear* defending you and me and all of America against all enemies, both foreign and Democrats. The number of videos of electric vehicles on fire that you have sent us just passed 1,000. EVs are piling up on dealer's lots. Another ship carrying electric vehicles from Europe is on fire in the Atlantic. Global warming is a complete scam and utter nonsense, even the co-founder of Greenpeace said so in a recent interview. The left focuses on things that nobody can see and makes up stories about them. Please send us your EV-on-fire-videos, and we'll post them on our page."

"This has been an exciting time in my life. I thank you for your support and encouragement. The next time we plan to be back will be on election night. Until then, get out and vote, don't let the crazies in the Democrat Party get you down, help is on the way. This is *Unfiltered and Unspun*! and Eastwood has left the building!"

•   •   •

Immediately after his podcast ended, Demetrius Eastwood opened the door to the suite and welcomed the moving company that would pack, move, and unpack his belongings at his new home in Texas. Another Duncan Hunter property. Where the air is free and clear. And maybe it would have a shower that could hose down a Longhorn.

EPILOGUE

August 15, 2020

Breakfast had been served on the lodge's massive deck overlooking the Grand Tetons. Nazy, Duncan, and Bong sat at a little bistro table as Therese Yazzie fussed with their breakfast orders. She knew what *Captain* wanted — always *huevos rancheros* with apple juice and coffee and cream. She didn't have to ask; Duncan would eat anything Therese would fix for him. Therese also knew what Miss Nazy wanted — scrambled eggs, hash browns, with thick, barely *limpy* bacon, toast, coffee and fresh-squeezed orange juice. She also didn't have to ask Miss Nazy, but, as a courtesy, she always did, and Nazy always confirmed her selection and thanked the old Apache woman for taking care of her.

Therese's problem was with the guest. *Bong? What sort of name is Bong?*

Bong had trouble deciding what to have for breakfast until Duncan offered, "Try Therese's French toast and country ham. You will not believe what she can do in the kitchen."

The trio enjoyed a home cooked meal among one of *Captain's* many science projects, hundreds of exotic plants were scattered about on the patio deck.

The double-garage-sized greenhouse was empty. Long after the snows had melted and when the weather had finally gotten warm enough at night where temperature-sensitive succulents wouldn't be killed from an unexpected frost, Carlos and Therese would bring all the plants of varying sizes and varieties from the greenhouse, and arranged them along the main deck. They were in individual Mexican pots; tiny pots to massive to handle the six-foot-high Madagascar palm. Most of the plants were unusual succulents or palms or cacti that Duncan had collected from his missions across the Middle East, Africa, and South America. Duncan always complimented Therese for her green thumb and for the exquisite care she took with his rare plants. *The Captain's* pride and joy was a six-foot-tall ponytail palm.

After breakfast, after Bong debriefed Duncan on the status of the business and other business operations, he announced Stacey Osceola had returned to Elmira, had been polygraphed, and was back at work.

Nazy remained at the table as Duncan walked out with Bong who handed him a note: *Ravens successful. Ti rods sent a message. Lost Jebriel. Maybe Dubai. Every corporate jet on PIA. FireFighters new home Amistad Lake in Del Rio.* Duncan nodded, pocketed the 3x5 card, and shook his hand. "We'll find him. We've done as much as we can up to the election."

"Are you going to stop flying?"

Duncan said, "I don't know. Much depends on the outcome of the election. *Bullfrog* should win easy. My back is a mess. We'll see. It's something that requires a lot of thought."

"It's been an incredible couple of months."

Duncan smiled and said, "Take it easy, Bong. And, thanks again."

Carlos Yazzie returned Bong to the Jackson Airport in one of the lodge's armored Hummer H2s.

The Captain returned to the table with Nazy and sat down. She had been so engrossed with the news she might not have noticed he had left for a few minutes. Duncan quietly admired the scenery; Nazy's delicate hands as she thumbed through the paper.

He chuckled and thought, *One month! By Presidential decree. Half-over. Blah.* After a two-week vacation touring Europe, Duncan and Nazy were ecstatic to be home at their ranch in Wyoming.

They rarely had time for themselves or time to relax. Duncan turned to admire their home.

The lodge had once been described as a *hideous accident,* as if Frank Lloyd Wright's iconic *Fallingwater* had crash landed atop the *Yellowstone Lodge.* The designer had called the 6,000 square-foot *masterpiece* of mammoth Western Red Cedar logs from Canada and huge stones from a local quarry, *Timber Rock*. Duncan's longtime friend and foreman, Carlos Yazzie, oversaw the remodeling of the property after *the Captain* had purchased it.

The retired Marine Corps Gunnery Sergeant, Carlos Yazzie managed the construction of a multi-car garage, horse stables, and an underground safe room complex with a shooting range. Yazzie also ramrodded the installation of an Agency-level security system of multiple fixed cameras, cameras on drones, night vision and thermal cameras, and hundreds of microwave and seismic sensors. Much of the additional labor and expense was in the construction of the considerable underground network of safe rooms, thousand-gallon propane and diesel tanks, and backup generators that could easily power the Jackson Hospital in an emergency.

The President said the best reward he could give me was some time off. Nazy and I had been going at it pretty hard. Not what Magoo wanted to hear. Nazy said Magoo about had a coronary when she said we were leaving for a month. His next coronary was when the President sent him to China. Which reminds me....

When the rustling of Nazy's newspaper interrupted his reverie, he turned to find her peering over the newspaper.

Nazy shook the pages of the *Denver Post* and said, "Before we left for Europe, Todd and I put a star on the Memorial Wall for Charles Lindbergh. The President directed we release the videos from Scorpii's *pumpkin* to Interpol and *Whistleblowers*."

Almost there. "About time. How'd you do that?"

"Diplomatic pouch to Brussels. Berlin Chief of Station pushed them to *Whistleblowers*. Interpol got copies. *Whistleblowers* said they would release a hundred names a day. I said not to release D'Angelo's name until the very end."

Duncan said, "That's good. We don't want to spook him."

"Exactly."

"A hundred a day will keep Interpol honest."

"The paper says European abortion clinics and their biggest biotech labs have shut down. They are all under investigation for harvesting and trafficking body parts. And, I almost forget, Dr. McIntosh left a few notes in her grandfather's file."

Duncan asked, "Really?" *Bullfrog said something….*

Nazy said, "One note hinted that Göring, the master of a hunting lodge, probably hunted Jewish children and took trophies."

Duncan said, "Oh. Sick bastards." *Lindy would never have been party to that.*

Her nose went back into paper and just as quickly, Nazy folded the paper and asked, "I think you were still in Alaska. Were you able to see the President's press conference?"

Duncan frowned and shook his head. *Eastwood texted me from the Capital Grill – MC.*

"Dr. McIntosh gave a speech and President Hernandez said in no uncertain terms that he would never allow experimental vaccines to be developed when there are FDA-approved drugs available. He asked for an investigation into the CDC, the FDA, and Dr. D'Angelo."

"About time."

"The President also sent Todd to China. To deliver a message." The newspaper flew back up for a dozen seconds.

Duncan asked, "Really?"

Nazy put the paper back in her lap and nodded. "Todd told them to dismantle their weapons of mass destruction program, specifically, their bioweapons lab at Wuhan. Cease research and development into ethnically targeted bioweapons. The President wanted Todd to emphasize that America cannot be defeated biologically, too ethnically diverse. No DNA homogeneity. However, over 98% of Chinese people share a common DNA. The Chinese proved the SARS was lethal to Chinese in Taiwan and Hong Kong. That the bioweapon they created to test on their own people could be released by another state actor and eradicate their population."

"That's ballsy! I think Todd is getting the hang of the job."

Nazy nodded, returned to *The Denver Post*, and found another article that was interesting. She talked at the paper. "Duncan, darling. I think this is you. Listen, North Korea's *official* Central News Agency reported one of their air bases had been completely destroyed in a U.S. drone attack. The Pentagon emphatically denied they had taken any action in North Korea. The Central News Agency claimed that what had precipitated the attack on their facility was U.S. Air Force Captain Darius Laskin defecting to North Korea with one of America's top fighter aircraft, an F-22 *RAPTOR*. The Central News Agency claimed Captain Laskin had been killed in the drone attack." She collapsed the newspaper when she was finished to ask, "Is that true?"

"I was too busy stealing a jet. I think they probably got tired of him whining about the fish heads and rice they call food or that he should be given a reward. Or maybe they just shot him because when he tried to convince them that America would not or could not respond appropriately after he stole our *wonderjet*, he was the catalyst that destroyed a dozen *Flankers* and an airbase and a couple of mobile SAM sites. North Korea got a whiner, not a winner. Baby, could you put some patches on my back?"

He certainly has a way with words. "Certainly!"

After applying lidocaine patches to Duncan's back, Nazy returned to the article. "Pentagon officials are mum on Captain Laskin's defection and showed video of Laskin's aircraft at Osan Air Force Base in South Korea after being repaired for its flight to Kadena, Okinawa. That was weeks ago. Air Force officials reported Laskin's F-22 had experienced a maintenance issue after aerial refueling and diverted to Oson Air Force Base in South Korea for repairs, Captain Laskin left the base and was never seen again. The F-22 arrived safely at Kadena Air Force Base in Okinawa, Japan. The official status and whereabouts of Captain Laskin are unknown."

Duncan nodded, smiled, and thought, *It may mean BlackWings did their job or the Koreans were pissed he was the cause of their base getting destroyed, and losing the RAPTOR.*

Nazy folded the paper over and asked, "Did Bill give you his Donovan Award?"

"No. I don't think so. I'm just holding it for him until he is done politicking and starts being Presidential. You know everyone who comes into the Oval Office will want to see it. I almost forgot about it."

"You forget nothing."

He grinned and tried his best Nat King Cole, "*Unforgettable, that's what you are.*" She threw him a kiss, rubbed his leg, and returned to the paper. Duncan sighed and stared off at the twin mountain peaks. *I'm no longer needed. I trained my replacement. Twice! No one on the Most Wanted Terrorist List. Maybe with Scorpii's tapes out in the open, Europe will curtail their child sex trafficking and the things the left did to satisfy their thirst for blood and children.*

I made the deal for the Curtiss. A man with a bad back and more money than sense has to stop collecting airplanes that can hurt him. Elizabeth took the 300SL. I knew she would.

He sighed. *I'm sure that foundation is still active doing Scorpii's work, like the dark state continues the work of the late but no-so-great Mazibuike. Europe will put on a show; we'll see how it goes.*

And no word on D'Angelo after his jet shit itself and the turd left the country. It wasn't too surprising that he found solace at the Althoff Grandhotel. I'm sure Scorpii gave him his own room. It was only about 400 clicks from Stuttgart and the Porsche Museum. Nazy said she wanted to see the cathedral in Cologne. We could do both easy.

Nazy was dozing when I tossed a couple of BlackWings out the window near the entrance of the Grandhotel. The dogs of darkness should find that criminal. If he doesn't first defenestrate himself when Whistleblowers announces his name.

Therese cleared off the table. Nazy finished her paper. She said, "I miss this. There is nothing like this place. It is so beautiful and quiet here." Duncan took her hand. He wrapped his arm around her waist and walked to the cavernous living room with a roaring fire in the fireplace. She sat in the sofa while Duncan poked logs. He removed a card from his pocket and tossed it into the fire.

He stood there for a moment as the note was consumed by the flames. *Fire has a cleansing effect. If the BlackWings find Dr. Science, good riddance. If they don't, I will find that pedophile bastard.* Hunter placed his Blackberry on the sofa table.

When Duncan joined Nazy on the large leather sofa, she opened her arms wide. The lovers embraced, stretched out. Therese Yazzie watched Nazy curl up on Duncan's shoulder.

Duncan's Blackberry buzzed followed by *Secret Agent Man* ringtone.

Duncan ignored the Blackberry and held Nazy tighter. *Magoo, I have two more weeks! Go away!*

The Blackberry rang again.

Nazy didn't move from her position and said, "You have to answer it."

Duncan sighed, unwound his arm and reached back for the cellphone. He answered without comment.

Director Todd said, "I need you, ya old fart."

The connection was severed. Duncan said, "Not again!"

Nazy snuggled deeper into his shoulder and said, "I think he's messing with you."

"What makes you say that."

Nazy said, "Well, Duncan darling, until I get the tasker, I can't give you the mission. So, I'm staying right here."

Duncan dropped the Blackberry on the table and squeezed Nazy. He said, "I have nothing else to prove. I trained my replacement.

There's no one left on the Matrix. I'm done. I can get used to this forever."

Nazy said, "No, Duncan darling. We still have a country to save."

"Well, then I'm going to need more patches."

ACRONYMS/ABBREVIATIONS

AACUS — Autonomous Aerial Cargo/Utility System

AB — Afterburner

ABO — Aviation Breathing Oxygen

ACP — Automatic Colt Pistol

AG — Attorney General

AGL — Above Ground Level

AI — Artificial Intelligence

AK — Automatic Kalashnikov

AM — Amplitude Modulation

AMTRAK — The National Railroad Passenger Corporation

APU — Auxiliary Power Unit

AQ — Al-Qaeda

ATLS — Automatic Takeoff and Landing System

AWAKE — Land or surface emitter activity detected via communications intelligence.

BANDIT — Positively identified as an enemy.

BCC — British Broadcasting Corporation

BINGO — Prebriefed fuel state needed for recovery.

BLM — Belligerent Leftist Mob

BMW — Bayerische Motoren Werke

BOQ — Batchelor Officers Quarters

BS — Bullshit

BUGOUT — Separation from a particular engagement, attack, or operation with no intent to reengage or return. Get the hell out of Dodge.

BUMP — Change power, plus or minus, from current power.

BUSTER — Fly at maximum continuous speed.

C — Cargo aircraft

CAF — Commemorative Air Force

Cal — Caliber

Cat — Category

CAVU — Ceiling And Visibility Unlimited

C-band — Ultraviolet wavelength from 100 to 280 nanometers

CDC — Center for Disease Control

CG — Commanding General

CHECK — Turn (number) degrees left or right and maintain new heading. CHECK SIX is to look directly behind you.

CI — Counter Intelligence

CIA — Central Intelligence Agency

CEO — Chief Executive Officer

CGI — Computer-Generated Imagery

CLEARED HOT — Term used when granting weapons release clearance to attack a specific target.

CN — Counternarcotics

COMM — Communications

CONTINUE — Continue present maneuver, does not imply a change in clearance to engage or expend ordnance.

COS — Chief of Station, Chief of Staff

CT — Counter Terrorism

CTC — Counter Terrorism Center

C-4 — Composition C-4; a variety of plastic explosive

DARPA — Defense Advanced Research Projects Agency

D.C. — District of Columbia

DEA — Drug Enforcement Agency

DELTA — 1st Special Forces Operational Detachment-Delta

DHS — Department of Homeland Security

DIA — Defense Intelligence Agency

DIC — Distinguished Intelligence Cross

DNC — Democratic National Committee

DO — Director of Operations

DOD — Department of Defense

DOJ — Department of Justice

D-21 — A supersonic reconnaissance drone from the Lockheed Corporation

Econ — Foreign Service Economic Officer work with U.S. and foreign government officials, business leaders, international organizations, and opinion-makers to promote national security through economic security

ETA — Estimated Time of Arrival

D.C. — District of Columbia

Dr. — Doctor

F — Fighter aircraft

FAA — Federal Aviation Administration

FARC — *Fuerzas Armadas Revolucionarias de Colombia*; the Revolutionary Armed Forces of Colombia

FBI — Federal Bureau of Investigation

FDR — Franklin Delano Roosevelt

Five Eyes — The anglophone intelligence alliance comprising Australia, Canada, New Zealand, the United Kingdom, and the United States

FLIR — Forward Looking Infra-Red

FSB — Federal Security Service of the Russian Federation

F-4S — Phantom

G — Gravity

G — Gulfstream aircraft

GITMO — Guantanamo Bay Naval Base, Cuba

G-IV — SP Gulfstream Model 4, Special Purpose

G-550 — Gulfstream Model 550

GMT — Greenwich Mean Time

GOP — Grand Old Party

GPS — Global Positioning System

GS — General Schedule

HAZMAT — Hazardous Materials

HEPA — High Efficiency Particulate Air

HK — Heckler & Koch

HQ — Headquarters

HR — Human Resources

HVAC — Heating, Venting, And Cooling

H2 — The Hummer H2 is a large SUV that was marketed by Hummer and built in the AM General facility under contract from General Motors

IC — Intelligence Community

ID — Identify/Identity/Identification

IED — Improvised Explosive Device

IG — Inspector General

IO — Intelligence Officer

IRGC — Islamic Revolutionary Guard Corps

IARPA — Intelligence Advanced Research Projects Agency

ISIS — Islamic State of Iraq and Syria

IT — Information Technology

IU — Islamic Underground

IV — Intravenous, the Latin number four

J — Jet Engine

JDAM — Joint Direct Attack Munition

JMO — Joint Military Operations

JPL — Jet Propulsion Laboratory

KGB — *Komitet Gosudarstvennoy Bezopasnosti*; the foreign intelligence and domestic security agency of the Soviet Union

LD — Laser Designator

LED — Light Emitting Diode

LIDAR — Light Detection and Ranging

LM — Lockheed Martin

LMCO — Lockheed Martin Corporation

LPU — Life Preserver Unit

MANPADS — Man-Portable Air Defense System

MBA — Masters of Business Administration

MERS — Middle East Respiratory Syndrome

MGM — Metro-Goldwyn-Mayer

MiG — Mikoyan

MIT — Massachusetts Institute of Technology

MM — Millimeter

Mode 5 – Identify Friend or Foe. Military only; provides a cryptographically secured version of Mode S and ADS-B GPS position.

MPH — Miles per Hour

MSL — Mean Sea Level

M-4 — Carbine version of the longer barreled M16

M-16 — M16 rifle, officially designated Rifle, Caliber 5.56

NASA — National Aeronautics and Space Administration

NATO — North Atlantic Treaty Organization

NBC — Nuclear, Biological, Chemical

NCS — National Clandestine Service

NCTC — National Counter Terrorism Center

NDA — Non-Disclosure Agreement

NE — Near East Division

NGA — National Geospatial-Intelligence Agency

NGO — Non-Governmental Organization

NM — Nanometer

No. — Number

NOB — New Office Building

NOFORN — No Foreign National

NOIWON — National Operational Intelligence Watch Officer's Network

NOTAM — Notice to Airmen

NRA — National Rifleman Association

NRO — National Reconnaissance Office

NSA — National Security Agency

NSC — National Security Council

NWC — Naval War College

N95 — The air filtration rating of the U.S. National Institute for Occupational Safety and Health, minimum efficiency level 95%

N100 — The air filtration rating of the U.S. National Institute for Occupational Safety and Health, minimum efficiency level 99.97%

O — Observation aircraft

O&M — Operations and Maintenance

ODO — Operations Duty Officer

O2 — Diatomic Oxygen, oxygen in our atmosphere

OPS — Operations

OSS — Office of Strategic Services

OXCART — The Lockheed A-12, a high-altitude, Mach 3+ reconnaissance aircraft built for the CIA

Pan Am — Pan American World Airways

PDB — President's Daily Brief

PDW — Personal Defense Weapon

PhD — Doctor of Philosophy

POAC — Pentagon Officers Athletic Club

POTUS — President of the United States

PPE — Personal Protection Equipment

PT — Physical Training

Q — Drone

QAS — Quiet Aero Systems

QD — Quick Disconnect

QT — Quiet Thruster

R — Radial engine

RAT — Ram Air Turbine

R&D — Research and Development

RC — Radio Control, Remote Control

RENEGADE — A platform that is assessed as operating in such a manner as to raise suspicion that it might be used as a weapon.

RESUME — Resume last formation, route, or mission ordered.

RETROGRADE — Withdraw while executing defensive procedures in response to a threat.

ROGER — Radio transmission received; does not indicate compliance or reaction.

ROLEX — Timeline adjustment in minutes for entire mission; always referenced from the original preplanned mission execution time. "Plus" means later; "minus" means earlier.

ROTC — Reserve Officers' Training Corps

RPG — Rocket Propelled Grenade

RPM — Revolutions Per Minute

RTB — Return to Base

SA — Situational Awareness.

SA2-37B — Schweizer single-engine low-noise profile aircraft

SAC — Strategic Air Command

SACEUR — Supreme Allied Commander Europe

SAD — Special Activities Division

SAM — Surface-to-Air Missile

SAP — Special Access Program

SAR — Synthetic-Aperture Radar

SARS — Severe Acute Respiratory Syndrome

SAT — Scholastic Assessment Test

S&T — Science and Technology Directorate

SCI — Sensitive Compartmented Information

SCRAM — FRIENDLY asset is in immediate danger. Withdraw clear in the direction indicated for survival. No further mission support from the FRIENDLY asset is expected.

SCRAMBLE — Takeoff as quickly as possible.

SEAL — Sea, Air, Land

SERE — Survival, Evasion, Resistance, and Escape

SES — Senior Executive Service

SIS — Senior Intelligence Service

SKINNY — Current survivor coordinates.

SL — designation from the German *Sport-Leicht* (English: Sport Light).

SMACK — Clearance to employ ordnance or fires on surface target coordinates.

SOCOM — Special Operations Command

SOF — Special Operations Forces

SPARKLE — Mark or marking target by IR pointer.

SPIN — Execute a timing or spacing maneuver.

SQUIRTER — A ground-borne object of interest departing the objective area.

SR — Strategic Reconnaissance aircraft; as in SR-71

STRANGERS — Unidentified traffic that is not a participant in the action in progress

STRATCOM — U.S. Strategic Command

STU-III — Secure Telephone Unit

SUSPECT — An identity applied to a track that is potentially hostile because of its characteristics, behavior, origin, or nationality.

SUV — Sport Utility Vehicle

TA — Table of Allowance

Tally Ho — A very old traditional cry made by huntsman to tell others the quarry has been sighted. Used by aviators to indicate other aircraft or targets have been seen.

TESLA — Mode 5 IFF.

10-4 — Message Received, from Ten Code

3M — President Maxim Mohammad Mazibuike

T — Trainer

TANGO UNIFORM — Tits Up

TROJAN — Deployment of an air launch decoy.

TS — Top Secret

TSA — Transportation Security Administration

TS2 — Terminator Sniper System

TS/SCI — Top Secret/Sensitive Compartmented Information

TV — Television

TWA — Trans World Airlines

UAE — United Arab Emirates

UAP — Unidentified Aerial Phenomena

UAV — Unmanned Aerial Vehicle

UFO — Unidentified Flying Object

U.S. — United States

USNA — United States Naval Academy

U.S.S. — United States Ship

U — Utility

U-2 — A subsonic reconnaissance aircraft from the Lockheed Corporation

UV — Ultraviolet

V — Fixed Wing

VHS — Video Home System

WAOC — Washington Area Operations Centers

WHO — World Health Organization

WINCHESTER — No ordnance remaining.

WILCO — Will Comply

WMD — Weapons of Mass Destruction

WTFO — What The Fuck Over

WWII — World War Two

Y — Prototype aircraft

Yankee White — Clearances for those staff members who work directly for or have direct contact with the president or the vice president

YO-3A — Prototype Observation aircraft, model 3, series A

Yo-Yo — Nickname for the YO-3A

Y-12 — World War II code name for National Security Complex in Oak Ridge, Tennessee

XK — A two-door 2+2 grand tourer manufactured and marketed by British automobile manufacturer Jaguar

XKE — Jaguar E-Type; the most beautiful car ever built by no less of an authority, Enzo Ferrari

Acknowledgements

I owe a special debt of gratitude to Barbara Hewitt, my editor and wife, for her careful reading and editing of my manuscripts, and her many excellent suggestions for their improvement. Her continuous good advice and encouragement has been invaluable throughout the making of my books. I am not afraid of her red pen.

I'm also deeply grateful for U.S. Air Force Colonel George "Curious" Fenimore, Retired, and the brilliant "recovering attorney" Rosemary Harris for their unfailing patience and good humor that helped turn my very rough ramblings and ruminations into something of a set of coherent thoughts and a better story. George must be something of a genius for his reviews and precise penetrating insights often leave me muttering to myself, "I am not worthy."

A hat tip to David King of Black Rose Writing for his incredible copy editing, book blocking, and cover art. I've seen other book covers and Dave's work is by far the best in the industry.

A personal thank you to Reagan Rothe, the consummate publishing professional. I will forever be in your debt, good sir.

Any errors found in this novel are my responsibility.

About The Author

Mark is a retired aviation executive, college professor, and military pilot. The ideas for his books spring from life experiences, his extensive international travel, and an admiration for the unique "quiet" spyplanes from the Vietnam War. Mark served in leadership positions with the U.S. Marine Corps, the U.S. Border Patrol, and the U.S. Air Force before leading and managing aviation activities and aircraft operations for international corporations in the Washington, D.C. area. He holds a Master's degree in National Security and Strategic Studies from the Naval War College and an MBA from Embry-Riddle Aeronautical University. His novels have been approved by the CIA's Publication Review Board.

Note From Mark A. Hewitt

Word-of-mouth is crucial for any author to succeed. If you enjoyed *Midnight Ops*, please leave a review online—anywhere you are able. Even if it's just a sentence or two. It would make all the difference and would be very much appreciated.

Thanks!
Mark A. Hewitt

We hope you enjoyed reading this title from:

www.blackrosewriting.com

Subscribe to our mailing list – *The Rosevine* – and receive **FREE** books, daily deals, and stay current with news about upcoming releases and our hottest authors.
Scan the QR code below to sign up.

Already a subscriber? Please accept a sincere thank you for being a fan of Black Rose Writing authors.

View other Black Rose Writing titles at
www.blackrosewriting.com/books and use promo code
PRINT to receive a **20% discount** when purchasing.

Made in United States
Orlando, FL
06 September 2024

51236532R00297